WANDERER IN A WHITE MAN'S WORLD

Salathiel Albine returns from a life among the Indians to that of his white forebears—a self-made outcast among the people who reared him. Under the guidance of Captain Ecuyer of the 60th Royal American Regiment he becomes a loyal servant of the English crown and an avid student of the arts and crafts of European civilization. But it is with the rugged, free-thinking Fighting Quakers that Salathiel Albine discovers his true identity: a free man with a conscience that may be ignored only at his own peril. Then, alone, he sets out to find his lost wife—and meets the headstrong runaway girl who is his fate.

BEDFORD VILLAGE

Hervey Allen

WARNER BOOKS

A Warner Communications Company

ISBN 0-446-81436-9

This Warner Books Edition is published by
arrangement with Holt, Rinehart and Winston, Inc.

Cover art by Jim Dietz

Warner Books, Inc., 75 Rockefeller Plaza, New York, N.Y. 10019

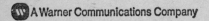 A Warner Communications Company

Printed in the United States of America

Not associated with Warner Press, Inc. of Anderson, Indiana

First Printing: August, 1978

10 9 8 7 6 5 4 3 2 1

Contents

	Prelude	9
1	Horizons Old and New	26
2	Official and Unofficial Views	37
3	Pendergasses'	42
4	In Which a Threshold Is Crossed	52
5	Fort Bedford	63
6	The Secret Story of Captain Jack	76
7	Captain Jack Associates Himself	99
8	Pandora's Pay Chests	117
9	The Lids Come Off	129
10	The Big Brawl at Pendergasses'	156
11	Conversations Overheard	174
12	Mr. Gladwin Comes Over into Macedonia	203
13	Garrett's Garret	226
14	The Women Underneath	247
15	Death at the Salt Kettles	287
16	Old Bonds Loosen	330
17	Summer	370
18	Wilderness Farewell	397

Prelude

ALWAYS, SOMEWHERE, it is morning. That bright streak of dawn extending from the arctic to the antarctic, the glittering boundary between day and night on this whirling sphere of ours, is always there. Dawn is not an isolated event renewed every day. It is a continuous astronomical performance.

To an unwinking eye gazing from far out in the cold and silent interspaces, Earth's day and night seem forever fixed. Apparently unchanging, neither the light nor the dark hemisphere shifts. The earth-star, dogged by her shifting moon, spins like a sleeping top leaning on nothing, casting a cone-shaped shadow into the void. Her bright morning-evening circlet tilts like a shimmering ring against the abysses. A ring jeweled with oceans. A marriage ring worn faithfully on a shadowy finger, where

9

Eternity is being made the bride of Time. Such at least is one view of our earthly situation, an eternal one.

But to eyes on earth that open each morning and close every night; to eyes that must close finally from one generation to another, evening and morning, morning and evening are the very stuff and symbols—the actual black and white counters—of the play of time itself. They provide another point of view of our earthly situation; the timely, the temporary one.

Wink at eternity, if you must, for winking is an involuntary human gesture—and you will not find the chance even in a lifetime to do much more than that about eternity—but whatever you do, keep both points of view firmly in mind; the eternal, and the timely one. They both exist, and they exist simultaneously. Combine them, or else you will understand very little of anything that is going on.

If you hang too much on eternity, even the most important event or poignant anecdote can seem trivial; with nothing but fleeting time in mind, every life and every story, even the best of them, may appear unreasonably long. For both life and books require a balanced seasoning, if you would enjoy and digest them. A pinch of the preserving salt of eternity, a dash of the pepper of time—there is your necessary modicum for pleasure in good taste.

Keeping the larger view in mind, then, let us at this point also recapture the timely one by descending out of the unending morning of earth's eternal dawn, into a particular daybreak at the exact place in North America where this part of a much longer story precisely begins. It is not so long ago. A comparatively few revolutions of our whirling top reversed would easily spin us back again.

The prelude is a strong, clear bugle call.

It is the morning of November 4, 1763; daybreak on the western frontiers of Pennsylvania.

The lively echoes of the English reveille die musically against the long, tumbling wall of the eastern face of the Alleghenies. Already the sun is thrusting fanlike ribs of light into the low cloudbanks and winter mists which hide and stipple the ranges and peaks near the village of Bedford, a half day's journey farther eastward on the banks of the Juniata.

In that direction, as the light grows, a rutted streak of muddy road can be seen twisting away through the wilderness; across the glades and through the thickets of a broad valley, long known even then as the Shawnee Hunting Grounds.

Characteristically, however, there is no one as yet to be seen on the highway. It is the only wagon road in America that leads from the settled colonies over the mountains into the western wilderness. But the times are such that few travelers are likely to be glimpsed there, especially at daybreak. And men take every precaution not to be caught there alone. Pontiac and all his warriors are on the warpath. The valley would be still and silent were it not for innumerable flocks of crows discussing the sunrise raucously, while drifting like dark clouds over the frosty clearings, from one patch of forest to another. Here and there a sudden flurry of wind falls in a swirl of autumn leaves. Only at one place in this wild, rolling landscape is human activity to be heard and seen.

On a graceful, tree-crowned mound in the midst of a natural meadow, and almost within hailing distance of the mountain wall itself, the red, flickering tongues of breakfast fires seem to be tasting the frosty morning air.

11

Dry branches crackle in the flames, horses neigh, and loud shouts of command addressed to man and beast alike are re-echoed in ironical confusion. A few more notes on the bugle, however, this time for assembly—and the confusion begins to resolve. So perfect are the echoes that for a moment it seems that several parties must be camped higher up on the mountain. But it is only at the old Indian mound, a place called Shawnee Cabins, that anyone is actually present. Evidently, quite a large party is there, preparing for departure. Examined more closely, the scene proves to be both lively and unusual, even for that part of the country and a dangerous frontier.

The grove on the flat top of the mound, a high and ancient one built by a mysterious people who have left no other trace, is of considerable extent. It is amid the tall black columns of its walnut trees that the encampment has been formed, one which at first sight seems to be surrounded by a ring of low entrenchment. But this "entrenchment" is not an earthwork. It is composed of a large number of bales, bags, and bundles of trade goods tumbled together in a rough circle. Some of these have been torn open and their contents spilled out on the grass. Articles of various kinds, hatchets, knives, bolts of cloth, flints, small puncheons, beads, mirrors, bedraggled blankets, and even some cheap brass jewelry, lie strewn about.

These scattered and wasted items appear now to be the principal preoccupation of a soberly dressed man in a broad Philadelphia hat. He carries the frozen fingers of one hand in a sling, and is addressed respectfully enough as "Friend Japson" by a trim, dapper little man, who, although evidently not a soldier, wears a small sword and pistol with an indefinable air of personal authority.

"Drop them!" he shouts suddenly and almost wasp-

12

ishly, at a couple of troopers in red jackets, who, thinking themselves unobserved, were about to appropriate a pair of new trade blankets from a torn bale. Touching their hats sheepishly to the gentleman, they move off.

"Aye," said the Quaker glumly, "thou canst see for thyself, 'tis all common property now. At the mere marcy of every stroller! And wilt thou really be leaving it all behind thee, St. Clair?" The question was addressed not to the small man with the short sword, but to a tall military figure with an open Scotch countenance, fine blond hair, and a dark-blue riding cloak.

"But there's naught else to do," replied St. Clair. "We'll have to leave it behind for a few days. We can send wagons back to fetch the stuff later."

The Quaker shook his head doubtfully.

"Give me one ranger, or even a trooper, and I'll stay to guard it myself," he insisted.

"I would advise *thee* not to try to do that, Friend Japson," said the little man a bit ironically. "You can't be certain the only Indians to find you here would be your friends. You might easily find a painful death instead, and all for nothing," he added earnestly.

"For nothing!" muttered the Quaker. "Why, here's a thousand pounds starlin' left on the ground for the crows to caw over. Now if . . ."

"I think you will have to take Mr. Yates's advice, Japson," said St. Clair, smiling wryly. "Remember, Ed Yates is the only lawyer for a hundred leagues about. And besides, it's not so often a Scotch attorney gives advice free."

"Don't undervalue it, Arthur, for a' that," grinned Yates.

"How can ye joke, St. Clair," cried the Quaker reproachfully, "when the loss is thine?"

St. Clair's face darkened.

"Be not so obstinate, my careful friend," he said sternly. "Do you think Captain Ecuyer will leave men behind to guard this stuff, when he'll not even lend a cavalry horse to transport it?"

"Correct, Mr. St. Clair," said a quiet voice directly behind them. "There will be no more lives risked by me for this merchandise."

Yates, St. Clair, and Japson all turned suddenly to face the newcomer. It was Captain Simeon Ecuyer of the 60th, the Royal American regiment.

Dressed faultlessly, and always as though ready to step out on the parade ground, the recent commandant of Fort Pitt walked that morning with a painful limp and leaned heavily on his cane. A flush on his olive cheeks, the glassy eyes, the extremely pale hand that shivered on his cane, all proclaimed the sick man. But neither pain nor fever had as yet shaken either his habitual firmness or his urbanity.

"Good morning," he added gently, raising his laced three-cornered hat above his trim powdered wig. "I'm afraid I've intruded unexpectedly on what must be the end of your conversation, gentlemen. But we leave immediately. I must reach Bedford early today."

Mr. Yates and St. Clair lifted their hats in return. St. Clair called to his colored servant to bring his horse, and went to mount. Yates accompanied the captain, offering him the support of his arm. Only the Quaker was left standing glumly with his hat still on.

"You will join me in the wagon, Friend Japson?" Ecuyer called back over his shoulder.

"Aye," said the Quaker, and raised his hand in acknowledgment—but stayed to cast a lingering look at the bales and merchandise so sadly scattered about. "I'll be

14

back for **ye ye**t," he muttered aloud, and then made his way after the others towards the captain's wagon, where a small group were now gathering to receive final instructions.

The big canvas-covered wagon with four heavy horses harnessed to it before, and a caissonlike cart hitched behind, stood waiting just at the edge of the grove on the very crest of the mound. Even from that low height the road leading eastward to Fort Bedford could be traced for some miles as an open muddy track through the thickets. On the misty meadows below, where wisps of night fog were still drifting towards the mountain, a detachment of light horse in scarlet jackets, leather helmets, and jackboots had already formed line and mounted, waiting for the signal to march. Their brass accoutrements and bright steel carbines winked and glinted in the morning light as the rim of the sun peered suddenly over a distant line of hills.

A shrill whistle from the grove marked the assembly place of a small number of provincial rangers. Men in the fringed deerskin shirts of the frontier with long rifle-guns now came hurrying through the trees. The cooking fires were hurriedly doused, and the roll called while the ashes were still hissing.

Meanwhile, Mr. Yates assisted Captain Ecuyer up a small folding ladder at the rear of the wagon. Nothing so much as the need of these steps showed how far Ecuyer had fallen from his usual vigor. This morning he was not able to mount even these unaided. He sat for a moment in a canvas swing slung from the ridgepole of the wagon, compressing his lips with pain, before he motioned to two mounted men, who were waiting near by, to come closer.

The contrast between the two who now rode up to the

wagon gate was so astounding as to force Mr. Yates, the attorney, to stifle a delighted grin, while he watched them solemnly receiving their instructions from the captain. It was surprising that the same continent could contain them both at once.

One, a young English officer in charge of the detachment of light horse from the fort, was scarcely more than a boy in appearance. His sabre was longer than the stubby legs he thrust into shortened stirrups. His leather helmet was jammed down on blond curly hair that escaped here and there around its edges. His nickname was "Cherub", and he had a milk-and-cherry countenance with large blue eyes. But Cornet Appleboy sat his lean grey charger with that native English combination of inborn modesty and imperturbable self-confidence, which has almost sufficed to conquer the world.

"Mr. Appleboy," said Captain Ecuyer, gravely returning his salute, "can ye remember the road back to Bedford?"

"Oh, yes, sir. We came that way only yesterday."

"Well then, you'll be in charge of today's march, and lead the way. Place half your men before, and half behind this wagon. And regulate your pace according to the directions of my driver."

"Burent, do you hear that?'

"Yes, sir," said a compact-looking man in brown boots and homespun, with a long whip in his hand, who stepped up and touched his cap with his whip handle, respectfully.

"We'll trot and we'll walk," continued Captain Ecuyer. "But keep going. Remember some of the militia are not well mounted, and none of them have wings. Whatever you do, don't forge ahead of your advance-rangers." The last remark was especially directed to Burent.

"I'll see to that, sir," said the driver, and went to take his seat at the front of the wagon.

"Have your men empty their pieces, Mr. Appleboy, and reload with good dry charges," cautioned the captain. "By the way, you should *never* neglect the usual morning volley in these damp woods," he added. "Now go and stand by for the wagon. We'll be moving directly."

The young officer saluted and rode off to join his men in the meadow below.

"Albine," said Captain Ecuyer, addressing the other horseman who was awaiting his instructions, "come closer. Even if I can't ride the mare, I don't want her to forget me." He leaned forward and began to stroke and fondle the nose of the spirited horse that now thrust her head under the wagon-top to nip at his hands.

"No, there's not a morsel of sugarloaf left, my fine lady," he said, and sighed.

These brief morning conversations between the captain and his beloved horse were almost part of the daily routine, since Ecuyer had been forced to take to his wagon. The hatchet-faced young giant who now rode her let the reins fall slack on her neck, while Ecuyer, who was a Swiss officer in the service of the English crown, whispered a few French blandishments into the mare's quivering ear, as she thrust her head farther and farther into the wagon and sniffed expectantly.

"Here," said Ecuyer, "here's a bit of a biscuit for ye. B'God, it's all I have!"

There was something genuinely touching, but embarrassing, about these interviews between the invalid soldier and his mount. They were the rare occasions when Ecuyer, who was a stoical disciplinarian, permitted himself manifestations of sentiment for the only creature left in the universe he could lavish affection on. This morning

17

a few terms of self-pity unconsciously crept into his talk and the tones of his voice, for he was now in constant pain and discomfort from a festering wound.

Partly for that reason, plus a native masculine diffidence in the face of candid Gallic emotion, everyone standing near joined in an instant conspiracy not to seem to see or to hear the captain. St. Clair and Yates suddenly lost themselves in a low-toned conversation. Even the Quaker stood respectfully by and looked away, moved in spite of himself, although he held a grievance against the captain. As for Salathiel Albine, the tall young frontiersman astride the mare, herself, he was not known as the captain's man without good reason, and he sat there with no expression whatever on his hawklike face, except that which might be attributed to the blade of a keen hatchet.

Yet Salathiel's friend, Mr. Yates, whose apt Scotch eye was swift to appreciate the humor inherent in nature, secretly much admired the scene before him. It was at once sentimental, ludicrous, and grim.

The mare with her head thrust under the canvas of the wagon stood sedately munching a biscuit. Albine sat on her back, dressed more like an Indian than a white man. His long, double-barrelled rifle was slung behind him. A fur cap with a buck-tail pompom on it drooped jauntily to one side to cover what Yates well knew to be the newly healed remnant of a bullet-clipped ear. There was a hatchet and a long knife in Albine's belt. A couple of fresh Indian scalps were drying on his pommel. Their black locks dropped disconsolately. And Mr. Albine sat there, temporarily at least, like a carved idol. Who but a man brought up among Indians could achieve so bleak a face? Only the grey eyes glittered. Mr. Yates was about to nudge St. Clair to be sure he was seeing the same thing—when the mare shied suddenly and withdrew her head violently from the wagon.

On the meadow below, Cornet Appleboy's dragoons had loosed a splattering, popping volley into the morning air, according to the captain's directions. The echoes crackled back from the mountain, causing the mare to dance.

"Just as I thought," said Ecuyer, "about half the charges were damp, and slow fired. Climb in now, Mr. Japson," he continued. "We'll be leaving. Where are the prisoners, Albine? You'd best bind them now that we're getting so near the fort. 'Twill be their last precious chance to desart again."

"I've bound them already, sir," replied the young frontiersman. "Here they come now."

A couple of hangdog militiamen rode up, their feet tied in their stirrups with a lashing passed under the horse's belly.

"Tell your van to move forward steadily and fast," continued Ecuyer. "It's only a few leagues to Bedford, but we can always be waylaid. You'd best hover about the rear yourself, Albine, but I leave the disposition of the rangers to you. You managed them monstrous well yesterday. Prisoners, follow the wagon. Mr. Yates and St. Clair, will ye keep an eye on them? Now prepare to move on."

Even a few words were great praise from Captain Ecuyer. Albine rode off elated. Just the day before he and his rangers had stampeded a whole caravan of traders back to Bedford. It was to this that the captain referred. With only a few men, it had been a difficult operation in the darkness of the early morning. How his rangers had yelled! They had sounded like Pontiac and all his tribes let loose. Salathiel had to laugh again at the thought of

19

the traders' wild scramble back to Bedford in the dawn. Two to a horse in some cases, *bumpety-bump*, and the pack horses' rumps bobbing away down the road. So the captain was pleased, was he? Well, he might well be. Ecuyer was determined to enforce the proclamations against trading. It was not likely that there would be more of it now for some time to come. The lesson had been a sharp one.

Albine found his rangers skylarking, but with their packs made up ready to move out. The simple orders for the day's march were quickly given. Two of the men who lived in Bedford, Nat Murray and one Tom Pendergass, whose father kept the principal ordinary and trading post in the town, were told to lead the advance. With the rest it was Albine's intention to cover the rear, as Ecuyer had suggested, for it was from that direction, if any, that they might still look for trouble. An ambush was unlikely for so strong a column so near the fort, but they might still be followed.

Two loud cracks of a whip like a couple of pistol shots, and the rumble of heavy wheels announced that the wagon was under way. Burent, who was actually the trusted assistant of Captain Ecuyer rather than a mere driver, nevertheless handled his horses with great skill. Mindful of the painful condition of Ecuyer's wound, he let the heavy vehicle, which had been especially built for the captain at Fort Pitt, roll down the long slope from the mound as easily as possible.

Seeing the column about to start, the rangers who had been chosen to lead the advance took a short cut over the meadows and raced along the road to Bedford in order to gain their distance in advance. Albine, and the rest of his riflemen, remained for a while on the mound, a vantage point from which they could oversee every detail of the departure and all the country about.

No one in the entire party looked forward to the arrival at Bedford with more eager anticipation than did young Salathiel Albine, or "Sal", as he was known to his friends. His life had been an adventurous one, but he had never yet been east of the mountains. Stolen at the age of six or seven from the cabin of his parents, who had both been murdered together with a younger child, Salathiel Albine had been brought up in the hut of the Shawnee chief Kaysinata, the Big Turtle. The boy had been adopted by the name of Little Turtle into that tribe. Since the adoption had been into the clan of the Turtle for ritualistic reasons, a small red turtle had been tattooed on the child's breast. All the affection he had ever known had been provided by his foster mother, a barren Indian squaw called Mawakis.

Purely by chance, a learned and pious Presbyterian missionary, also a captive, had undertaken the boy's education, and thus saved him from barbarism. The Reverend James McArdle had lavished on his forest pupil all that ample time, devotion, and intellect could confer. So Albine, although his story was not so unusual for that time and the frontier, was nevertheless a curious combination of Indian upbringing and white "book larnin". It was his peculiar pride that he could read, write, and cipher.

A clear mind in a huge, strong body was the gift of his English and Irish ancestors, about whom he knew little but was now very curious. Indeed, the murder of his mother—he had heard her screaming under the hatchet—was the primary impression of his soul. At moments of emotional crises he would seem to hear her scream again, "from underground".

In the troubles accompanying Pontiac's rebellion, Sala-

21

thiel had shaken off his Indian character of the Little
Turtle and escaped from the Shawnees, partly with their
connivance, to take refuge at Fort Pitt. In a brief forest
interlude he had been thrust, by the overly conscientious
McArdle, into a hasty marriage with Jane Sligo, a young
white girl whose story was somewhat similar to his own.
They had escaped together with some other refugees,
women and children, but Salathiel had lost Jane in their
flight from a Shawnee village while on their way up the
Ohio River to Pittsburgh. Whether Mrs. Albine was now
in the hands of Indians or had been taken in by friendly
settlers, her young husband did not know. He had lost
an ear by an Indian bullet, trying to find out. But he had
been forced to return and remain at Fort Pitt alone until,
owing to good luck and circumstances, he had been taken
into the personal service of Captain Ecuyer, the commandant. Albine had been trained in his manifold new duties
by one Johnson, a skilful valet and a servant, but also
an independent and vigorous man, who was taking up
land on the frontier in order to found a family in America.

Albine had gone through the entire siege of Fort Pitt
during the summer of 1763, when Captain Ecuyer had so
distinguished himself as a gallant man and an able officer.
In fact, he had saved the Pennsylvania frontier for the
English crown. Salathiel had thus learned to know the
captain as few others could, and to revere him. And he
had also matured rapidly both in mind and in character.

The siege of Fort Pitt had been raised in August, after
the bloody battle of Bushy Run, by the relief expedition
under Colonel Henri Louis Bouquet. Bouquet was now
preparing a further expedition westward into the Ohio
country for a final blow at the hostile tribes, especially
against the Shawnees on the Muskingum. But savage
desultory warfare was still harassing the frontier. Colonel

22

Bouquet needed more men and a constant stream of supplies at Fort Pitt. It was vital to keep open the road over the mountains to Pittsburgh, and for that reason Bouquet had prevailed on Captain Ecuyer, despite the captain's physical condition and his desire to resign, to remain in the English service, in order to devote himself to the task of furthering transport and speeding up supplies and reinforcements across the mountainous wilderness.

For this task Ecuyer was given all the authority possible. Much, indeed almost everything, connected with the immediate defence of the frontiers and the proposed Ohio campaign depended on how Captain Ecuyer should perform his mission. He knew that, and so did those who served him. Their anxiety for the little Swiss captain was therefore not one of personal sentiment alone.

In the late autumn days of 1763, accompanied by Albine and Burent only, Ecuyer had sent out from Pittsburgh for Fort Bedford in the face of mountain winter and growing weakness from his wounds received at Fort Pitt and in the campaign against Montcalm. Unable to ride his own horse, the captain had rebuilt an old wagon and filled it with every rough comfort and rude contrivance for prolonging existence and ameliorating living which the frontier could afford. Albine had ridden the captain's mare; Burent drove the wagon.

At Frazier's cabin, a licensed ordinary near Pittsburgh, they had encountered Ganstax, a Seneca chief, a party of drunken Delaware Indians, and Japson, the trader. Serious trouble was avoided only by the captain's adroitness. At Frazier's, Albine was appealed to by Frances, an Irish girl, for protection against Mrs. Frazier, her brutal mistress. He could do little at the time to aid her, but left the girl a pistol to protect herself.

23

On the way east, they had nearly been frozen to death in a sudden mountain blizzard.

Halfway to Bedford, at the important outpost of Fort Ligonier, Ecuyer had been forced to pause in order to enforce discipline. The unpaid garrison was in dangerous ferment: miserable settlers had been troublesome. It had finally been necessary to hang a mutinous Irishman. There had been other serious complications with merchants and traders who insisted upon trade as usual, whether their savage customers were the king's enemies or not. All this the captain had dealt with as best he could, and on the whole very well.

Taking a few of the Pennsylvania militia along with him to act as rangers and additional escort, Ecuyer had then pushed over the mountains from Ligonier towards Bedford as rapidly as the difficult road would permit. At a way stockade called Ray's Dudgeon there had been a brush with lurking Indians, trouble complicated by the news that a large "caravan" of the traders lay at the foot of the Allegheny Mountains, camped on the mound, waiting an opportunity to get through to Ligonier.

It was here that Ecuyer had placed Albine in charge of the rangers with orders to try to panic the traders back to Bedford by making a pretended Indian attack upon them. The ruse had succeeded beyond all expectation, and the traders had fled in terror to Fort Bedford. Cornet Appleboy and his troopers had then been sent by the commandant at Fort Bedford to rescue the goods abandoned by the traders and to drive away any lurking savages. Instead of Indians, Appleboy and his men had met Captain Ecuyer and his escort at the Shawnee Cabins.

Now the entire party—including Mr. Yates, an attorney active in land surveys for the province of Pennsylvania, but in the personal service of the Penn family; Japson, a

24

trading Quaker from Philadelphia; and Arthur St. Clair, an ex-British officer and a gentleman deeply concerned in land and the settlement of that part of the frontier—were setting forth to Fort Bedford together. Captain Ecuyer's haste was now personal as well as official. If he could not obtain the services of a surgeon immediately, the delay would be fatal.

All this tangle of events and circumstances was the reason that young Albine now sat the captain's mare and watched over the departure of the wagon and its escort from the top of the mound called Shawnee Cabins. To his restricted experience and unbounded expectation, Bedford Village loomed as a metropolis. Who could tell what new vistas it might hold for Salathiel Albine, alias the Little Turtle?

It was therefore with no small satisfaction that he now saw the cavalry swinging into place before and behind the wagon, and the escort led by Cornet Appleboy heading down the Bedford road.

A short blast on the bugle set the echoes to rolling briefly and brought the column to a brisk trot.

1

Horizons Old and New

BEHIND towered the Allegheny and before them the long wall of Will's Mountain, with a riot of peaks farther northward where the blue Juniata rushed through its water gap. Between lay the broad valley known as the Shawnee Hunting Grounds. This they would have to cross before reaching Fort Bedford on the river, something over a half day's journey eastward.

The morning sun glittered on the frosty mountains; shone through the mighty black skeletons of the winterbare forest, tracing blue shadow figures on the snow. Deer bounded away from them through the open glades. From time to time the trumpeter of the troop of rangers sounded a brazen note. They were going fast now, trotting; half the troop of horse before the wagon and half behind.

After the mountains the road seemed easy, rising and

falling over the gentle swales of the valley floor, sweeping around great bends of the streams.

In the wagon Captain Ecuyer devoted himself to holding on—with his teeth to a cigar, and with his hands to the seat.

Outside, Salathiel ranged about on the mare pretty much as he pleased. She was stepping high and whinnied to her old teammates of the wagon and the troop horses ahead. Cornet Appleboy, the young English officer in charge of the cavalry, was responsible for the command, and there was small chance, in such force, of being ambushed now. With much of the responsibility that had accompanied him all the way from Fort Pitt thus shifted from his shoulders, Salathiel felt like a free man once more. He looked about him eagerly for the first signs of settlement.

He had often heard of this beautiful valley from the Indians who had adopted him. In the old days, only a generation before, it had been the father of Kaysinata, the Big Turtle, who had built his village at the grove on the mound and so given the name of Shawnee Cabins to the place. Only a few fire-scarred stones of the Indian hearths remained now.

Then the valley had been a paradise of game. Every stream was alive with beaver and fish. The brown bears had battened on wild honey and chestnuts. Buffalo and elk drifted undisturbed through the succulent glades. Not a smoke showed on the mountains. All was undisturbed silence, except for the growling of thunder in summer, the croaking of frogs, or the high, hornlike *honk* of the wild geese in autumn, flying V after V down the long valley between the channelled mountains, heading for their winter feeding grounds on Chesapeake Bay. There had

27

been blessed years of this for the Shawnees; a treaty which said solemnly that it should always remain so.

Then the white man came. Chimneys smoked at Rays-town, as Bedford was then called. Rifles cracked. Axes rang. Indians were found murdered. White men did not return home. The game grew shy and scarcer. Again the red man flitted westward.

But he remembered. He hated this remove more than any other. He had greatly loved the valley. He schemed to come back again.

In the tales told by the Shawnees in their cabins of exile down the Ohio, on the Beaver and the Muskingum, this high, heavenly, mountain valley had been spoken of as their happy hunting ground, as the perfect homeland of their fathers, who then had had teeming wives. The Big Turtle had told Salathiel where the grandfathers were buried. He had spoken of the signs of the hills and of the stars by which one could find them sleeping in the quiet places by the streams.

So Salathiel looked about him now as they rode across the valley as though he half remembered having been here before: as if the whispers of a voice lost, but still familiar, had something to say to him which he could not quite overhear. Indeed, these sensations were very real and deep in him, even if they were not wholly conscious. It was a kind of dim awareness of his forest-self that rode with him that morning over the road through the Shawnee Hunting Grounds.

The three mounds shaded by the three great sycamores —they were no surprise to him. Or the level by the stream where the village of Mawakis must once have stood. With-out thinking, he expected these landmarks. He was not surprised to find them there. He passed them like something remembered from another lifetime; with a kind of familiarity of which he was not fully aware.

More consciously, he was looking for signs of white settlement. For every mile of the road eastward brought him nearer to those towns and cities, and pleasant, long-settled farmsteads about which he had heard and read so much, and towards which his imagination and curiosity constantly outsped his frame.

So far he had been disappointed, for the country through which they had passed seemed as wild, untouched, and primeval as that along the Ohio. Leave out the road, and there would have been scarcely any difference, except the mountains. He had heard of many settlers in this place. Yet he was to be disappointed again, for there were none of them left in the valley. They had fled, the spring before, back to the fort at Bedford. Or they had given up and gone even farther eastward. For if anything, the frontier was more dangerous now than it had been for some years. It was haunted by small raiding bands of Indians bent purely upon mischief and vengeance. They were harder to cope with than organized tribes or large disciplined war parties, because there was no rumour of them that went before. They came and went capriciously, without notice or sign. And they came to exterminate rather than to plunder. So the valley of the Shawnee Hunting Grounds, like all the frontiers of Pennsylvania that fateful year, lay desolate and desolated.

Here and there, as they approached Bedford, an old clearing appeared. But the weeds stood high amongst the stumps, and the cabins and barns were burned. Not a smoke from a chimney rose anywhere. Even the houses that had been built near the road were nothing but fire-marked cellars, filled in some cases with the leaves of many autumns. A few well sweeps remained lonely and

29

gallowslike. The only sign of present occupation and use was the camping places every few miles; the breakage and litter of wagon trains and convoys left behind in dangerous journeys to and from Fort Pitt.

Towards noon they stopped at such a place and prepared a meal on the wide, stone hearth. Then they were off again, rapidly. About two o'clock they came down suddenly into the vale of the winding Juniata and crossed it on a stout bridge of logs. Here there was an outpost, not often occupied. A couple of miles beyond, at the crest of a brisk rise, they were suddenly rewarded and cheered by their first glimpse of Bedford.

Murray, who was riding ahead, gave a shout and beckoned to Salathiel to ride forward. He did so eagerly, and this time he was not altogether disappointed.

The fort and the settlement about it seemed, to Salathiel's eyes at least, a surprisingly large town. The first thing he noticed was an astonishing number of chimneys all belching smoke. The whole place, indeed, was overhung by the blue haze from its own wood fires.

They were standing here at the top of a considerable hill that overlooked the town. The river made a wide loop at their feet. Some miles to their right, and eastward, the north front of Will's Mountain ceased abruptly in a sharp abutment like the prow of a ship. Here the road swung north to follow the east bank of the river, and about two miles away on a high bank of the Juniata, so steep that it almost amounted to a cliff, stood Fort Bedford and the jumble of roofs and chimneys clustered about it that was Raystown.

In the clear, quiet mountain afternoon the wood smoke hung over it like an immense hazy umbrella. A few windows flashed in the sun. But that was all. For encompassing the village in every direction, from the crests of the mountains down to the banks of the stream, over a vast area of valley and hills, stretched the illimitable forest.

Except for an open swamp in the channels of the river immediately before the fort, the settlement was a mere hole in an ocean of trees. A few cleared fields and pastures near the town made small checkerlike patches. Under a light snow, they looked like handkerchiefs laid out to dry in the dark forest by the inhabitants.

The only prominent building was the fort itself. It had five bastions and a peculiar gallery like a big ice chute, but roofed in and loopholed. It led down the cliff from the north gate to the river, so the garrison could draw water directly from the stream or make a sortie in that direction if besieged. This log gallery was the outstanding feature of the place, a genuine military curiosity.

For the rest, the view of the fort reminded Salathiel not a little of his first glimpse of Fort Pitt. The roof of the barracks shrouded with busy chimneys studded the interior of its five-pointed star. But the ditches around the place were smooth and grassy. And just across the fort was a cluster of long shingled roofs of quite considerable proportions.

"Them's the hospitals," said Murray, pointing out the features of the place, "and they're mostly alers full; smallpox or the like."

"That's my pa's place," announced young Tom Pendergass, riding up. "Ye see the two big houses with a bridge between em t'other side of the fort? One's his store and taproom, and the far un —that's home! All of us Pendergasses is gathered thar sence the troubles. But we do have big nights round the fire in the bar. Hit's the biggest chimley west of Carlisle. You'll see some good times there, or I'm a liar." He clapped Salathiel on the back. "Will yer be stayin' on with us agin, Mr. Yates?" he asked as the young lawyer joined them. " 'Speck ma's saved yer the river room whar you left your things. Cap'n Ourry's adjutant wanted to hire it off her, but ma's a woman of her word."

"I hope she *has* kept it for me," said Yates. "It's the nicest room in town."

"It is!" Pendergass agreed enthusiastically, and went on to boast about the town of which he was naïvely proud. "It was my pa found the springs," he said. " 'Course the Injuns knew 'em fustest. They're over the hill there in the valley beyont. Gawd, but one of 'em stinks! And t'other will turn a man into a shitepoke in a jiffy. Clears you out in the springtime fine; better nor boneset tea for the blood. You ought to hev saw the place when Gineral Forbes was here with nigh eight thousand men. The surgeons put a guard on the water then . . ."

"But the Pendergasses have even stronger water than that," said Murray, laughing. "Comes in barrels."

"You bet," agreed Tom, "and we have a worm, too. Pa cooks his corn juice in it. Its fine white spring water comes out. Ever taste it?" He smacked his lips.

Just then the wagon drove up and halted. Captain Ecuyer slowly got out and took a look at the place. He gave a grunt of satisfaction like an Indian, much to the amusement of the rangers, and climbing painfully back, shouted to Burent to get on.

The whole cavalcade finally tore down into the place, Burent putting his horses through their best paces.

They came down the little street past the sutlers' houses where officers stood smoking in the doorways, and women and children hung out the windows, gawking at the rumble of wheels and the clatter of cavalry. A gust of surprise and curiosity ran through the place at the sight of the wagon. People came shouting, more people than Salathiel had ever seen. Some of the houses were built of stone and had painted doors and shutters. There were flat river stones to walk on beside them. A few dooryards had strange tended shrubs in them. It was amazing. The houses seemed riddled with windows and openings.

They thundered across a bridge over a gully and drove along by the walls of the fort. The gate opened over a dry moat and onto the street. The bridge was down, and they swept in, leaving the sentries challenging foolishly behind them. There was no time for the guard to assemble.

Captain Ecuyer climbed down in front of the large officers' quarters and looked about him. It was the most luxurious building Salathiel had ever seen. It might have been in a European town. An officer buckling on his sword came running out of the door.

"Where's Captain Ourry?" demanded Ecuyer.

"He's gone to Carlisle to fetch the pay chests," said the lieutenant, saluting.

"I thought so," said Ecuyer, "and I see ye keep the gate open so he'll be welcome any time with the cash!"

"Not after sundown, I assure you, sir," replied the lieutenant. "The gate's always closed then."

"B'God, I'm surprised you go to all that trouble," blurted the captain. "Albine, get my things into the house here, and be smart about it. Put some men on them to help Burent. And come in and tend me, for I'm mortal ill." He limped up the steps, threw the door open into headquarters, and staggered in.

The adjutant and the quartermaster's clerk were working over some papers together at a desk. The room stank of whisky and old candles. The clerk stood up and blinked at the captain. "Whadja wan?" he said.

"Congratulations to the second battalion," shouted Ecuyer in a fury. "Your gate's wide open, lieutenant, and I've been received with all the honours of a sutler. We *do* manage it better in the first—at times."

Captain Stewart's adjutant, Lieutenant Spenser, made no attempt to reply. Stewart, the commandant, had gone east to meet Ourry. Spenser was familiar by long correspondence with Captain Ecuyer's official opinion of the discipline maintained by the second battalion of the Royal American Regiment, and there would be small chance, he felt, to controvert it now. The men hadn't been paid for over a year and the new recruits sent from Philadelphia were the dregs of society. In his opinion at least, the garrison at Bedford was on the point of mutiny. He hoped to God Captain Ourry would arrive with the pay chests soon. Ecuyer was obviously a very ill man with no patience left.

Maybe he could get him into bed—quick!

Without further ado he led the way to Ourry's quarters, had a fire built there, and sent for the surgeon. While they waited, Salathiel set about making the captain as comfortable as possible during the interval the things from the wagon were being brought in. Mr. Yates came in to offer his services.

Even in his pain, Ecuyer was "much obleeged". He thanked Yates, and he finally thanked Spenser handsomely.

"You're an adjutant I'd like to see in my own battalion, lieutenant," he said. "But for God's sake, *do* see that the gate is closed, or we'll all be scalped in our beds some night. And hurry the surgeon, for the anguish of this wound is inexpressible."

It was Yates who finally found Dr. Boyd, the battalion surgeon, at Pendergasses' and returned with him. Salathiel spent an afternoon of sympathetic agony while the captain's wound was lanced and a probe thrust into his groin. A small piece of iron shell which had lodged there since the fight on the Plains of Abraham was extracted.

"You'll get better now—or you'll die," said the surgeon, sniffing the fragment doubtfully.

"That's the universal prognosis for all mankind, Dr. Boyd," grinned Ecuyer. "You're a good prober, but be damned to ye! I must sleep. Can't you give me a powder?"

The doctor complied.

The captain slept, but with a mounting fever and laboured breathing. Salathiel sat by him until late in the evening, when the surgeon called again and Burent came to relieve him as "nurse" on watch.

Dr. Boyd stopped over the captain, listened and shook his head.

"Sounds like inflammation of the lungs," he said.

"I 'opes not, sir," said Burent, rearranging the pillows so as to raise the captain's head, and looking anxious. "Me old mother died o' that."

"I suppose you know what to do then," said the surgeon. "Call me if he starts gasping." He turned to Salathiel. "A bit of supper would do *you* no harm, I imagine," he remarked with a kindly smile. "Mr. Yates tells me you and Burent are devoted fellows. I like that. There's not a better officer in the service than Captain Ecuyer. But come, some of your friends have been waiting outside for news. We'll be at Pendergasses' if you want me, Burent."

They went out, to find Yates, Murray, and young Tom Pendergass waiting anxiously in the hall. A door opened. Captain Stewart, the commandant, who had just ridden in from Fort Loudon and was still mud-splashed, came out to enquire about Ecuyer.

"He's sleeping, and I'll not know much till tomorrow," replied the surgeon. "Any eastern news, captain?"

"General Amherst's resigned, and the pay chests are on the way," said Stewart, grinning.

"Good! 'Twill cheer even a sick man," said the surgeon. "As for me, I'm penniless. I've been living on your father's bounty, Mr. Pendergass, for three months past."

"Oh, Pa's used to thot," laughed Tom.

They walked out through the sally port talking.

"Good God! so Cunctator Amherst's resigned," exclaimed Yates.

"And a damned good riddance," said the doctor.

There was not much to be seen of Bedford except locked doors, dark streets, and stars overhead. Every house was barred like a fortress. The Reverend Joseph Jenkins and his family had been murdered that afternoon only two miles east of the fort, and their scalps taken.

"Pa told 'em," said Murray, "but they would light out for Big Cove. And now they've lost their har. Delawares, I hear. I 'low them rascals air still hangin' round. We was pretty durned lucky gettin' through from Ligonier ourselves."

To this all agreed with prophecies of more trouble to come.

2

Official and Unofficial Views

BEDFORD may have been only a hamlet lost in the forest to the eyes of the authorities and to the European officers in the garrison, the last outpost civilly inhabited before plunging into a tangle of murder haunted and mysterious wilderness. That, at least, was the way it appeared to Captain-lieutenant Lewis Ourry, Esq., of the Royal American Regiment of foot, deputy quartermaster general for his Majesty's troops, and to Captain Stewart of the Royal Americans, commandant at Fort Bedford. That was the way they thought of the place when they looked westward from the river-front bastion to the wall of the Alleghenies glittering in winter snows over the cheerless distance.

Bedford was certainly the end of the world to them. There might be military posts beyond, even an unthinkably vast territory. But it was all "useless" territory; a matter of savagery and savages. To these officers and their ilk it was incredible that their world should ever catch up with this place. That it would ever overflow it and spill over the mountains into the country beyond was no more in their thoughts than an assembly of apes in Westminster Abbey. The mountains were a barrier set—and they would remain. When the war was over, Ourry, for instance, would return to London. Even on half pay, and the remains of a small estate, he could sit and read his newspaper in the morning and live like a gentleman at one of the coffeehouses, a long pipe and a long glass before him. Not a bad prospect at all, if you considered it rightly.

But to even the least of the new settlers and older inhabitants about Raystown—they were now beginning to call it Bedford—both the town and the landscape wore a different aspect. Nothing they looked at was permanent. It was all a beginning, a natural condition subject to immediate change. Their angle of sight was cast into the future. The present village, rude as it was, was a triumph over what had *not* been there only a few years before, and they could see fields where once there was nothing but forests, a right-little-tight-little-city only a few years hence, where was now a fort, a few log houses, one or two stone dwellings, and a road.

It was the road, the road! People, more and more of them, came by the road. As for the mountains, they were merely an inconvenient wave in the ground, something to surmount that would soon be surmounted.

All their dreams, even their unconscious feelings, were set towards the future. And the future was as endless and vast and as full of opportunity as the land to the westward. Anyone who came as far west as Bedford had already dropped the feeling of old security and of unchanged, stable living that had been achieved on the eastern seaboard for a century or more. Ships, for that matter, never came into their minds. They had dropped all that. They expected nothing more from Europe and the past. They had come to make a new beginning of things, and they did not care to think backward, because that was a waste of time.

They would begin where they stopped with an axe to change the face of things; to slaughter and subdue. Nor was even that a move towards permanence. They all expected to go on farther or further, into the west or to better things. For they travelled in space as they travelled in time, into an ever-shifting mirage of the endless beyond. That was the future to them. And that was the difference between the native-born Americans and the Europeans. They thought differently in a different direction. "Now" was dim in America, "then" had faded into nothing, "to-morrow" was everything.

If Captain Ourry could have borrowed the eyes of, let us say, young Tom Pendergass even for a moment he would have been confounded; amazed. But he couldn't. He couldn't even get a glimpse through them. He was an Englishman, a Londoner, and the spectacles he had been born with were irrevocably glued to his long nose.

Mr. Yates had been able to shift his spectacles. He was already looking through a pair of American lenses, although with a slightly backward glance from time to time. But Yates was a Scot and had been cut loose from his roots by fate. For him a shift of view was not only possible, it was imperative. And it was deliberate.

Most surprising of all, perhaps, was the view of Bedford seen through Salathiel's eyes. It was no mere hole in the forest to him. It was a portent, a small but infinitely interesting and surprisingly complex sample of the wonders farther eastward as yet to come.

First, there was the excitement of many people. To one from the forest a few hundred people, not mere soldiers and Indians, but the folk of a neighborhood and a town, were a multitude. All the many crosscurrents of emotion and thought which ran through them, now ran through him. There was something extraordinary about that, something he was not entirely able to cope with at first, for his own emotions were greatly increased, reduplicated, and made more complex by being reflected back from others, and by being thus unexpectedly changed.

For the first few days he scarcely knew what to do about so many people. Sometimes he felt inclined to boast and shout, at others to fling himself about or even to start a fight. The self-control which had been sufficient to keep him silent, self-alert, and cool when he was alone with animals and trees, or squatting with laconic Indians about a fire, was now frequently surprised into letting him go on the loose. He was always on the verge of some new and unforeseen excitement.

It was hard to cope with this situation. He began by doubting himself, and hence, for such was his nature, he also began to put a firmer bridle upon his mind, muscles, and tongue. He avoided crowds where too much that was unexpected might overwhelm him, and talked, when he did talk, to individuals alone. In a crowd he found it best to remain silent, because for a long time, until he grew more used to people, he could never tell what he might say.

This, however, did not give him the feeling of being a non-entity. He was so large, his bulk and appearance were so startling that he did not need to say much. His presence was felt. And he felt that it was felt. Mr. Yates, on the

40

contrary, being a dapper fellow, a bit short on the scales of physical being, made weight for himself only by the skill of his tongue. With that he accumulated, wherever he was, considerable momentum and his impact was felt.

Thus in one way or another both Salathiel and Yates managed to feel at home. Luckily for them, there was a place to feel at home in—Pendergasses'.

3

Pendergasses'

CENTRE and glowing heart of the neighbourhood and of the new world in which Salathiel now found himself, the point of vital radiance, so to speak, for all Bedford and its vicinity was the tavern taproom with its huge, warm hearth, kegs of genial and fiery liquors, and equally inspiring friendly encounters and talk known as "Pendergasses' ".

Garrett Pendergass, "Prendergás, Pendergast or even Pendergaster", you could take your choice, for everyone knew him, was the host and patriarch of the establishment that overlooked the banks of the river just beyond and eastward of the fort.

While the formal sovereignty and nominal rule of the country roundabout still remained with the king's commandant at the fort, the actual governance, control, and influence of the entire neighbourhood for a day's journey on all sides resided, at least in normal times, in the mind and hands of Garrett Pendergass himself, a hale and hearty, still powerful, and white-bearded man of seventy years.

Time and experience had stored up and kept for him the rarest of all commodities, wisdom and happiness, and in no small measure. Somehow in himself he did personify the achievement of what so many had come into the wilderness to get: freedom, ease, and abundance.

To look at Garrett as he stood just a bit bowlegged before his own vast chimney, and in the midst of his possessions and family, was to realize what time, patience, and genial zeal could wring barehanded from the reluctant but exuberant forest.

Garrett teemed. He teemed with children, grandchildren, and things. And his excess ran over and solidified in hospitality.

Whatever one might think of Bedford, whether one was a European or an American, there was only one single opinion about Pendergasses': it was a good place to be in, in this or in any other kind of world. Even Indians liked to come there, when allowed.

It would be hard to describe the establishment exactly. For Pendergasses' was its own peculiar self, and so such set terms as tavern, inn, trading post, ordinary, public house, mill, or general store could precisely apply; since it was all these things or any of them, depending upon what a man's bent or business might be. And it was all of them at once, and so proclaimed itself by the songs that emanated from the taproom, the hum of business about the store, the clink of iron from the blacksmith shop at one end near the road, and the intricate voices of the men, women, and children that came from the hive—for it was that, too—and perhaps best described by Murray in a simply homely term as a "goin' consarn".

Its houses, for there were two of them, faced the road on one side and the river on the other. And the level riverbank between was covered with a medley of small buildings devoted to various domestic, business, and farm uses.

From the midst of these shacks and outhouses the two main buildings towered up like two swans leading a flock of cygnets to the water. But that is not to say there was anything fragile or graceful about them. On the contrary, they were massive and substantial, built of the materials at hand provided by the original clearing of the land.

The lower stories were of large river stones set in lime-puddled clay, and the upper of walnut logs, vast fellows, the remains of a grove cleared from the ground on which the houses stood.

"Such trees will never grow here again," said Garrett, when he and his sons cut them down. "They are the kind the Lord makes when he works all alone"—and he had refused to have them burned as the general custom was when making a clearing.

Instead, he had made the frames of the houses out of the mightiest of these trees and used the comparatively smaller ones to cabin him in. Nothing but adzes, axes; nothing but wooden pegs had been used in building. But they had been used skilfully, and both the massiveness and the neatness of the place were the pride, envy, and model for the whole neighborhood and its inhabitants.

Not that many other settlers could profit by the example set by the Pendergasses. Garret had seven sons and four daughters. His wife was a little woman. But great and small they had all laboured together upon the place. And a great deal can be accomplished when something is done every day by thirteen skilful and devoted people for twelve years.

Such in fact was the natural genesis and continuing reason for Pendergasses', and why, perhaps, it was always named in the possessive plural. For it was a hive of family industry and a store of local plenty, one that inevitably attracted travellers; that overflowed with news, gossip, and the benefits of trade, sustenance and furnishings; a veritable wellspring of sociability and primary necessities to the town and garrison, and to the pioneers in the coves of the mountains and the valleys about. For many years Mrs. Pendergass, for instance, had been the main, if not the sole, source of seeds, eggs, yeast, kittens, puppies, and even of fire itself, as the settlement spread.

Prime and vital nucleus of the establishment was the long room on the ground floor of the store building nearest the fort, known to the Pendergasses themselves and to all the older settlers as the "hearth room", and to others as the "taproom" or "general store". Combine the three, and a complete description of the function, indeed a history of the place, could be had, except for the fact that before the fort was built the main dwelling had also served on several occasions as the blockhouse or rallying point of the whole Raystown neighbourhood for defence against the Indians. A few louvres and loopholes in the stone walls of its lower story and the heavy log section above, now all carefully stoned in or blocked up, was all that remained to tell of a time of precarious, private conflict with the savages, which had already passed.

Pendergass and his seven sons had built the hearth room originally for the ample living quarters and kitchen of an equally ample family, to which, seeing the capacity of his copious loins already increased by a Biblical number of sons, to say nothing of his daughters, Garrett had

45

prophetically seen fit to provide the largest and widest proportions that the hugest specimens of his giant walnut trees would permit.

Hence, the beams supporting the ceiling were twice the thickness of a man's body. The floors were of mighty planks ground smooth by the passing of time, innumerable feet, and the action of clean, white river sand. The windows were not numerous, but enclosed by shutters, iron bars, and glass, the first to be brought into the community. If anything, the apartment suffered from a certain lack of light. But this was at least partially offset by the fact that the long walls were plastered and whitewashed, and that at one end of the place burned continuously and forever a fire that was never less than twelve feet long and might be nine feet high, depending upon the weather and the exigencies of cookery.

Indeed, the actual dimensions of the fireplace were even larger. A whole ox, a stag, or an elk could be roasted there, or a bear upon occasion. There were several stone ovens provided with separate flues in the body of the towering chimney, and the hearth itself, made of the whitest, smoothest, largest of boulders, rose a good two feet like a stage at one end of the apartment above the level of the rest of the floor.

To enter the hearth room therefore, was to become immediately, although perhaps unconsciously, a spectator of a comforting drama of life. And the spectacle at Pendergasses' seldom failed to be interesting, since not the eye and mind alone were engaged, but food, drink, appetizing odours, and lively company also made their appeal. Perhaps, more than anything else, *that* was the secret of the place.

As time went on, and the community had grown, the hearth room had gradually become a general store. Garrett had first begun as a trader in peltry, and he had imported goods to exchange for skins, both with the Indians and with the settlers, liquor being not the least of items. He had formed connections with merchants at Harris's ferry and later at Philadelphia, and he had prospered.

In due course of time a counter had been run along one side of the big room. Barrels and kegs with spigots, shelves heaped high with cloth, notions, and sundries lined the wall behind the counter. An abacus for doing sums, and several smooth, painted shutters covered with chalked names and amounts constituted the immediate bookkeeping of the establishment, or that part of it which went on before the eyes of customers. And the counter itself, now stained and worn, had long performed in the dual capacity of a merchandising table and a drinkers' bar.

Only one important change had marked the coming of the garrison, a silent and not an entirely complimentary comment: the installation of a large grille made of hickory bars that could be let down from the ceiling, and behind which those who tended the store and served out liquor appeared, when it was let down, to be so many felons or wild beasts pacing the length of their cage.

Transactions for drink at least were now always in coin. Money, both metallic and paper, had appeared with the coming of armies and the presence of important personages and officers. A cashbox, into which a large part of the contents of the paymasters' chests was eventually transferred, was installed. Trading in kind gradually became rarer, except with hunters and pioneers. Fights and disorders occasionally troubled the room. Truculent and notorious characters dropped in. The precaution of the grille was necessary.

But while Garrett was secretly troubled by the comment which its bars seemed to make on the hospitality of his house, he had tried to offset the somewhat grim message which its presence implied by a sign hung from a beam midway along the counter. On this an "artist" from the garrison had depicted in thrilling colours and in crude heraldic style a hive surrounded by busy bees with a homemade verse beneath them:

> Here in this hive we're all alive,
> Good liquor makes us funny.
> If you are dry, step in and try
> The flavour of our honey.

And this, if it lacked genius, at least evoked a universal, popular admiration.

The transition of the place from a dwelling house and store into a general inn and tavern had been gradual, inevitable, and scarcely noticed. Travellers, at first as guests and then as boarders, had sought and obtained shelter at Pendergasses'. Newcomers, magistrates, and itinerant preachers came frequently. With the cutting through of the road westward, with the establishment of the fort and the passing of regiments, "everybody" who had business in the Western Parts, and quite frequently Somebody and his servant, stopped there. And some of them were inclined when they wrote home about this "haven" in the wilderness to insert an "e" in the word.

The family had for long inhabited the log story above the hearth room. It was divided into a large number of small but comfortable chambers. Here at first they had tried to accommodate guests by the simple process of doubling up. But the constant crowding and disturbance had at last become intolerable, and Garrett had finally, and at the urgent representations of his wife, erected a second dwelling house next door, thus doubling his living space and filling the old tavern building to capacity, while his family privacy and domestic intimacies were preserved.

The marriages of his sons and daughters and the arrival in due course of many grandchildren had at last filled even the second building—and had also provided the hands to continue the establishment.

In addition, there were several Negroes owned outright and two Indian families, Cherokees fooled long years before by a governor of Maryland into leaving their native parts and now forever stranded, after a sad experience, in Pennsylvania. Their status was dim but their dependence and services plain. They and the Negroes had cabins in the yard amid the cattle, poultry, wagons, horses, and dogs.

From time to time the pressure of numbers had been relieved by the departure of one son or daughter or another, with children, to settle on outlying lands. Thus Pendergass cabins and clearings dotted the hills around. But Indian forays and troubles drove them back again. And they were always glad to return "home".

For a constant din of life, partly natural, and partly an unconscious protest against the monotonous, threatening silence of the wilderness, forever arose from the place. A delicious confusion, a jostling of many people, quarrels, loves, and perpetual animation provided a balm and antidote for lonely frontier souls. Here were people instead of trees. And even the trees roared cheerfully up the chimney. In the course of years a whole forest of them had vanished here.

Queen bee of the hive, and, as her days went on, more and more inclined to stay hidden in her cell, was the mother of the place, Mrs. Rose Pendergass, an apple-cheeked, brown, little Englishwoman from Devon. Some-one must pay for so much exuberance, and it was Mrs. Pendergass who did so. As the din, vigour, and complexities of life were increased about her; when each period and climax of accomplishment by her tremendous husband proved to be only the vaulting stance for something more, she resigned quietly, enjoyed the seclusion of her room whenever she could—where she somehow induced hummingbirds to hover at her window sills in summer—talked comforting nonsense to the babies, wiped their mothers' jealous tears away, and cultivated her garden. If she sometimes sighed for the quiet and simplicity of her pioneer beginning, when her cabin first stood by the Juniata and the Juniata sang to the stars, or for the earlier and more solitary devotion of her husband, she said nothing. Deafness had at last come to her rescue and she now moved in a silence and with an inner peace and patience which the fullness of life had brought her. In fact, she blossomed again faintly in a kind of poised Indian summer of the soul. And to look at her was inevitably to be reminded of the flower she was named after, and its quaint habit of reburgeoning in the fall.

As for old Garrett, he was completely devoted to his Rose. As she grew a little feebler he had built a kind of covered way on trestles between the store building and the house to save her steps, especially in winter, and to ensure the ease and privacy of her passing to and fro. This bridge was also appreciated by all the other women on the place, who could thus do their chores about the upstairs rooms in the inn without descending to the bar below.

To Garrett and his wife the bridge was the visible symbol and link between the two parts of their lives, the domestic and the public, and a reminder that each was dependent and inextricably linked with the other. The bridge was not, as later days would have it, a "protection from Indians". It was much more than that. It was a tie that bound. To the very last Mrs. Pendergass continued to use it and to appear upon occasions even in the tavern by her old hearth. Her presence about the place lent an intangible touch of natural refinement and an indestructible respectability. She was adored by her sons and grandsons and their wives and daughters. Her matriarchal prestige, indeed, was already legendary. In her presence even the boldest and rudest spirits were prone to rememreb whatever manners they might be said to have forgot. And if not—there were the tongues, fists, and rifles of her tribe to remind them.

Such was Pendergasses' by the banks of the Juniata at Bedford, its men, women, buildings, and repute, when, on the night of November 4, 1763, Salathiel Albine, accompanied by Edward Yates, Dr. Boyd the surgeon, Murray, and young Tom Pendergass approached its main entrance from the riverside, saw a hint of young moonlight on its silver shingles, heard the near-by rolling of waters— pushed open a heavy double door, and entered in.

4

In Which a Threshold
Is Crossed

AND THIS TIME Salathiel was not disappointed. He had found what he had been looking for; something that was not of the wilderness. Certainly that night the hearth room at Pendergasses' was as far set apart from the forest, the winter, and the loneliness outside as anything man-made could be. There was peace, warmth, light, security, abundance, and happiness there.

Old Mrs. Pendergass sat at one end of the long, low-ceilinged room with a spinning wheel, her chair on the raised hearth, with her back to the glowing embers of the great fire. The white yarn was coming off the wheel steadily to a low humming sound and the clack of the treadle, and being wound in a hank about the white, extended arms of her golden-haired granddaughter, Phoebe Davison. The girl, about sixteen years old, had a laugh like clear water poured from a silver urn. An old Negro woman with a corncob pipe in her gums sat dozing on a stool near the chimney, her withered face showing the outlines of her skull. Garrett and two of his men were taking stock behind the hickory grille and re-arranging the goods on the shelves in anticipation of the arrival of the pay chests, when trade might be expected to reach a copious pitch.

"Stack the playin' cyards high fer all to see," old Garrett was saying as the door opened; "even the English parsons will be wantin' 'em. Thar's not a pack left up at the fort that ain't marked or worn thin." The cold draught from the open door struck him. "Come in, come in, gentlemen, I've been expectin' you these two hours and keepin' the coffee soup hot. How's the little captain, doctor? Pina, stir your stumps. What'll it be now, gentlemen, what'll it be?"

"Hot rum and butter," said Yates. There were no vetoes. Salathiel stood looking about him while the old coloured woman brought the rum and mugs.

The main area of the room, provided with one huge oak table and three smaller ones, had a floor scattered with gleaming white sand laid in patterns and evidently fresh put down, for there were few footprints upon it. Several dip candles set in homemade sconces cast a yellow glow which, mixed with the firelight, was reflected softly but cheerfully from the white floor and the long white-washed walls.

In one corner, at a small table of his own, sat an Herculean figure of a man dressed in fringed buckskins. He was playing checkers with a small boy whose resemblance to his sister by the spinning wheel was so striking as to be unmistakable.

"Crown me, Cap'n Jack. I'm in your king row again,' piped the youngster. "Oh, goody!"

"Pizen me ef you hain't," rumbled the big man through a wealth of grey-streaked beard. "Here, Garrett, send this grandson of yours to his bunk. He's beat me again worse nor the French did Braddock."

"Go to bed, Arthur, it's dreadful late," said his grandfather. "And you too, Phoebe. Kiss your granfer."

The young girl tied her yarn carefully, and ducking under the counter stood on tiptoe to kiss her grandfather good night. As she did so she caught Salathiel's eye upon her and blushed violently.

He had no eyes for anything or anybody else. He had never seen anyone like Phoebe. She seemed like an angel escaped from some golden heaven. His breath came quicker. She turned as she left the room and looked back at him with eyes as calm and innocent as blue mountain lakes.

"She's gone!" he exclaimed tragically and aloud, before he was aware of speaking.

"Like a doe in the woods at twilight," said Captain Jack, laughing, "but cheer up, young feller, mornin'll come again."

Old Mrs. Pendergass laughed musically. She could hear little, but she saw everything that went on.

"You boys from the forest," she said, "you be like zailors home from the zea."

Mr. Yates appeared delighted at Salathiel's being the centre of curiosity and attention, and slapped his large friend encouragingly on the back.

"You're coming along, Sal," he cried. "Demme, you're coming along!"

Salathiel was intensely aware of but somewhat overcome by all this. For him it was a confused and crowded moment, one forever memorable. He was conscious of achievement, of having finally stepped over the threshold of the wilderness into the world of his own people that he had longed to see. He was amazed and moved by the vision of Phoebe. He was confused by so many people; embarrassed by having spoken his feelings about Phoebe aloud; pleased and surprised that Yates should care that he was "coming along". He was also bowled over by the incredible "wealth" in goods and comfort of the room in which he stood, and by the, to him, well-dressed, neat, and confident people present. He felt his mind swimming triumphantly in the surprising comfort and solid ease of the place, lapped in the palpable glow and warmth of its large, bright floor and walls. And all this had come upon him and was to be digested at once and at one time. The net result was a feeling of rising exhilaration.

His people had done all this—and he was one of them! They were accepting him.

He felt an all but overpowering impulse to give the triumphant scalp helloo of the returning successful warrior. The impulse rose in his chest like a solid thing trying to escape through his mouth. He put his hand to his throat, remembering what the captain had said about indulging in savage yells, and stopped it just in time. Then he stood for a moment with his eyes closed.

Captain Jack was the only one who understood what was happening to Salathiel.

"Come over here, young feller, and set down with the rest of us," he said. "Murray and Tom Pendergass has been tellin' me about you. Garrett, hev you met Tom's friend, Sal Albine, him they was talking over this evenin'?"

Garrett Pendergass came dodging under the counter and across the room to shake hands.

"I hear ye turned a smart trick on the traders from what the boys say," he remarked. "Yer little captain's a clever man. Liken it will hit friend Japson hard, though. By the way, I was sayin' to the old woman I kin only recollect hearin' your name once before. 'Twas a young couple, a smith and his wife, stopped off with us when we were living out at Path Valley. They were 'tarnel bent on goin' clar to the Ohio. Leastways he was. And that was long before the road was opened over to the forks of the Yough. From Connecticut, I think they were. It's a long time ago now. 'Bout a score of years. But I remember we wanted 'em to stay on with us. The missus was in a family way. Liken you're the baby?" laughed Garrett, looking Salathiel's six feet four up and down.

"I'd hardly know, sir," replied Salathiel. "You see, I was taken by the Injuns when I was a young'un. Why, it's only kind of by luck I remember my name."

"Wal, I jes thought it maunt be," said old Garrett.

"So you was kerried off by the varmints," said Captain Jack excitedly. "Wal, now, that's curious! Now, so was I. We'll have to talk some together, young feller. Tell the truth, I got suthin' in view. Suthin' might interest ya, and . . ."

"Gentlemen, gentlemen," called Yates. "Come over and sit down with the company or you'll miss the grog," at which the three, who had been standing in the middle of the floor talking, adjourned their meeting and joined the rest at the big table near the fire.

It stretched halfway across the room, a massive piece of oak furniture with two heavy wrought-iron sconces bolted into it at either end. The candles in these were now halfway burnt down, but shone none the less brightly on the red English phiz of Dr. Boyd, the tanned, lean faces of Murray and young Pendergass, and the engaging countenance of Mr. Yates. Salathiel, Captain Jack, and old Garrett now settled themselves at the same board with their feet stretched out under the table towards the warmth of the fire.

Mrs. Pendergass bade her husband good night and excused herself, after seeing that the old coloured woman had the hominy, venison, and bacon smoking on the table; hot water, butter, rum, and a spice pannikin going around. A large chicken pie as yet uncut smoked near the fire for further reference. Dr. Boyd filled the only glass tumbler in the place with rum and water, eyeing the proportions with the nice eye of an apothecary—and tossed it off.

"Two-thirds to one," said he, "is a proper night potation—hot."

Advised thus by the doctor, the meal began. Mr. Yates produced some dice from his vest pocket and began to throw.

" 'Pon my word, Edward," said old Garrett. "I was in hopes you'd lost 'em at Ligonier. They cost me half your board last time you came to stay here. Wal, what is it now?"

"Low cast takes care of the company." Yates passed the dice along in a cup and prepared to keep score.

The surgeon cast extremely high throw with a sigh of relief. Murray won from young Pendergass, and Tom from his father. Old Garrett then rolled with Yates.

"What did I tell you!" said Yates. "These things are as good as a legacy to me."

Old Garrett grumbled and then lost to Captain Jack—and the last throw remained between Salathiel and Garrett.

Salathiel lost.

"Maybe he ain't got no money, pa," said Tom. "Liken you got some pelts, ain't you, Sal?"

So it was money they wanted. Why, then he had some. He began to fumble in his bullet bag. Some cartridges, some tobacco, one of five louis d'ors he had taken from the Delawares near Ligonier, the medal, and the two newly dried scalps came out on the table.

An appreciative roar went up from the company.

"Go on, go on. Ye can't tell what ye might dig up out o' that yit," said Captain Jack.

Old Garrett reached forward, touched the gold piece, and then began to fondle the two scalps with his stubby fingers. "They're worth a king's pound apiece in Philadelphy," he said. "That's the provincial bounty. I'll give ye two pounds Pennsylvania for 'em or your change in credit. That'll be enough to keep you goin' here for some time, ef you don't cast dice with Yates."

Yates nodded to Albine. Salathiel shoved the two scalps over to old Garrett. "It's a bargain," he said. He also extended the gold piece doubtfully. He had no idea what the supper would cost.

"Best keep it," said Garrett, after hesitating a moment visibly. "Reckon you're not paid yet, eh? I know the captain ain't."

"We'll all be paid when Ourry gets here with the chests," grumbled the surgeon. "I've three-quarters due myself. It's a scandal, I say! Amherst wouldn't certify the paymaster's account. The papers lay in his bureau for months, I hear. We're nigh mutiny here, and no wonder! The least a general can do is to sign his name. Well, I hear Ourry's due at London with the chests and train tomorrow at latest. That puts him only two days away. They say he has nearly fifty wagons in the convoy and they can't make haste."

"And Captain Stewart told me the roads were strewn with desarters all the way back to Lancaster," remarked Yates. "The commandant expects half of the recruits will be gone 'fore they get here."

"Speck so," agreed Captain Jack. "Them 'umble fellers from the east counties never would fight. It's riflemen, the Macs and Bucktails, the Presbyterian psalm-singin' stronghearts, not a passel o' pressed Dutchmen and pacification Quakers they want. Some o' those fellers looses their bowels when they hear a papoose howl for a squaw." He spat and looked up. The door had opened.

"Were you referring to me, sir?" demanded an angry voice unexpectedly. They all looked up now to see Maxwell and two militia officers coming in through the door. It was Neville and Aiken.

"Why, no, I can't say I was," drawled Captain Jack, " 'cause ye weren't here to refer to."

This being manifest, Mr. Maxwell swallowed his hurt pride with a jumbled explanation, and sat down with the two Pennsylvania officers at the far end of the room. Young Tom went over to serve them.

"I'm not payin' fer *them*, Mr. Pendergass," said Salathiel firmly.

"No, no," replied Garrett. "Of course not."

Mr. Yates looked pleased. He was exchanging horrid glare for glare with Lieutenant Neville.

"Still under arrest?" the little lawyer asked mock-sympathetically.

"Yes, Mr. Attorney, but we'll not be retaining you," said Aiken.

"Innocence needs no advocate, I suppose," countered Yates—and turned his back on them.

A certain constrained atmosphere had now fallen on the room. The two tables ate their respective suppers separately with a gulf between. But the silence rapidly became onerous. After some prodding, Salathiel consented to tell the story of the trip from Fort Pitt to Bedford, and finally warmed to it. He was not sparing of facts and drew forth considerable laughter. Mr. Yates joined in with his own version of things from time to time. The gentlemen at the other table soon had faces like thunder clouds, although their names were never mentioned. Maxwell's chagrin was only equalled by his brooding desire for revenge on having his suspicion confirmed as to who the "Indians" were who had stampeded him and his men.

"Ef'n that Irish gal from Frazier's ever shows up here, I'll be on the lookout for her," said Murray to Salathiel when he had ended.

"Yer might find her handy round the place, pa," suggested Tom.

"I know the place ye'd be handlin'," replied his father. A shout went up.

"It hain't the joke ye think," joined in Captain Jack. "I've knowed Frazier and his old woman off en on from ever since Braddock's time. And I alers says murder is jes settin' on the ridgepole of his cabin, waitin' for ter climb down the chimney." He spat into the fire for emphasis. "I'm plumb sorry fer that colleen. And I doubt the pistol you left her, Sal, will do her much good. I doubt ef she gits away even when her time's sarved out. Wal, good night to yer all."

He rose and took his rifle and pouch down from some pegs on the wall. "I got some miles ter ride before I kin hole up," he remarked, and came over to shake hands with Salathiel, the butt of his rifle cuddled over his arm. "Thanks for the supper, young feller, and don't forgit you and me has a powwow comin'."

"I'll not," said Salathiel, much flattered at the old

60

hunter's civility and attention. The rifle butt, he noticed, was decorated with a series of notches. Sometimes these occurred in groups of three or four, and there were several lines of them cut into the wood. Noting his eyes upon them, Captain Jack smiled.

"Kind of a hard time to be riding many miles alone around these parts tonight, ain't it?" suggested Salathial as the door closed behind the powerful figure of the old hunter.

"Not for him, son," said old Pendergass. "He's jes hopin' he'll be follered. The only thing worries him is thar's not much more room left on his gunstock fer notches."

"Don't yer know who he is?" asked Murray, looking astonished. "Hit's the famousest story—"

"Excuse me for interruptin'," said the surgeon, "but I think I'll just step up to the fort and have a last look at my patient before turnin' in."

"I'll be goin' with you, doctor. The captain might need me before mornin'," said Albine.

"Good," replied the doctor. "Your friend Burent must know more about horses than sick men."

They bade the company good night regretfully. Yates was beginning to relate an anecdote.

"That's him, that's him," Salathiel heard Maxwell saying as they closed the door behind them and stepped out into the keen, star-flashing night.

The low, rushing sound of the river filled their ears. Somewhere in the town a dog barked. They climbed the steep path to the postern gate and answered a surly challenge.

"Advance friends and give the God-damned countersign," said the sentry.

"Cumberland."

"Cumberland, it is," muttered the sentry inside, and the chains rattled. The dim rays of a filthy lanthorn were flashed into the surgeon's face.

"Why, it's only Bones—and a scalp," said the corporal, and he grinned impudently.

With some difficulty the surgeon restrained his impulse to knock the man down. He wiped his forehead as they walked across to headquarters.

"This detachment of grenadiers," the surgeon burst out, "are the damnedest, most insultin', mutinous, pox-riddled . . ." His feelings choked him. "By God," he added, finally getting his breath again, "I hope Ecuyer *does* get better! What we need is a man that's death-bane for impudent rascals around here."

They entered the sickroom.

Burent and the captain were both sleeping soundly. In the thin shine of one low-burning candle Ecuyer's face on the pillow was like a wax cameo. He was breathing easily and a dream had laid a smile across his lips.

The surgeon again swore—softly. This time with relief.

5

Fort Bedford

FORT BEDFORD overlooked the rolling valley lands westward to the distant Alleghenies, and that tumbling range of blue mountains seemed to march southward and gaze back at the fort. Between, like the shades of monsters cast on the bottom of a translucent ocean, swam dissolving cloud shadows, the gloom and gleams of weather, ever changing and ephemeral, against something still and eternally the same. That sameness was the backdrop and ground plan of the bowl of forest into which the stub ends of long, high mountains thrust themselves like the broken ribs of a fan or the hubless spokes of a disordered wheel.

Here, in some dim age before human time began, had been the centre of an earth convulsion riving and waving the land all around it into a sprawl of wrinkles on the surface of the star. But this force had suddenly subsided, ceased; leaving, like the cooling purpose of a mad, impulsive artist, only the hinted outlines of design—and now the fort and town stood where the hub of the wheel of mountains might have been.

There, as if to make room for the puny works of man, the spokes of the hills gathered in, but stopped short, broken off abruptly. One long range, that must once have been closed in the valley to the northward like the rim of a wheel, had been neatly sliced in two as though by the stroke of a knife, and in the gorge between the severed hills the keen, blue steel of the river still gleamed; flashed at noon brightly.

Perhaps the hint made by the valley lying westward that it was once the bottom of a sea was a genuine whisper from the remote past. For at one time, before the river broke through its gap, there must have been a lake there, brimming like an overflowing cup to the very rim of the surrounding mountains. Indeed, for Dr. Boyd, who fancied himself as a geologist and dabbled in several other sciences besides his own, there were limestone deposits all about to prove his theory.

This substance, certain mysterious sinkholes, curious springs, a lush rainfall, and probable underground streams and rivers, still gave to any discerning eye, whether a well-informed one or not, a luxurious and comforting sense of a cup running over; in summer especially, of forests of a darker green, a nobler outline, and grass fresher and more luscious to crop. Nor was this impression merely some romantic reflection in the fashionable looking-glass of the time. It was similarly noted by other than human eyes for purely practical purposes. Animals and birds delighted in the neighbourhood for their own reasons. Game had, and still continued, relatively, to swarm in this favoured swirl of the Pennsylvania hills.

It was this suggestion, made by the region itself, of bountiful plenty and pleasant grandeur that had endeared it to the Shawnees and preserved it in their firelight legends as a happy hunting ground. And it was all this, plus a certain inexplicable, but certainly auspicious drama in the surrounding landscape, that had caused Garrett Pendergass to enter in his diary when he first came to spy out the land as a young man, "a marvellous beautiful valley I covet dwelling in someday, God prospering me."

That prayer had been amply granted, prosperity being added. Garrett at least could say, "my cup runneth over", and thank God and the country in which he dwelt for his blessings. Its grandest grove of walnut trees had gone to make his dwelling, but in his case justifiably.

In the course of time many other pioneers had also paid the vicinity the undoubted, but more dangerous compliment of settling down in it. Armies had come and gone, as armies do. But there was as yet little to mark either their passing or the presence of settlers. The region was still naturally pristine, essentially unspoiled. Only the fort with its flag flaunting by the river, the village clustered about it, Pendergasses', and the trace of the military road reaching westward, made visible the encroachments of man.

But that there was something inherently noble and quiet in the arrangement of the hills about Bedford, that this coign of the mountains presented an image of peace and foretold abundance even in troubled times, was evident to some degree and in some way to everybody but the blind. Even harassed and homesick soldiers had been known to succumb to its spell and to settle down contentedly when discharged.

As for Salathiel, Bedford was the first place in which he ever felt thoroughly at home. And the memory of it remained with him permanently and significantly, etched deeply on the fresh tablets of young memory by the hand of time. If there was something deep-bitten and indelible about the picture, that was due both to the beautiful lay of the hills and to the scalding acid of events which fixed them forever on his mind.

For a while, too, it had seemed as though Ecuyer might recover. For Dr. Boyd had not been altogether mistaken that evening when he had sworn with relief at finding Ecuyer apparently better, and his fever subsiding. The removal of the shell fragment from his old wound had at first done wonders for him. He had not developed "inflammation of the lungs", and even the wound from the stone arrowhead, which had become inflamed, "sympathetically", as the surgeon said, had subsided during the week or ten days in which the captain lay abed after his first arrival at the fort. In fact, Ecuyer had seemed in a fair way then to get on his feet again.

"Rest and quiet is the prescription," said the doctor; "exhaustion and threatened blood poisoning, the diagnosis." After which Dr. Boyd bled his patient profusely. That at least did keep him quiet for a while. He was left quite too weak to get up. The trouble was that both the driving will of the captain and events were wholly against the patient's being able to take the surgeon's advice.

Ecuyer felt himself personally responsible for the organizing and forwarding of men and supplies to Colonel Bouquet at Fort Pitt. He knew that even the possibility of the expedition down the Ohio largely depended upon him. He had been given full authority to keep supplies and men moving over the roads, and in using it mercilessly he was not one to spare himself. Nor was he being merely fanatical about it.

Authority was largely personal on the frontier. Those

who could apply it and get results were rare. Few things were done for government out of patriotism, much for a man.

Now it was already apparent to Ecuyer, even in November, '63, when he had first arrived at Fort Bedford, that Colonel Bouquet's expedition against the Indians in the Ohio country, then scheduled for the following spring, would have to be delayed, might indeed never leave Fort Pitt at all, unless he, Simeon Ecuyer, greatly bestirred himself at Bedford. In this crisis a painful body was to his mind only one of the minor difficulties before him, and a trivial and personal one at that.

He, and Salathiel, and Burent had arrived at Fort Bedford on the 4th of November. Luckily for the captain, it rained, snowed, and froze again the following week. Nothing much could be done under the icy circumstances. Everyone, friend and enemy alike, was stopped. Ecuyer had stayed in his bed in Captain Ourry's quarters, where he had first been taken. He lay there while his wound closed and the fever left him. He dozed and recuperated. From time to time he would come to himself and work feverishly. For, while he lay abed, that is not to say he got nothing done.

Captain Ourry had also been delayed by the weather with the pay chests, supplies, and recruits at Fort Loudon, some miles to the east of Bedford, and on the other side of the mountains. The roads and weather being what they were, it was impossible even to try to get through. But it was not impossible for Ecuyer to send Burent on to Fort Loudon to help get the wagons repaired and under way as soon as the weather should break.

Burent had a positive mechanical genius for organizing repairs and devising ingenious tackle for getting transport out of the mud. Again and again Ecuyer had tried to get an officer's commission for Burent, in order to use his talents more effectively. But no attention as yet had been given to his many urgent requests, and it was only by various subterfuges that the captain could manage even to get Burent paid.

He had already put him on the payroll as a military servant. He now entered him as a "road contractor". He again promised to try to obtain him his commission, and with a final, personal appeal to the devoted little man, dispatched him to Ourry with a letter demanding that strict attention be paid to his recommendations, and the necessary assistance supplied.

So, two days after they arrived at Bedford, Burent had said good-bye, and departed in the midst of a blinding snowstorm, reluctant to leave the captain, but convinced that it was his duty to do so.

As a consequence, for the first few days at Bedford the entire care of the captain and his now multifarious affairs fell upon Salathiel. He was kept busy all day, and he got little sleep at night. There was not only the body care of Ecuyer; meals, the horses, and equipment to look after as usual, but there were also endless letters at night, errands to be run, details to be checked, and messages to be taken. Although Ecuyer was ill in bed, he was, nevertheless, able to drive those about him at the fort, and Salathiel in particular, to the limit. And what weather it was! Raw, arctic cold; then rain and snow; then an ice storm to top it off.

It was in this welter of affairs, weather, hardships, and various new difficulties and responsibilities, that Yates stepped in to lend a hand. He had come to the fort from Pendergasses' regularly every morning to enquire after the captain's health. He would sit for a quarter of an hour or so and talk. Ecuyer was now looking about him for anyone he could get to help speed affairs along. He rapidly came to depend on Yates for a trustworthy account of what was happening from day to day. More than anything else, the captain felt his inability to get around and keep in touch with the state of mind in the garrison and the town. With a keen ear for talk and rumour, Yates seemed to have the state of the community and what everyone thought and said at his tongue tip. He was honest and straightforward. He liked the captain. They had both come to trust each other at Ligonier. Thus the young Scot's comments were both helpful and shrewd. Salathiel learned a great deal by just listening to what was said.

It was during one of these morning conversations that Ecuyer reminded the young lawyer that he had never told him what the favour was Yates had said he was going to ask him at Ligonier.

Yates laughed.

"To tell the truth it was a trivial one I more or less made up at the time. I was making talk that night, you may remember, and I just wanted a point to bargain on."

"Nevertheless, out with it, man," insisted Ecuyer.

"Ahem," said Yates, considering. "Oh, yes, I do recollect now. You promised to let me have the receipt for the soup Albine served us that night St. Clair and the two militia officers came storming in. It was the best soup I ever tasted, and I rather fancy getting such things into my notes and diary as I go about."

"Ah, you keep a diary, do you?" smiled the captain. "I rather thought as much. Well, 'your Grace', the favour is granted," he said in a low tone.

"Albine," he called, "give Mr. Yates that receipt of Johnson's for the famous Queen of Scots soup."

Salathiel sat down and copied out the long receipt from

the captain's memorandum book. He handed it to Yates, who looked at it, whistled, and expressed his thanks.

"Perhaps you have done me more of a favour than you know," said he. "By the way, I hear that Burent has arrived at Loudon and has already put the smiths to work forging snow runners for the pay-chest wagon. Captain Jack brought in the word only this morning. He's been east for a week."

"Good!" exclaimed the captain. The news cheered him greatly. "I knew I could depend on Burent," he added. "Now if we can only get these surly rascals at the fort paid, how *that* would help! The grenadiers are much the worst, I hear."

Yates agreed. "They do need a curb," he said. "But pardon me, I am not so rash as to try to advise you there. I am not of the military."

"To some extent we must *all* be of the military in these times," replied Ecuyer. "I was wondering if *you* would undertake to help Albine here with the correspondence, and give me your assistance in some other matters while I am laid up. The letters are now more than both of us can manage. Also, frankly, as matters now stand here at the fort, I do not wish to call in a new officer from a battalion that is not my own, or a raw military clerk. Certain matters of policy and promotions are involved. There might be leaks, I am afraid." He plucked the covers nervously.

Yates smiled encouragingly. He quite understood the predicament in which the captain found himself.

"Let me advise you," he said, laughing, "in matters concerning the civil and militia laws of Pennsylvania. In that capacity I could be more or less at your service, sir. And most happy to be so."

Ecuyer looked grateful and relieved.

"Very well, I shall consult you," he said. "On detached

service I am entitled to certify fees for 'necessary and unavoidable' civil aid. I take it this is both."

"I, too, can be ingenious," laughed Yates.

"Ask Captain Jack to come up to see me about this time tomorrow, if he is still about," the captain suggested as Yates rose to leave. "Tell him it's important."

"He'll be here, I warrant you," replied Yates.

The captain looked doubtful, however. "I am not so sure," he said. "That may require all our ingenuity."

"Thanks for the receipt for the Scotch soup," replied Yates. He grinned at Albine, and went out whistling loudly, much to the disgust of Captain Stewart at work down the hall.

That officer was not feeling so mortal cheerful. He thought he had a fine, young mutiny on his hands and was dandling it nervously. Good God, would the pay chests never come!

Thereafter, for many nights, and for some time to come, Salathiel had the able assistance of Edward Hamilton Yates, Esq., in the difficult drudgery over the captain's letters, records, and correspondence. Or rather, to be exact, Mr. Albine became the assistant and pupil of Yates, for the astute little lawyer took over wholeheartedly, although with great wisdom and restraint, and became in effect, though unofficially, a kind of civilian adjutant to Captain Ecuyer, and a careful and modest adviser in his affairs.

It was a purely personal arrangement and relationship amongst the three, Ecuyer, Yates, and Albine. It was rather typical of Ecuyer, who had a way of getting things done by the people who could do them and be trusted, whether they were official or not.

Headquarters, for instance, might have been astonished had they known. But, as Ecuyer said, "Why trouble them?

71

Their social duties about the metropolis are already overwhelming."

So the light burned late at Captain Ourry's quarters, where Ecuyer lay those first days at Bedford, and the letters and orders, the messengers and orderlies went in and out, and back and forth, while the garrison seethed with discontent.

For an invalid, Ecuyer did astonishingly well. Only Bouquet, who knew his true condition, commented. "I see that you write letters with both your right and left hands now," he once remarked in a postscript. "But your new, third hand does puzzle me, though it's a right professional scrawl." This provided a much-enjoyed private laugh for the three conspirators in Captain Ourry's quarters. Outside, the sleet and snow still beat at the window. It was a mercy the last messengers from Fort Pitt had come through. Trouble was reported again on the road between Bedford and Ligonier. A party of Delawares, it was said, perhaps some of Japson's old friends. Nevertheless, the weather and the captain's enforced quietude did provide an opportunity to catch up with the clerical work.

Now all of these apparently minor arrangements and small affairs were actually of prime importance and consequence to Salathiel, whose life and future were shaped by them to no small degree. The presence and help of Yates in the captain's quarters helped to ripen and solidify the friendship between him and the young lawyer. It might easily have had the opposite result, but the good nature, understanding ways, and invariable tact of Yates carried the day.

From the first he seemed to understand instinctively what great store Albine set by his ability to help the captain as a clerk. It was the one thing that obviously raised

72

Salathiel above the status of a personal servant. Johnson, good servant as he had been, had never been able, and, of course, never presumed to meddle with the captain's papers. But Albine from the first had been a help there. And in working with the records and correspondence Salathiel had been obliged to use and improve every jot and tittle of whatever skill in writing and what little practical education McArdle had been able to impart to him. That portion of his forest experience alone Albine regarded as his ladder to climb to the status of a civilized man.

As a consequence he had worked long and painfully, but accurately and laboriously over the captain's accounts and at copying out his letters. He had often been slow and ponderous as a schoolboy. But he had always been faithful, and ever quick to learn and improve.

True, Ecuyer had often helped, pointed out or corrected mistakes when necessary, and he had frequently had to explain. Yet the captain valued loyalty and faithful work more than facility, and he had been secretly quite proud of, and always amazed at, young Albine's ability to cope with the correspondence at all.

But at Bedford more and more of the captain's affairs had now to be conducted by correspondence. He was in touch with officers and officials from Philadelphia to Fort Pitt, and upon urgent matters. At Bedford he was threatened with being swamped. Only the slowness of communication for the time being saved him. It was imperative, none the less, for him to have assistance. So it was no dissatisfaction with Salathiel that had prompted him to turn to Yates for help. It was necessity.

Yates, however, fully realized a delicate situation. He did not step in and try to supplant Albine, or relegate him to the duties of nurse and valet. He came to help. He had nothing but compliments, sincere ones, for the at least neat and accurate way in which he found the captain's papers had been kept. He shared the work and responsibility instead of pre-empting it. He acted as an equal and brought a welcome sense of companionship and a relief in difficulty in doing so.

A mutual devotion to the captain, understood between the two young men, but never commented upon, provided all the lubrication that was necessary under the circumstances. Yates and Albine got on. The correspondence, as Ecuyer said, "began to arrange itself". If Yates finally took the lead, it was only natural and seemed fair in a field where he excelled professionally. And when Salathiel finally left the captain, as he did soon afterward, he felt that no one except his forest mentor, McArdle, had helped him more with pen, book and candle—for they worked long and late together for many weeks at Bedford while the captain was ill, or was absent.

There were two other consequences of this time which also were vastly important to Albine. One was his move from the fort to bed and board at Pendergasses', the second was the beginning of his association and work with Captain Jack. The first came about quite naturally, and of itself. Captain Ecuyer carefully planned the second, not only for Albine, but for far larger reasons. It was in fact part of a scheme long cherished between the captain and Colonel Bouquet, nothing less than the formation of a corps of woodsmen and rangers. In that enterprise Captain Jack's help was vital. Ecuyer therefore awaited his coming with vivid anxiety. For Captain Jack might simply disappear into the woods as he had done before.

But Captain Jack eventually presented himself at the fort one morning, as he had been requested, although diffidently and with a certain amount of indignant bravado, the result of a combination of conflicting impulses which altered his usual long, confident hunting stride into a more severe *clumping* gait, since, for the weather and the occasion, he wore boots over his moccasins.

It was impossible for Captain Jack to enter a fort where the English flag flew and his Majesty's troops and officers strolled about in their scarlet or green, without a tightening of the throat, a flood of sorrowful and poignantly tragic memories that lay buried deep in his own and his family history. In fact, he was extremely reluctant to enter a military post at all, or to have any truck or traffic with royal officers, particularly with Englishmen.

Because Ecuyer was a Swiss, and therefore turned out of a different mould, Captain Jack had finally swallowed his hesitations and prejudices. In short, he was making a personal exception in Ecuyer's case, because he liked and trusted him. But he disliked the surroundings and atmosphere of the fort none the less. Nor was the old ranger being merely eccentric in all this. He had ponderable and powerful reasons peculiarly his own for feeling as he did. Only those who knew who and what he was could fully understand him. And there were few who ever really knew his secret. Many stories were told about him.

6

The Secret Story of Captain Jack

CAPTAIN JACK'S last name was Fenwick. He was either a grandson or a grandnephew of that Sir John Fenwick, who, in the reign of good King William, had lost his head on the block for his fanatical loyalty to the banished James. Sir John had headed a dangerous conspiracy in England and taken a leading part in a bitter affair. He had grievously insulted the queen, and that most dreadful and potent of all legal devices for punishment and destruction, an act of attainder working corruption of blood in his heirs and descendants, had, along with the axe, descended upon his devoted head.

Because the situation is so unusual, few can realize the predicament of those of the Fenwick blood who survived Sir John. They were physically alive in a world in which they did not legally exist. Even the fact that they occupied space was officially denied. Their name was erased, their estates confiscated. They could be robbed or assaulted, but no court could hear their complaints, or even see their persons, if they appeared before it. For an act of Parliament said they did not exist, and the consequences of this act, like the wrath of Jehovah, descended unto the third and the fourth generation of them that had loved King James too well.

In this condition of social no-men, the Fenwicks, if such they still were, had fled to the North American colonies with what apparel and small personal belongings they could collect by the combined mercy of their friends and the indifference of the authorities. There they had forthwith lost themselves in the kindly oblivion of the forests amid the Alleghenies. So succesful were they in this that most of them disappeared; and reappeared, if ever, only under different names. They were literally forgotten and forgot.

Under these circumstances it is, therefore, not possible to say whether it was a son or a nephew of Sir John Fenwick who first built a cabin on what, in later times, became known as "Jack's Mountain", about a day's journey east from Bedford. Only Captain Jack, the cabin builder's son, knew. And he was not likely to tell. Above all, he would not set anything down or confirm any rumours. Indeed, he went down in local history and legend without a surname, known as "Captain Jack" alone.

And very much alone he was. Neither a sense of obligation to the society from which his family had fled nor a feeling of loyalty to the house of Hanover and the Protestant succession was a lively sentiment in his family. His father had died a hopeless and embittered widower, leaving his son a cabin, some pre-empted land, a sockful of old hoarded guineas, and a little corn meal. There were also the memories and secret pride for an ancient vanished name, which, to Captain Jack at least, had almost the force of an infernal legend in shaping his character.

It was this family secret, perhaps, which gave him at times a certain Luciferian, a dreadful, but a heroic aspect; which enabled him to fight all his life against men, authority, and the universe successfully and alone. In this kind of career, and in the forests, he was towards the end of his life to achieve, apparently at least, a certain grim happiness, a sort of dark halcyoninity in a satiety of revenge. Those who knew him best recalled moments in his latter days when he was said to have been both kindly and urbane. If so, such manifestations were reserved for his intimates alone.

"Alone" was indeed the word which always best described him. His giant size lent itself to setting him apart from the rest of mankind. In a roomful of people he towered above them, singled out and remarkable. His iron-grey beard, his steely-blue eyes, the peculiar axelike feel of his profile and contour, outlined and made cruelly soft by the faded blood-red fringes of his buckskin hunting shirt and trousers, all contributed both to distinguish and to isolate him.

His voice was deep, suggesting a capacity to roar, while it remained disconcertingly soft and pliable; full of echoes, as it were, of the tones of experiences unknown and uncanny to most men. His few words came memorably from a red mouth ruled like a straight line under his thin nostrils, and finally, and perhaps most unconveyable in its meaning, except to those who actually saw it, he carried his rifle in his left arm like the proud father of a murderous child.

Yates said that Captain Jack looked as though he knew where the trap door of hell was hidden; that he had been there, come back, and wouldn't tell. And in this, as in several other matters, Mr. Yates was only being quite precise.

For Captain Jack (Fenwick) *had* been in hell. He had returned with difficulty, and he had devoted the rest of his time on earth to hunting down the devils who, he conceived, should be sent back to the infernal regions to which they essentially belonged.

It was quite simple if you knew why. It was this way:

When his father died, Captain Jack, then a lad of about seventeen, had buried his gloomy parent under a neighbouring oak, where it seemed likely to the boy that he might attract thunder even when dead. Jack had then taken the hoarded guineas and the corn meal on hand, arranged the meagre contents of the cabin for a long absence, sealed the latchstring with clay and resin, and scrawled on the door with charcoal, "This is Jack his place. Beware."

As to what his youth had been before leaving this sinister greeting on his rude ancestral portal, there were afterward many rumours afloat. According to some, he had once been carried off by the Indians as a child, lived amongst them for some time, and then returned to his father. Some said he had been rescued, others that his father had ransomed him. Once or twice he was later heard to refer somewhat cryptically to such an experience. However that may be, it is certain at the time of leaving home he was already an accomplished woodsman, familiar with the ways of savages, but also possessed of a grim resolution to get on in the world, retrieve the family fortunes in more civilized surroundings, and make a new name for himself. In short, he was of a far more manly and resolute character than his age might indicate. And

79

the threat that he left on the door for any who durst disturb his property was no idle one.

After taking a final look about at the wild scenery of the place which had detained his boyhood, and reading again for the grim satisfaction which it gave him the message to the world that he had left on the door of his home, he departed eastward accompanied by a fierce, old hound, an axe, a musket, and the family Bible with some pages torn out, both of which latter articles harked back to Cromwellian times. He paddled down the Conococheague branch to the Susquehanna and stopped at Harris's, where he traded his musket and one good guinea for a horse whose youth had been spent, not idly, but in an extremely remote antiquity.

Thus mounted on a four-legged myth, he took the trail along the river to Lancaster, remarking casually before leaving that his old man was dead; that he himself expected to come back someday, and that he would certainly kill anyone who might happen to be occupying his cabin when he returned. To lend emphasis to his amiable thought he twinkled his axe in the air, easily, twenty feet up—and caught it by the handle when it obediently returned. At which all present bade him Godspeed with relief and alacrity, and he rode off without looking back.

At a small settlement called Paxtang, the first village at which he arrived on his course eastward, a pack of curs ate his dog after a memorable fray, fragmentary in character towards its close, owing to the intervention of the axe. Without waiting to ascertain the probably unfavourable opinion of the villagers in regard to the matter, he wiped his axe off on some moss, and continued on to Lancaster. There his horse died of sheer inability further to continue in a state of equanimity.

Noting, not without a certain self-importance, that

death seemed to dog his steps, he also concealed his uneasiness at that fact and the increasing evidence of civilization which now began to surround him. But he was of a keen and noticing turn. He looked about him, and took measures to cope with his new surroundings. He had his hair cut and done into a neat queue. He bought himself the discarded wardrobe of a gentleman and a pair of new boots from a Jew peddler. He paid him with the worst guinea he had, and pushed on to Philadelphia. The lamentations of the peddler were necessarily restrained, because he had stolen the boots.

Fate is lured by small bait. It was the clothes thus obtained that caused a sober Philadelphia merchant to direct Jack to the respectable London Coffee House near the market. He took lodging there, found himself in good company, and before long was able to become the assistant to a surgeon-barber and dispenser of nostrums for a small down payment and a note of hand. Mr. Williams, the surgeon-barber, had taken Jack for the son of a plantation owner of means, which by both speech and manner he seemed to be.

This impression Jack was at no pains to correct. He had a few guineas left, and fortune in the form of death still followed him. An outbreak of ship's fever added suddenly to both reputation and income. His own services and the nostrums of his partner were in constant demand. Of those whom he attended some died and some recovered, but he was faithful in his rounds when others fled and his deathbed manner was always most reassuring and respectable.

As a consequence, both his fame and his fees were enhanced. And before his note came due the second time, the fevers had claimed his partner. This was luck in a shroud, but he stepped into his partner's shoes willingly enough.

Thus within the short space of two years "John Morton", as he was now called, found himself in actual, if not legal possession of a small cottage on the outskirts of town, a business that throve on calamity, and a reputation for the cure of all those who survived his semi-medical attentions, abetted by the silence of those who died.

Nor was John Morton a mere charlatan. He diligently observed, read, and experimented in the field of his art. He was clever, and he used herbs and bark medicines instead of powders. Add to this, that he never bled any of his patients either of gold or of the liquid in their veins, and there was much to be said for him in contrast with the run of regular practitioners of the time.

He finally made one innovation of medical moment. He kept in his service for a trifling regular stipend, and at his beck and call, several respectable and experienced widows who had nursed, buried, and survived. These women he let out as nurses, at a considerable profit to himself, to be sure, but also to the great comfort and satisfaction of his growing clientele. It was something no one seemed to have thought of before, even in Philadelphia, and it was profitable.

In short, Dr. Morton was genuinely successful. He aided his patients as much as any man then could—and was well paid for his trouble.

"Dr." Morton's success, for he had now assumed the title or had it bestowed upon him, can be gauged by the fact that he was already the envy of, and would soon have been the subject of denunciation by, the regular fraternity of licensed medicos in the city, had not a series of unfortunate events removed him at once from both their jealousy and their ken.

Not long after his partner died, John Morton had married a successful tradesman's daughter, one Mary Caldwell. And it so happened that soon after they were married, Mr. Caldwell chanced to die in great pain and internal discomfort—but unfortunately, not until he had been treated and well dosed by his son-in-law.

The medicine used had been a harmless concoction of slippery elm bark, alum water, and aloes, a soothing and astringent affair at worst. But Mr. Caldwell, who had a nice little property, had died *after* taking the medicine, and apparently quite suddenly. The property went to his only daughter Mary, he being a widower, and it was Dr. Morton's "widows," the nurses, who began to talk. Their bitter eloquence was not easily to be silenced.

In a few weeks the pearl of Dr. Morton's reputation vanished in vinegar. Calls for his services and medicaments ceased. Instead, there were threats, anonymous letters, and suspicious looks from old friends. In brief, he was ruined by specious gossip. And he now went about in great fear of being called to account before a jury of neighbours, who would necessarily be prejudiced.

In this crisis all comfort forsook him, save the consciousness of his own innocence and the constancy of his wife. Desperate, he finally consulted one Maria Carfax, an English "wisewoman" of somewhat unsavoury and occult reputation, who lived with an Indian at Conshohocken and had often sold him herbs for his medicines. She told him that because he had cheated Death of many upon whom the Black Shadow had already laid his hand, he had been called to personal account by the Grim Reaper and his own life was undoubtedly in danger. Death, Maria Carfax said, would not be denied, and if Dr. Morton avoided paying his forfeit now, it would be required of him thrice over in the future. Perhaps it would be just as well to let some of his patients die, she suggested. The grounds for her assertions were those in the bottom of a teacup, but Dr. Morton was nevertheless impressed.

Remembering that death *had* dogged his steps, he was both alarmed and depressed by the old woman's babble. He had gone down to Endor, and he returned to his house thoroughly frightened for the first and only time in his life. Every step in the street now seemed to announce the approach of constables, and the sound of the door knocker would all but stop his heart. He lost weight. He brooded. He recollected now that he was a Fenwick with a legal curse on his head. He descended into the valleys of melancholy.

In this hopeless state of affairs his wife came loyally to the rescue. She disposed of their property and of the small inheritance from her father, quietly and at a loss. From the proceeds she bought a stout German wagon and a sound team. Into this she persuaded her husband to load their household goods during the hours of darkness, and to leave Philadelphia. The early dawn of a spring day found them rolling southward for Maryland.

Lord Baltimore's province proved to be another and a hospitable country. On the western borders of it, at a small but growing settlement called McCullough's Town, they eventually found peace, plenty, and happiness. Indeed, the ensuing five years lay afterward in the perspective of Captain Jack's experience like a shaft of sunlight across a long corridor of gloom.

The return to the familiar life of the forest and fields revivified and made a new man out of him. He drew a line through the sentence of the past. He changed his name again merely as a sensible precaution, but he continued his practice much as before. He was now known as "Dr.

Caldwell", and he seemed in fact, and not only in name, to have achieved a new personality. The words of Maria Carfax did not apply to Dr. Caldwell. They had been meant for Dr. Morton. Perhaps even the Black Shadow could thus be thrown off the path. At least Dr. Caldwell felt so, and life at last seemed to have claimed him with no penalty attached.

He farmed, he rode about the country with his simples, and dispensed his herb medicines. He became much respected in the growing Scotch-Irish community. He and his good wife eventually became beloved. They did good and prospered. And in the course of time they had two children, a son and a daughter.

The Caldwells lived in a small valley that ran down to the Susquehanna, where the doctor had built a snug log house with his own hands. There were flowers in Mrs. Caldwell's dooryard and a carefully tended herb garden for her husband's practice. A stream sang its way past their door, expressing, along with the voices of the children, their quiet happiness in married solitude. A new rifle bought from a Pennsylvanian constantly enriched the larder. The Caldwells and the community in which they lived prospered. The doctor in his prayers frequently acknowledged his blessings.

Then a certain Indian summer came. The French and English across the ocean were going to war. No one at McCullough's Town remembered exactly what the quarrel was about. That it was an ancient one, they knew from what their fathers from the old country had said. But few in America cared any longer about it. In the spring there was fighting somewhere west of the mountains, but that, too, was far, far away. Then Death with a painted face came out of the forest.

Dr. Caldwell had been away on a two weeks' trip to

Baltimore for supplies. He was bringing home, in addition to a fine chest of carpenter tools, which he had long scrimped and saved to obtain, some English taffeta for his wife's gown and presents for the children. There was a rag doll for the baby girl, a painted toy trumpet for the little boy. There was white flour, household sundries, and a year's supply of powder, a roll of lead, and a new bullet mould. Such a fine wagonload showed how well the doctor had been getting along in the world.

He had heard humours of trouble on the way up but the war was young as yet and there had always been rumours of Indian trouble. He took the usual short cut over a woods road to his farm on the river, and thereby missed what would otherwise undoubtedly have attracted his attention; the fact that McCullough's Town had ceased to exist.

It had been burned two days before and every soul driven away or massacred. The dogs had been shot and eaten, the cattle killed, and the horses stolen. That was the reason the doctor had not met a soul on the road on the last lap of his journey. That, however, was not so unusual. It was as yet sparsely settled country.

The massive silence of the forest along the high banks of the Susquehanna was all that met the doctor on the drive down his own valley. He did not hear any cowbells, and he thought that strange. He blew on the painted toy horn at the stream crossing as he had promised his little son to do. But there was only a brief echo and the complaint of the stream which here ran under a log bridge. No dogs barked. There was no running figure in a sunbonnet with the two children toddling along behind her.

Suddenly he saw that his house was roofless and the logs seared by fire. The being of Dr. Caldwell seethed within him like a volcano. Some things he found out later, some he saw for himself at the time.

His was the last cabin that had been taken in the raid. The valley was lonely. The party of drunken Hurons and five half-breed Frenchmen had stopped in security to celebrate and be ingenious before moving on. The record of their brief visit is not conveyable in letters. It can best be understood by holding some member of the body in a flame—and not withdrawing it. Mrs. Caldwell had finally been hanged. She was still there, scorched. What had been a little boy was shaped like an egg.

As darkness came on, the person that had achieved being Dr. Morton and Dr. Caldwell dissolved, or sublimed, in a kindly oblivion of madness. An insane man presented the rag doll to the remains of his baby girl suspended over the talltale ashes in the fireplace.

Then the little girl came out on the hearth and danced for him in the grilled streaks of moonlight streaming between the burnt-out intervals of the logs.

The hallucination was final and complete. He was never able entirely to shake it off. He thought he gathered his child up in his arms and drove away. He felt her weight and he saw and heard her. She remained in the wagon with him for some days. He must have fed the horses sometimes and existed mechanically. Some weeks later, exactly how long he never knew, he lost the little girl. She vanished. Occasionally she called to him. She went off to join other voices in the forest, which he thought might be those of his wife and little boy. But he was not sure of it now. He began to realize he was wandering both mentally and physically. What had happened? Somehow he had crossed the Susquehanna. God alone knows where.

Eventually he found himself with a team of emaciated

horses covered with sores, wandering northward through the woods on a packers' trace. The outlines of the mountains were the first thing he began to become fully sensible of and to remember. The hills where he now found himself were vaguely familiar. He was also conscious now of an incredible fatigue.

He rested, fed the horses and himself, and then went to sleep in the wagon. His sleep was like a dip into death. When he awoke he was more sensible. Part of his memory came back. He began to realize the situation, although not fully. He first remembered things that had happened some time ago. He came to a familiar spring and crossing of wood paths. He knew he was on the way to Harris's from the south. The man he remembered best was Jack Fenwick. He could see that was who he was when he looked in the spring when he stooped down to drink. His face had much altered. He looken drawn but younger, despite his beard. He had returned to his original self again—alone.

But eventually Jack Fenwick remembered in every detail what had happened to Dr. Caldwell.

Shortly after this the stories began to gather about his name that later turned him, even during his lifetime, into a legendary character.

Most people are diffuse or diverse in their interests, fortunately. What in the end attracts permanent attention and fixes a reputation in memory is a man with a single end in view, one which he pursues relentlessly. This lends a precision, and eventually an economy to his actions, in comparison with which the diffuse activities of more normal contemporaries seem trivial and merely time-passing. That a certain insane tenseness frequently accompanies the man of one purpose seems only to cast a more focused and strange light upon his doings. It accentuates him by contrast. And if, as frequently happens, the man with one idea has no fear of consequences in the attainment of his object, a "hero" is in the making. Such a man can be completely rational about one thing alone. But he can often be superrational about that, and to be superrational is a characteristic of genius.

Captain Jack, for so he eventually came to be called, was a prime, although an obscure, example of the type described. From the time he recovered his memory after the massacre of his family until the cooling hand of old age fell benignly upon him, he pursued one object, was possessed of only one mastering desire, to accomplish which all else, both people and things, were merely means. The end, of course, was the extermination of Indians. In that line he became both a hero and a genius.

Nothing could have caused more astonishment at Harris's, for instance, than his arriving there at the time he did. The place had been turned into a fort, a stronghold for the whole region. Only a few miles westward the frontiers had been swept clean in the first triumphant raids of the war on the hapless inhabitants. The cabins along the Conococheague had vanished in flames, and all those who had not fled in time perished or were dragged into captivity. Garrett Pendergass and his numerous family had taken warning and abandoned their homes. They now made part of the garrison at Harris's. They had saved some goods; their houses had been burnt. Watch was being kept at the crossing with regular discipline and anxious care—when out of the forest, and on the dangerous southern bank of the river, one summer day emerged a loaded wagon and a lone driver. It was pure chance that Jack had come through from Maryland without being scalped, literally a crazy chance. It looked like fate. The advent of a British 74 on the Susquehanna could not have caused more astonishment at Harris's.

But that was nothing to what followed. Jack did not stay at Harris's. After a rest and a brief period for reflection and cogitation he set out for his cabin that he had left years before with "Beware" scrawled on the door. Argument, prayers, even well-meant insults to detain him were all in vain. On a certain Sunday morning before dawn he had himself and his wagon ferried across the river and disappeared up the now-abandoned road into the western fastnesses.

It was now that the incredible-in-reality began. The second day out he was taken prisoner by a war party of fourteen Indians. Apparently he let himself be taken prisoner. He either was demented or he appeared to be so to the Delawares who took him captive. They deferred his fate to confer later about it. Exactly what happened is not clear. But about a week later Jack Fenwick arrived in his wagon at the cabin his father had built, with the scalps of fourteen Indians. A string of the more usable Indian horses was attached to the wagon. That was the beginning.

The Fenwick cabin was still standing. It had long been taken over and inhabited by a family of Christian Indians who had been converted by the Moravians. They had planted considerable corn and cleared the fields about. Raids had passed them by. They were red men, and they had not been molested by their kindred. The word "Beware" was no longer visible on the cabin door, but it might well have been, for the returning owner killed them all with his hand axe and buried them in the adjacent cornfield. One old woman, out berrying in the woods, alone escaped to bring the news to Harris's. She was the last survivor of what had once been a numerous tribe.

At the cabin Captain Jack set up a base for his lethal

one-man forays. The terror of him gradually spread until his reputation became little short of supernatural. His principal strategy was to attack, always at a remote distance from his place of abode, an Indian village or a war or hunting party. He approached unseen, struck and fled. He outran, outshot, and outdid his enemies in all things and particulars. His strength was gigantic and inexhaustible; his cunning and strategies innumerable and seldom repeated. Chiefs died, shot at the council fire. Young warriors, women, and children vanished. His name became a synonym for fatal misfortune. War parties were scattered in long and vain pursuits and were cut off individually as they turned back. In the end any who returned unscathed were counted lucky.

Finally Captain Jack took to wholesale methods of harassment. In dry seasons and high winds he set the forest afire. He burned out hunting grounds, cornfields, and whole villages. He ranged from Virginia to the New York borders, and at times and for intervals he disappeared entirely. Purely for expedient reasons he let the Iroquois alone. Only occasionally was he known to act in concert with other white men. Here and there were a few lonely characters who knew him, whom he trusted, and who followed him when he called.

His favourite method was to manœuvre for hours for a clean, fatal shot, and he killed at a quarter of a mile. He used exactly the right charge of powder for the distance, and there were many who never heard the report of his rifle. The Indians called him "Silent Gun", and this trick more than any other seemed to them to be diabolical.

It took some time for his reputation to spread among the whites. He did not care whether they knew about him or not. He worked for his own satisfaction. Also, most of the witnesses of his feats were thereby provided with graves. He desired a reputation among the Indians alone. But the cabin of many a white settler was warned in the middle of the night by a voice from the darkness in time for its inmates to take flight or to put themselves in a posture of defence. And all the frontier forts of the Blue Mountains saw him from time to time.

Eventually the mountain where his cabin stood came to be known by his name. It will remain as an everlasting monument of his personal war long after his legend fades. The legend is dim now, but at the time those most intelligently interested in the defence of the province of Pennsylvania knew and understood the fiery lustre of his name. "That bloody man", as certain Quakers called him, was regarded by the more knowing authorities along the frontiers as the equivalent of a regiment, as an individual bastion of defence westward. Among those who understood his worth best were Washington and Franklin.

In the year 1755, in the early summer when the British army advancing against Fort Duquesne was only a few miles west of Frederick, Maryland, but already tangled in the wilderness, a sinister figure emerged from the forests at twilight and demanded to be taken to the commanding general. He would tell neither his name nor his mission. It was Captain Jack, his face blackened for murder at midnight, his belt fringed with dangling scalps, and his already legendary rifle nursed in his left arm with a composite epitaph of nicks upon its stalk. In the company of a sergeant he passed between the campfires of evening towards the tent of the general, which stood on a small knoll.

Captain Jack bore a letter from Benjamin Franklin, and he was presented by Colonel Washington to General Edward Braddock about the time the general and his staff were sitting down to mess. The staff, dressed in scarlet and gold lace, looked at this apparition from the woods with astonishment and horror. Even the younger officers, usually inclined to laugh, found nothing funny in the grim frontiersman. They were even astonished that he spoke the same language they did.

"This is the man whose reputatiion I have enlarged to you, sir," said Colonel Washington. "Far west of the mountains, which we soon hope to cross, the cries of Indian children are stilled by the syllables of his name." Colonel Washington then withdrew, leaving Captain Jack alone with the general. The colonel had already learned that his presence might prejudice as well as predispose.

The general shook the hand of the savage figure presented to him, not wholeheartedly. He could not conceal his astonishment and reluctance. In any event, he regarded handshaking as barbarous. And the mien of Captain Jack was anything but cordial, neither was it subservient or respectful. The general felt repulsed. He was angry before a word passed between them. He was not in a good mood anyway as he had been forced to give up his coach that very afternoon and to send it back to the governor at Annapolis. What kind of campaign was it going to be in which a general could not even sleep in his coach! Captain Jack seemed gloomily to personify the grim and barbarous hardships ahead. The general glowered at him.

He then read the letter in which Franklin urged him strongly to retain Captain Jack as the leader of advance rangers. Before he reached the end his indignation rose. He had not thought of having any advance rangers at all. Mr. Franklin was helpful, but who was he to give military advice to a veteran British general? The terror of the name of English regulars would clear the way for the army. Franklin seemed to think they might be surprised, might even suffer defeat! "You are overconfident, I opine," read the general. His gorge rose.

"Humph, humph," said he, "pshaw!"

He put the letter under a candlestick, and looked up at Captain Jack.

"So you wish to serve his Majesty?" he asked.

"You have read Mr. Franklin's letter, general?" replied Captain Jack, restraining another reply with difficulty.

"I have, sir!" shouted the general, turning scarlet above his collar. He snatched it up again, rose, and led the way out of the tent, followed by Captain Jack. The mess were now all regarding the general uneasily. Braddock choked . . .

"And my reply," shouted he at Captain Jack, "is that his Majesty's troops can do without your eminent services, and still conquer for a' that"—he rustled Franklin's letter angrily. There was a pause while for a moment the general and the woodsman glowered at each other.

"Farewell, sir," said Captain Jack prophetically.

"By God, Halket, you'd think *I'd* been dismissed," complained Braddock to one of his majors as he sat down at the mess. "I'll have to instruct Colonel Washington not to bring low characters like that to headquarters."

"A portent, a grisly portent from the woods," said Sir Peter Halket, and shivered uncomfortably.

"Nonsense, damned impudence!" snorted the general, crumpling up Franklin's letter. He tossed it into the fire kindled before his tent, and began to eat heartily . . .

In the years that followed Braddock's defeat Captain Jack continued to fight his enemies as relentlessly as ever, but without the help of the British army which had perished in the same attempt. Later Forbes endeavoured to enlist him as a leader of rangers, but in vain. The experience with Braddock appeared permanently to have alienated him from the royal authorities. Only as time went on did Captain Jack come to acknowledge the advantage of a few trusted assistants.

Gradually, without there being any formality about it, a group of young hunters and woodsmen became his followers, and at times, and in special instances, assisted him in his forays.

These young hunters, for some of them were scarcely more than that, were, nevertheless, all sons of old settlers and tried frontiersmen whom Captain Jack knew. There was a decided element of secrecy about this "forest brotherhood" of young men who had gradually gathered about him as their acknowledged, but unofficial leader.

All its members were Masons, or "sons of the widow". All came of families who had been harassed by the savages. All of them spent a time of probation in training with Captain Jack. Many of them lived with him on the trail or at his cabin at various times. No fools or hapless hotheads were included. The membership seems to have varied from year to year. But it was an honour to be associated with Captain Jack and it was regarded as a kind of accolade in woods skill and forest fighting, a warrant of dependable character to be asked to join.

Whether there was a password among them is doubtful. That rumour seems to have risen from the fact that most of them were Masons. The wisdom of keeping their plans and their deeds secret, and the reputation and personal authority of Captain Jack, were all that was necessary. Essentially the "brotherhood" was simply the keen admiration of youths for a great older man who enlisted them in a wise way in a cause to which they could give their enthusiasm. The rest was rumour and talk, gossip sometimes envious.

Yet some kind of organization, formal or informal, there must have been. Colonel Bouquet contributed arms, powder, and rations at least once. He knew about the "Mountain Foxes", and so did Ecuyer. In Pontiac's war Captain Jack came to stay at Bedford, probably to be near his friend Garrett Pendergass. For many years they had been associated in one scheme or another. Jack finally built himself a cabin not far from Bedford. There he gathered his young Foxes about him from time to time, as the need arose. Part of this activity may have been for Masonic reasons. Masonry was then spreading along the frontier and both Captain Jack and Garrett Pendergass were furthering it.

At any rate, the old fighter now spent much of his time at his new cabin and about Garrett's place at Bedford, where he was much less alone than ever before. Indeed, the hearth room at Pendergasses' had served to soften even his embittered heart. Perhaps, too, the memories of many years before were growing less poignant and unbearable. Captain Jack was fond of the children at Pendergasses'. He was seen to whittle things out for them in the evenings, play games, and even to smile. Garrett considered this his greatest triumph in hospitality. Undoubtedly, too, a great many schemes were arranged before the fire at Pendergasses'.

It was Garrett, for instance, who had brought Captain Jack and Colonel Bouquet to speaking terms. In the colonel Captain Jack saw the nemesis of the Indians, and he ended by not only tolerating, but actually liking him.

In this pact of mutual respect Ecuyer had also gradually come to be included as the colonel's man, as a Swiss and not an Englishman. It was in the summer of '63 that Captain Jack had finally received arms and assistance

96

from Bouquet. That at least was a beginning of co-operation with the authorities. And the king's powder had not been wasted.

It was now Captain Ecuyer's plan to enlist the aid of Captain Jack and his young men in a closer collaboration with the military. The test of the whole matter was whether or not Captain Jack would come to the fort to talk with him. There had been considerably more than appeared in Ecuyer's apparently casual message asking Captain Jack to pay him a visit.

Few important things are ever arranged simply. Ecuyer had asked Yates to speak to Captain Jack. But Yates was forced to work upon the old hunter through his friend Garrett. Captain Jack had at last consented to listen to Garrett's appeal. Only then had he overcome his reluctance, and finally promised Yates to come to see the captain.

What to say to him, in case he did come, was something Ecuyer had long and carefully considered. He knew most of the tragic story and Captain Jack's prejudices. He realized he would have to tread warily and make a powerful personal appeal. It was, therefore, with no small satisfaction, but also with some anxiety, that he finally heard the old hunter arguing with the sentry outside.

"Here comes the old devil now!" exclaimed Ecuyer as the heavy boots came stamping down the corridor. In their tread he recognized both the hesitation and the bravado.

"No, no," he exclaimed to Yates, who rose hurriedly, prepared to leave. "Pray stay, I may need you! And you, Albine, this talk will certainly concern you. Have the goodness to listen carefully."

With which preliminary remarks the captain settled

back in the pillows and managed to look even a bit sicker than he actually was.

Captain Jack knocked sturdily at the door.

7

Captain Jack Associates Himself

SYMPATHY is always an excellent opener. It is the oiled key that turns many a rusted lock. When Captain Jack entered Ecuyer's room he immediately forgot his own hesitations and prejudices in a generous solicitude for his friend.

The expression on Ecuyer's face, his deadly pallor, the very position of his body under the bedclothes managed wordlessly, but in totality, to convey the extreme helplessness and sad predicament to which a brave and indefatigable man had at last been reduced by forces beyond his own control. Captain Jack understood exhaustion when he saw it. Here was a silent and personal cry for help, not for a cause, but for a man.

Albine was surprised that to some extent the captain was obviously arranging this effect. Not that Ecuyer was play acting; he was simply making use of his actual condition. But Yates was fascinated. He admired greatly the strategy of employing a state of helplessness to provide an opening for placing the first blow. And Captain Jack's guard was certainly down.

"Man, man!" exclaimed the old hunter in consternation, "I'd not dreamt they'd reduced ye to *this!*" He shook his head ruefully, and then tried to smile.

Ecuyer extended his hand and smiled back at him patiently.

"I do *much* appreciate your coming to see me," he said. "Albine, a chair for my guest! By the way, do you know each other? This should be a young fellow after your own heart, Captain Jack. Mr. Yates will bear me out in that, I know."

"That I will, and gladly," chimed in Yates. "But I know that Captain Jack and Sal have already met."

"Good!" said Ecuyer.

"Oh, aye, that we have!" exclaimed Captain Jack. "I had a good talk with him only the other night. Old Garrett thinks he knew his pár and mar. However that may be, happen I could put him to better work than you can, captain."

"I've no doubt of it," agreed Ecuyer. "Prop me up, Albine, Captain Jack and I are going to make big medicine together to snare some of your red friends, and I never heard it could be done lying down."

"Only Quakers, pacificators, and suchlike try to make medicine in wartime by lying down," drawled the woodsman.

"It's a good position to place the feet of your enemy on the back of your neck, and not good for much else, as far as I can see," laughed Ecuyer, who was now sitting up and looking brighter.

"It is, it is," cried Captain Jack, smiting his knee. "Plague take 'em!"

"Colonel Bouquet and I are bothered by a good deal of half-hearted medicine making," continued Ecuyer. "The sad truth is we get no willing help, only forced aid, grudgingly given. None of the country people volunteered last spring when the colonel advanced here from Carlisle. Not one!" he exclaimed. "The terror of the Indians lay too heavily upon them. And to some extent they were right. For if Bouquet had been defeated at Bushy Run, the savages might well have descended upon Philadelphia or Baltimore. The people of Pennsylvania are only too willing to let others do their fighting for them—and to trade behind the backs of their defenders with the enemy." The captain had become vehement as he went on. He smacked his fist into his hand weakly, but with emphasis, and flushed spots appeared on his cheeks. "You, yourself, they call a man of blood, sir," he said to Captain Jack. "I hear they have even been niggardly about paying you the bounty on enemy scalps you have taken," he added.

It was now Captain Jack's turn to flush angrily.

" 'Tis true," he said. "As for what they call me along the Delaware, I care not. The eastern counties have ever been indifferent to the sufferings of the frontier. As long as their own precious scalps were well glued on all was well, as far as Philadelphia was concerned. Mr. Franklin and his friends have been a noble exception to such base slavery. And the instinct of the Scotch-Irish on the borders has always been to strike back at the redskins and to stop the Quaker caravans loaded with whisky and scalping knives for the varmints. But what do the authorities do? They license the traders! And they regard the riflemen, those who could best strike the enemy in their own way, as mere provincials, as unfit to associate with the noble British regulars." Captain Jack's voice had gained in volume. "Now in Braddock's time," he began, "I . . ."

"I know all about that," said Ecuyer, reaching out and laying a restraining hand on the old frontiersman's arm. "But much blood and tears have rolled under the bridges since Braddock's time. Defeat is your great corrector of abuse, Captain Jack. So it's different now. Come, admit it. Don't you find it so?"

"I do, I do," admitted the old fighter—after a pause. "For instance, you have received me here like a man, like a gentleman. We talk face to face, and on the same floor. But you are a Switzer, Ecuyer. An Englishman would not be able to see me. Many a whippersnapper, whose fathers were less in England than mine, looks at me like a blind man." This last was said with great bitterness.

"Now, there I can sympathize with you," interrupted the captain. "Both Colonel Bouquet and myself have felt the blue blindness of English eyes, of which you speak, and so has Mr. Yates here, I warrant you. Why, he is *only* a Scot!"

At this they all laughed together.

"Yes, it *is* difficult to bear," Ecuyer continued. "What you speak of is the curse of empire, perhaps its nemesis. The Frenchman born in France, the Spaniard in Spain, the Englishman in England—all feel themselves, no matter how ignorant they are, superior to the provincial on his native ground. Such is the pride of paternity combined with the air of the metropolis, and I suppose it will always be true—to the end. After all, it's natural. Few fathers ever come to regard their children as equals, much less take advice from them. But let us try to forget that here. We at least can agree on one thing. The common enemy must be defeated. The people of these frontiers must be harassed no more. And, sir, there is now an opportunity to strike back at the enemy in his own country, a chance to bring peace to these beautiful hills forever. Bouquet would strike home at the Indians down the Ohio, release the captives, dictate a lasting peace. He has learned to conquer by using the savages' own method of warfare. He has turned their own cunning upon them, and improved upon it. That I think is what you have been doing, too. Colonel Bouquet is a great man, Captain Jack. You already know him. His cause is your own. But he will fail if we can't keep the road to Fort Pitt open. I am responsible to him for that. It was my thought that you might see fit to aid me. You could be of invaluable help. As for me, I am all but spent in the service of the king. And time flies, flies away for a lame man." Ecuyer sank back into the pillows, keeping his eyes fixed on the face of the man before him. It was some time before the frontiersman replied. His reluctance was still evident.

"What is it you would have me do?" he finally asked.

"Why, range the road from here to Ligonier," replied Ecuyer. "Prevent ambuscades, and bring us news of the savages."

"I could not do that alone," said Captain Jack. "It's a large territory, and a difficult one to cover."

"I did not suppose you could, although the terror of your name is great,' said Ecuyer. "But you have great influence with some of the best young riflemen and woodsmen in these unhappy parts. You could enlist the aid of such young fellows as Albine here, and put them to valuable work. Come, come, Captain Jack, you know that. No one could do more. In fact, no one but youself *can* do it."

But the old frontiersman still hesitated.

"Pray consider what the captain says, sir," put in Yates

at this opportunity. "Murray, the Pendergass boys, my friend here would all esteem it a privilege to follow you. I, myself, would wish to volunteer if you would let me." His enthusiasm and seriousness showed in his face.

Captain Jack was now undoubtedly moved. He cut some tobacco from a twist and cogitated it.

"Wal," said he, lapsing into the country jargon as he turned to Albine, "an' how do you take to the proposition, young feller? You know more about the Injuns than most, I guess. Say your say."

"I say *do* it, Captain Jack," exclaimed Salathiel. "As for me, I have an account to settle with the redskins anyway. Mr. Pendergass was tellen me the other night he thinks they shot my pa in the back one Christmas Day when I was little. I reckon they did. But I'd follow you anyway, if you want me. And I do know something of the Injuns' ways." He smiled. "Do it, sir, I say. Do it! Ever since I came to serve Captain Ecuyer he's always been right."

"That's the talk," cried Captain Jack, again smacking his knee. "Young man, I like your style, and, captain, I'm inclined to jine ye. But I'll do so only on my own terms."

"I never thought you would do anyhing else,'" laughed Ecuyer. "Well, sir, what are your terms?"

Captain Jack sat pondering. His face darkened for a moment; seemed to cloud over with a rush of blood. Memory was strong. It was hard to come to terms even with Ecuyer.

At this juncture a curious thing happened. Ecuyer made a gesture with one hand. It seemed, unless one happened to be watching carefully, a natural one. Salathiel, who was watching carefully, could not be sure, but it looked to him like a certain motion of secret sign language that had been taught him as a finishing touch to his lore by Nymwha, the Shawnee medicine man. It was the plea of one warrior to another when stricken upon the field of battle. Only some warriors in some tribes would know it, Nymwha had said. For it was an ancient, a much-cherished and powerful sign. It was a motion not lightly to be made. Had the captain made it? If so, how did he know? Perhaps, after all, it was a mere coincidence. But at that moment Captain Jack replied. There could scarcely be any doubt of it now. How extremely curious! And these were white men.

Just then Captain Jack found the weed in his mouth more of an impediment than a help. He rose, went to a window, hoisted it deliberately, and spat out the wad, much to the astonishment of the sentry on duty outside, who looked downright disgusted.

"Don't let it fuss ye, young man," said the old hunter, still keeping the window open. "Worse things than that might come your way."

He paused now with his back to the room, seeming still to be considering. The wintry, mountain air swept in, reminding Ecuyer of the difficulties still ahead of him outside. He shivered and drew the bedclothes about him resignedly. He had done all he could. He had made the last appeal.

At last Captain Jack closed the window and returned. He was more at ease now, almost affable, as he resumed his chair by the captain's bed.

"This is how I see it, captain," he said. "Young Jimmy Smith over at Conococheague valley is raising a company of rifles by subscription. They'll enlist, and take the oath to the king probably. He'll be commissioned, and he'll desarve it. But I won't do that. I'll never jine up with the royal army. I'm an old wolf and I hunt alone. If you can manage to supply me with powder and shot, arms if I want them, and rations for, we'll say, ten, I'll undertake to associate some likely young fellers like your man Albine here, and I'll promise to patrol the road from here to Ligonier, and make it hard for the redskins in the adjacent parts. And I'll stick to it until Colonel Bouquet returns. And if he doesn't return, I will stick to it just the same for a year. As for pay—that would help. We'll be giving our time, maybe our lives. Manage something with the paymaster, if you can. But I must make this plain, pay or no pay, I'm to do the drivin' of my own wagon. No drillin' at the fort, no musters, and no oaths. Just tell the Britishers we're fighting Quakers and it's agin our conscience to take an oath. That'll stop questions, and they won't know any better. Also, all the scalps, booty, and bounty belongs to us, and I take instructions from you or Colonel Bouquet, but from no one else. And, sir, you will listen to no complaints about my cruelty to the savages. We won't be cruel, we'll be quick—and they'll be dead. The best way of all to manage this affair would be for nobody to know anything about us except the 'savages', as you call them. Talk that advertises surprises is a scalping knife in the enemies' hand. Now I'm done. That's my say, and I never thought I'd say it!" He looked at Ecuyer and smiled with a frown.

"But it's fair enough," replied the captain. "And I think it can be managed, even the pay. I'll write to Colonel Bouquet tonight for his consent. All shall be confidential, and I'll make a special express of it. Do you think you can find me a volunteer to carry the letter to Pittsburgh? Meanwhile, since time passes, will you go ahead with your plans on my word alone? I agree with you, the less said outside the better. I'll begin by releasing Albine to you as soon as you want him. That is a real earnest on my part that I am interested, for I value his services greatly.

And now, sir, my best wishes and profound thanks. I trust you will soon be able to strike some shrewd blows for your country. I doubt not you will." Captain Ecuyer extended his hand from the bed.

Captain Jack pumped Ecuyer's arm cordially, with considerable emotion. He also shook hands with Albine and Yates as though he considered them part of the pact.

"Now that this powwow's over," he said, "I feel better. I'd like to see you both at Pendergasses' tonight, if the captain can spare you," he added. "We can start right away making our plans."

Mr. Yates and Mr. Albine were delighted and showed it. Captain Ecuyer smiled with relief, and Captain Jack clumped off down the corridor, this time without a trace of hesitation in his tread.

"Sir, I never can thank you enough," said Albine to Captain Ecuyer as the old woodsman left the room.

"Every dog has his day, or should have," laughed Ecuyer. "But never mind wagging your tail now, Albine. Wait—and see how it goes."

"But I'll never stop wagging my tail," exclaimed Salathiel. "I'm a lucky dog, and I know it, thanks to you."

Mr. Yates, thus forced to regard his friend as a large dog wagging its tail, leaned back and laughed.

And so, pleasantly enough, that was how Captain Jack's "Mountain Foxes", or the "Fighting Quakers", began.

That also was why Salathiel came to live at Pandergasses'. For while the Fighting Quakers, as they came to be called, because it was known they would not be sworn into the king's service—and that was about all that most people ever did know about them—were not wholly a Pendergass organization, they were predominantly so.

It must be remembered that old Garrett Pendergass

had seven sons and four daughters. There was Charles, the oldest, already grey, and married to an invalid; there was Tom, a few years older than Salathiel; then there were two sets of twins, Matthew and Mark, Luke and John. There was only a year between the two sets of twins, and they were all strapping young cubs. Tobias, or Toby, the youngest child, had been born halt in the left leg. He was bright as a whip, however.

As for the daughters, Polly was the oldest girl, a little younger than Charles. She had married one Murray, who had been caught out and scalped near their cabin in the Juniata water gap. Young Nat Murray was her son. Bella was next in age, but she had never married. She was her mother's favourite, perhaps because of her nature, and had remained constantly in the house to help her. Rachel, the third daughter, was now Mrs. William Davison, the mother of Phoebe and young Arthur. She lived at Fort Loudon, where her husband was a prosperous tanner, but her children spent half their time in their grandparents' house. Sue, the youngest girl, was a bright, upstanding young woman, much given to fancy clothes and the vapours, as she was in doubt as to who was the best chance among many who came sparking. As Garrett would not put up with any bundling in his house, she found her choice difficult, and was sometimes inclined to pout or even weep a bit over the matchless strictness of her lot. Really, she was not able to make up her mind to leave her father's house and was inclined to keep on consulting her Bible or a pack of cards about her swains and her future. When these authorities disagreed, as they frequently did, it was like to be a bad day for the entire family.

Owing to the dangers of the times, most of the Pendergasses were again living with the old man at Bedford. It was not regarded as a hardship to come back to the establishment where plenty and peace reigned. For, although family troubles sometimes threatened, old Garrett still ruled with a rod, which he seldom used. The boys, who had taken up land and built cabins, all but Toby, had returned till times should be better. They all worked hard for their father, who kept them busy. But Captain Jack's proposal that some of them should now become regular members of his gang of "Mountain Foxes" was not unattractive to old Garrett, despite the danger involved. He admired Captain Jack and thought well of the discipline and training both in character and as woodsmen that his sons would get. In addition, he was public spirited and felt that his family should do something for their friends and neighbours.

As a consequence, that evening in the big hearth room Garrett, his son Charles, and Captain Jack sat long over their supper, discussing in low tones the ways and means of putting Captain Jack's proposals into effect. They were joined about eight o'clock by Salathiel, who had been released by the captain for the occasion. But he had left Yates toiling over the correspondence, in particular over the letter to Colonel Bouquet, which was to go out that night.

It was arranged that Charles, who had no children to care for, should set out for Fort Pitt with the letter as soon as it was finished, and bring back the reply. He was an expert woodsman and knew the route to Pittsburgh well. Of the other Pendergass boys, Tom and Matthew and Mark were to join Captain Jack, along with Nat Murray and Salathiel, at the cabin which Captain Jack had recently erected near Bedford. This was a small "strong place", more like a blockhouse than a cabin, which the old hunter had built for himself some miles down the range of Lookout Mountain, close by a limestone spring. The boys were to act as a "garrison"" of this place, and be ready for any duty Captain Jack might call them out upon, day or night. Also, they were to practise and undergo certain trials and tests he insisted upon before taking the trail with him.

"For," said he, "I don't look forward to accidents. And even you bright young fellows might make just one mistake. I make a pint of never making—none. *None*," said he, smiting his knee, "not one! As for the several boys who'll be coming over from the Big Cove pretty soon, they're old hands, and they know my ways. But I'll not send for them till we hear from the colonel at Pittsburgh. You can never tell what the army will do till they do it. Not that I don't trust Ecuyer," he added, looking at Salathiel, "but we'd best wait to hear from Bouquet."

It was at this point that old Garrett stepped into the breach with a kindly offer.

"Don't wait," said he. "No matter what the authorities do, I believe this is an excellent plan for ridding ourselves of the red varmints. And we might also stop any trading that pops up." He lowered his voice here almost to a whisper and looked knowingly at the table across the room, where Lieutenant Neville and some of his friends had just come in for a round of hot grog. "I hear that some of your friends over there, Albine, are pretty mad. You and Yates had better keep a sharp eye on them. But maybe we can nip any little deal they cook up before it gets ready to serve up hot. Now, my idea is not to wait till you hear from Fort Pitt, but for you young fellers to go out to Captain Jack's tomorrow. I'll furnish ye with all that's necessary for livin' and shootin' out there, and I'll guarantee it, even if Bouquet won't carry out Ecuyer's plan. He will, though, if I know him. But anyway the road

110

must be kept open, and the good people of this town have their neighbourhood freed of varmints so they can go to church and plough their fields without being scalped. There's an army at the fort trying to prevent that, but you boys can do better for our people by yourselves than all of the soldiers put together. So, I say, don't wait! Begin tomorrow. And I'll back ye. Back ye to the limit." He brought his fist down on the big table so that the dishes crashed and the candles guttered in their iron holders.

Everyone in the room jumped.

For some reason or other the party at Lieutenant Neville's table, which had recently been joined by several other officers, was considerably disturbed and apparently annoyed. Their mutterings, subdued laughter, and conversational oaths were suddenly cut off, given a period, as it were, by the crash of Garrett's fist. They were nettled, and they showed it. It was tacitly understood by everybody that the conversation thus interrupted was one that somehow concerned those gathered about Garrett at his table—and not favourably. All this was quite suddenly, but quite plainly, in the air,

"Blast me!' said Lieutenant Guy, a young officer with an impudent face, red from too much drinking. "Let's go back to my quarters, gentlemen. I'll guarantee at least y' won't be interrupted by havin' your host crash the dishes.'

"I'll warrant ye won't," put in Captain Jack, "because, gentlemen, at Lieutenant Guy's quarters there aren't any dishes to crash."

"Nor any chairs to sit in, gentlemen," added Charles Pendergass.

"Nor any cups to pour liquor into," mourned Nat Murray.

"Nor any liquor to pour," added Garrett.

111

Now, this was quite true, since Guy had lost everything but his clothes at cards, and a general laugh at his expense went around.

"I see you're all against me," said the red-faced young officer, hiccuping sadly. "What—what can I do?"

"Well, you might pay for the suppers you ordered," suggested Garrett.

"Ah, so you might, since you ordered them," agreed Neville in spite of himself, but not anxious to foot the bill. He rose hastily. They all rose, leaving the red-faced lieutenant alone to face the music.

"All right! Post me for it. Put it on your damned charges, Garrett," said Guy, with a reckless gesture. "I'll pay you—when the pay chests come." He laughed loudly and stumbled out, helped towards the door by the others.

"Gentlemen," cried Garrett suddenly, just as they reached the door. He brought his fist down again hard.

They all stopped and gawked at him.

"The pay chests will be here tomorrow, and I shall expect every one of you to settle with me as soon as you're paid. Whatever you may have had to complain about tonight," he added ironically, "I've fed you, warmed you, and set good liquor before you for months past, and I've never dunned you, but I remind you of that now. Captain Ourry is camped just east of the water gap tonight. He'll be in tomorrow morning. Good evenin'."

This was news indeed. It would change the whole face of affairs at the fort. Salathiel was anxious to take the tidings to the captain.

"He knows about it already," Garrett assured him. "I sent young Toby up with the message to Yates some time ago. Burent brought the news this afternoon. He's upstairs in bed now, clean tuckered out. They had a hard trip,

112

but they've got the chests and about fifty other wagons, too."

Just then the door opened and Yates came in with Toby. Evidently he had stayed only long enough to finish the letter to Bouquet, which he had brought along with him.

"What's the trouble with that crowd outside?" asked Yates as he sat before the fire warming himself. "I met that mob of Neville's on my way down from the fort. They were all gathered at Baker's corner arguing, but they dried up like hardtacks when I passed. A conspiracy, I'll be bound," he said contemptuously.

"I don't think so," said Garrett. "I told them about the pay chests."

"I wouldn't have," said Yates.

"I want to collect what's due me tomorrow, Ned," said old Garrett, "so I thought I'd just let that news get about, too."

"I've got some news for you," said Yates. "And most astonishing it is. I think it will interest Sal, here, more than most. When you left the fort this afternoon Ecuyer was in Ourry's quarters, wasn't he? Well, he's not there any more. When Toby came in with the news just before supper that Ourry and the wagons would be here tomorrow, what do you think the captain did? Why, he got up out of bed. Then he sent for Captain Stewart and had himself moved over into that tent next to the hospital, right at the head of the street of battalion huts. It's the grenadiers' row. And there he is now—and no one to look after him but Captain Forbes's orderly, who is an impudent rascal if I ever saw one."

"Why, in God's name, didn't Ecuyer come here!" exclaimed Garrett. "He could have had the big river room

113

on our side of the house till he got well, and young Phoebe to nurse him."

"That's what I told him," said Yates, "but he says he won't put Ourry out of his quarters, even if he does rank him, and that too many of the company officers have neglected the troops and taken lodgings in town. There'll be trouble when the men are paid, he insists, and he wants to be among 'em till he starts back for Pittsburgh. And he says he thinks he will be well enough for that in about a week."

"I suppose he'll leave anyway," said Captain Jack. "It's just like him. And to think of Lieutenants Guy and Neville, and suchlike, boozing about and toasting their shins at every hearth in the town that'll let them!"

"Captain Jack," said Salathiel, who had been listening to all this with sensations varying between astonishment and consternation, "I'm going to stick by the captain till he leaves for Fort Pitt. It's the least I can do. Do you think you could get along at the cabin without me for a few days?"

"Wal, now, I've managed without ye for about fifty years," drawled Captain Jack, and then changed his tone: "We certainly kin, and you ought to be with Ecuyer now, that's sartin. He'll need ye. And you'll only be doin' what's right to stand by him for a while."

Garrett agreed. "As far as that goes," he said, "I think all of you boys had better put off goin' out to Jack's cabin for a day or two. You'd better stick at the store and help you old pa. Charley can go with the letter, but I'll need the rest of you for tendin' store and keepin' an eye on things. Maybe Captain Jack would just kind o' set in the room here till the worst of it's over."

"Happen he would," said Captain Jack.

"Now, Charley, you make ready to leave at daylight,

before Ourry and his men get in," continued Garrett. "That letter's important! And mind your hair west of Ligonier."

"I'll go by way of the Turkey Foot instead of Ligonier," said Charley. "The old trace ain't like to be so frequented by lurkers."

"No, it hain't," agreed Captain Jack; "you'd better come back that way, too."

While this discussion was going on, Salathiel had borrowed a couple of blankets from the shelves, and rolled up a small parcel of cooked food.

"I don't know how the captain will be fixed," he said to Garrett. "You might ask Burent to come up first thing in the morning."

"I'll see that he does," said Yates.

Old Garrett followed Salathiel to the door.

"Get your own things together and bring them down here first opportunity," he said. "You can have that little room nigh the corner across from Yates. Tell the truth, I want ye in the house as much as ye can be when you're not off with Captain Jack. Ye can help out and it kind o' seems like old times with one of your name about." Old Garrett paused. "Well, well, now, be off with you. The captain will be needin' you, too. Did you ever see a garrison payday, Albine? No! In that case you've got a surprise comin', and likely it won't be a pleasant one. I expect trouble here for the next few days. Keep an eye on your friends. They don't love ye too much. I'll tell Dr. Boyd about the captain's leaving his bed. He won't like it, I guess. I'll give your compliments to Phoebe, too."

With that old Garrett, who had seemed to be detaining him, laughed and let Salathiel go, closing the door behind him. Salathiel heard the bar fall in place and for a moment felt alone out in the cold. It would be good to have a room in that house, he thought. He'd certainly move his stuff down tomorrow. Now that the captain had left the fort there would be no place for him except the tent, or one of the huts. Well, he'd see how the captain was.

The silence of midnight had fallen on the fort and little town as he breasted the rise towards the hospital. It was only after an argument with a grenadier sentry that he got past the barricade and into the captain's tent in the camp near the parade ground. Ecuyer was still awake and a candle burning. He made no attempt to conceal his satisfaction at seeing Salathiel.

"Did you expect me, sir?" he asked after a while.

"Not exactly," replied the captain, "but I did think you might come. It's good of you. You're your own man, you know."

This reply affected Salathiel greatly. He put the tent to rights and made Ecuyer as comfortable as he could. The blankets and cooked food came in splendidly.

"Ourry will undoubtedly be here tomorrow, and the next few days will just be the devil," said Ecuyer. "Mark my words. As for me, a man never knows how strong he is till he gets up out of a sickbed and walks. And now, good night. I must get all the rest I can."

Salathiel went and slept in the ark where it had been left behind the hospital yard. The roll of drums awakened him at reveille. For a moment he thought he was back at Fort Pitt with Bustle beside him in the casemate. Then he thought of Phoebe. Maybe he would be seeing her before the day was over. But for the next few days there was small time for dreams or running after maidens.

8

Pandora's Pay Chests

MEDICINE is not the only field in which the cure prescribed frequently produces complications. Half the easements of life only introduce aggravations, and so it proved with Captain Ourry's pay chests.

Ask any subaltern hanging about the bar at Pendergasses' what the trouble was with the garrison at the fort, and he would probably tell you all they needed was to be paid. That explanation seemed reasonable, for the Royal Americans and the grenadiers had not been paid for over a year. Some of the militia companies had never been paid at all. There, undoubtedly, was adequate cause for grumbling, and the root of much trouble.

But to assert that all would be well as soon as government settled its accounts with its armed servants would be quite another matter. Ourry, Stewart, Ecuyer, who had all been through paydays before, had no such easy view of the matter. They knew that the most serious trouble often came afterward. And in this case their gloomy expectations were more than realized.

For every one of the good, round gold and silver pieces with the dull, but honest faces of Hanoverian kings minted upon them acted like so many imps of Pandora, once they had left the paymaster's chests, and seemed to multiply and fructify trouble, disputes, hard feeling, and even violence as they flew nimbly from hand to hand. The paper notes of the province of Pennsylvania let loose amongst the militia were even worse. They were a bad trouble in themselves to begin with.

Still, who would have thought that the mere paying of the garrison would result in a few days' time in having two men shot and twelve flogged; a barracks gutted by fire, a riot at Pendergasses', twenty-two desertions, and a mutiny of the grenadiers. Not even Dr. Boyd, who was something of a cynic, would have prognosticated that—although Captain Ourry, for one, and the commandant, Captian Stewart, for another, might have. Ecuyer wasn't exactly surprised. He had long had his own opinions about the state of discipline in the second battalion of the Royal Americans. And he was treated by the grenadiers only the morning before Ourry got in with a sort of premonitory glimpse, a kind of dress rehearsal in advance of what might be in store.

Rumour, of course, was exceptionally busy. Everyone knew even before the line-up for reveille roll call came that Captain Ourry's column was coming through the water gap with the pay chests that very morning. A thousand expectations, innumerable long-deferred hopes for release and revelry danced like fox fires in three thousand excited minds,—for such was about the combined number of the

118

garrison and townfolk assembled—the former before their barracks at the fort, and the latter in eager, gossiping knots about town. "The pay chests are coming. They'll be here today." Everybody kept repeating it. Pendergass and his boys had worked all night. The solid grille by the counter was firmly in place. They were ready to serve, sell, and collect.

So was nearly everybody else. For the government was not the only debtor in the community. It was merely the principal one. Every officer, every soldier owed. They owed one another, they owed the townsmen. They all owed to Pendergass. They had all lived on hope, on credit, by borrowing, by begging—finally, in some cases, by stealing. And now coin was coming; money minted and printed. And money is one of the principal excitements and irritants of life. Also, for once, it was a beautiful day. Ourry would undoubtedly get through safely with the wagons. Still, nerves were taut.

Despite the good weather, the day, nevertheless, got off to a bad start. Several small war parties had been hovering around Ourry's column from the time it left Fort Loudon. But Ourry was wary, and the column proved too strong to attack. The Indians had reluctantly given him up at the water gap. Yet it would never do for them to return without any scalps. Consequently, on their way towards the mountains, and just before dawn, they had stopped to make a combined surprise attack on an outpost at the Juniata crossing, two miles west of the fort.

There was a detachment of grenadiers on watch at the ford, and they had been caught napping. Four of them were scalped and murdered, a fifth was scalped, but revived to stagger in with the news. It set everybody's nerves on edge. Indeed, the cries and groans of the unfortunate man could be heard coming from the hospital just as reveille sounded. Dr. Boyd was trying to prevent him from bleeding to death by sewing his head skin across with catgut. The muscles clear down the neck would retract.

Salathiel provided Ecuyer with an extremely early breakfast that morning. He helped dress him as usual, and reloaded the pistols carefully at Ecuyer's particular behest. He also provided himself with one of the pair of hand guns of which Frances, the Irish girl at Frazier's, must still have had the twin. He then cut the captain a stout hickory stick for a cane, since Ecuyer was still quite lame. Just as an afterthought he returned Kaysinata's tomahawk to his belt and kept it there.

"Now," said the captain, "stay close by me and do use your eyes in a circle. Trouble often comes from behind."

With that, Ecuyer hobbled out of the tent onto the muddy grass street before the huts, where two companies of the grenadiers were assembling. It was from these men, if from any, that trouble might first be expected, and it was Ecuyer's intention to nip the flower of anarchy in the bud.

The scene, to begin with, was a somewhat disorderly one. A red-haired Scotch sergeant was in charge, but seemed not to be very serious about it. The man in the hospital kept cursing and screaming at Dr. Boyd. The sergeant bellowed perfunctorily at his men. The assembly ceased to beat. But the formation was slow and the men indifferent and surly. Some of them had to be dragged from the huts by cursing corporals. A good many appeared to be absent. Lieutenant Guy, who was supposed to take the report, was in bed in town, and everybody knew it. A cheerful light of dawn glowed from the mountains, but everybody felt ugly. A nameless sense of grievance was in the air. Into this centre of sleepy and surly difficulty Ecuyer, followed by Albine, came hobbling from his tent.

For a moment the silence of surprise fell heavily. Everything stopped. The sergeant was now busy arguing about something with five or six grouped close around him. He didn't see or hear Ecuyer, nor did those near him. The altercation was too absorbing. But all the rest saw him.

"By God, it's an officer!" someone shouted.

"He must have been up all night then," yelled another. A laugh went up.

>"They stay abed in the mornin';
>They won't get up in the mornin' . . ."

a fresh-faced young soldier began to chant. Several others took up the refrain.

"Collar that lad for me, Albine," said Ecuyer, pointing his cane.

Albine took the young soldier with a rush. He was surprised and made little resistance. A hearty bully with a horribly scarred face came to his rescue. With his hands on the young soldier Albine was forced to use his feet. He lashed out and kicked the newcomer in the stomach and laid him flat and gasping. The sound of chanting ceased. The young soldier who had begun it now faced Ecuyer and began to whimper.

There was another moment of ominous silence broken only by the loud dispute around the sergeant, which was getting hot and hotter. Some of the men looked ugly and seemed about to close in on Ecuyer, to release the prisoner.

But it was not yet time to draw his pistols, Ecuyer decided. It might precipitate matters. He intended to save the pistols for the general rush, if and when it came. That was the way every mutiny began, a rush usually followed by a murder. Officers are always in the minority. Sometimes they are a nervous temptation.

What prevented the rush from getting under way automatically was probably the clanging argument being carried on by the sergeant and his friends. It seemed to be just about to reach the state of violence. It was a strong distraction. Most of the men stopped to listen.

Sergeant McIntosh, it appeared, had loaned money to his friends. According to him, all loans were to be paid back in full that day. But they were *not* all to be paid back, according to the debtors who surrounded him. Violent appeals to the Deity indicated that only part of any loan was to be paid back. The sergeant was no longer red; he was purple. As yet he had not noticed Ecuyer. He now flatly demanded his rights, cursed, and squared off for blood and money.

"Fight!" screamed a young drummer.

"Sergeant!" roared Ecuyer.

It was then, for the first and last time, that Albine heard what the little captain was mysteriously famous for—the furious voice of a lion. It was mysterious, because his small body seemed incapable of producing such a sound.

The sergeant staggered under the shock of the captain's voice as though someone had handed him a blow.

"Sir?" said he, brought up standing, and hopelessly astonished.

"Get your damned yeomanry into line," thundered Ecuyer.

The furious bellows of the sergeant were now added to the angry roars of Ecuyer. Everybody was suddenly reminded terribly of authority. The two voices seemed to beat the men into line as waves form sand on a beach. The companies began to assemble. Several scared late-sleepers came sneaking out of the huts to fill up the gaps.

" *'Shun!*" bellowed the sergeant.

"Call the roll," roared Ecuyer.

The loud, nasal clang of names, mostly Macs, began. Apparently, there were eight deserters. No one would be simply and casually absent on payday.

Ecuyer realized that these deserters must have been absent for some time, and that they had not been reported. The men saw that he knew. Just what the captain would have done under the circumstances, Salathiel wondered many a time afterward. But to a certain extent immediate decision was now taken out of Ecuyer's hands. Events intervened.

The sergeant faced about to report, and in doing so, of course, turned his back on the men. That simple action was the deciding factor. Perhaps the irritating screeches of the man in the hospital helped. At any rate, Ecuyer sensed that a crisis was at hand.

"Tie that man's hands with your belt, instantly," he said out of the side of his mouth to Salathiel, who still held his man.

Almost at the same instant three men left the ranks and made for the sergeant, whose back was now turned. They were three from the group with whom the sergeant had just been arguing. They came fast. One of them drew a knife.

"Jump!" roared Ecuyer to the sergeant, and pulled out his pistols.

The sergeant turned just in time to tackle the man with the knife and throw him violently.

Salathiel slipped in and felled another. The third, who was just closing in, now hesitated. He began jumping about in a circle with his knuckles touching the ground.

Meanwhile, Ecuyer was left facing the two companies alone, with drawn pistols. It was plain that he would shoot the first who now attempted to leave ranks. Some parts of the ranks leaned forward; recovered themselves.

No one broke.

The third man, who had at last made in and tackled the sergeant, now broke loose and came at the captain. Salathiel caught him by the foot and broke his leg. He lay writhing and cursing on the ground directly in front of Ecuyer. The captain, however, did not move.

Every eye was on his pistols and if he had shifted them even for an instant the rush would have followed.

There was one of those moments of crisis and tension which seemed to be suspended in the air on nothing, but like a palpable thing. It lasted possibly ten or even fifteen seconds, then—

Captain Stewart, the adjutant, Captain Forbes of the grenadiers, and three sergeants of the Royal Americans came from between the huts and ranged themselves beside Ecuyer. A company of infantry with fixed bayonets soon followed and stood at the ready at the foot of the street.

Ecuyer put up his pistols. He poked a moment in the ground for a firm stance with his cane and leaned on it.

"A remarkably fine winter morning, gentlemen," he said. "How did you hear about it?"

"Corporal McCallum brought the news," replied Captain Stewart, wiping the sweat off his face despite the frosty air.

"Promote him," said Ecuyer. "March these mutinous rascals to the brick barracks in the fort and confine 'em there, Captain Stewart. Have you called the rest of the garrison to arms?"

124

"Yes, sir, they're standing to now," answered the adjutant.

"Send out and round up any stragglers or loiterers in the town," continued Ecuyer. "Now take these rascals who tried to attack us, Captain Forbes, put irons on them and clap them in the guardhouse. I'll attend to them personally, and promptly." Ecuyer pointed to the soldier who was groaning on the ground with a broken leg. "Send for a surgeon and have him set this man's bones. In his case a splint will do even better than irons."

While these arrangements were being made, the two companies of sullen grenadiers had been marched off. The officers now stood alone.

Captain Ecuyer stepped back and faced them. He took off his hat and bowed from the waist. "My obligations, gentlemen, for saving my life," he said quite simply. At the same time he looked at Salathiel and smiled.

Captain Stewart wondered. Not a word of reproach! What kind of man was Ecuyer?

They all walked over to the fort and into headquarters together. Outside on the parade the battalion of Royal Americans and the company of grenadiers, which had not been concerned in the incident of the morning, stood to arms and at attention. The other two grenadier companies were already confined and howling in their barracks, where the smashing of benches was going on. Several officers came in from the town hurriedly, sweating at reporting late. The commandant, Captain Ecuyer, Forbes, and the adjutant consulted earnestly together over a big table at one end of the room. Something was suddenly decided. All but Ecuyer rose and hurried out.

Ecuyer came over to Salathiel, where he stood waiting by the orderly table next the door.

"You have done well, Albine," he said. "Come to me

125

after the pay is over and you shall receive your reward. Two pennies a day was the arrangement, if I remember correctly." The captain smiled. "But that is not *quite* all, is it?" He shook his head. "No, in this case there is something more. This is it." He reached out and shook Salathiel by the hand. "Good-bye," he said quietly. "I shall not require your services again. Remember me sometimes in the years to come as a friend."

Salathiel could not reply. Tears came to his eyes. He wrung the captain's hand and dashed out the door.

So it was over.

But he and the captain were friends. The savage boy from the forest had achieved that. In how many days? The pennies would tell exactly. He had forgotten how long it was. It seemed years. He was a man now. Ecuyer had made him that. And he was free! He would never serve again. There would never be another Ecuyer. One gave one's self that way—and learned—once only. Now once more he was alone. But not alone in the forest. The inhabited world eastward, the towns in the dawn-light by the great water, lay before him.

While these things passed like lightning through his thoughts he strode mightily across the square where the troops were lined up. He scarcely saw what was going on there.

At the gate he realized that people from the town were pouring eagerly into the fort. He thrust them aside almost rudely. A punishment had been ordered. Word of that, or of a hanging, always flew about like wildfire.

But Salathiel did not wait to see the mutineers meet the cat with nine tails. That could remain, for all he cared, the privilege of the garrison and those from the town who came to look over the heads of the soldiers into the hollow square.

There had been no court-martial. It, and possibly some hangings, would come later. Ecuyer and Stewart had acted instantly on their own authority in ordering the floggings.

Several people shouted at Salathiel that he was missing a good thing as they passed him, hurrying frantically up the hill. But he doubted that. He kept on his way. He felt he was glad to miss whatever he might be missing. He was glad he was through with all of it and free to go where he liked.

He went directly down to Pendergasses' and pushed open the heavy door into the main room impatiently. The contrast of the interior of the tavern with the scenes he had just left was a pleasant surprise. The big hearth room seemed lapped in undisturbed peace. At first glance it looked to be almost deserted. A fire flickered and smouldered on the hearth. Phoebe and two of the Pendergass girls were seated knitting in a far corner. Captain Jack was dozing on a bench. At the big table Yates had his cards laid out, studying some intricate combination. Behind the grille at the counter, old Garrett and three of his boys were making a final check of the goods ready on the shelves. Except for some giggling from the girls and the ticking of a big clock, the place was silent. All that had happened at the fort, all that had ever happened to him before, seemed suddenly as though it had never been. His private drama and the elation of the moment of his release vanished as he stepped over the threshold.

Phoebe looked up at him and smiled. For a moment he forgot everything he had been thinking. He stopped. Yates looked keenly at him as if he sensed something unusual. He shuffled his cards quite easily, and laughed.

"*Well,*" said he, running the cards through the air from one hand to the other fluidly, "so you've come to stay, Mr. Albine!"

127

"Why, yes," admitted Salathiel astonished. "But how did you know?"

"Oh, just by this and that," replied Yates, running the cards back again with a loud snap.

"Eh, what's that?" exclaimed Captain Jack, coming out of his doze on the bench, and sitting up.

"Why, Sal's one of us now," exclaimed Yates.

"Why, of course he is. Sartin! I knew that all along," cried Captain Jack, smiting his knee. "How about a little toddy before the crowd comes roarin' in? Money and thirst will turn this place into a bear garden before the afternoon's over."

" 'Spect you're about right, Jack," said old Garrett. Leaning on the counter, he addressed the girls. "Now, the very first stranger that comes in here I want you young women to go upstairs right away and look after your mamma. And don't you pay any attention no matter how much noise you hear. There's like to be plenty!"

9

The Lids Come Off

CAPTAIN JACK proved an accurate prophet. Ourry's column poured rumbling, splashing, and clattering into Bedford about eleven o'clock in the morning. By one o'clock Pendergasses' was doing a roaring business with the new officers and men who came with it. They had been paid before leaving Fort Loudon; money burned their pockets, and they now hastened to take full advantage of their first opportunity to spend. Once again solid coins rang on Garrett's tables and counter; bounced into his till. Fifty-four wagons with their crews and drivers were in the convoy, besides the reinforcements for Bouquet, of both regulars and militia, who had acted as escort for the paymaster's chests.

Everyone in town, and anyone from the fort who could get away, including wounded and sick from the hospital just able to hobble, lined up along the level stretch of highway before Pendergasses' to see the column come in along the road from the water gap.

Smith's Associators, a company of volunteer, militia riflemen, dressed like Indians in breechclouts, coloured headcloths, and long, fringed, leather leggings, were in the van. They strode ahead nonchalantly but in good order, their long rifles slouched horizontally over their shoulders, led by the vigorous, half-savage figure of Captain James Smith himself, a youthful replica of Captain Jack, looking more like an Indian than a white man. These riflemen were all frontiersmen raised from the vicinity of the Conococheague and Path Valley. They had many friends and relatives in Bedford with whom to exchange greetings and profane repartee as they passed by.

Captain Ourry, Mr. Fagg, the paymaster, and several officers of the staff of the incoming troops came next in a body, mounted on rather sorry-looking nags.

Ourry himself looked tired and harassed. He was a tall, cadaverous man. He rode gallantly, but with the inevitable, exasperated embarrassment of a man with very long legs on too short a horse; an air that even suggested the woes of Don Quixote. The boisterous half cheers, half jeers of the crowd were visibly hard for him to bear. In reality, most of the inhabitants meant only to be roughly complimentary. "How j'do, cap'n? How's it?" But Ourry replied to no one except Burent, who, upon hailing him, received a cordial word and a smile with, "Well, sir, you see we're arrived. And we didn't have to use your sled runners after all."

But the mere commander of the detachment was by no means the centre of attention.

Following him came the main attraction: three heavy,

ron-barred, and mud-splashed coaches, each with a triple-padlocked pay chest firmly lashed behind. They were closely guarded and surrounded by a troop of mounted rangers in leather helmets. From the windows of these ponderous vehicles, as though from the barred casements of a county jail, peered the smooth, pink, and well-fed countenances of the English clerks of the paymaster. They, in particular, received an uproarious but good-natured ribbing from the crowd. But like Captain Durry, and for much the same reason, they failed to reply.

Some people were unable to resist the apparently magnetic attraction of the metal in the chests. They followed the coaches to the very gates of the fort. But most of the crowd remained to watch the rest of the procession pass by, and these on the whole were the better rewarded.

For immediately after the coaches came a battalion of grenadiers in sparkling new equipment; scarlet and polished steel, colours flying, snare drums and trumpets crying aloud. These men were going forward to reinforce Bouquet at Fort Pitt. They marched with a verve and with so much vigour and obvious good discipline as to suggest that victory was already in their grasp. Their mien of cheerful confidence was both infectious and surprising. No such troops had been seen on the frontier for many a day. Their leader, Major Moncreith, rode by erect with the keen look of a sparkling but dangerous blade. An indomitable dandy, he brought forth the admiring huzzas of the crowd.

"By godson!" exclaimed old Garrett to Burent. "I've seen many a detachment pass to the frontiers since Johnny Forbes's time, but never more proper soldiers than these. And to think they belong to the same regiment as the present grenadier battalion at the fort! It only goes to

show what idling in garrison will do. I hope the example
of these new fellows will spread. But here come the
wagons, and a slew of them! Why, it's the finest convoy
and the best loaded I ever did see. Burent, your hand
shows here. And all newly painted, every one of 'em!
The idear!"

Garrett was only voicing what many another thought.
This was the most considerable and hopeful-looking effort
government had made for years. It looked as though the
authorities had at last remembered the frontiers effectively. It boded well for Colonel Bouquet. Here were
men, arms, rations, pay, and ammunition; and in considerable quantities.

For over a mile down the road the big white-topped
and canvas-draped Pennsylvania wagons stretched off
into the distance like a fleet come sailing home. Four-
and six-horse teams, the bells on their yokes jingling confidently, paced and stalked into town. Whips cracked,
and the relieved wagoners, happy at their own safe arrival,
shouted and sang. Indeed, a company of no ordinary
voices brought up the rear with a volume of true harmony.
It was a detachment of the Royal Americans, Welshmen,
recruited exclusively from the Welsh settlements along the
Delaware and in the Welsh Hills about the sources of the
Brandywine in eastern Pennsylvania. They looked fit.
They even looked glad at returning to active service. And
they made the valley ring.

"Ecuyer will be glad to see these lads back again,"
mused Burent. "And look, Mr. Pendergass, there's a
special nod of Fortune for you!"

"What do I see, what *do* I see?" shouted old Garrett,
the wrinkles on his face suddenly registering a pattern of
incredulity together with delight and surprise. "Burent,
I'll not forget this. B'God if I do!"—three wagons at the

132

ail of the procession were just then detaching themselves
rom the column on the road and driving down into the
nnyard. Garrett fairly galloped off on his old feet to meet
hem.

They proved to be, as Burent well knew, three loads
f goods and supplies from Harris's and Philadelphia, the
rrival of which, owing to the disturbed conditions of the
ime and the horrid state of the roads, Garrett had long
espaired of. At Loudon Burent had "pressed" them for
he convoy and passed them on through. Now they came
n the precise nick of time to replenish Garrett's store-
ouse and shelves. The old man could not do enough to
how his gratitude to Burent or his appreciation to one
obe Stottelmyer, the chief wagoner, who had rounded
p his recalcitrant drivers, taken advantage of oppor-
unity, and brought home the bacon.

So now the big wagons and their teams stood steaming
n the yard by the river, with their loads mountainous
pon them. Garrett roared for hands to come and help
nload, stopping only now and then during the process to
nit his fingers together with satisfaction. Even the
vomen joined in, carrying away the lighter articles, and
t was not long before everything was unloaded, checked,
nd under lock and key.

Yet fast as the Pendergasses had worked, the news of
he arrival of the three trade wagons spread faster. A
umber of local traders and small merchants, who had not
een so lucky as to know a Burent or hire a Stottelmyer,
ame to stand about watching; talking out of the sides of
heir mouths, plainly disgruntled and envious. Here was
nother proof to them that Pendergass and the authori-
ies had a mutually profitable understanding. Well, they
ad always said so!

In the troubles of the days which immediately followed,

undoubtedly some of these men played their small trouble some parts. But so on the opposite side of the stage did Stottelmyer and his drivers, seven good men and true who were now temporarily added to the house garrison at Pendergasses'.

Perhaps, both Albine and Yates contributed unthink ingly to a hidden resentment, of which they were not aware, by their possibly too zealous assistance in helping to clear the yard of all idlers and strange lookers-on. But Captain Jack and his assistants were not in a delicate mood. They were even forcefully hasteful at times. Dig nity was somewhat disregarded, even thrown sprawling out the gate when it violently protested. There was small time to argue. In a few moments the first rush of Ourry' thirsty men might be expected to break like a wave against the bar, as soon as the convoy was dismissed.

Its arrival at the fort was already announced by the salutes and the outbreak of cheering which greeted it. The first not entirely sullen noise, which, as Yates remarked the garrison had been heard to make for some months past. In fact, what was going on at the fort could from then on be accurately followed at Pendergasses' both by the kind of noise prevalent in the garrison and the suc cessive waves of various commands and detachments that descended upon the place as the troops were paid

Ourry's hungry, thirsty, but fresh and good-natured men were the first to appear. They hastened to make the most of their advantage over their comrades in the garrison, who could not all be paid until the next day at least, and from shortly after one o'clock until early evening they thronged the bar, drank steadily, ate heartily and bought curiously of the most unexpected and useless articles, as soldiers do. In general, they comfortably pos sessed and overran the place.

Big as the huge hearth room was it could accommodate only a certain number. From Garrett's standpoint the art of coping with a garrison pay successfully therefore consisted in serving rapidly and keeping the crowd moving. Otherwise, those who had already emptied their pockets would continue to occupy the big room and block the counter and bar with dicing, cards, guzzling, and gossip.

Hence the man with the interminable narrative or the too lengthy and lugubrious song was always moved after a time, he scarcely knew how, out onto a stretch of greensward along the riverbank.

Some space there had been fenced off and provided with benches, a couple of fiddlers, a dancing bear, fighting cocks, and old Cloud Face, the Creek, as its master of ceremonies. That office—with a few drinks in him—the old Indian managed to fill expertly with an ironical dignity and a consciously comic air in the performance of it. His squaw and younger progeny brought pipes, tobacco, and liquor. They also proved to be, to newcomers at least, a curious and native novelty in themselves.

Indeed, the attractions of the "yard-garden" were much counted upon to empty the big room and to keep the crowd passing along. When nothing else sufficed, and the jam became too thick, the announcement of a round of free drinks being served outside usually emptied the house. The cost of such strategic treats was small, and it was always amply repaid by the throng of new spenders for whom room was thus made at the bar.

The officers and "gentry" were much harder to handle. They constituted a problem in themselves. The tables in the big room were reserved for them, and, while it was one thing to move out some grenadiers or artillerymen for a few drinks or a cocking main into the yard, it was

135

quite another to try to disturb a party of commissioned officers in epaulets, a gathering of traders and local parsonages, or substantial and self-important residents of of the town.

Here in short, here in the big room, was the weak point in Garrett's arrangements. Here, and not among his more humble patrons as might be supposed, had trouble—quarrels, disputes, duels, and even more serious disturbances—arisen in the past. Officers would linger over their cards and liquor. Traders, farmers, hunters, and wagoners gathered, drank, ate, talked, and disputed. Deals and bargains were made. Lawyers, even ministers, were sometimes present. For all thronged to town on payday. And everybody found some occasion and excuse to drop in at Pendergasses'. Liquor flowed: wine, rum, and whisky. Of late, Garrett had also imported much Holland gin. Inevitably there was some trouble. And the hearth, or common, room was always the crux of the situation.

To cope with the various situations which might arise there required tact, firmness, good nature, and a knowledge of local character. Sometimes, though not often, a swift and judicious use of force was in order.

Captain Jack, Yates, Salathiel, Nat Murray, and Ma Pendergass were told off by Garrett to have the big room on this occasion in their special care. They began—and this, said Captain Jack, was quite usual—by weeding out certain idlers, old topers, penniless loafers, and borrowers who otherwise, on one excuse or another, would have infested and monopolized valuable space. This first unpleasantness having automatically been got over with, the establishment cleared its decks for more profitable action.

It was during the brief pause before Ourry's men arrived, when for a few minutes, and for the last time for

136

several days, Salathiel had a short interval of leisure to look about him, that he first began fully to understand what a crisis in the affairs of Garrett, and of his family and establishment, the occasion of a garrison pay provided. At such times the old man's friends, neighbours, and debtors rallied about him to prevent his being overwhelmed. But troublemakers also assembled. Hence, his dispositions and arrangements for meeting possible complications, and most eventualities, were both ingenious and of long standing.

The sheer convenience and wisdom of the two separate houses with the bridge between them now became more fully apparent. All the women and children, all purely domestic activities, were now completely withdrawn and cut off from the tavern side of the establishment. The door giving access across the bridge was barred, and everything that was delicate, feminine, or private was confined strictly to the residence. The animals and poultry were brought into the barns and sheds and left there under the strict care of the younger Indian servants and of the watchdogs. The last by no means to be despised.

In the notable pay of '63, Garrett was enabled to put an extra guard on his horses and wagons and outside storehouses, owing to the presence of Stottelmyer and his drivers. Deserters were especially liable to become horse thieves, but the loss of a valuable draft horse and yoke-mate from the wagons was not to be tolerated. Knowing the state of the garrison, however, Garrett anticipated at least some attempts on his stables. In fact, this pay he looked forward to trouble in general, and was glad to be able to count upon Stottelmyer and his men, not only for extra watchmen, but also as a general emergency reinforcement to be kept in reserve.

The rest of the arrangements were simple, but effective enough. Like most good arrangements they seemed to have suggested themselves.

The Negro slaves, men, women, and youngsters, were assembled under the able tyranny of Agrippina, their grandmother, to cook, serve, and run errands for "de quality" in the hearth room. Pickaninnies turned the spits there and replenished the fires, while old Pina sat on the raised hearth, switch in hand, watching the roasting meats, cooking, and overlooking the services of the tables. In the course of time Pina had reaped a small fortune from such occasions. All tips must be deposited in her apron, to be buried afterward beyond hope of resurrection under her cabin floor. Woe to the smart youngster who tried to hold back a penny from her. She could read their faces.

Behind the counter and grille Garrett and his sons stood ready to supply drink or display the goods on hand. A small movable section of the bar permitted a sally onto the floor of the big room, in force, if necessary. And it was through this gate that the better customers at the tables also were served wtih the more select vintages, brands, or brews in Garrett's stock, while the crowd satisfied itself at the bar.

Captain Jack, Yates, Albine, and the others assigned to watching the progress of events and business in the big room, sat at the gigantic table with the iron candlesticks at both ends, near the hearth. Or they moved about the room, mingling with various groups from time to time. To the casual eye at least, thus lost among the crowd, they appeared to be only ordinary guests of the tavern who had momentarily dropped in. But they were always there, either in full force or in relays, and especially after dark when the frictions of the day often tended to burst into flame. Prevention of trouble was, of course, the ideal; maintaining good feeling and the usual flow of affairs. Force was a last resort when all else had failed. For those who peacefully fell by the way, overcome by their own potations, the floor of a near-by shed had been covered deep with hay and softly set apart.

Such were Garrett's preparations for the moments of crisis in his life and business marked by paydays. And if his precautions and arrangements seemed to discover an undue apprehension, or to be fatuously elaborate, the answer is that they were not so. They arose out of necessity by experience. The need for his foresight had only too frequently been proved.

To be sure, he might have obtained an armed guard for his premises from the commandant of the garrison. But to have done so would have been to confess that his liquor business was the cause of disorder with which he could not cope himself—and above all Garrett was independent. The purveying of liquor Garrett regarded simply as a necessary, though a somewhat regrettable, function of his establishment. Its other activities were to his mind much more vital and important.

Between the Blue Mountains and Fort Pitt his was the only place where an exchange of civilized commodities went on on a large scale; the only place where those small but essential comforts that make life bearable even for soldiers and hunters could always be amply obtained, and at a fair price.

Take tobacco, for instance, or salt: he practically supplied them wholesale to the entire frontier. And then there were cloth, thread, small cutlery, and tools. Harris's, a hundred miles eastward, was the next place where a woman could get a thimble, or anything else feminine for herself. And the indwelling and social aspects of his establishment had long assumed an importance that was even political. In short, a bright light shone from Garrett's windows into the darkness of the surrounding wilderness.

All of this, the work of his mind, heart, and hands, the result of the patience, toil, and collaboration of his good wife and remarkable family, was not to be casually committed to the indifferent care of an "armed guard" at times of crisis. It required a more careful and yearnful policing, a diplomacy which only its proprietor could invent and supply, for despite his popularity in the vicinity, Garrett's position was often a ticklish one.

Between the good natured indifference or the somnolent toleration of the military authorities, and the thinly veiled hostility of a certain portion of the community, those who either envied or as small traders tried to compete with him, Garrett hoed a difficult but expertly planted and cultivated row. Like all good husbandmen he had to garner his harvest when the season came. At such times he had, to be sure, the support and sympathy of all those, either soldiers or citizens, who had enough sense to realize the importance of his establishment to the territory at large. But he also had would-be rivals who would ruin him if they could.

To say, then, that Salathiel profited from his experience at Pendergasses' would be understatement. Rather, he was enlarged and informed by it. He came; he saw; he copied. Years later his own notable establishment of "Gunset Hall", at Richfield Springs in upper New York, could be traced back, in many of its features, to Pendergasses' at Bedford. Not least in Albine's memory remained the unforgettable days of the garrison pay during the anxious autumn of '63—or the hours of it, rather; hours filled with events that flowed swiftly one into another.

To Salathiel these events disclosed themselves with

the curious quality of a continuous combination of inevitability and surprise; that is, they seemed kaleidoscopic. To the more sophisticated and lettered mind of Edward Hamilton Yates, they seemed to occur like a naturally arranged but fiery little drama with its complications, violent climax, and final tragedy—for him a poignant personal tragedy which completely changed his view of things for life.

As remarked, the serving and entertainment of the new men who had come with Ourry went off well enough. They had begun trooping in about one o'clock and by four or thereabouts they were well satisfied. They had drunk, eaten, bought what goods they desired, and generally exhausted the possibilities of the place. Many of them had then strolled off to loiter about the town and camp. A few grenadiers still capered with the bear to the shrill strains of the fiddle in the yard. A small group of officers lingered over their wine in the common room. But the excitement and novelty, the crowding and rush were over. Even the townsmen and wagoners who had gathered in felt this, and the bar was beginning to be quiet and comparatively deserted again.

"Well, you see how it goes, boys," said Captain Jack, putting his feet up on a chair, "just keep 'em happy and your eyes cocked, and it will all pass off all right." He looked unexpectedly relieved, however.

"Yep, looks like a quiet day after all," remarked John Nogle, the miller, whose mill lay only a half mile up the river from the fort. "Guess I'll go home now. Give me a tuppenny twist and a new clay pipe, Garrett. Beats all how the women kin smash 'em." Nogle nevertheless looked about him a bit disappointed. He had privately hoped for at least a *little* trouble. Milling, although not sedentary, is often monotonous.

141

Garrett smiled, knowing how well his hearty neighbour loved a fight. "If they don't begin to pay the rest of them today, belike it will pass off quiet enough," said he.

But they did begin to pay.

The first evidence of it was a continuous hubbub going on up at the fort, and a message from Ecuyer asking Burent to report to him immediately.

"I guess the captain has his hands full and the pay must be going forward. But that ain't exactly an easy and reassurin' noise up at the fort, is it?" remarked Garrett to Burent, as the latter prepared to leave.

"No, it's not," agreed that neat, brown little Englishman, who obviously left reluctantly the shelter of the comfortable room he had been occupying upstairs. He bade Salathiel, who carried his leather hand trunk halfway up the hill for him, a regretful goodbye, and trudged on with the trunk on his own shoulders towards the postern.

Salathiel stood for a moment listening. Underneath the normal sounds of cheerful excitement, which might be expected to proceed from a garrison being paid, rose a steady angry roar, a kind of threatening and continuous protest.

"What d'ya make of that, Albine?" demanded Captain Jack, who was standing before the door listening when Salathiel returned.

"I allow they've decided to pay the Royal Americans first, which means the grenadiers last. And the grenadiers confined to barracks are raising the roof," Salathiel replied.

This surmise was soon more or less painfully confirmed. A rush of customers from town; keepers of officers' boardinghouses, sutlers and others, were soon besieging the counter for goods. It was merchandise rather

142

than drink that they wanted. Their accounts had suddenly been settled by the officers of the Royal Americans, they said, and they had hurried to Pendergasses' to be the first to replenish their long-depleted supplies. They also reported considerable trouble at the fort. The battalion of Royal Americans was being held under arms, and there was a rumour that the mutinous grenadiers might not be paid at all. What the confined grenadiers thought of this was already patent to anyone within a mile of the barracks.

Doubtless it was this tense and disturbed state of affairs at the fort which accounted for the fact that the militia, which liked to be called the "Pennsylvania line", but for all that was usually paid last, nevertheless appeared next at Pendergasses', waving their paper bills and anxious to turn them into coin almost on any terms —or at least to obtain some goods and diversion for them.

Garrett was considerably put out and disconcerted by this development. He must now be prepared to act as a banker on a considerable scale. Ordinarily he was willing to honour the paper currency of the province of a little over half its sterling exchange value at Philadelphia. Of the rate, his correspondents regularly informed him. So advertised and warned, usually he made a good thing out of trading in paper money, despite the risk.

But the present case was different. The notes for the pay of the provincial militia in '63 were in the form of a special emergency issue authorized by the legislature for the purpose. No one as yet had had the opportunity to find whether they would pass current or not. The privilege of first making this patriotic experiment was now to be Garrett's, and Yates thought it only right to inform the old man that the proprietors of Pennsylvania had not yet approved the issue, and that they might not do so.

Here was a quandary. If the notes proved valueless, Garrett would be in for a shocking loss. If he refused to take them, riot might ensue.

Around the big table before the hearth, Garrett, Yates, several officers of the militia, and one or two local Solomons gathered in solemn and nervous conclave. The argument went on and on. Meanwhile, the militia and their numerous creditors, plus about fifty wagoners, became more and more impatient and importunate, damned the authorities as cheats, the legislature as Quaker bastards, and Garrett as a Shylock. Unless trade began soon, it was plain there would be pillage and violence. Only the trickle of a small quantity of liquor over the bar was serving to stave it off.

"We've been had," roared a big, moonfaced corporal in a bottle-green coat far too small for him. "It's just pretty paper with a promise on it; paper for our blood! That's what it is. Here's what I think of 'em." And with that he twisted up a pound note and lit his pipe. "But there's no tobaccy in my pipe," he roared, pausing in the act. "No, I can choke on the smoke of liars, and damn well like it!"

A menacing growl of agreement went up. The crowd surged forward and several laid hands on the grille and began to shake it.

"Just a moment, men," said a commanding voice. Major Cadwalader, a large florid man, impressive in his fine-fitting uniform, had mounted on the big table and stood aloft facing the crowd.

"Now listen, Mr. Pendergass and I have arrived at an agreement," he continued. "His house will take your notes up to half their face value in trade. I might say I've given my personal bond to him to cover the amount. So you can see *I* think the notes are good. Jennings, you can put *that* in your pipe and smoke it," he called to the big corporal, who now stood thunderstruck with the burnt stub of the bill smoking in his hand.

A roar of laughter at the look of woebegone consternation on the corporal's face, and a cheer for the major shook the room.

At the same moment young Arthur Davison sprang onto the counter behind the grille and began to parade up and down it, shouting, "Well, well, what d'ya lack?" The crowd surged forward laughing, this time good-naturedly, and the trade began.

"You young devil, I'll have the hide off your behind for that," said old Garrett, going after his grandson. "Didn't I tell you to keep in the house whar ye belong?" The boy fled upstairs laughing, for he knew Garrett was really pleased with his presence of mind.

Selling over the counter continued briskly, despite a lack of change and small coin. But the halt in affairs had nevertheless been unfortunate.

Cadwalader's patriotic offer had prevented a riot, but the major was known to have more political ambition than estate. So actually it was Garrett who took the risk on trading goods and hard liquor for soft money. How soft, no one yet knew. And the resentment of the men had, despite his taking the main risk, been focused temporarily upon Garrett and his people. Some of this resentment remained and certain people continued to cultivate it.

Captain Jack and his helpers, more especially Albine and Yates, began to be conscious of this as the afternoon wore on and the militia and their friends continued to monopolize the big room. Their officers, a number of traders, clerks, and the more prosperous wagoners and leaders of the teamsters occupied the tables which they could scarcely be asked to vacate before their betters and superiors, the ranking officers of the garrison and the more substantial citizens of the town, should arrive.

Among those present, obviously inclined to trouble, and being as unpleasant as they dared, were Lieutenant Neville and Ensign Aiken, Maxwell, Japson's disgruntled clerk, and several other characters, friends of free trade, whom Salathiel thought he remembered having seen not long before at Ligonier. Three or four of the teamsters from Japson's scattered caravan also were among the crowd, and they especially seemed bent on making things uncomfortable for Salathiel and Yates.

Yates, in particular, was hard put to it to keep his temper at times. Unfortunately, he had been overheard warning Pendergass about the doubtful nature of the notes, earlier in the afternoon. Neville and his friends were making the most of that. The word was even being passed along to newcomers. Without its actually coming to a head, both Salathiel and the young lawyer could plainly feel the atmosphere of gathering hostility that followed them and seemed to be closing in upon them as they moved about.

Captain Jack was also soon aware that a train of powder was deliberately being laid. To his mind it led back plainly enough to Neville and Maxwell. But that would have been hard to prove. He nevertheless took measures to prevent some spark from setting it off, by calling Albine and Yates over to the big table and introducing them to Major Cadwalader. The major engaged them briskly in talk, which probably prevented the flash that was soon bound to come. At least he delayed it. Or perhaps the delay in the impending explosion was only accidental after all.

For a ferocious growling and scared shouts, the hoarse, agonized screams of a man in mortal trouble just then brought most of the people in the room to their feet and rapidly emptied the place of friends as well as enemies.

Jennings, the note-burning corporal, had, it appeared, undertaken an amicable wrestling match with the dancing bear. Something, as someone lucidly explained, had gone wrong. Corporal Jennings now lay on the ground, groaning hoarsely. Part of his face, most of his clothes, and a portion of that valuable part of the trunk which so conveniently covers the ribs had been clawed off him and lay about in bloody flecks and patches on the ground. The angry bear, feeling unable to explain himself, had departed across the river.

So notable a fight and a shambles, however; the lamentable condition of Corporal Jennings and the tales of eyewitnesses, protagonists of either the corporal or the bear, sufficed for some time to detain the undivided interest of the crowd.

Into the midst of this excitement now descended the first companies of the Royal Americans who had been paid, given town leave, and dismissed. They fell upon the place like locusts, and apparently in equal numbers. Whatever had been the plan of Neville and his friends was rapidly obliterated by the Royal Americans. Other people and other interests took the places of Neville and his troublemakers and occupied the common room.

A number of the regular officers from the fort, even some of the staff, now appeared, settled their accounts with Garrett, and sat down to occupy the big tables and to enjoy the finest vintages and fare which the house afforded.

Towards evening Captain Stewart, the commandant, accompanied by no one else than Ecuyer appeared. The latter was assisted by Burent. Ecuyer looked pale but more vigorous. He was welcomed by Dr. Boyd as the "best living example of my skill".

Room was indeed eagerly made at the big table for the two ranking officers whose presence, together with the expressions of obvious relief which they both unconsciously displayed, was a warrant that the affairs of the garrison must now be in a more satisfactory way.

Thus, with the rest of his customers either satisfied or in process of becoming so, Garrett himself now came over and joined his more distinguished guests at the big table before the hearth. Conversation went on, and a feeling of greater ease gradually pervaded the place.

But the pay had not passed off entirely without incident. That was soon learned from both Stewart and Ecuyer. Stewart, indeed, was still labouring under considerable excitement. "After the lesson we gave those mutinous rogues this morning," said he, "Ecuyer and I both hoped the day would go off quietly enough. But we underestimated the capacity for deviltry in the grenadiers confined to barracks. I admit I thought, when we told them they would be paid tomorrow the same as the rest of the regiment—all except those had up for courtmartial—that it would quiet 'em down. And it did, until some of your men, Major Cadwalader, smuggled in liquor to the first company of grenadiers. A touching instance of fraternizing between the line and the militia, you will observe. As a result, someone set fire to the barracks, where the first company was confined, on fire from the inside. Half the roof was scorched before we could subdue those fellows and get the flames quenched. And it was some of your whiskey, Mr. Pendergass, I am afraid. I hear you have two kinds; the fightin' kind, and the cryin' sort. *Do* try and see that the grenadiers get only the weeping variety hereafter. It's contrition and tears we want to encourage amongst 'em from now on."

Some of the grenadier officers laughed a bit wryly at the commandant's wit, which was somewhat at their expense. They were sensitive about the record of the grenadier battalion that had long been in garrison at the fort. It was a sorry one, and now shone in dark contrast to the bright discipline of the other battalion of their regiment which had just arrived. A moment of uncomfortable silence ensued.

"I'll take the worst of these rascals along with me over the mountains to Fort Pitt in the first convoy," said Ecuyer, who cared very little what the grenadier officers thought. "We can't try them en masse, and the severest punishment they can have will be to go forward to the seat of war, and to Colonel Bouquet, who has peculiar powers of persuasion."

"Fightin' for to keep on wearin' your own har is wonderful soberin'. I've known it to turn the pertest idjets plumb thoughtful," added Captain Jack.

"We'll see, we'll soon see," said Ecuyer dryly, and licked his lips.

"I trust the pay of the grenadiers will pass off without further unfortunate incident," said Captain Frazier, who also looked annoyed at the turn the conversation had taken about his men. Ecuyer respected Frazier, and now tried to turn the matter aside.

"I know at least one man who won't be led into much temptation by his pay," laughed Ecuyer. "Burent, give Mr. Albine his bag of pennies. I'll be bound, Albine, if you're not the most princely rewarded man, next to myself, that I know."

The captain then hastened to explain that Salathiel was receiving two pennies a day for his services, according to the agreement made between them when Salathiel had first been taken into Ecuyer's service at Fort Pitt. He put considerable humour and gusto into the story. Everyone was amused and laughed at him.

Salathiel took it in good part. He bore the grins and laughter of the company by joining in. That Ecuyer seemed more like his old self, that he was able to come down to Pendergasses' and enjoy the company, would have made ten times the chaff that Salathiel received welcome to him.

". . . and I had a hard time convincing the paymaster I really needed so many pennies," concluded Ecuyer.

That there was something else in the bag which Burent had handed him, besides pennies, Salathiel soon discovered. He could feel a fairly large object wrapped up inside. He didn't care to open the bag before the company, but he nodded gratefully to the captain, who looked pleased by his obvious gratitude. It remained for Neville to introduce the only deliberately sour note that marred the evening. He was sitting with the rest of the militia officers about Major Cadwalader at another table, and remarked as he watched Salathiel heft his bag.

"A whole bagful of pennies, eh! Well, I guess in the end we all get paid just about as we deserve."

"Maybe that's what makes you look forward to your court-martial so confidently, lieutenant," countered Salathiel.

Yates chuckled; it was an answer after his own heart. Neville turned a fiery red and started to rise. Major Cadwalader laid a detaining hand on his arm.

"Now, now," said Garrett, "let's not spoil a nice quiet day. I wish you young cockerels would quit foining at each other. Do, do! You might find that bear and try to throw him, if you feel so ornery. Personally, I'd like just a little peace over my mug tonight."

Several others voicing their hearty approval of these sentiments, Neville was forced to sit down and contain himself.

"You might try some of your wit pleasant-like," chimed in Captain Jack, supporting Garrett. "Now, they tell me *you're* quite a hand at a story, Mr. Yates."

"Tell 'em that one about the new dog in the old town," suggested Nat Murray.

Yates raised his hand, afraid of further suggestions. "No, not *that* one," he said. "It might shock Dr. Boyd."

"Pshaw!" exclaimed the surgeon, "do ye think I'd faint away?"

"Well, I don't know," said Yates—"but that reminds me. And this one is about a tavern, Mr. Pendergass. It's called 'Gooseberries'."

Mr. Yates placed both his hands on the table and leaned forward impressively. His eyes glittered like an actor's, and he cast a spell.

Ecuyer grinned to himself. Yates could have made his fortune as a preacher, he thought. His voice reached out and held them.

"When I was living at Pennsbury," he began, "I used often to talk with the lumbermen who came down the Delaware on their rafts from the mountains. Nothing was so funny to them as something that must have been painful to somebody else. That was the way they boasted of being men going downriver. They proved their thesis to themselves going back.

"At Philadelphia, as you know, they sell their tall trees for good money, and every tavern along the road upriver is successively the scene of their enormous revelry going home. At the water gap into the highlands is the last

151

place where they find anything that even resembles an inn. Here a final farewell to pleasure, drink, and the last of their cash is marked by a series of personal encounters which gradually merge and enlarge into one rafter-loosening and universal brawl. After this is over peace descends. The maimed then lead the blind back into the hills to cut down more trees for the next spring freshet.

"Now, some years ago a macaroni acquaintance of mine in Philadelphia lost an election bet and was forced to ride into the backwoods as far as the Delaware water gap as a forfeit. He was one of those exquisites whose voice was higher than his courage, a gentleman with a delicate turn to both wrist and mind. And it so chanced that he spent the night in the inn at the water gap during the extreme climacteric of the lumbermen's annual brawl.

"Our dandy instantly realized that the furious relaxations of the barroom were more dangerous than a minuet. He therefore withdrew into the comparatively genteel solitude of the garret, where he listened all night, trembling, to the rending, smashing, and shattering concussions going on below him, and to the hyenalike howls and laughter that accompanied them. Only dawn, he said, brought at last a majestic and, to him, reassuring silence.

"So—after listening carefully, and hearing nothing more alarming than a few dying groans or drunken snores, he at last ventured to descend into the barroom, carrying his buckled shoes in his hand, in order to avoid making a noise.

"But he was unable to cross the floor in his stocking feet, for a horrible mixture of something in the sand and sawdust, small round, oozy objects, barred his way. Also to his terror, when he put on his shoes he wakened the only other man in the room, a large towheaded ruffian sleeping on the bar. When the man sat up he recognized

152

him as the landlord, and hastened to settle his reckoning for fear he should be thought to have been trying to sneak out. The man bit the coin with considerable satisfaction, since it was a large one, but offered no change.

"He did ask, however, 'Don't ye want yer breakfast before ridin'?' in a deep voice while pocketing the coin.

" 'I don't feel much like breakfast,' squeaked my friend, looking at the floor queasily.

" 'Yer don't want *nothin'*, then?' demanded the landlord, grinning. His apparent affability gave courage to the dandy.

" 'Why, yes,' said the latter, 'there is something.'

" 'What's it?' growled the landlord. 'What do you want now?'

" 'Why, I wish you'd tell me why you scattered gooseberries all over the floor last night.''

" 'Gooseberries? Gooseberries?' mumbled the landlord, looking about him. Then he shook with laughter. 'Gooseberries!' he yelled. 'Them ain't gooseberries. Them's eyes!' "

Yates glanced about him. There was no laughter; no understood though silent applause. The story was not being received as he had expected. Apparently Dr. Boyd really was shocked. Stewart and Ecuyer sat and sipped their wine thoughtfully. Captain Jack seemed strangely annoyed. Only among Smith's Associators, some of the other militia, and the Pennsylvania officers was the anecdote finally accepted with all the enthusiasm which a professional appreciation of the sport of gouging required. To cap the climax, Neville, of all those present, was the only one to voice a compliment—and that seemed to carry a concealed threat.

"That's a *bloody* fine story, Mr. Yates," said Neville. "B'God, I think I'll remember it for future use." He grinned at Maxwell, and that disgruntled trader burst into a knowing laugh.

"Use it if you want to," replied Yates. "There's no use my objecting to your purloining a trifle, after . . ."

"Gentlemen, it's closing time," said Garrett abruptly. "I hate to break up the company, but you can scarcely expect me to disregard regulations when the commandant himself is here."

With that he and the boys began closing down the bar. The room gradually emptied, and in a few minutes the door was barred for the night.

Yates and Albine went upstairs to their rooms above the inn. It was the first time Salathiel had occupied his room overnight. He lay in the comfortable feather bed before blowing out his candle, turning over the contents of the bag Burent had brought him from Ecuyer, and looking at the simple, but to him luxurious and remarkable furnishings of his little chamber. There was a white curtain in the window, a rough pine bureau, several jars and basins, and a rush-buttomed chair. In the bag were nineteen score pennies, tuppence, and two bright guineas wrapped in paper with the small dictionary he had used so often in toiling over the captain's papers. This out of Ecuyer's stark poverty constituted, he knew, a princely gift. How could he ever thank the captain? In fact, how could he be grateful enough for the way things were turning out? He lay back wondering, lost in gratitude, and profoundly pleased and surprised at the comparative eminence and wealth to which he felt he had attained. He luxuriated in the enormous comfort of his surroundings. What a bed! How well things were going!

Across the hall old Garrett had paused before retiring to say good night to Yates, and apparently to admonish him about something, judging by the tones of his voice. Yates's door opened . . .

". . . no one thinks you're afeared of them," Garrett was saying, "but it *was* a damn fool thing to tell that story. Ye might well put them in mind o' something. That's what I mean."

"Well, well," replied Yates deprecatingly, "well, so it was."

Garrett tapped at Salathiel's door as he passed.

"Good night to ye, Albine," he said. "Don't ye go to sleep with your candle burning. Ye might set the place afire. Best get plenty o' sleep, too, young fellow. The hardest day's ahead of us tomorrow—and it's late now."

Salathiel took the hint. He reassured old Garrett by blowing out his light there and then.

If he had known how hard a day lay before him he would not have slept as soundly as he did. It was, as Garrett expected, "the hardest day", remembered for years afterward as the day of the big brawl at Pendergasses'.

10

The Big Brawl at Pendergasses'

THE REMAINDER OF THE GRENADIERS, those who had long been in garrison, were paid next day. That provided difficulty enough in itself. The grenadiers were in a subdued but still an ugly mood. They threatened to take out their sense of indignation against the universe in general on helpless bystanders, since the authorities at the fort had made it plain that whip and gallows, with all the other paraphernalia of order and justice, were on tap there as usual.

This mood of the still half-mutinous grenadiers was a complex, but not an unusual one. Ecuyer had seen similar situations with other troops on the frontiers before. It was the result mainly of a vast boredom with life under considerable hardship with the mysterious, silent forest looking on, gloating like a sinister spectator. It was the result of untimely laxity, of selfish indifference on the part of some of the officers, of petty tyrannies, and the grinding of one personality on another in the gloomy barracks.

This feeling of disgruntled indignation had come to a head and the crisis had passed the day before, when Ecuyer had prevented its spreading into a general mutiny. Those who had become violently active in discontent, or too vocal, were now laid by the heels or had deserted. The chief grievance of not being paid had been removed. The suppressed resentment that remained was now forced into another path. It was now directed at the grenadiers against the other troops in garrison, more especially at the new arrivals, either because they had helped suppress the mutiny or because they did not sympathize with those who had taken part in it. The result was a continuous series of personal and individual fights, grenadiers against the world, that unrolled through the morning like the sputtering out of small packets of fireworks after the main exhibit has been fired.

From early morning, therefore, everybody at Pendergasses' had his hands full on the second day of the pay. The main effort was to prevent fights and to maintain some kind of order and decorum in the big hearth room so that trade could go on.

Captain Jack and his helpers had a lively time. Once or twice it was necessary for Garrett and his sons to emerge from behind the counter and join in the skirmishes. Shortly before noon an attempt was made on the stables, probably by men intending to take horses in order to desert. But this was promptly squelched and put an end to by Joe Stottelmyer and his drivers. Three grenadiers and two militiamen were turned over to Captain Stewart at the fort. He confined them.

After that it was "better". Most of those whose sense of grievance tended towards muscular outbreak had by noon been tired out, thrown out, subdued, thrashed, or overpowered. They now retired to tend to their abrasions or to sleep off the effects of their celebration. Milder and less indignant natures, even some grenadiers, remained to fraternize with the rest of the crowd; to eat and drink heavily, and to buy tobacco and small comforts while the rapidly diminishing stock held out.

About two o'clock trade rose to a crescendo. Most of the officers now came forward and settled their accounts with Garrett. Some of them even thanked him for his patience and generosity. By three o'clock it looked as if everything would end fortunately and the pay pass into local history as a strenuous but profitable interlude. Garrett was even seen once or twice to be rubbing his hands with satisfaction behind the bar. So far only one man had been seriously injured and a dancing bear lost. The bear might come back later. As the flood tide of custom began to ebb it became evident that a large sum in good hard cash had been washed in and would remain behind the bar—with little wreckage to mark it.

"So far so good!" confided Garrett to Captain Jack during a lull. "We must have grossed nigh six hundred pounds."

"So good so far," answered Captain Jack, "or that's the way I'd put it, if you see it as I do."

Just then a large number of militia and wagoners came in, mostly for trade and small articles, and Garrett was recalled to his place behind the counter.

Captain Jack's remark, however, was not merely a cynical aside.

He had begun to notice that, as the officers and soldiers from the fort satisfied themselves and departed in time

158

for the evening parade, their places were gradually being taken by customers less welcome and less profitable. And these customers, it seemed, as the scarlet and green of uniforms gradually departed, had come to stay, for the brighter military colours faded out entirely at last into nothing but homespun, the grimy deerskin shirts of some of the more bedraggled militia, or the soiled butternut of certain odd characters from town. Many of these were hangers-on of the garrison, doubtful and ugly-looking customers, for whom Garrett had little use.

Conversation gradually lagged, or was conducted by groups that appeared to know a dangerous secret withheld from the rest of mankind. They grumbled about it. Then there would be an occasional laugh, suddenly stifled. Tobacco fumes grew thicker as the silence grew more dense. Now and then someone else came into the room, bought a drink for himself and sat down, preferably in a corner.

"I can't make head or tail of the way the trade's going," said Garrett. "Many of these gentry I never did see before. Probably they're drivers come with the convoy, or some of that scum that Japson left behind him. They buy by the hap'orth, and they act like they wanted to string it out."

"Likely somethin's brewin'," suggested Captain Jack. "I kinda feel it 'cumulating like rheumatiz in the fall."

"It seems to me I see a remarkable number of our former friends and acquaintances," growled Salathiel to Yates. "Look, there are five or six of St. Clair's people from Ligonier bunched over in that corner around that Irishman O'Toole, the one whose nevvy got himself scalped top o' the mountain. Remember?"

"And shot, too, by one Albine, I believe," remarked

Yates. "Didn't O'Toole swear he was going to get you for it?"

"He did," agreed Salathiel. "And two of these fellows from the militia we brought here to be tried for desertion seem to be in the room now. I'm not sure, though. I don't remember them so well."

"Probably they've been turned loose by their officers after being lightly admonished," suggested Yates. "That's about the size of it."

"Quite a parcel o' the rest of this gang is traders and drivers from Japson's caravan, the ones we driv off," added Murray, who was standing nearby. "And their friends from roundabouts, too."

"Doubtless," said Yates, "friends and friends' friends. Well, our sins seem to be catching up with us."

"All we need is Japson and St. Clair sitting here to be sure of a fight," mused Salathiel.

"Japson and St. Clair are both in Philadelphia," answered Yates, "but I suppose their memory is still kept green. I'll bet you'll find Neville, and Maxwell, that hang-dog clark of Japson's, droppin' in soon. And Lieutenant Guy and Ensign Aiken—with their friends. That's when the trouble will begin, I opine."

"Speck you're about right," drawled Captain Jack. "All this gatherin' needs is a leader to start mischief. Nice fix you young fellers got yourself into, if I do say it! Now all of you keep settin' behind the big table. Have Pina bring you a plate of victuals, and jes keep settin' and act natural like you was havin' supper. Don't *you* start the ball rolling. Leave that to them. I'm going over to speak to Garrett behind the grille, and I'll be back in a wink."

For some moments Captain Jack continued to talk earnestly with Garrett, who at first shook his head and then appeared to agree.

Meanwhile Yates, Albine, Nat Murray, and Tom Pendergass were served by old Pina. They all sat along one side of the big table next to the hearth, facing out, and keeping the table between themselves and the rest of the room. "Like a breastwork," said Murray, who had no trouble in giving a lively and convincing appearance of a man eating his supper naturally.

Presently Captain Jack came back and brought Stottelmyer with him, who also sat down and ate heartily. That made six of them together behind the long table.

Nothing had happened so far. It would have been hard to say just why the temperature seemed to be rising, but it was. They sat quiet, smoking, ready for any moves. The surly and muttered conversation in the room buzzed on. Finally Yates got out his cards and laid them before him for solitaire. He was inventing a new game.

None of them ever forgot that evening.

To anyone dropping in casually it would perhaps have seemed as though a half-fuddled company of fifty or more congenial topers were frowsting in the warmth and strong tobacco smoke through which the candles burned dimly and the lanthorns along the counter glared like dim but disapproving eyes. Draughts, chess, dice, and various card games were going on here and there. There was some conversation, but on the whole the company was a remarkably silent one. It was that which gave those on watch about the table and behind the bar a strong impression that they were on guard; that they, and everybody else in the room, were waiting for something to occur; that the tension was growing.

Once or twice a complete silence fell.

Then the low soughing of the chimney could be heard and the cloud of tobacco smoke domed up in the ceiling; arched itself into a beautiful curve above the long mantel;

flowed downward into the fireplace—and then poured upward into the flue like a scarf of fog.

For some time now no one had even pretended to buy anything at the counter.

"What d'ye lack?" cried one of the Pendergass twins. "What d'ye lack?"

A laugh or chuckle here and there was the only reply.

But since everything so far was orderly enough, there was nothing to be done about it. Finally Captain Jack got up and suggested to Garrett that he might close the place for the night. But Garrett refused.

"I can't do that," he said. "It's fairly early yet. Word would go round we cater only to big spenders and close our doors on the poor ones. It's the worst thing they could say about us. Besides, if they are going to start anything, putting them out would only bring it to a head."

Captain Jack went back to the table and sat down. He had to acknowledge Garrett was right. But it seemed to him that everybody had been hanging on the result of his conversation, and that they had guessed what it was about.

There was now a complete silence in the place except for some snapping of new wood on the fire. Nat Murray leaned forward and mopped his brow.

At that moment the door opened, letting a great draught of fresh air in, and Lieutenants Neville and Guy, Ensign Aiken, Mr. Maxwell, and three tough-looking followers entered the room. A number of profane greetings were exchanged while the three strangers lost themselves in the crowd, and the officers and Maxwell came forward and sat down opposite Captain Jack and his company, whose plates had now long lain empty before them.

"Howdy, gentlemen," said Captain Jack, "we've kind o' been waitin' for ye."

"That's uncommon nice of you," replied Guy, seating himself about opposite Yates, and glancing down at his cards.

"Why, yes," put in Neville, "we hardly expected so much courtesy as that—and to find you all together! It's an unexpected pleasure." He ran his eye warily along the line across the table, but sat down unabashed across from Captain Jack.

Aiken faced Murray. And Maxwell, looking pale, sat down across from young Tom Pendergass.

"Don't believe I know *that* gentleman," said Aiken, indicating Stottelmyer.

"You wouldn't, he comes of a fine old family," replied Captain Jack.

Everybody was pleased to laugh at this. Although Aiken turned brick red, he said nothing.

"Don't we get served?" cried Guy. "Let's have a round. Hot rum, Garrett."

Old Pina hastened to comply.

"Cap'n Jack, did you ever see a pure-white fox pelt, white as snow?" demanded Neville, as though to keep up the conversation.

"Can't say as I ever did," answered the old hunter. "I've heared half-breeds from the north say they cotched 'em in Canadee."

"Well, I've got a skin here. Like to see it?" said Neville. And without waiting for reply, "Gunther, bring that pelt over here and show it to the capain."

One of the men who had come in with Neville now emerged from the back of the room with a bundle in his hand.

Guy was attempting to talk to Yates. "Tellin' your own fortune?" he asked, indicating at the cards.

"Solitaire," said Yates.

"Always reminded me of mental masturbation," sniggered Guy.

"Can't say I have the same memories of boyhood," smiled Yates.

At that moment Gunther, the man with the pelt, reached the table and stood by Neville.

"It's as curious and pretty a fox pelt as you'll ever see," Neville was saying. "White as the driven snow! Show it to the captain, man! Unroll it!"

Everyone leaned forward.

A pure-white, albino fox pelt rippled down from the hands of Gunther as he undid the bundle. It hung dangling with its nose towards the floor.

Instantly everybody in the room rose as one man and crowded forward towards the big table.

"Look out, look out!" shouted Garrett.

Yates disappeared. His head cracked loudly on the floor.

Gunther had yanked him off his chair by his legs, drawn him under the table, and shot him out into the middle of the room. Three ruffians fell on him before he could get up.

Salathiel leaped on the table, picked Neville up by his sword belt, and hurled him like a log into the faces of the oncoming mob.

Captain Jack upset the table before him so that it now stood over breast high with its legs thrust back towards the hearth.

Salathiel leaped back behind it.

All this had been instantaneous. Salathiel only had time to hear Yates give an agonized scream, and then a wave of fist-fighting rabble came over the table and engulfed him.

His one idea was to get to Yates. He was sure they would kill him. For that reason he wasted no blows or small tricks for inflicting minor injuries on those who came at him. This was no time for tearing off ears. He picked men up and hurled them back where they came from. It was instinctive. For the first time his giant strength, now fully unleashed by furious anger, came into full play and being. For the moment it was effective. Few among the attackers had expected to be used as weapons against themselves. Luckily Captain Jack and Stottelmyer, who roared like a bull, followed suit. At either end of the long table men had Murray and young Pendergass down and were worrying them. In the centre all those who crossed it had become ammunition to be shot back into the faces of their friends.

Heads cracked, shouts, curses, and animal yells filled the tavern. There was another concerted rush against the three giants behind the table. A splintering crash announced that Stottelmyer was using a bench on the heads of his enemies. He used it up. The strong oak was splintered on skulls. The war whoop rose in Albine's throat, and this time burst out. The sound of it seemed to madden Captain Jack. He wrenched a leg off the table and freed Murray of his tormentors. At that moment the grille came down with a sound like the wreck of a ship on a rocky coast and the Pendergass boys poured into the flank of the crowd.

Their rush cleared half the floor, and Salathiel was able to pick Yates up and half pitch, half carry him behind the bar, where he sank down either lifeless or unconscious, his face covered with blood.

For an instant as he sprang up on the bar again

Salathiel was aware of the hideous clamour let loose in the place; of the groans, curses, and shrieks; of the roarings of Stottelmyer and the half-musical rhythmic moaning of old Pina and her family cowering back against the wall of the chimney with white eyeballs glistening in sweating faces; of the thud and smack of blows and the splintering crash of bottle glass all blent into one enormous devil's symphony. This he saw and heard in the bat of an eye, standing on the bar. But there he did have a second or two in which to think, and he could oversee the whole room.

The sortie of the Pendergasses from behind the counter had been enough of a diversion and surprise to drive the crowd back halfway down the room. But the Pendergasses could get no farther, no matter how desperately they fought. The sheer weight, the mass and numbers of the crowd stopped them. Only those near the front could be reached, and those behind kept coming on. The Pendergasses were being pushed back towards the hearth, fighting like mad angels, but giving way. In a minute or two it would all be over. A howl of triumph burst from the crowd. Salathiel was just about to leap back into the forlorn hope, when, like the ground knocks of an earthquake in a furious storm, he became aware of a series of house-shaking blows at the back door.

Could it be . . . ?

He raced along the top of the counter and leaped off into the rear corridor that led by way of the back door into the yard.

The back door was bolted—bolted!

How the hell . . . ? What the . . . ?

He threw the door open, and Stottelmyer's drivers, who had been trying to smash it in with a log, almost crushed him as they rushed into the corridor.

He managed to lead them back into the big room, leaping ahead.

Even in the few seconds that he had been away things had gone from bad to worse. The Pendergasses and their friends had been pressed back and behind the table. They were making a last stand there before the hearth. Blood flowed down old Garrett's face from a nasty gash. Captain Jack staggered and reeled. Even Stottelmyer was gasping now. He and three of the Pendergass boys alone delayed the end.

So evident was this that towards the rear of the room some of the crowd had turned aside to loot the bar and goods counter. Bottles and merchandise were crashing down from the shelves. Bales of cloth were flapping. All this could be seen at a glance.

It was the glimpse of empty space at the far end of the room that gave Salathiel the idea. The sight and impulse seemed one—the impulse to pick up the huge oak table and rush forward with it into the crowd. Stottelmyer saw the plan in a flash. He bellowed hoarsely to his men to help. Out of long habit they obeyed his roars instinctively. Someone slogged Stottelmyer over the head with a bottle and he went down. But his men had heard him. Five of them stooped and laid hold of the table. Salathiel had one end; Captain Jack the other. The massive planks rose slowly from the floor, a barrier and shield for those behind them; started forward; gained speed; came down the room like a moving wall with the iron pronged candlesticks sticking out before like stags' horns.

Old Pina jumped from her chair by the hearth, sobbing with excitement. The thing was totally unexpected. Men went down before the table like ninepins; were swept under it; trampled upon. With the impetus of an avalanche, their feet going like mad, the seven powerful men behind it slammed a half ton of sixteen-foot oak planks into the bunched bodies of the crowd caught at the far end of the room—rammed and jammed it home.

Puffs, oaths, hoarse breathings, a sound like falling grain bags, the frantic howls of a man pinned against the wall by the iron prongs of the candlesticks—bone crackings marked its sudden halt. Its weight fell with a padded thud on arms, on feet and legs trying to wriggle from under it.

"S—t, f—k, goddam . . . oh, Christ, I'm kilt . . . let me up, you ornery bastards. Jesus! God! I'm done . . . varmints . . . sons of bitches . . ."

There was no end to it. But words were no defence. The determined men behind the table turned back and began knocking down every man who now tried to get up. The Pendergass boys rallied again, joined Stottelmyer's drivers, and continued the fight. They trampled on those who lay prone, while for a few seconds the battle swayed furiously up and down the room. The odds were now about even. Stottelmyer's six drivers were fresh, new, and terrible. They were enjoying thmselves.

Someone wriggled out from the crushed mass of humanity behind the table, opened the door, yelling murder, and fled out into the night. More followed. Panic spread. Those who had been looting the shelves now cowered behind the counter. At the rear of the room the wide-open door suggested at once the end of the fight and the only possible exit, to marauders and defenders alike.

At the last there was a kind of gantlet running. Boots now came into full play. The Pendergass boys chivied those who remained caught in the room like rats around and round; routed out the skulkers from their hiding places. They knocked them silly, and sent them spinning down the line of Stottelmyer's waiting men, who booted them out through the open door with roars of delight.

Suddenly, except for those lying quiet on the floor, the room was clear of strangers. The defenders burst into a breathless shout of relief and triumph. On her knees by the hearth old Pina "bres' Gohd-a-mighty," fervently, and without end. She was also heard later on asking His forgiveness for having locked the back door as usual, and for forgetting to say anything about it.

According to the clock, about six minutes had passed since the nose of the white fox had pointed at the floor.

The big brawl at Pendergasses' was over.

". . . all except for the helpless and injured," said Captain Jack, looking about him and licking his bruised lips. "Now let's get rid of 'em. Let those poor bastards under the table up first."

It was remarkable how difficult it was to lift the table now. What they had done with it only a few moments ago now seemed impossible. It was already a legendary feat even to themselves.

Those who were caught behind or under the table begged for mercy and were allowed to leave the room unmolested. Some walked and some crawled through the open door. The man caught by the candlestick was helpless. He could only moan a little and curse. They carried him out and laid him by the riverbank to be looked after by his friends, if any.

"We've got one or two of our own to nurse," said Garrett bitterly, mopping the blood from his own face. "Yates has lost an eye. It was that big, gouging lout of a Gunther

169

that Neville set on him. He got away, too! Cleared out airly, the scum!"

"So did Neville and Aiken, along with Guy and Maxwell. They'll swear they had nothing to do with this; that they left as soon as the fight began," said Murray, feeling his bruises and loosened teeth.

"That'll all be true enough," said Garrett. "I thought I saw that redheaded Irishman O'Toole sneak out with them, too."

"Did I ever see a white fox?" mumbled Captain Jack dreamfully. "Did I? Well, I'll know one now. I'll get that white fox pelt yet!"

And curiously enough, although it was not quite what he meant, Captain Jack did get the pelt. It was picked up by Mark Pendergass in the yard only a few minutes later and brought in to him. There was blood on it.

In the little corner room upstairs over the inn, Yates lay stretched out on his bed, where he had been carried by Albine. Phoebe Davison and two of the Pendergass girls were hovering over him. He had come to once, but luckily was unconscious again. He was terribly beaten up. He had a frightful blow on the back of his head and his left eye was irretrievably injured. In fact, it was gone out of its socket.

Salathiel stood looking down on his friend, filled with wild fury and regret. He was half out of his head with anger and chagrin. Only Phoebe and old Mrs. Pendergass, who came in to see what she could do, were able at last to prevent Salathiel's running out to do murder in the town. Captain Jack also helped to restrain him.

"It won't do you no good, son," said the old hunter, who had come upstairs with a strange surgeon. "You'll have to let things take their course now. Captain Frazier with a provost guard is downstairs and they've taken things

170

over. Now you go down, too, and get your own gashes and cuts fixed up. Dr. Boyd's looking after his friends in the big room. I'll be down myself in a jiffy. I've got a bad arm I want him to look after."

Thus cajoled, Salathiel left Yates to the care of the girls and the hot compresses ordered by the surgeon, and descended into the big room again. A provost guard from the new grenadier battalion was in charge with Captain Frazier. Bayonets glittered and lanthorns flashed on much scarlet and gold lace.

Captain Frazier, a precise little Scot with a sandy moustache, was making notes in his pocket memorandum of what was being told him by several people at once. He regarded Mr. Pendergass as a much-abused and outraged man. Arrests were being made in the town of anyone connected with the military suspected of having been in the fight. That was the best Captain Frazier could do under the circumstances. Warrants would have to be sworn out for any of the others.

But everybody knew that would never be done. Who and where were the miscreants? Where was a magistrate to be found? How could the warrants be served if once obtained, and who would serve them? On the harassed frontier the civil government of the province was not even a convenient fiction. It was only a hope waiting to be born. Except for taking out land warrants, no one ever thought of the civil law seriously.

Captain Frazier talked of warrants as though he were in Britain. The commandant was indignant, he said.

Garrett and Captain Jack looked at each other and smiled through their injuries. They knew they would have to protect themselves, and what measures they must take. The big brawl would only serve to hasten their plans. It would make the necessity of a secret combination of good

171

citizens against rascals more patently evident. In the end, it would be a help for what Captain Jack and Garrett intended to do.

Dr. Boyd was kept busy for some time. There were a couple of arms to be set, a case of broken ribs, cuts and bad contusions to look after. Black eyes, swollen faces, and loose teeth could be left to cure themselves. Salathiel had a knife slash from his shoulder to his wrist. But it was a scratch. The man had somehow missed him.

"I wonder there weren't more lethal weapons used instead of fists," remarked Dr. Boyd.

"I think I know the reason for that, doctor," said old Garrett. "I'll tell you later. It fits in with what was behind the whole thing."

"Well, it's lucky for you people, that's all I can say," answered the doctor, as he finished bandaging Garrett's forehead. "The gash will heal without a stitch. You and Captain Jack got off light. He's bruised but not dangerously. Damned bad business, this brawling. I'm mortal sorry about Yates."

It was typical, however, that Captain Frazier scarcely seemed to notice that several people in the room had been rather severely injured. His indignation and worry seemed to be totally concentrated on the loss of goods and damage to property. The double loss exhibited by bolts of cloth soaked in wasted liquor struck him especially. The partially looted shelves were to him so many gaping wounds.

"Now what do you think your total loss might be, Mr. Pendergass?" he kept asking.

Driven at last to answer, Garrett finally replied, "Offhand, I should say about thirty pounds."

"Thirty puns, thir-r-r-ty puns! Mon, think of it!" the captain kept exclaiming.

Captain Jack and Garrett, followed eventually by the others, went upstairs to bed.

" 'Mon, *think* of it!' " said Captain Jack, smiling ruefully, and laying his hand on Garrett's arm affectionately as they said good night.

"Why, we'll do that, old friend. We'll think of it considerable, won't we?" said Garrett, and laughed painfully. "Good night."

Salathiel looked in again at Yates. Phoebe sat by his bed with one candle burning. He wondered if there was anything he could do. But Phoebe looked up at him and shook her head, her finger on her lips. He whispered good night to her. For the first time in his life he felt thoroughly exhausted, not only in body but in mind.

Under the official care of Captain Frazier's sentries Pendergasses' at last lapsed into the silence of a hard-earned peace. But even in the sleep of nervous shock and exhaustion great green, yellow, and red sunflowers bloomed and burst and spun through seething darkness inside the skull of Edward Hamilton Yates.

11

Conversations Overheard

FROM THE TIME of the Big Brawl, which, like Braddock's defeat, left an indelible mark on the calendar of Salathiel Albine, his days through the winter and spring of 1764 alternated between the woods of the deep wilderness and the, to him, fascinating and absorbing life of the small frontier town of Bedford, for so it was now called by nearly everybody, except the oldest settlers who clung to "Raystown" to the very last.

The story of those days comes down to us at once vividly and puzzlingly told. For, as might be expected, the tale reaches us only in fragments, with the emphasis upon what most interested the actors in the stirring drama of their own lives, and not at all, necessarily, upon what would most interest us. Yet from the very nature of what was set down and recorded by them much is to be in-

174

ferred. Here, at least, are the things which must have most concerned the recorders—or they would not have left a record of them.

There is, of course, the invaluable, long-continued diary of old Garrett Pendergass, somewhat diffuse, odd, even a bit senile, if you insist, towards the end. And there also remain fragments of the accounts from his store and tavern together with a few warm family letters, scattered now, as his tribe is scattered, from sea to sea. These are helpful records, corrective in taking a view backward over the shoulder—the left shoulder, since on that side lies the heart. And they also provide a kind of focus for illumination in reconstructing the cyclorama of a lost country, once, since it belonged to our fathers, in some sense our own.

Otherwise, most of the story comes down to us from Salathiel himself, although not directly, heaven knows!

At best, Salathiel's own story emerges only with difficulty, and after much rearranging and mind prodding, from that curious mass of notes, journals begun and left off, letters, bills, receipts, old newspaper clippings, Continental money, commissions, and handbills—a very devil's welter and human jackdaw's hoard assembled haphazard during his long and disturbed lifetime, papers which Major Albine was always going to put in order "someday", and never did.

It could only have been Yates who found them hidden in the old deerskin sack in the pine desk at Richfield Springs after Salathiel was lost in the great storm, for the precise notes and fine handwriting of the little, one-eyed attorney fairly stream through them. Some of the material Yates sorted, sealed into bundles, and then endorsed upon them. He seems to have contemplated making a kind of

175

chronicle of the olden time, a *Personal History*, as he somewhere calls it.

It was evidently to have been a work of love and leisure, something to while away the peaceful hours and perhaps the tedium of the long, calm summers and longer comfortable winters at "Gunset Hall", after his friend Albine was gone. But old men have often sat down thus to preserve the scenes of days that are no more, only to lose themselves in dreams of being young again. So it has often been, and so it must have been with Yates, who left only fragments of his story completed here and there.

There was a beginning, a few favourite scenes his pen lingered over, and the notes, more notes, projects for chapters, cryptic reflections on pieces of paper meant only for himself. And yet sometimes from one of these "reflections" glances a helpful ray, illuminating the whole picture puzzle, once you have taken the trouble to put it together.

In straight narrative Yates got only as far as the days of Braddock, a good bare story. But we must be thankful even for that. For he knew the old frontier as none of us can ever know it, brood upon it as we will. He had seen and he had heard. He remembered. And all the lost country down the Ohio valley where Salathiel spent his youth, and the strange story of the Albines, Yates put together from what Salathiel and old Garrett told him, and he checked and added to it as only an attorney would, and as he in particular could.

Thus we are saved a deal of petty fiddling with the personal past, and futile excursions into that forest morass of old Indian country; twilit, tangled vistas, thickets where *Antiquarius sapiens* himself might find nothing but fox fires to follow and false trails to tread.

For this time at Bedford one is forced to depend mainly

176

upon certain passages in a brief journal Salathiel began to keep about January '64, but left off suddenly, and in mid-air. One thing emerges quite plainly here: Salathiel Albine was interested mainly, not in his frequent forays into the forest with Captain Jack, but in the all-absorbing events of life in the town. This flashes back crystal clear from occasional bright fragments of his journal, pieces of mirrors, as it were, left in the jackdaw's nest of the past.

Putting all these pieces together like so many jagged fragments of a shattered looking glass, and not neglecting to fit other important parts of it, such as Ecuyer's letters, records of the fort and town, and Surgeon Boyd's *Notes & Queries*, each into its proper place—suddenly the thing is done. The whole picture emerges. The past is reflected back to us in the light of other days from fragments of itself. And our reward is great.

It lies not only in the fascination of having successfully fitted together the remains of a scattered puzzle. It is greater than that. Now we can ourselves supply any small missing parts; extend and enlarge our being into the past. The breath of the imagination quickens for a moment; fogs upon and mists over the cold mirror of the past. Then, as it clears, the miracle happens. The shattered surface is revealed as healed and glassed over. Movement is there; depth in space; sound, sights, and odours. The pale faces of phantoms glow with the hues of life. The sphinxlike lips of silence move to words and song.

From the valley of the Juniata the sound of a cow bell comes from behind those misty willows. Wind catches in the trees along the mountains. The long forests shiver. The river flows musically again past Garrett Pendergass's door.

After the Big Brawl, things rapidly settled down at Pendergasses'. Those most concerned either left town by a return convoy of empty wagons to Fort Loudon or so comported themselves as to be monstrous inconspicuous. In short, it was remarkable how difficult it was to find anyone who would admit that he had even been near Garrett's place the evening of the big brawl, especially if he bore a black eye or a ripped ear. Some of the more seriously injured claimed they had been hurt in accidents on the road. And they were prepared to produce witnesses, if necessary. But it was not necessary.

For all this diffidence suited Garrett well enough. Maxwell and his friends had received so notable a check that it was not likely they would be looking for more trouble for some time to come. Besides, both Garrett and Captain Jack were planning to protect themselves and the town from the repetition of any similar outbursts in the future in a manner much more far-reaching and fundamental than the punishment of this or that individual could provide.

At the fort, Ecuyer had Neville and Guy well in hand. Ecuyer was taking them west to Pittsburgh and Colonel Bouquet. Discipline was now being enforced amongst the Bedford garrison by the exasperated commandant with an iron hand. Court-martials were functioning with a reassuring precision.

To show that peace had returned, the damage in the hearth room at Pendergasses' was repaired and the grille hung even more securely than before. Trade with the garrison resumed shortly and went on quietly and profitably again. Garrett and his whole household celebrated Christmas '63 before a roaring fire with old English custom and cheer: roast beef, plum pudding, fiddlers, and all. Thirty-eight people great and small, including some of the officers from the fort, sat down about the great table in the hearth room.

It was hard to believe that so secure and happy a festival could be held on that troubled frontier even under the protecting ramparts of the fort. But held it was, with reels and dancing afterward; with toasts to everybody from the king to Phoebe Davison, not forgetting poor Yates, who was still unable to leave his room but somehow contrived even in his pain and misery to send downstairs a rhymed message to the whole company:

> Though Storms without like wild Beasts howl and rave,
> Yet still to Cyclops frowsting in his Cave,
> The Sound of Music, coming through the Floor,
> Reminds him of new Friends—and days of Yore.*

To Salathiel these days spent at Pendergasses' as the year '63 grew to its close were the happiest he had ever known. As his first really domestic experience, it was a revelation to him. He was in the house, and as a member of the family. For ever since the night of the great fight in the hearth room he had been accepted as such without further reservation. He saw Phoebe every day. The Pendergass boys regarded him as a welcome and giant accession of strength to their tribe. They could never get over talking about how "Salathiel and Cap'n Jack jes picked up the little old table like nothin' at all and rin down the room with it."

---

* "Few will ever know the pain which this small effusion cost me at the time," says Yates, in a note evidently made many years later on a copy of these couplets he had saved. "Christmas '63 was my nadir. I thought I should have gone mad with misery, homesickness, and despair. Blind perhaps. Cyclops indeed!"
This is the only bit of verse in the whole bundle of papers found in the deerskin bag.

That was the form in which the legend of the Big Brawl finally crystallized, for when Stottelmyer and his drivers departed eastward, as they soon did, their gallant part was conveniently forgotten. It was Captain Jack and Salathiel who remained to become local heroes. The story spread through the whole neighbourhood and they began to be pointed out around the camp and streets as tall Samsons whose rage was a terrible thing.

Thus the slaughter of the Philistines lost nothing in the telling. And, to tell the truth, neither Captain Jack nor Salathiel did anything to belittle it. In fact, they enjoyed the reputation they had painfully earned. The younger children of the establishment climbed over them and swarmed about them whenever they sat down, until old Mrs. Pendergass herself interfered in behalf of their peace. The women of the place were admiring and grateful. Old Pina was forever frying, stewing, or simmering "suthin' tasty" to tempt them. It was almost embarrassing, but it was also exceedingly pleasant. From Salathiel's private standpoint nothing more lucky for him than the big brawl at Pendergasses' could have occurred.

How much of his swift and cordial acceptance into the ordinarily jealous and closely drawn circle of the Pendergass tribe was due to old Garrett's affectionate remembrance of his father and mother, Salathiel at first had no idea.

Like many young men, Mr. Albine tended to regard his own desirability as rather inevitable. But Garrett's frequent and close questioning of him in regard to his early memories soon brought about two results: it convinced Garrett that Salathiel was certainly Lemuel's child, and it informed Salathiel himself of many things which he might otherwise never have learned about his parents.

For his part, he could never hear enough about them.

He was particularly curious about his mother, and both Garrett and old Rose were frequently called upon to repeat in minutest detail the story of the sojourn of the giant blacksmith and his pretty Irish wife with the Pendergasses in what now already seemed even to them an era in the remote past. This both the old people were glad to do. For they had long arrived at the place where they loved to linger over the now romantic scenes of their early married life in Path Valley and in the older settlements eastward.

Mrs. Pendergass from the first had entertained no doubts as to Salathiel's being the child of the young couple she had once so happily known. There was the name. And there were certain resemblances, traits of gesture and expression in Salathiel, which recalled both Lemuel and his wife forcefully to her mind. As a woman, Mrs. Pendergass "knew". She needed no further circumstantial evidence. Salathiel seemed to have come back to her like bread cast upon the waters. His physical presence was a vigorous denial of any futility in the kindness and affection which Mrs. Pendergass had lavished upon his mother in the past. For once, the wilderness almost seemed to have given up its dead.

Mrs. Pendergass's long-repressed grief over the disappearance of the Albines had never ceased to be a real sorrow. Secretly, she had continued to hope against hope that they might be heard from. She had even argued against Garrett's common-sense "I told you so", when the news of Lemuel's murder by the Shawnees on Christmas Day of 1748 had later been brought in by a Mingo hunter. She had fondly hoped that it was only a rumour, of which the woods were full. Garrett, however, shook his head conclusively. He accepted the tragedy as complete—and the years had seemed to justify him. Finally, it had all grown dim, a far-off painful music in memory like dreaming of long-dead children.

And then Salathiel had walked in out of the forest, a surprising, a comforting and satisfactory fulfilment for nearly vanished and vainly cherished hopes.

His welcome, therefore, was really not quite so mysterious as it might seem. He was welcome even in Mrs. Pendergass's own room, to be admitted to which was a kind of accolade of family approval. He came there often to hear about his mother and father and brought the "old lady", as she was affectionately known, seeds for her birds that languished in the winter, a new cage whittled out for them by his own hands, and special billets of hard wood for her chimney fire.

She could not hear very well all that he had to say. But on account of that she talked all the more herself, and seemed to enjoy it. Indeed, she always talked as though in conversation. Seated in possibly the only upholstered, wing chair west of the Susquehanna, her warmly stockinged feet secured from the draughts on a high, stuffed carpet stool, old Mrs. Pendergass would lean her white-kerchiefed head against the knotted head piece on the back of her chair and reminisce of her own past and everybody else's in a strong Devon accent that, despite the lapse of her years in America, might still have passed muster at Zeal Morachorum in the moor.

Phoebe and Arthur Davison, her favourite grandchildren, frequently came and sat in the room to hear their grandmother's stories. And if Phoebe sat a little closer to Salathiel on the big oak bench in the corner than she did to her brother Arthur, Mrs. Pendergass, although she noted it, had no comment to make. Her eyes were better than her ears, however. She could see how it was.

A pair of fur-lined moccasins made by Salathiel and

embroidered by Phoebe confirmed her tacit approval of so natural a situation by being accepted and worn. When Salathiel repaired and reshaped an old wig of Garrett's, one which his wife had seldom been able to get him to wear, Mr. Albine's star approached its zenith. Garrett grumbled a little, but he too, like his wife, was amused and confounded by the domestic skill of a "wild man", who took scalps and dressed "artificial har" with equal felicity. In the end, Mrs. Pendergass did what she had never permitted herself to do before any of her own boys; she took out a small clay pipe from her reticule and smoked it while she talked to Salathiel.

Deafness, a certain failing of lively energy were the only natural crosses age had so far laid on the trim shoulders of old Rose Pendergass. She was hale, silver haired, blue eyed and rosy. She still had all her teeth sound in her head. She still took a constant interest in the emotions of other people, particularly in their loves, hates, and passions.

She was aware, for instance, that jealousy appears with infancy and lingers to the last senile flicker; that it is the most pervasive motive in life, the most constant and the most subtle. For it always unconscously assumes itself to be something else and its disguise is therefore real. She saw that men and women were both equally swayed by it. And she had discovered and confirmed all this for herself. It was, indeed, the juicy orange amid the dried golden apples of wisdom which she had gathered into her now overflowing cornucopia of experience. Sometimes she thought she could more or less run her family on this one item of knowledge alone.

When conduct became apparently mysterious or unexpectedly and perversely provoking, she attributed it to jealousy—and she was seldom wrong. In this way she was able both to prevent and to predict family conflicts in a manner that seemed Sibylline. So, while she was beloved, she was also feared and respected, two adjuncts without which lasting affection is impossible.

Thus, after a long, active, and useful life, Mrs. Rose Pendergass's now passive role as a female spectator and mentor of existence in her own ample family was an interesting one. Yet it was interesting not only to herself but to others. Her deafness, she thought, was a positive advantage, for it enabled her to watch things happen without the prejudice of overhearing emotional sounds about them, and to arrange her conclusions on the already ample basis of her own experience, nicely and to the point.

She was actually able to impart usable advice not alone to those who asked it, but also to those who needed it. And the whole family came to her from time to time, from young children with sore bottoms or warts, to those much perplexed about mating or with the ancient troubles of new husband and wife. Since her advice was given not in words only, but was frequently accompanied by gifts —clothes, medicines, furniture, and even money—to enable it to be put into effect, it was no wonder that her room was both the confessional and the oracle of the whole establishment by the Juniata, and of the outlying cabins and family settlements about Bedford, when times were safer.

Of course, all this interest which she kept up about her was quite satisfactory to Mrs. Pendergass herself. She had in fact solved the chief problem of women: How not to become superfluous after their children grow up and age leaves their husbands free to comparatively undisturbed sleep and self-consecrated days. She had unconsciously at first, and later deliberately, placated fate against her being left lonely, discounted, and neglected in deaf desuetude. And she did so by the deft and copious use of the two best agents for preventing so natural and likely an end to any decent woman's life: children and property.

Property she therefore now gave away along with her advice, and in order to reinforce it, in somewhat the same way that children had been bestowed upon her, painfully but with prodigality. Her gifts great and small she thus avoided dispersing in a mere impulsive scattering. They were instead anticipations of two facts, facts which she had long realized; that both her children and possessions *must* be left behind, and that to begin to divide her property now among the several divisions of herself whom she would leave perambulating the world after her own baby lay still was merely to prolong and enlarge her enjoyment of her things in the possession of her children.

Thus few were ever either disgruntled or debased by her giving. No one in effect felt himself bribed. Her gifts as a grandmother seemed, even to the eager recipients, merely to anticipate the inevitable division of mortal justice and to restrain rather than promote the inevitable jealousy which the bestowal of usable objects that occupy space always engenders in humanity, to restrain it by the salutary thought that the giver was still present, still able to reward or withhold.

All, even very small grandchildren, had finally come instinctively to understand this and to act and abide according to her matriachal desires. And they were all the more willing to do so, because, as they grew older, it was gradually borne in upon them one and all that the inner and finally ruling motive in this wise old woman's conduct of affairs was a kind of passionate selflessness, an unfathomable capacity for quiet self-sacrifice and yearnful patience, which desired that none should be hurt or harmed in order that all should survive and prosper together.

This is in effect only to say that Mrs. Rose Pendergass was an exceedingly womanly woman, that the outer shell of her protective common-sense and right self-satisfactions was inhabited by "a wondrous tender, involute, and astute creature" that knew by instinct when to open and when to close its shell against the world.

The reasons for her decisions, which affected many people, being instinctive or founded upon a depth of experience not always immediately self-evident, were acquiesced in by her tribe out of long habit and confidence. But not always without a good deal of discussion, especially by the in-laws, some of whom were inclined, at first, to carry their own cherished points of view before Garrett in a family dispute. But only once, for the "old man", while he would listen, would never act either to veto or to interfere with any long-settled policy of his wife. And so in the end it was the same as though Mrs. Pendergass had quietly reviewed her own case.

She remained, therefore, secure in her key position. And her character and peculiarities were consequently the subject of constant interest and frequent review, not only in her own family, but in the neighbourhood at large and about town.

Certainly amongst the women of the community she was more discussed, applauded, attacked, envied, and defended than anyone else. Possibly there was something mysterious in the influence and authority which she seemed to possess by unassailable natural right, the gift perhaps of time and fortune. Or was it luck? Was it not rather her fortune-compelling character? She accepted life so calmly that there was a hint of eternity about her. Yet it was strange to find something only delicately robust so enduring. Where was one to look? Outwardly there was only her cool room and her garden, both pretty and plain. There were her birds that sang in winter and the flowers on the window sill. In summer there were white blowing curtains. But there was always Mrs. Pendergass herself, asleep perhaps in her chair, while the clock ticked on and on on the mantel. Yet somehow to her descendants that clock seemed to be ticking theirs and not her life away.

Officers from the fort, guests at the tavern, strangers who came out of a lonely wilderness to warm their feet or their hearts before the Pendergasses' fire, felt and noticed this pervasive, timeless quality in Mrs. Pendergass. They sometimes wrote home about her, or discussed her quietly, while Garrett was absent, over pipes and tall glasses. Something so eternally feminine in the forest, something so permanently human was both intriguing and refreshing, a balm to lost or homesick men. Nor did it seem to make much difference that Mrs. Pendergass was no longer young.

Surgeon Boyd, for instance, who had seen a great deal of life, both men and women, from the Punjab to Pennsylvania, including a surprising number of countries scattered between, speculated about Mrs. Pendergass considerably by both mouth and pen—as, indeed, he speculated about nearly everything else from stars to gallstones with ingenious and even whimsical comparisons and analogies.

It was he who maintained he had never seen anything to compare with Mrs. Pendergass, except in some Hindu households, where all the family, sons, new wives and their offspring, retainers and animals lived in one vast compound where the oldest couple ruled them all. And how curious to find something similar, although much more matriarchal, on the banks of the obscure Juniata.

187

An accident, of course, something unusual in the colonies, Indian troubles had kept the family together. But how would it be, the doctor wondered, if more English settlers lived like the Pendergasses, instead of wandering off couple by couple into lonely cabins lost amid the hills?

Few really understood just what the doctor was talking about. But this problem of lonely families in America, and women in general, Dr. Boyd discussed frequently with Yates in the lawyer's small room just across the hall from Salathiel's, where the surgeon came évery afternoon to bathe and dress his injured eye, bringing a basin, sponges, bag, bandages, and instruments. Sometimes he also brought an old newspaper or an interesting book and read from them. Or he read from what Yates found to be even more interesting; from his own *Notes & Queries*. The door of Yate's room was usually left open into the hall.

Lying on his bed, Salathiel could thus overhear the doctor. And Salathiel frequently lay on his bed then even in the afternoon. For it was now dark and snowy outside. There was little to do at that time of year, and he had never quite lost the habit of sleeping or dozing, when time served, like a savage or an animal. He would come up to his room, curl up like a wolf making his nest in the leaves, and settle himself down on the deep mattress, revelling in the comfortable feathers and the sounds from all over the house, listening to the tags and snatches of talk as the women went up and down stairs. He could tell people by their footsteps. How strange and pleasant to be in a house like this, and with women. And Dr. Boyd was nearly always interesting. He talked and read to distract Yates, of course. But it was good talk and good reading, for all that. One learned things from it.

It was that way in fact, lying on his bed one winter

afternoon, that Salathiel first heard about "the wondrous tender, involute, and astute creature" that inwardly inhabited the outward shell of Mrs. Pendergass. It was Dr. Boyd talking to Yates. And Salathiel, as he listened, chuckled quietly.

". . . and this creature—" explained Dr. Boyd, who as a scientific philosopher took all his analogies from nature, and tried them upon Yates, whom he considered an understanding patient—"this creature is nothing less than the spirit of human mercy, the ultimate female sanity from which all animal affection and decency originally proceeded, and upon which, in the final analysis, society still rests.

"It is a something obstinate and enduring too, my half-blind legal friend," insisted the doctor. "You lawyers would persuade us in these days that society was formed by men making a contract. Contract!" he snorted. "Contact, I say! Society was formed by *a* man making *a* contact with *a* woman, and by her having children and preserving them from his brutalities. For that matter, the process still goes on. Society was never founded. It is always being refounded. You have only to look about you, especially in this very house, where Mistress Rose Pendergass has this saving quality of female mercy about her to a remarkable degree. And by God Almighty, I say as a medical man, as a sort of despised male camp follower of armies," the doctor spluttered, "that we contract-making and contract-breaking men need all of this quality the women can provide.

"For instance, I myself have seen seven pitched battles and the Lord only knows how many small night exercises and day excursions in military murder and pillage, from the filthy Ganges to the virgin Ohio, and the wonder is to me that the teats of female mercy never go dry. So when

189

I say that this female quality is a marvellously enduring and obstinate one I mean exactly that, for if you had ever seen a field of battle heaped with green, rotting corpses, or regaled yourself with the infernal panorama and stench of burning villages and massacred inhabitants, such as I have had forced upon the contemplation of my eyes and nose both in India and in France, I say that you would then appreciate what I mean, and never cease to marvel, as I do, that the product of women's bodies can replace so much unnecessary mischief and replenish and re-enliven the earth."

Here the doctor wiped his face with a cambric handkerchief after so sustained a period, and looked at Yates, who lay with his eyes closed almost as though he were asleep. Perhaps he *was* asleep, after all? It had happened to the doctor before.

So Dr. Boyd murmured to himself as though adding a final after thought not necessarily to be overheard. "Of course, the women have one initial advantage. They get the babies first and teach them to talk. Language is essentially at first, and so fundamentally, a female affair. Philosophers merely warp it to their manly ends years after the mothers have settled all the vital meanings of the important words. Thank the Lord the philosophers are always too late. Because it must be when the children are small that the women indoctrinate 'em with the only decency and mercy they ever really learn. Quite fortunately, of course, over half the children are always girls. For only some of the boys remember some of the things they heard from their mothers, after they grow to be men. Let's say half of 'em do. The rest become warriors, parsons, politicians, thieves, drunkards, whoremasters or patriots—or name any other profession you like . . ."

"Medicos and lawyers, for instance," said Yates, opening his one eye with an amused gleam.

"Yes, God rot 'em," said the doctor, "I wouldn't expect them either. Contract makers and breakers, let's call 'em. You see my point is that about one quarter of the human race, after you leave out the girls and some of the boys, are bound to be purely destructive and obstructive when they grow up, according to my reckoning. That just about maintains an even balance between the forces of male destruction and those of female repair. Give us a few more murderous weapons, or turn the nursery over to Janizaries for nurses, and what do you think would happen? Where would your beautiful contract for holding society together be then?"

Thus appealed to, although in a somewhat whimsical rhetoric, Yates none the less could not fail to respond. He sat up, leaning upon one elbow, and shaded his injured eye with the other hand.

"You make out a bad case for the social contract, doctor. But, as a lawyer, it is my lot to defend the accused even in mortal difficulty. As a matter of fact, there is a good deal to be said for the contractual view of the case. Just as your medical men's minds invariably run to bodies, which you like to dissect, so we lawyers are incurably documentarily minded. And when we take society apart, as you do a cadaver, it is convenient for us to find a contract at the bottom instead of merely a fructified womb. Such a human and fundamental view of society as you take could scarcely, my dear sir, be contemplated by the comfortable male dignity of a bewigged and bewhiskered court. For the sake of the court itself anyone who maintained it would have to be held in contempt. What you advance is a mere meeting of bodies instead of a meeting of minds."

191

"What is a *mere* meeting?" snorted the doctor.

"Well, then you must remember," explained Yates, who was now warming to his own argument, and had forgot his eye enough to wave his free hand eagerly— "you must remember that all these views of society, contractual, cadaverous, or whatever, are only at the best *merely* convenient fictions of the male mind. From time to time different theories are in mere male fashion. But they are always male theories. No one yet has ever seen or heard of any general female view of mankind as a whole. Such attempted comments as we have upon it from the women always lapse into the particular. If not, they are really the secondary comments of men rehashed by virginal or whoresome ladies whose lack of offspring or golden leisure has provided them opportunity for idle correspondence. Letters, you know, memoirs, and poems! What are the women whose names one remembers? Not philosophers. They are Sheba, Sappho, Cleopatra, Zenobia, Joan of Arc, Elizabeth; in our own time, Queen Anne. Most of them troublesome parties—and who knows what they thought? What folly from the lips of women could you base the state upon? Since *some* folly must be taken in order to explain the state, all one can say is that, so far, they have all come from bearded lips. So I stick up for the president Montesquieu and his contract. It's as good a theory as any. I imagine it will see us through our day. Actually I prefer it to that of Hobbes with his holy oil dripping from heaven upon the anointed head of a royal lawgiver. If you want to skip several steps up the flight of argument, who in our time can even begin to think of a female God? But I would prefer not to think about that," said Yates, interrupting himself, "my eye begins to pain me."

"I would prefer not to myself," said the doctor, open-

192

ing up his instruments and laying out a basin and sponges at which Yates winced. "But as a son of Aristotle I would ask you to remove yourself from your high, male, rarified, and platonic generalities of law and religion and descend once more to the scientific case of something in particular; to wit, a woman, one Mistress Rose Pendergass."

"Ah, that *is* so," said Yates, "once we were talking about her, weren't we?"

"We were," said the doctor; "and since you are naturally not a little nervous about my swabbing out your eye this afternoon, I propose for a bit to go on talking about Mrs. Pendergass." He hitched his chair closer to the bed, arranged the basin, and sat down.

"You see, Mrs. Pendergass exemplifies quite nicely what I want to say about the women," he continued in a confidential tone calculated to put Yates more at his ease. "Now you complain that no woman has left us a record of what she thought about things in general. And, in general," laughed the doctor, "I imagine that is true. What female philosophers we have had have more or less said their lessons as the apt, parrot pupils of men. But if we don't have a record of what women think, or rather how they think, that is largely the fault of book-minded male philosophers somewhat weak in the reins, who prefer to study the subject on parchment rather than in the glorious original. And as for the rest of us who are always interested in women directly, that is to say, in one woman from time to time, we are attracted to them for our own purposes and satisfactions rather than theirs, and in only one way. And it is a curious thing, too, that the women men are most intensely interested in and who therefore cause most comment, talk, writing and otherwise, are only part women, doxies of sundry various types, females fascinated by going to bed with a man but consternated by being brought to bed of a baby, girls who keep on being diddled by lovers without ever becoming women and dandling a child. These are really nothing but coquettes, causes without due effect, I call 'em. And that's what most of your poetry and romance and rumour and talk of love is about," said the doctor; "yes, most of the comment men make about women is about that kind."

"Naturally," said Yates. "Girls like that are interested in men instead of babies, and you can't blame us for responding cordially. But after all there are only a few of that kind, comparatively. Not enough, maybe," he added, grinning.

"That's exactly the point," insisted the doctor. "There are only a few of that kind, they're exceptions, and yet they're the most studied and talked and written about. Men are mostly absorbed by them. It's natural we should concentrate on the role of going to bed, it's pleasant and it's self-important, but that's the very reason in the end we know so little about women. We realize how a woman looks at us in particular, but we never try to find out how women look at things in general."

"They don't," said Yates; "did you ever hear women giving testimony?"

"Yes," said the doctor, "I used to deliver them before I joined the army, and at such times the women usually give a good deal of testimony."

"But not as disinterested witnesses," said Yates.

"No, no, just as accessories to the crime," smiled the doctor.

"I say they only look at each item in particular," insisted Yates, "look how they look at babies, for instance. You'd think every baby was a unique specimen instead of being one of a kind."

"Now you're wrong!" exclaimed the doctor. "They

194

always talk about particular items but every particular is viewed from one grand general standpoint. You can always trace anything a full-grown, completed woman talks about, all her attitudes, and all her motives back to one thing," insisted the surgeon; "that's what often makes married life so monotonous, I say so not only as a medical philosopher, but as a widower."

"Come, come," said Yates, "now, doctor!"

"But it's a fact," insisted Boyd. "Now take old Mrs. Pendergass . . ."

"By Jove, we were talking about her, weren't we?—as I said before!" laughed Yates.

"We were," replied the doctor, "and now at last I get around to her again as my scientific specimen in particular of the complete woman in general on which I base my hypothesis. And Mrs. Rose Pendergass is a good specimen and example, for she's unusually complete on a large scale, so to speak, a kind of magnificent typicality of the female humane."

"For the sake of argument I'll accept her as such," sighed Yates.

"Well," continued the doctor, "did it ever occur to you, then, how things in general, and therefore anything in particular, would look to you—to put it broadly, what your attitude to life might be if you were Mrs. Rose Pendergass?"

"No, I can't say that I've put in any time considerin' that particular proposition," admitted Yates.

"Exactly!" countered the doctor. "And that's just the trouble. Too few men have ever really tried to imagine what it would be like to be a woman. They're only interested in their own feelings, the ones women arouse in them. They call that 'knowing' women. Now, in the former age 'knowing' was the word for lying with them.

195

The two were, and I say still are, usually mistaken for the same thing."

"Carnal knowledge," suggested Yates, "a meaty acquaintance, is the way you might translate the legal phrase, I suppose?"

"Yes, you put it nicely. That's about all there is as far as most men's knowing women goes," agreed the doctor. "But suppose you were Mrs. Pendergass—how curious that would be!"

"Damn curious," admitted Yates. "It looks physically inconvenient to begin with. But go on—how would it be?"

"Not so inconvenient as you think, probably more compact," replied Dr. Boyd, "but instead of having a wound in your head, like that eye of yours, which will eventually heal but even then leave your view of things permanently affected, instead you would have a wound between your legs that would never close, and out of which from time to time would have slipped away into the world certain portions and replicas of your own precious self. And although they were finally detached from you somewhat painfully, and therefore memorably at the time, you would still follow them about in every action, motion, and want with an interest and an absorption akin to your preoccupation with yourself, just as great if not greater. Yes, I think, unless there were something the matter with you so that you were in some way insensate, that would necessarily follow.

"For you must remember that these children are not like anything else. They are not like anything in thought, say some cherished theory or great ideal; they are not like some precious object possessed or even a work of art by your hands and mind. Man has no equivalent for them, because they are alive first within the woman, alive after-

196

wards with her life and their own in the outer world, part of her, an enlargement, a duplication and a multiplication of herself into something astonishingly new about which everything without exception in her existence is arranged and referred to item by item with a constant, unconscious, invariable, instinctive reference.

"This is entirely true, certainly while the children are infants, perhaps only less true when they grow up, although the wound from which they came is always there as a tender reminder, urgent to repeat the performance, mind you, even when the source dries up and the fountain fails. For an old woman is simply a fountain that has stopped and yet never ceases even in her stillness to be an image of the source and outlet for the sustaining waters of life.

"And what a satisfaction, what a sense of completion the woman has, all provided for in the organs of her body and the mind that goes with them. What moments of relief and accomplishment, and surcease—of fulfilment after pleasure and after pain. What great ambitions and right expectations she has that can be naturally fulfilled instead of, as with us, only teased into a phantom being in thought."

Yates reminded silent for a moment. The doctor had surprised him out of himself. But he now returned to the only original comparison.

"For a woman to lose her children, then, would be something like the loss of my eye to me, I suppose."

"I thought I might bring it home to you that way," suggested the doctor.

"But how about childless women?" mused Yates.

"That would be very much like not having ever had any eyes at all," replied the surgeon. "All your life would have to be arranged about that primary fact. It would be

197

different, although still about the same thing in a negative way."

"And how about the half-blind?" asked Yates obstinately.

"Half of anything is almost as much as the whole," laughed the doctor. "At least you can generally make it do."

"Hm—I suppose so," agreed Yates doubtfully. Suddenly he was aware that Dr. Boyd was looking at him with more sympathy than he liked to have. He closed his good eye again and smiled. "Go on," he said. "How would I look at things if I were Mrs. Pendergass? You'd better finish it."

"Why, you'd look at things with one eye," asserted the doctor, getting up now and beginning to fill his basin with water, while arranging a few items out of his kit. "You'd look at everything with the eye between your legs. Your eye would come peering out of that maternal tunnel on a kind of long stretchable; on a sort of snakelike spiritual neck. It would therefore have to examine things item by item but always from the same point of reference. And it would always return at length back into the tunnel to think things over. I once had a conch in the West Indies put its eye out from its shell and examine me carefully that way, and withdraw."

"Suspicious animal?" suggested Yates.

"No, just wisely apprehensive, I think," said the doctor. "You see, I was holding it in the hollow of my hand. Now the curious thing about that experience was that the eye of the conch looked like the eye on the end of a long red finger, but it indubitably had a female point of view."

"What's the book to be called, doctor?" demanded Yates, laughing.

"*Medical Meditations and Philosophical Cogitations,*"

replied Boyd. "I'll print it in Edinburgh in my ripe old age. Meanwhile, suppose you let me look at the place in your head where your eye used to be."

"By God, I don't know whether I will or not now," said Yates. Then he lay back and braced himself for what was to come. The surgeon's fingers laid hold of the two drooping lids and gently pulled them apart.

"*Hum*," said he. "The inflammation is almost gone. It's marvellous what the body will do for itself, if you let it alone. The scarred flesh inside is nearly glossed over. Perhaps you were lucky the patent London unguents and apothecaries' washes have all been smashed in the hospital chest. God alone knows what they put in some of those compounds at home. I have used nothing but plain salt water. At first a tincture of laudanum to keep the pain down. That fool Kirby, who had you at first, was all for packing your eye with lard and tobacco. Some old wives' remedy he said he heard about in Southwark. They send them out here to carve the troops, you know, before they're through walking the hospitals. Influence. He's connected with the Lord Ligonier on his mother's side, I hear. Lucky for you I took over. I'm going to make a note of my success with the salt water. Gad, what a blow you got! The whole eye clean out of the socket. Fell out on your cheek, Kirby said."

While this was going on, Yates lay tense but still. He was aware that Dr. Boyd was expert in using conversation to keep his patients' minds off themselves, yet he had been interested in spite of himself. For some days he had not felt much pain. The hole in his head during the last week had become numb, stiff rather than sensitive. It was the use of the other eye alone which now most troubled him. The doctor continued his ablutions carefully. Something tinkled in the basin metallically.

199

"Not the tweezers again!" exclaimed Yates apprehensively.

"No, no, the necessity for that has long passed," said Boyd reassuringly. "You're doing remarkably well. The principal difficulty in these cases is to pack the cavity. It is important, too, for other reasons than appearance. A proper filling of the empty cavity enables you to use the muscles of your other eye with less strain. Now I have something here which might do at least temporarily. At any rate, I want you to try it. See if you can learn to tolerate it." With that he dropped something cool, round, smooth, and heavy between the eyelids and brought them down over it.

"That *looks* better," said the doctor doubtfully. "How does it feel?"

"It's cool, rather soothing, in fact," admitted Yates. "What is it?"

"A stone," said the doctor.

Yates lay quiet with both his eyes closed. The coolness slowly died away. He could feel nothing now but stiffness and weight and the gradual sensation of nothingness as the laudanum water in which the doctor had bathed the stone began to take effect.

"It's lucky for you I'm a bit of a geologizer," said Dr. Boyd presently, while observing the expression on his patient's face. "Were we in London or Edinburgh or Paris now, I could get you a fine glass eye. But I doubt they're to be met with anywhere in the colonies. I was going over some of the specimens in my natural collection the other day and just happened on this stone. It was curiously eye-like in some respects, except for one protuberance which I ground off with the gunsmith's rasp. Further alterations could be made if necessary. How does it feel?"

200

"Not at all," said Yates. "The strange thing is that it seems to put my other eye at ease."

"Excellent!" exclaimed the doctor. "Better than I'd hoped for. Take it out if it troubles you, but do try to get used to it. I'd keep it smooth and clean. It's a kind of volcanic stone, lava-glass. Oh, the Lord knows what it is! I picked it up in Sicily once when the transports lay at Palermo."

"A very *costly* specimen?" inquired Yates, grinning.

"No, my Scotch friend," said the doctor. "You can say I came to treat you with charity, and gave you a stone.

"And now I must leave you," he added. "Ecuyer is anxious to get off to Pittsburgh and I want to put some sense in his head and get his wounds closed before he goes."

So saying, the surgeon poured the water out the window and gathered up his things.

"Give the little captain my best," said Yates, "and by the way, doctor, apropos of Mrs. Pendergass, don't you think all her family ought to be great mathematicians?"

"Now," said Boyd, "now why so?"

"Well, their father must have had an eye for a figure," said Yates, "since their mother is so distinguished for multiplication."

"Tush!" said Boyd, and ran downstairs, laughing to himself.

He climbed the ascent to the fort thoughtfully, however, considering what he should say to Ecuyer. "If he doesn't take some rest and give himself a chance to recuperate while his wounds close, he'll die of exhaustion," muttered Boyd. "But I might as well talk Greek to a grenadier, I suppose. No, he's bound to be off with the next convoy. Duty!" sniffed the doctor. "Duty!"

The sentinel at the postern saluted, this time respectfully, but later on passed the word that Surgeon Boyd was cracked and could be heard talking nonsense to himself

"Of course, I talk nonsense," said Boyd, when the rumor finally got around to him, "but it's the prerogative of every learned profession to talk nonsense. And after all, compared to what the clergy proclaim from the pulpits every Sunday, my nonsense is like an exercise in logic by the Spirit of Clarity."

12

Mr. Gladwin Comes Over
into Macedonia

AFTER THE SURGEON left him that afternoon Yates lay quietly preoccupied with the new problem of the geological specimen in his head, trying to open and shut both his eyes together to get used to the stone. Somehow he felt that he ought to be able to see through it as if the stone were a part of a pair of spectacles. It seemed at times as though he could.

This effect, or illusion, was probably due to a compound of his great desire to see and the fact that when he did open both eyes together he could see with one—and then quite clearly. Most of the muscular strain of focusing was gone. Finding the inward problem of his own sight thus solved to some degree, he now began to wonder how he might look to other people. After a while he called to Salathiel across the hall.

"Are you awake or asleep, Sal?"

"Awake. I've been listening most of the time."

"I thought you might be," said Yates. "I heard you come in an hour or so ago. Come over a minute or two, won't you? I want you to see something."

Presently the form of his tall friend Albine filled the frame of the door.

"A great little talker is Surgeon Boyd," Yates went on. "Like most widowers, he is philosophical about women. And he's a medical widower to boot. We young fellows can't afford to be so philosophical yet. At least not until we get what we want. But look here—throw that shutter around, please. Now, what do you think my chances are?"

The cold winter light reflected from the snow outside fell on Yates's face where he sat against the white pillows. He opened both his eyes, looking at Salathiel.

It was impossible for Albine not to be startled, and not to show it.

Yates was pale and sallow from his ordeal. His broad forehead, sunken cheeks, and pointed chin gave his face the effect of a triangle. And from the top of it, from under arched and brown silken eyebrows, gazed a pair of eyes whose combined effect was astonishingly disconcerting. The grey of the living eye seemed to blend with the smooth ashen grey of the stone.

"Fascinatin', eh?" prompted Yates, watching his friend's face.

"You're a devil," exclaimed Albine. "Why, you're like a rattlesnake with the face of a doe!"

"Dear, dear," groaned Yates dramatically, "good Lord! Suppose you hand me my shaving glass over here."

Into that he gazed long and carefully, turning it to various angles.

"I opine you're more truthful than comfortin', Sal," he

said at last. "I'm afraid I'll have to do my wooing either after nightfall or with gold. But I do see professional advantages in this. Now suppose you were a judge, or the jury, and I looked at you like this—and this?" He closed one eye, and then the other. The effect was truly astonishing. He seemed to be two different people.

"Well," said Salathiel, after considering, "I'd be willing to do about anything you wanted. I'd almost be afraid not to."

"Precisely," said Yates. "The evil and the good eye put off or on. Now, of course, I can't see how I look with only the stone one open, but I must be a regular remora, or a Medusa." He laughed uneasily—and then went on to explain to Salathiel just what a Medusa was, in a jocular way. During the process two tears escaped him and ran down his cheeks.

"It—it don't seem to make any difference with the gals," said Salathiel awkwardly, trying to comfort his friend. "Sue Pendergass is always talking about you and telling your jokes over. She likes to be in your room as much as she can. That's quite plain. And as for Phoebe, why, she's so devoted she stays watching you even when you're asleep, I notice."

"Ah, I'm afraid you won't need to be jealous about Phoebe any more," sighed Yates. "It must be your bulk she likes, Salathiel. There's so much of you it makes an undying impression. It can't be just that hatchet-faced, mangle-eared, grey-haired young man I can see even with one eye. There, there now," he hastened to add, "you *have* got a nice smile, an honest, level gaze. A bit piercing. But two eyes, both of 'em! And your hair tied behind in a queue with a neat bow, and that smooth deerskin shirt with the red muffler! All that's an improvement. Yes, it's effective. By the way, how are you coming on with Phoebe?"

Salathiel coloured violently and stirred uneasily. "To tell the truth, a little too well," he said.

"*Too* well!" exclaimed Yates. "Why, that's monstrous. She must have been flattering you worse than even I did just now."

"No, no, not that," replied Albine, "but happen I just remembered something this morning. Burent brought me a letter from a man at Pittsburgh. It came in the bag with the last express. You see . . . Well, the truth is I'm a married man!"

Yates put the mirror down on its face before him, lay back, and laughed.

"You get a letter from a man in Pittsburgh—and so you're a married man," he chortled.

"It was a letter from the Reverend James McArdle, the man who married me," explained Salathiel indignantly. Then he told Yates the whole story of the forest wedding on the island with a kind of hangdog air, ending with, "So you see, Jane's safe in Virginny, hired out, I s'pose, in the settlements there. And McArdle says he'll be coming east with the first captives Colonel Bouquet rescues and sends back home. But I wonder if he really *will* come," he added thoughtfully—and with a sigh.

"I'm rather certain he will," said Yates after a bit. He was no longer inclined to laugh, seeing his friend was in a real predicament.

"I'm afraid McArdle will come east and find Jane for you. You seem to have been a youthful sacrifice to respectability on a forest altar down the Ohio. It's too bad you couldn't have bedded down under the leaves a few minutes without having to marry the girl."

"I liked her, it went very well when we were together, and it was really the first time," said Salathiel.

"It's surprising what trouble a few moments' pleasure can get you into," mused Yates. "I wouldn't be surprised if it quite ruined your life. It might, you know."

"But I really didn't know exactly what I was doing," explained Salathiel. "It was McArdle and that fox-faced woman who insisted we must be married. It seemed an easy way out. It is curious to think that was only about a year ago. I was only a wild boy then. I'm a man now. You know, I really forgot all about it. I haven't thought of Jane for months. I seem to be a different person now. It must have happened to someone else. Or maybe when I saw Phoebe she made me forget."

"Are you going to tell Phoebe?" asked Yates.

"Well, I'll think it over for a while," replied Salathiel, taking a deep breath or two and looking terribly troubled. "I'll have to sooner or later, I guess."

Yates nodded. "I wonder," said he; "it depends on how you love her."

"I love her *right!*" exclaimed Salathiel.

Yates looked relieved.

"Do you think that marriage is good in law?" asked Salathiel, after a pause.

Yates pondered a moment. "I'm afraid so," he replied. "Your wife has that writing on a piece of elm bark with the witnesses' names on it, and her ring. And there's the Reverend James McArdle. It's not likely yours is the only marriage he ever performed. Too bad, too bad! I once had a devil of a narrow squeak myself at Edinburgh. Nice little split-tail with a soul, or a heart, or whatever it is Dr. Boyd says is inside 'em. She had it. I felt sorry for her. But that's my story. I ought not to tell it to you now.

"Cheer up!" he insisted, seeing how depressed Albine looked. "Let's change the subject. Now, what's going on downstairs these days? B'gad, it will be a relief when that strained muscle in my back lets me up again! I can see pretty well, as far as that goes. Well, has anybody new and interestin' turned up lately?"

"Six Creek Injuns sent by the governor of North Carolina. They have a blood feud with the Delawares and say they want to join Bouquet. They tried to pitch in the yard-garden, but Garrett wouldn't let them and sent them back to the fort. He's afraid Cap'n Jack or some of Smith's Black Boys might do away with, well, with six Creeks accidental. They had a new blanket apiece from Garrett and a drag of Jamaica, and just stood around stinkin' by the fire."

"Must be a pungent addition to our fireside circle," yawned Yates. "Do they belch or grunt when formally addressed?"

"Both," laughed Salathiel.

"Princes of repartee, eh! Anybody else?"

"A man by the name of Gladwin from Philadelphy, who seems thick as thieves with Garrett and Cap'n Jack. You know, one of *those* fellows."

"How do you mean?" demanded Yates.

"Oh, you know," said Salathiel, and he made a certain gesture in sign language.

"Now where the devil did you learn *that?*" exclaimed Yates, sitting up again suddenly, despite his bad back.

"From my Shawnee uncle Nymwha in a medicine lodge on the Ohio long ago," answered Salathiel. "But I didn't know the white men had it till I saw Ecuyer and Cap'n Jack talking together that day in the captain's room at the fort."

"A medicine lodge!" said Yates. "Well, I'll be damned!

208

Now that *is* a new one. Either you are a very observin' man, my friend, or—"

"Oh what?" demanded Salathiel.

"Oh—maybe the Injuns *are* the lost tribes of Israel," ended Yates cryptically.

"The Reverend James McArdle thought so," replied Salathiel, to whom by pure accident the theme of the lost tribes of Israel happened to be an enormously familiar one.

"Did McArdle know the signs? This one?" asked Yates.

"Comin' to think of it, I guess he did," said Salathiel. "Now it never struck me before, but maybe that's why the medicine men let him alone to preach and to go around pretty much as he liked. Now that's curious, isn't it?"

"My friend," asked Yates very seriously, "did you ever hear of the Masons?"

"Masons? You mean stoneworkers, builders, the kind King Solomon borrowed from Hiram of Tyre to build the Temple—in the Bible, you know?"

Now it so happened that Salathiel could not have made a better answer by asking a question if he had tried a thousand years.

"I think," said Yates, "that we'll certainly have to talk this over together, and the sooner the better. Suppose you go downstairs now and ask Garrett and Captain Jack to come up here after dinner to sit with us in my room. Bring up my dinner yourself, Sal, if you don't mind. We don't want any women pokin' in. And you might ask Mr. Gladwin, too. Hurry now! Try to get them all before anybody steps out for the evening. Tell them it's important. It *is* important, Mr. Albine, for you."

And so it proved to be.

For when Salathiel went to bed that night, or rather

early the next morning, he knew that all the masons were not the subjects of Hiram King of Tyre.

Captain Jack's delay in gathering his chosen young men about him and going out to his cabin to begin raids on the redskins, as agreed with Ecuyer, was by no means accidental. There were several controlling reasons why he continued to linger on at Pendergasses' well into the winter. The winter itself was a powerful deterrent to action of any kind, either by the Indians or on the part of the whites. Through January and February the snow lay in neck-high drifts in the mountains and communication westward was temporarily severed, except for a few plucky expresses who managed to struggle through.

Toward the end of November, 1763, the indomitable Ecuyer had attempted to get through with supplies and reinforcements to Colonel Bouquet. But he had been attacked at the top of the Allegheny ridge, forced back to Bedford, and compelled by the condition of the roads, the insistence of Surgeon Boyd, and his own infirmities to delay and to rest himself. That, and the weather, had held him at the fort well into the beginning of '64. But, exasperating as this delay was, it undoubtedly prolonged the captain's existence. For even if he had been able to get through to Ligonier, he would have been stopped there by the snowdrifts, and he must certainly have perished at that bleak outpost away from all medical help.

Salathiel, however, saw very little of either Ecuyer or Burent that winter. They were at the fort and he was at Pendergasses'. As time went on, Captain Jack began to prepare for his coming raids westward, and in the early mornings at least, kept his "Fighting Quakers", as they still loved to call themselves, busy in advance prepara-

210

tions. The various supplies which Garrett had agreed to contribute were secretly carried out to the cabin that lay some miles east of the town in a deep fold of Lookout Mountain near a fine limestone spring.

In this unobtrusive manner flour, corn meal, lead, powder, and salt pork, with a considerable quantity of other necessaries, including plenty of new flints, were quietly transferred to the cabin and laid up against the day when its "garrison" should live there withdrawn and in seclusion for weeks at a time.

An ell with bunks for eight was added to the original small building and a small but secure storehouse built. This labour in the deep snow and mountain frosts was no small task, especially since everything had to be done with the greatest secrecy amongst an observing population. Yet no one so far had been seen either going or coming, and the stocking of the place was nearly accomplished.

"These mountains have big ears," said Captain Jack. "The best way to fool the enemy is to let him think nothing at all is going on until the blow falls. And then let only the destruction and not the destroyers be seen. The hatchet is always its own best advertisement. That kind of no news is a good way to keep on growin' your own har. If a rumour of what we are about gits round, even among the Black Boys, we'll find ourselves ambushed as soon as we step over the river. The Boys have friends amongst the traders. And the traders have friends amongst their customers, who are only too anxious to trade furs for bullets and powder while the war's going on. So remember, when we start protecting the road, we're also going to stop a lot of trade in furs that's goin' on right now. I saw six pelts only yesterday in the hands of a man from Philadelphia, and I know where they came from. So mum's the word, and don't be seen goin' to the cabin. At any rate, don't any two of you go there together at any one time."

Salathiel, Nat Murray, Tom, Mat and Mark Pendergass were chosen for the work in hand. Two older men, Calvin and Sid McClanahan, had come over from the vicinity of Loudon to take part. But they remained constantly at the cabin from the very first and never came to town for any reason. It was known they had been on raids with Captain Jack before. They were strangers at Bedford, and their presence in town would immediately have given an inkling of what was up.

Perhaps the best guarantee against anyone's suspecting what Captain Jack and his boys were up to was the constant presence of Captain Jack himself, talking and smoking with his old friend Garrett sitting in the big hearth room at Pendergasses', and apparently taking his winter ease there before the fire.

That this ease was not quite so easy as it looked, Salathiel was now able to understand. And he was also able to see what both Captain Jack and Garrett were doing, not only to prepare supplies at the cabin, but to put the affairs of the whole community in better order.

Mr. Gladwin frequently sat with them. He was boarding at the inn, "snowbound," he said, from returning to Philadelphia. What his mission was, gradually became evident. But only to those who were properly informed. The mystery was finally imparted to Salathiel by Yates, who had been designated to prepare his friend for taking the first degrees in Masonry when opportunity should serve and a lodge could be held.

Mr. Gladwin, it appeared, had come from the Grand Lodge at Philadelphia to organize the loose "Blue Lodge" Masonry, prevalent along the frontier and in the back country, into what was then called the "Ancient Arch", where ties were more binding, selection more particular, and higher degrees could be conferred. He was to be assisted in this work by certain of the officers at the fort, who had a military or travelling lodge charter under a grant to the 17th Infantry. And he was, of course, being helped by Garrett and Captain Jack, who were both Masons of high degree, and had first arranged the whole matter with their brethren in Philadelphia by long and urgent correspondence.

Now all this stir about Masonry was not a mere matter of love of ritual. Nor was it due simply to a boyish fascination for secrecy and a longing to be mysteriously distinguished in a society where conditions had levelled most men to a common plane of existence. Those allurements were there, as they always have been in Masonry from the beginning, but there was infinitely more than that to the movement which was then going on. In North America, especially in the newer settlements, Masonry in sundry and various ways filled vital and long-felt wants.

It was in essence at that time an association of chosen good men to make common cause together for the protection and fostering of the more hopeful social instincts. The mysteries which it purported to unfold gradually were not trivial ones of mere sign, grip, and knock-on-door. They were successively, as one advanced in degrees, moral revelations of the Fatherhood of the Creator, and hence also of the brotherhood of man. And these concepts, so fundamental to any society, were brought home to the mind of initiates by a system of education that is wedded to the nature of mankind; that is, by imagery elucidated through ritual and by memorized precept, all at some time presented in drama. The drama from ancient times had been of two kinds: the ceremony in which the initiate was himself both an actor and a spectator; and actual plays, "morality skits", exploiting an episode whose plot at least attempted to explore and expose some incident in the immemorial conflict between virtue and vice.

No more apt and carefully devised scheme for bringing about a modicum of social cohesion in what was then virtually a state of anarchy on the frontiers could have been devised. It was admirably suited for the time and place.

On the frontiers, both religion and the state had largely been left behind. The state was visible only at times of extreme crisis in its spasmodic military efforts to survive. Religion, that is, Protestantism, where it still functioned in congregations with a minister supported to preach it, was violently sectarian and existed mainly by virtue of long-cherished theological differences, antipathies, and historical antagonisms. The ideal of a universal church and the communion of saints had practically been forgotten.

Besides, there were many in the remoter settlements who had never been inside a church or chapel in their lives, people who had never even heard a sermon. With such families religion, when it lingered at all, was a sheer idolatry of Bible worship. People believed the Bible "printers' errors, fly specks and all"—and they were their own interpreters of it.

But everyone did not have a Bible. And great numbers could no longer read it, even if they had one. With them religion, or some dim memory of it, was kept alive only by the women, or, except for profane cursing, was no longer verbally remembered at all. And of people in this condition there were many more in the western settlements than anyone ever liked to acknowledge. In brief, the European Christian tradition of nearly eighteen cen-

214

turies had all but lapsed. It was part of the inheritance that had been left behind.

In the terrible years of 1763 and 1764, when Pontiac's Indian raids had brought hideous confusion into lives that were only beginning to achieve some traces of human order in the savage scene of the wilderness, something heroic was needed to preserve the root ideas of civilization then in the precarious process of being transplanted. The frontiers needed to be replanted. It was itinerant preachers of religion and of Masonry who eventually supplied the seed. They did so at fearful personal risk, hardship and sacrifice. But the messengers came and the message was delivered. Mr. Gladwin, for instance, was an apostle of Masonry. He wished to see it firmly and widely implanted.

The effect of its propagation was to bring a sense of order and to give a point and direction to the existence of many who had heretofore been without either, unable to see anything in the universe but the chaos of nature in the wilderness that surrounded them.

But it did more than that. It raised many a poor lonely individual from a purely physical to a moral and social plane of existence. It pointed out and emphasized what was mental and human in man from what was purely animal and physical. Like the ancient mysteries, it pointed to the spiritual and the divine at the apex of the pyramid. And this process of rekindling the torch was not coldly institutional. It was always personal and personified, latent and living in the individuals who devoted themselves to the task. Missionaries, whether lay, Masonic, or clerical, were therefore revered, valued, and respected by all who were not already lost in barbarism, fools, or too insensate to understand. Indeed, it was at this time that the almost superstitious respect for teachers and learning, an

215

immoderate expectation of their fruits were first engendered in the land.

It is not to be thought strange, then, that even though Mr. James Callowhill Gladwin, a Philadelphia merchant, was only a benign-looking, grey-haired old man with blue veins on his hands and temples—it was not to be thought strange that as he sat talking with Garrett and his older friends, Mr. Albine and *his* younger friends, who were in the secret of Mr. Gladwin's mission, should see something heroic in him and feel that he was to be revered.

They knew, for instance, that at the fraternal behest of Garrett and Captain Jack, Mr. Gladwin had mounted his horse at Philadelphia and, despite his age and growing infirmities, had ridden by Indian-haunted roads through deserted country to the extreme border settlement of Bedford in order to spread and establish the message of his brotherhood. They knew he had left a comfortable home and a profitable business to do so, and that the success for his mission could be his only possible reward. Therefore, to them, there was something "worshipful" about him.

Salathiel also saw that all the older men who came to consult with Garrett and Mr. Gladwin—who so casually dropped in—but who sometimes lingered overnight at the inn at the express invitation and solicitation of Garrett, were of the stanchest and most trustworthy, altogether the pillars of the community. And this in a similar way was true also of the officers from the fort, who in one way or another seemed involved in the stir of what was going on. There was Captain Lewis Ourry and Dr. Boyd. There was Major Cadwalader from the militia, and several officers from Captain James Smith's Black Boys, lieutenants and subalterns of whom Salathiel knew little, except that they bore a good reputation. To his great surprise, some of the noncommissioned officers and soldiers seemed also to be included.

But it was not only the older generation or officers from the fort who were involved. Quite a number of young men his own age, the friends of the Pendergass boys, who came to the inn from time to time from the town and country about, were evidently like himself going to be initiated. They, too, were talked to by the older men and received with that good-fellowship and equality that was so heartening to their age.

That he was not alone but belonged to this class of young men, the sons of the respected citizens of the town and trustworthy farmers of the neighbourhood, was gradually borne in on Salathiel and served to encourage him and to give him a feeling of having an honourable place and a part to play in the community. This was a feeling that was scarcely to be overestimated in its influence for good in his particular instance. Less and less he now felt himself to be a lone wolf, a wild product of the woods. More and more he was becoming a citizen.

Pendergasses' was, of course, the ideal place and common meeting ground for organizing any movement in the neighbourhood, from politics to a hill revival, or a benefit lottery. There everybody male, who was not too young and who behaved himself reasonably, came and went with no questions asked. In furthering his favourite project, Garrett was thus only taking advantage of the fine opportunity which his own establishment provided. And in the bitter winter of '64 the opportunity both for broadening the base and "erecting upon it some of the higher structures of Masonry", as Mr. Gladwin put it, was unusually favourable.

Everyone who had not fled the frontiers at the earliest alarms had been forced by the terrible series of Indian attacks of the year before to gather in or about the town of Bedford close by the fort. Many families from places even quite remote had eventually come to take shelter under the wing of the only regular troops in that part of the province. The passing to and fro and the gathering of considerable reinforcements, both militia and the royal regiments, had brought not only the soldiers themselves but various supernumeraries and followers to the camp, barracks, and dwellings of the town of Bedford. The long pack trains required many horses and drivers. There were now more wagons in town than were seen there again for years to come, more refugees and strangers.

Much of this gathering array, men and animals, was to move westward to Colonel Bouquet as soon as the roads should be open over the mountains in the spring. In the meanwhile it gathered, dammed up, as it were, behind the mountains at Bedford. In fact, that place had once again become what it had been only a few years before in General Forbes's time, a quite considerable military base. And it was now doubly crowded with the entire civil and refugee farm population of the Juniata district, together with a large number of traders from the East, attracted to what Captain Ourry impatiently called "This, our beautiful, accidental, mountain metropolis".

Both farmers and traders were only biding their time. The farmers to return to their lonely cabins and fields, the traders to repair to the fur-bartering Indian villages as soon as the state of affairs on the frontiers should permit.

But that time had not come yet. Despite Colonel Bouquet's victory at Bushy Run of the previous summer, the crisis still persisted. Indian raids and rumours of raids were frequent. And both were in their own way hair-raising. Scalps were frequently taken within a few miles of the fort by wandering war parties. As yet only the hardiest and bravest of the settlers dared to venture anywhere alone. No family or individual exodus had begun. On the contrary, there was still a constant accretion of population. From as far south as the Virginia border and north to the Susquehanna all who had not fled eastward had taken shelter about the fort.

It would be hard to estimate their total number, two thousand perhaps. But new houses were being built in the town and temporary huts and shelters hastily erected. Farmers, hunters, deep woodsmen, and their friends became used for the first time to a kind of town life, to existence with many "nigh neighbours" with whom they rubbed shoulders every day. The traders profited as much as they could by the occasion—and time went on.

As the sense of immediate fear and disaster was slowly replaced by confidence in Colonel Bouquet and the eventual return of peace, various forms of excitement ran through the necessarily idle population. There was gambling of all kinds, fights, and speculation. Land, to which the owners did not yet dare to return, was sold and resold, nevertheless. Horse trading went on continually. There were prayer meetings, games, and frolics. This time was afterward well remembered, often regretfully by women who went back to lonely mountain farms. It was called "*the* '64". There were more people at Bedford then than for nearly a half century after. It was a disturbed, a fearful, but an exciting time. The Big Brawl at Pendergasses' was indeed only a symptom of the period. Farther east the Black Boys and their doings were another.

In March '64 the news came of the murder of the helpless Conestoga Indians at Paxtang, and of the later assault of the mob and massacre of the Indian survivors in

Lancaster jail. The rioters threatened to march on Philadelphia. The alarm and excitement over these affairs were great and had repercussions even in the western hills.

Hatred and contempt for the puerile Quaker government of the province was stirring into restless revolt. The legislature at Philadelphia having sat with their hats on, mulishly disregarding the frantic pleas of the governor and the royal army officers to vote supplies for defense, had at last been compelled to look at a wagonload of scalped and mangled corpses riotously drawn through the streets of Philadelphia past the doors of the State House. Still remaining obdurate, despite the whiff of death under their very noses, they were at last forced by armed risings on the outraged frontiers to take cognizance of a universe where it had pleased God to release force.

Presbyterian Scotch-Irish, fortified by whisky, by prayers to the God of Battles, and armed with curses and long greased rifles, descended with blackened faces and Indian costume upon the Quaker city of Brotherly Love. Abject pacifism and Christian resignation in the face of other people's troubles could no longer maintain a dreamful silence in a meeting of Friends. The irresistible fact of their personal appearance brought home with incontrovertible logic even to Friends the conclusion that there were people in the world whom the word "enemy" accurately and precisely described.

The Quaker utopia by the Delaware, which had firmly closed its eyes upon the outer world in order to follow nothing but the inner light, blinked—and found itself in North America with a horrible glow of burning cabins on the frontiers. A "gift" was made to his Majesty in order that the legislature might shift the guilt of military expenditure from their own to a crowned head. The combined prayers, curses, and beseechings of Governor Penn, General Gage, and Benjamin Franklin, together with the petitions of angry city gentlemen and the shouts of gathering mobs, finally prevailed.

But not notably.

Hearing that Colonel Bouquet had "borrowed" two hundred Virginia riflemen from that province anyway, "Friends abstained from voting", and a thousand militia were authorized to assemble at Carlisle in the spring of '64.

By the Lord [wrote Bouquet to Ecuyer, who had sent him the news], not since the Diet of Worms have so many pious mules and asses been assembled to bray all together under one roof. The murder of the helpless Indians at Lancaster can also be laid at the door of the Assembly, for had they raised a sufficient force to protect the frontiers there would have been no cause for the indignation of the rioters against those innocent people. It is fear that begets cruelty, and a scapegoat must then be had. The most helpless are always nominated.

I am now paying the riflemen from Virginia on bills of exchange I negotiated on my own credit, and being hounded in Philadelphia, when they go to protest, by some of the same pious rascals who refused to vote supplies. Why such as you and I sweat and bleed for these bemused, grasping numskulls remains the wonder of all time. It is out of pity, I hazard. Among the English there have always been sects and parties, men of moonlight, who would meet the grisly shambles of this world with words or tears —and keep their shillings in their pockets. Such have before talked the crown off the king's head, and the head off his shoulders. But it may yet be writ in des-

221

tiny that upon some occasion they will sniffle and protest too long.

I do verily believe that if Pontiac himself had appeared on Front Street with all his feathered host, not the dismal screeching of their wives and babes in the fires of their own houses would have convinced these devoted fools. 'Tis an axiom that faction is always above reality, and beneath contempt.

Now as to your request in your last letter—I cannot, my good friend, deliver you from your labours in the vineyard until the grapes of wrath be pressed. There can be no furloughs this year for any of us. And if I know you, you would but eat your own heart out in retirement. As it is I may see you at Fort Bedford before you see me at Pitt. I must come east this spring to meet the new levies at Carlisle. You can help me wipe the mothers' milk from the lips of these unwilling babes of peace delivered to us in a world of universal war. 'Tis your profession, *mon vieux*. God send the snow on the mountains melt soon.

I remain, etc., etc.,

Your obdt serv and much obliged colonel,

It was in this condition of external war and internal confusion that Garrett and Captain Jack had determined to revive and strengthen the Masonic bonds which held many men of orderly and moderate opinions together, so that they could co-operate in mutual good will and common sense.

It was not that Garrett expected his fellow Masons to take direct action in this or that affair or instance. The lodges seldom did so. Their meetings provided rather a means and opportunity for the discussion of problems and the formation of influential opinion, a solemn free discussion under the protection of an oath of secrecy.

For under the compulsion of vows to do good and to serve their fellow men, sectarianism, personal prejudices, and violent party feelings were to some extent laid aside when the lodges met. A constant reminder that the doings of every individual take place under the all-seeing eye of the Creator was provided both by the regalia and by the ritual. The dignity of the gathering, the presence of some revered and worshipful master made ranting and hysterical appeals, lying, and intolerant tirades difficult if not impossible. Hence decorum, moderation, and tolerance were in order, and not their opposites.

Above all, those who were thus gathered together in the name of charity in conduct, as well as for the care of their brethren and families, looked about them, and saw that they were not alone and helpless, but many, powerful, and organized. And a careful correspondence bound the lodges together. Authentic news and opinions that could be trusted were constantly being exchanged.

Thus Masonry operated on individuals largely by the force of opinion, a secret but a well-informed and implemented opinion. It was powerful enough, if ably directed, to uphold and protect a brother in an effort to do right or to check and make difficult the operations of troublemakers and villains in the community at large. If necessity arose it could even boycott or effectually ostracize an individual. And it was all the more feared and reverenced because the deliberations on its policies were not even rumoured and its decisions were mysteriously enforced. For once, secrecy and organization was on the side of right doing instead of evil. How powerful and far-reaching were the effects of Masonry, the secrecy in which it operated successfully concealed from one generation to another.

If Captain Jack, Garrett Pendergass, and others whose stake in the welfare of their community was more than usually considerable found their own interests best served by promoting peace, order, and good understanding amongst the more solid and thinking men of their neighbourhood—and if the lodges they cherished and organized tended to make property safer and the way of the transgressor hard, that is only to say that they marshalled public opinion effectively on *their* side, but also to the general benefit of everybody except rascals and rioters.

As a matter of fact that is precisely what they were engaged in with the able assistance of Mr. James Gladwin, who had had long experience in planting and propagating Masonry along the frontiers and throughout the western settlements of the old Pennsylvania border. Like other missionaries he, too, was totally convinced of and devoted to the gospel he preached and propagated. He had answered the call of his brethren to come over into Macedonia and help, with sacrifice, it is true, but also with alacrity. And he was quick to grasp the idea that, while the temporary concentration of population at Bedford brought difficulties, it also provided an unusually ripe field from which to garner grain. That prospect had in fact been the most telling argument in Garrett's letter to the brethren of the Grand Lodge at Philadelphia, asking for help.

After Mr. Gladwin arrived and had discussed the situation thoroughly, things began to move rapidly. His plan was to reorganize and straighten the Blue Lodges, or the "Hill Lodges", as they were called at the time, because they usually met in the woods under open heaven, by starting meetings, by bringing scattered or detached Masons together again, and by initiating a large number of new and younger men as far as the first three degrees. After the first work should be accomplished, Mr. Gladwin had in mind taking some of the more promising brethren farther along the path that led under the Ancient Arch.

Thus it was that in the garret at Pendergasses' the first meetings began.

13

Garrett's Garret

GARRETT'S garret was, as might be expected, a long, low room extending under the roof of the main building of the inn for its entire length. But everything else about it was unexpected. Even to call it "low" is to be comparative. It was "low" only in perspective when the eye ranged along its surprising length and breadth. Without a single break or obstruction, it comprehended in its dimensions the entire foundation space of the building below. Actually, the rooftree was a good fourteen feet above the garret floor. And the house was hip-roofed. The giant walnut beams of the lower spill rose therefore at any easy angle from the floor, providing ample space to walk underneath them.

It was the dust-moted twilight of this loft that at first glance perhaps made it seem mysteriously larger than it was. Or was it the really ample area of its smooth plank floor? There was only one window, that in the south gable, since the chimney effectually blanketed the entire north end of the house. But a warmth from the flues was thus pleasantly diffused through the place, a fact which winter travellers who had occasionally been given beds there, when the inn beneath was overcrowded, had been delighted to note. Indeed, in General Forbes's time some twenty-odd officers of the Virginia Line had used it quite comfortably as a dormitory, until their stock of gentlemen's candles gave out.

The garret was approached from below by a steeply pitched stair resembling a ship's ladder which rose from the south end of the second-story hall. To ascend this through a trap door into the long, dimly lit room above was always a surprising and an unexpected experience. For the eye first took in an astonishing area of clear floor space as it came to that level, and then, as one shouldered one's self into the apartment above, and stood by the window, the entire untrammelled area of the place housed under its ribbed tracery of massive beams gradually became apparent like the arched reaches of a Gothic hall. It was a family joke of long standing with the Pendergasses that no gentleman had ever been brought there who had failed to exclaim as he first looked about him, "Well, I'll be damned!" "And yet," said Mrs. Pendergass, "they are really nearer heaven there than in any other place in the house."

However such exclamations were natural enough, for the very existence of the garret itself came as a surprise. From the outside of the house, unless one stopped to think, there was nothing to suggest it. There was only a bare, windowless expanse of shingled roof, a sight scarcely calculated to arouse speculation, if it were noted at all. A roof, of course, was taken for granted. And the garret beneath it therefore provided more genuine privacy and aloofness, more space for convenient secrecy, than any other place in town.

Hence, it was in Garrett's garret, and not in one of the barracks at the fort, as Captain Ourry had at first suggested, that the lodge meetings in Bedford village began sometime in February, 1764. But careful preparations and alterations were made beforehand to put the garret in order.

After midnight, when the bar was closed and the last patrons had departed from the big room below, the sound of the saw and a muffled hammering in the heavenly regions disturbed the women and children asleep in the dwelling house next door. Nothing was said about this, however, because the women were cautioned by Mrs. Pendergass to keep quiet about what they heard—and the work in the garret proceeded apace.

Under the superintendence of Mr. Gladwin and the critical eyes of Garrett and Captain Jack, the Pendergass boys, Murray, and Salathiel pitched in during the small hours of several nights and ran a panelled bench clear around three sides of the room. A low stage or platform was raised at the north end across the chimney, and on this dais was placed a wooden altar made to a design furnished by Mr. Gladwin. There were two smaller altars, or lecterns, situated opposite each other halfway down the room with a special chair behind them let into the bench. And there was also a simple but more massive chair set behind the altar on the platform.

Mrs. Pendergass, not without a sigh, lent one of her most long-cherished domestic treasures, a small width of Turkey carpet, to cover the platform. And Mr. Gladwin produced from his kit several rolls of canvas, which, upon

228

being unrolled, proved to be oil paintings of mystical import. These, an all-seeing eye, apparently enraged by what it saw, a divine hand coming out of a cloud, grasping a compass, with a beam of light and a bolt of lightning darting through misty chaos on either side, were hung above the platform and against the chimney face at the end of the room.

But what was even more admired were three small pewter chandeliers, each containing a half dozen candles that, with due precaution against fire, Garrett had suspended on short chains from the rooftree, with tin reflectors above. The resulting illumination was truly astonishing and could only have been contrived in Philadelphia, whence the chandeliers had come.

In addition to three lights about the altar, there was a seven-branch candlestick set on a special stand by the worshipful master's chair, but this Luke Pendergass had to make himself out of bar iron under Mr. Gladwin's direction. Luke was the blacksmith of the family, while Mark was the carpenter. All the Pendergass brothers, even lame Toby, were skilful with their hands, but Mark excelled.

Mark owned a great chestful of carpenter's tools, including a remarkable variety and selection of planes provided with infinite chisel blades and gouges to be set in them to make mouldings and tongue-and-groove joints. Salathiel had seen axes, adzes, draw-knives and saws before, and had upon occasion used them. But he had never seen mitre boxes, squares, angles, small-saws and such a bewildering array of augers, bits, chisels, and gimlets. Mark Pendergass's carpenter's chest fascinated him. He made himself its owner's constant assistant, and during the renovation of the garret learned all he could from Mark, who was much flattered by the admiration which his skill evoked.

Between them, Mark and Salathiel not only made the intricate mouldings for the altars but also the panels for the seat that extended about the three walls. And not content with that, they sawed out in the old saw pit by the river enough pine boards to sheathe-in the ceiling, standing up to their waists in snow in the pit, and sweating at that, to do it.

Luke forged what bolts and iron nails were essential. Still, iron was both scarce and expensive, and the sheathing for the ceiling of the lodge room was not only planed on one side and tongued and grooved, but finally set in place by white oak pegs driven home into the beams. And for every peg a hole had to be made.

All this took many nights of long, hard labour and afternoons in the saw pit. Yet the improvement was great. The rough underside of the roof shingles was entirely concealed and the room given a smooth finished appearance, even an elegance, which completely bowled over all those who first thrust their heads up through the trap door and looked about them. Finally, the floor was painted with triangles for a border surrounding the main design, an expanse of black and white checkerboard squares.

Mr. Gladwin, who knew exactly what a lodge room should do, had urged the work on eagerly, and he was especially pleased at the sheathing-in of the ceiling which so completely changed the whole character of the place.

Mr. Gladwin had been present and presided at over a hundred initiations, and he regarded the first impressions of a neophyte as crucial. The instant when the lodge-assembled first burst on the view of the new initiate he called the "moment of great awakening". It was for him the supreme moment of existence. He remembered vividly the strange "memory" that had been aroused in him on the occasion of his own initiation, and he watched the face of every newcomer eagerly, when the light first burst upon it, in order to renew and to reassure himself vicariously of his own profound, initial sensations.

To many a simple frontier youth, in particular, the experience of initiation was frequently overwhelming, and in the back-country districts at least, Mr. Gladwin was often not disappointed, unless young faces lied. That the room at Pendergasses' was now peculiarly well fitted to produce the impressions he so much desired, Mr. Gladwin felt sure. And he had good reasons for thinking so.

For, instead of arriving in some rude loft, showing in the rough, exposed materials of its crude construction the outer bark of the forest trees and the poor barbarism of the woods surrounding them, the new initiates would now seem to have been translated into the finished cavern-like abode of some powerful magician or spiritual personage, a being superior to and aloof from the wild self-planted nature without, and yet, obviously, one who was always close by, lurking and immanent—for merely by ascending a garret stairs and coming through a trap door had they not found him and his worshippers at home? Only a missing password had been needed—and they had at last gained entrance to his very house.

"At last"—because this place and the spirit that dwelt there must after all have always been quite close by. Indeed, they had often suspected that; felt that someone must know the secret of the path here, and that it had been withheld from them. They had heard of it in overtones of talk and thought of it dimly. In the recesses of their lonely minds they had sought this dwelling through forests of dream-afflicted nightmare. Somehow, somewhere it had been lost. Now they had suddenly come upon it—again!

So they would be duly astonished as they came through the trap door into the smooth, unexpected light; astonished at the seven candles burning in the many-branched tree near the altar, at the all-seeing eye looking at them, and at the double row of the familiar feet and faces of the worshippers. "Why, this was not a garret! No, this was that old place!" They would be astonished. But that was not what would astonish them most. It was this:

Each would suddenly feel that he had been alive for ages. He would instantly "remember" that he had often and often seen this familiar place before.

Whether the conferring of such high moments of mystical hindsight on initiates was a fact actually experienced by them or only a hope that it might be so, cherished by Mr. Gladwin, it would be hard to tell. He had faith. He was ambitious. And the effects he produced even by simple arrangements and in quite humble surroundings were seemingly always out of proportion to the poor means at hand. Those who first received their degrees under his presidence remained forever inspired by them. For it was the curious effect of Mr. Gladwin's personality to deepen and bring to life a mysterious presence in the ritual, until even literal-minded brethren were at times made aware of a soundless passing of unseen wings. It was some quality of imagination which he released, a door that he opened into otherwhere. It was intangible, but it was there. Somewhere behind the bland, though rather rigid, face of this old Philadelphia merchant was a mind masterful in a priestly art. Men remembered him. And it made no difference that after a meeting it was only a simple old man on a homely horse, who was seen to be riding away.

Somehow he had conveyed part of his secret. And he managed to leave it behind him, operating.

At Bedford, at first, except for his actual physical presence at the table and about the hearth room, Mr. Gladwin had made no particular impression at all. He was pleasant and tactful, but essentially a quiet and an unassuming man. If it had not been for Garrett and Captain Jack's obvious reverence for him, Salathiel would scarcely have remarked his presence, beyond accepting him for what he actually was in this world, a merchant draper, one who had come to sell Garrett a bill of goods in a moment of great demand; to replenish his shelves with calicos, Osnaburgs, and English woollens that arrived in due course of time in a wagon from Philadelphia.

It was only natural that Mr. Gladwin's departure should seem to be delayed by the bad weather. He was an oldster waiting over for spring thaws and good company going down. And no one who was not otherwise informed thought anything more about him, unless to say, " 'Scuse me, grandfer," if they got in his way. But to those who did know, it was quite different. It was remarkable how in a short while Mr. Gladwin's quiet presence seemed to pervade and hold possession of the place; how easily and without attracting notice he became the vital centre of a far-reaching influence.

Within a short time after his arrival all the recognized Masons of the neighbourhood had been seen by him and interviewed. They simply dropped in and talked with him by the fire. Meanwhile, the usual eating, drinking, and selling business in the hearth room went on. Once or twice at night Mr. Gladwin paid a visit to the fort, or he went out for a few moments to see an "old friend" in the village. That was all.

And then the meetings of the newly organized lodge began.

They began before the alterations in the lodge room were entirely finished, and the only reason Salathiel was sure of it was that he had been asked to help carry up some paint to the garrett and help spread it on the floor.

That evening a more than usually large number of "customers" gathered in the hearth room. Some even came early and had supper. Others dropped in after dark and had a glass. Perhaps the company was more distinguished than usual. But there was nothing especially noticeable about it. Apparently it had no business as a whole. Individuals just happened to be there. Quite a few kept coming in and out. Mr. Yates was said to be giving a party upstairs. Nice but unfortunate young fellow with many friends, was Mr. Yates. Well worth while having a drink of Monongahela whisky in his room. The hearth room gradually thinned out, leaving the usual wagoners, members of the garrison, and late town customers leaning over the bar or counter.

The two Pendergass boys who remained to serve seemed extremely affable and kept everybody well supplied and happy. Four Creek Indians who came for warmth and tobacco had three free drinks apiece by the fire. They stank quite normally. Members of the militia thumbed noses at them behind their backs, and departed. The bar closed a little earlier than usual. At eleven o'clock Mark clamped the grille down and locked the big door, after getting the Indians to leave. Then he and his brothers went up to join the lodge meeting in the garret, which had now been going on for some hours.

Salathiel went up and lay on his bed. The whole place seemed wrapped in sleep. Yates's room was empty, although his candle was left burning. At two o'clock in the morning Salathiel heard the muffled shuffling of feet on the planks overhead as the meeting broke up. People came quietly down the stairs and along the corridor past his room. Yates looked in on him, and they had a nightcap together. "It's good to think that you will soon be with us now," Yates said, as he nodded good night. Except for a few dogs barking here and there, outside there was no commotion at all.

Apparently nothing had happened.

But in the course of that winter and early spring there were upwards of fifty young men about Bedford village who thought differently. They were the new material upon which Mr. Gladwin and Garrett and Captain Jack counted so greatly to broaden the foundations of their order. It might be, and as it turned out it was, many years before so many people were so conveniently gathered together again on the frontier. Mr. Gladwin could now see his prospective flock as a whole, black sheep and white. He and Garrett could pick those who promised to be leaders and men of influence. The opportunity might soon pass, so the work went on ardently.

The group of scattered brethren who had first been assembled and organized into a lodge in Garrett's garret rapidly turned in effect into a school of missionary Masons in which each one of the accepted brothers became a zealous member of an active teaching faculty. Here and there about town, at the fort, and at Pendergasses', young fellows and a few older men were constantly being prepared for the first three degrees.

There was no general or active solicitation. News of what was afoot was most carefully passed on from one responsible person to another. Fathers brought their sons, uncles their nephews. Youths applied to Garrett or Captain Jack, and brought in their friends. The Pendergass boys alone accounted for a round dozen. Not everyone was accepted. And the distinction and honour of being chosen for initiation had a telling effect. The element of secret ordeal provided its own fascination.

After some preparation, the candidates were finally passed on to Mr. Gladwin, to Garrett, Captain Jack, Dr. Boyd, or some other brother of high degree for final preparation. These final interviews were quite solemn, but they were also impressive. And the older men seldom failed to make friends and admirers of those who came to sit at their feet.

Salathiel, for example, was first prepared by Yates. Yates was able to get up and move around now, although he had not yet left the house. For the most part he and Salathiel sat together in his room, while the young attorney explained to his friend the meaning and implications of the step he was about to take. He also helped him become letter perfect in those things which Salathiel must memorize, going over the words again and again. But they did not remain mere words. Yates expounded as they worked. He opened up and extended the meaning of ancient texts and lessons like an intellectual fan.

Here again the early groundwork laid by McArdle proved invaluable. But Salathiel was able to appreciate that he was now enjoying the benefit of instruction by a much broader and clearer mind. Yates's flashes of humour and original insight were both helpful and startling. His well-informed but lightly cynical wisdom was convincing. It was still the unfrightened wisdom of a young man, despite his maiming. Yates was never pious, but he could still be reverent. So these talks, instead of proving an ordeal, turned out to be a good time well spent.

In fact, it was in these intimate talks together at Pendergasses', while Salathiel prepared for his initiation, that the friendship between him and Yates was finally cemented and the broad basis for its long enduring firmly laid. Yates was always amused by the natural simplicity of his friend Albine, but he was also impressed by it in its complete honesty of purpose and directness of understanding. Here was a genuine naturalism, thought Yates, but here also was a wary simplicity that was instantly on guard, and seemed to be intuitively aware it was being abused.

This habit of scouting a mental landscape in advance Salathiel never lost. It remained, probably, as a heritage from his Indian upbringing, which gave him a keenness of sensation and immediate realization of everything natural, but a care and deliberation in examining anything artificial or abstract that constantly stood him in good stead.

Much that was old in the world was pristine to Salathiel. That intrigued Yates, who found a zest in re-examining everything through the new eyes of his friend. But if Salathiel was curious and avid, eager to know and even broad-minded, and though he was completely lacking in most of the prejudices of conventional thinking—he was also alert and enormously careful about being fooled or taken in. He looked at things directly and saw them in their natural, unclouded reality. But he approached them first with an all but savage circumspection.

Now it was this circumspect quality which Yates admired above all in Albine—above every other quality save one. Neither of them was afraid of anything. They could decide on something together, and carry it out against time, fortune, and the devil. And they both sensed that as a good basis for successful partnership almost from the first.

"It's curious," said Yates one evening as he and Dr.

Boyd, Mr. Gladwin, and Garrett sat together before the fire in the hearth room, talking over their experiences and comparing judgments about various candidates; it was the first time that Yates had come downstairs into the big room again—"It's curious, but now take Albine. Sometimes I think his lack of what we would call education and my loss of an eye make us just about even in common sense. You see, by sheer accident we'll both always be forced to take a remarkably single-minded view of any proposition. And I find that's the way he looks at most things, including joining the lodge."

"I wouldn't worry so much about that lost eye of yours," interrupted Dr. Boyd. "You can still see a good deal with one. It's not going to be—"

"I'm not worrying," interrupted Yates. "As a matter of fact, I was thinking of certain compensations"—and he favoured the doctor humorously with a stony glare. But Garrett was anxious to hear what Yates had to say about Salathiel.

"How much did your friend Albine really learn from his Shawnee uncle in the medicine lodge?" asked Garrett. "I've often wondered about that. You hear all kinds of tales about what the Injuns know and don't know."

"Oh, not much," replied Yates. "I went into that pretty carefully, too. You remember we were all a bit startled—annoyed, I suppose—by finding he knew the greeting sign. Well, the Injuns know that, and they know this sign, and this. Only a little different from ours. They give them like this, Albine says. And they have various grips. I couldn't recognize them when Sal showed me, but it's the same idea. The redskins are particular on ways of shaking hands, anyway. Sal showed me one grip by which all the Turtles would know one another if they met up crawlin' about. Are you a Turtle, sir?" he asked Mr.

238

Galdwin suddenly, leaning forward and shaking him by the hand with an arrangement of three fingers and a thumb.

"I'm afraid not—but I might be something else," replied Mr. Gladwin, looking surprised, for he had recognized the grip.

"Well, that's it exactly," continued Yates. "It's all a bit similar but never the same. There is only one thing we should all recognize as something in common. All the Injuns acknowledge the Great Spirit, and Sal thinks there are certain men in every tribe who could know each other by their Great Sign, and be bound to acknowledge it. Such men are called 'The Children,' he thinks—now that's funny, ain't it? But there's only a few of them. It's their highest degree, or you might call it that. And Nymwha, Sal said, would never show it to him or talk much about it. It's the great secret of great chiefs and medicine men. And no one has ever known it who would not be too proud to abuse it. They make sure of that by some pretty severe ordeals, I opine."

Captain Jack sat listening somewhat gloomily during this talk about the Indians, but Mr. Gladwin nodded in agreement. "I'll tell you something about that," he said, after some cogitation. "I think their Great Sign is our Mercy Sign. An old Injun who was begging on the streets of Philadelphia, and dying too, as it turned out, once gave it to me. How he knew I might recognize it, I can't say. He was a Moravian convert, but he never learned it from them. I took him into my house, warmed him and fed him, and he died there. I was much condemned, of course, by some people for helping an Injun. There was trouble about a place for him in the cemetery. A certain vestry thought the potter's field would do. The Friends finally gave him decent burial. I never said anything about this before, naturally."

"I've heard it's like that, too," said Garrett. "As I remember, it was Nymwha or his brother who once gave me the greeting sign. I entertained them, too. It was in 'fifty-eight, I think, and I didn't know then—"

"I'm glad you didn't," exclaimed Captain Jack impatiently, "for it was that same Shawnee Nymwha and his brother Kaysinata who murdered this Albine boy's father in cold blood." Captain Jack paused to mutter something into his beard, and then continued. "I heard about that from Chris Gist and he wasn't ever a liar. It happened nigh the Turkey Track crossing away back about Christmas, 'forty-eight. What's the difference what signs such varmints know?"

No one cared to argue with Captain Jack about that. Indeed, the conversation appeared to be about to bog down in sudden gloom. In the unexpected pause all of them noticed for the first time the tortured howling of a winter gale outside. It was no common storm. Finally, Mr. Gladwin looked at Yates and smiled.

"Send that boy to me before he's initiated," he said. "I'd like to talk with him. It's a strange story, isn't it? Send him tomorrow afternoon. He goes through with six others tomorrow night, I believe. Is he ready?"

"Ready," said Yates.

"I'm sure of it," said Garrett. "I've spent some time with him myself. He's a fine boy, and I think Yates here has done an honest job preparing him."

Dr. Boyd took a pinch of snuff.

"Tomorrow will make twenty-seven new ones so far," he said. "A remarkable record for a lodge in a howling wilderness. Now I was telling this Albine lad only yesterday, myself, that I've no doubt the Injuns would think that they could *make* their Great Spirit listen by carrying on high hocus-pocus in a medicine lodge. And I said a white man's lodge doesn't think that. I thought Albine might still hold some savage notions. But I found he hadn't. In truth, he gave me some startling good answers. So I went on further to tell him that the chief difference between a white man's lodge and a church is that in a lodge we fear God but stand up before Him and serve Him by helping our fellow men; while in a church we are afraid of God, grovel before Him, and try to save our own dirty souls."

Old Garrett laughed heartily. "It's a bold distinction, doctor; you'd better not try to make it with the chaplain."

"The trouble with you scientific men," said Mr. Gladwin," is that you're always going about corrupting the youth."

"*Must* it be hemlock?" asked Dr. Boyd, waving his empty mug enquiringly.

"Make it hot buttered rum this time," suggested Yates, shivering. "It's a damned cold night and a wolfish wind goes prowling around."

"Why, a drop of rum makes a good period to any discussion," agreed Mr. Gladwin. "Garrett, can you manage it?"

"I know Pina can," said Garrett, leaning back in his chair and looking at his old slave's countenance wreathed in wrinkles and sleep, where she sat by the chimney.

"Pina, Pina," he called. "Stir your stumps! Hot buttered rum, double all round."

The mutter of the old woman, grumbling sleepily over her preparation of the gentlemen's drinks, and the fumbling of the winter wind in the chimney seemed now to be making a conversation of their own. The long roll of the tattoo beating at the fort came only fitfully through the winter blasts like interrupted thunder.

"Wonder how long this fur-thickenin' weather's goin' to hold?" mused Captain Jack after a little. "Somethin' we just talked about reminds me I've got a work to do. And it's well-nigh the first of March." He stirred his drink impatiently, and looked gloomy again.

Remembering what the work was, the rest of the company drank silently, and with brief good nights retired.

"So the blood fit has come over you again, Jack," said Garrett as they climbed the stairs together.

"Aye, that it has!" answered the old hunter huskily. "Did you hear those voices in the storm tonight?" He stood in the hall, shading his candle and listening.

"Hark to that, would you?" His eyes glittered.

Garrett left him standing alone and went across the bridge to the other house to bed. Captain Jack's "fits" depressed him. He was glad to climb in beside his wife and be warm. Outside the snow drifted clear up to the lower window sills.

Captain Jack sat smoking alone in his room wrapped in a blanket. In his mind's eye he saw a place beyond the mountains called the Salt Kettles. There was a river and a high cliff. A wisp of smoke rose through the trees that were in misty spring foliage. Several canoes were drawn up along the riverbank. It was a peculiarly peaceful scene. Captain Jack pondered it carefully for several hours.

"Yep," said he at last to himself, "we kin! The whole kit and passel of 'em."

He knocked his cold pipe out thoughtfully and turned in. . . .

Salathiel had his little talk the next afternoon with Mr. Gladwin. He never forgot it. He came away with the firm resolution to try to lead a better life. He saw now why that was desirable. No one had ever talked to him quite like Mr. Gladwin. He felt prepared now for the ordeal of the evening. He felt chastened.

On account of the deep snow the lodge members were slow in assembling that night. The drifts lay belt-deep in places but the wind had died away at noon. There was a hard frosty stillness abroad in which the bells of a pack train, that had taken all day to make the few miles from the water gap, rang like chimes. The half-frozen drivers crowded the bar and left before evening, well warmed. After that few except lodge members came in. They had the place pretty well to themselves.

The seven candidates for the initiation that night took supper together in a corner by themselves. Besides Salathiel, there was his friend Nat Murray, Cornet Appleboy from the fort, John Nogle, the miller's son, William Smith and John Banner, farmers, and one Jonathan Dickson.

In view of the ordeal ahead, they were all somewhat silent and subdued. But after a jug was passed around by John Banner their spirits improved, and full justice was done to Pina's hoecakes, ham, and potatoes. Garrett came after supper and sat with them. He told them he had been initiated when he was only eighteen at Colchester in England, according to the old York rite.

"It is the most ancient rite of all, they say," he continued. "Some people think there has been a lodge at York ever since Constantine's time. Dr. Brandsford was a very learned man at Colchester in my day. He it was who wrote a book about old King Cole and Queen Helena, and he was also a very high Mason. I once heard him tell my father he had seen Masonic carvings on old stones along the Tyne River, that went back into

243

heathen times. How that may be, I don't know. But what you are going to learn and see tonight is not new. It has held men together in brotherhood for ages past. All of them were not fools," smiled Garrett. "It is important we should keep on remembering in this new country what they knew at home."

All of them sat listening attentively. They were surprised to hear old Garrett talk this way. He seemed to have grown younger as he spoke of his youth in England. Something happened to his tongue and voice, and he spoke for a moment with an earlier accent. Meanwhile, the lodge was assembling upstairs.

Presently the sponsors came for their candidates and drew straws for the order in which they should appear. Yates drew the shortest for Salathiel, and that meant he would be last.

"Come on upstairs," he said to Salathiel. "It will be some hours yet before our turn comes, and my eyes pain me in the light."

So they went upstairs and sat in Yates's room with one candle burning dimly on the floor. From time to time the footfalls of the other candidates passed them, going along the corridor and ascending the stairs. They heard the knocks, and the trap door open. A shuffling of feet went on in the tanbark overhead. There were voices, and the door closed again.

It was nearly midnight when Salathiel was finally summoned and followed Yates up the ladder into the stifling room. The lodge rose to meet him, and he stood looking down the entire length of the place past the long, double row of faces to the worshipful master in his collar and apron, standing on the platform.

It made no difference that he had lately helped to fashion this room with his own hands. The golden light of the candles, the presence of many people, the rows of aprons seemed all to have united into one thing that was something else. The ladder and the comfortable house beneath it had disappeared. He was translated into another world. Its walls seemed suddenly completely to surround him and to make him a part of it. And even as he stood there, its strangeness died away. He began vaguely to remember a forgotten acquaintance with this chamber like something he had seen before in childhood, like a familiar apartment recognized in a dream. He had come back here. How? It seemed to him that he had come down into this place, that he was now deep underground.

Yates vouched for him.

Through the yellow fire of the candles on the altar the master was now saying something to him.

He remembered how to reply.

The questions and the responses began.

What was happening seemed to be taking place outside of time . . .

An hour later he took his assigned seat among his brethren, a Free and Accepted Mason.

Afterward, when they went downstairs, Mr. Gladwin looked pleased. They were all pleased. They made him welcome among them. Old Garrett and Yates were positively happy about it. It was like a final home-coming. And about the fire in the hearth room, where they gathered that night before leaving, it was still the same. He belonged. He would always belong now, he felt.

For about the initiation of Salathiel Albine into the lodge at Bedford there was something which even its worshipful master and Garrett never suspected; could not, indeed, be expected to understand. But Captain Jack did.

"My boy," he said, while they sat together near the

big chimney looking into the flames, "you are a free white man now. Never forget it." Then he passed his pipe across the table to Salathiel, who took a great puff and blew the smoke out through both nostrils ceremoniously. Captain Jack did likewise, and they sat watching the wreaths of smoke curling together into one cloud over their heads.

Captain Jack laughed cannily. "You damned Injun!" he said, "now *we've* got you," and he slapped Salathiel on the back.

14

The Women Underneath

AROUND, and underneath the business and doings of the men at Pendergasses', through the village of Bedford —and for that matter, everywhere else—flowed the activity of the women, constant, sinuous, and everlastingly and instinctively insistent that, no matter what the men did or were up to, life should go on.

The frontier war, as all wars do, had greatly disturbed and harassed the women. It had uprooted them from their lonely cabins, where a wife could be busy all day, and half the night too, making and keeping children alive. Now for the time being many of them, both women and children, were concentrated about the fort and village at Bedford, while the white man settled his bloody accounts with the red, while colonels disappeared westward with regiments intent upon the business of killing. And everything the men did was necessarily arranged, at least temporarily, about that.

But the aim of the woman had not changed. Their problem remained the same. Only the scene of their labors had been shifted. Mating, getting, suckling, cooking, and cloth making; sewing; nursing the young, old, and sick; cheering and cherishing; tricking, cajoling, and persuading life to go on and smile with dimples even in the net of death was what, as usual, the women were eternally, each in her own way, busy and very busy about.

Theirs was not a business, it was not a job. It was not a game or a symbolic something that engaged them. It was not a drama, or anything about something else. There was no remove. It was nature and the thing itself; the thing that must go on. And the women were part and parcel of it.

And what a din; what a deal of talking, gossip, whispers, laughing, and crying about it there was in the village of Bedford! How the children shrieked at play and the babies wailed! What a gamut of the kind of noises that life makes there was! The dogs and the cattle replied in kind. And to everybody, but to the women especially, who felt exactly what the noises meant, how encouraging the sounds of life were.

To a lonely woman and her brood, who had fled suddenly from a dark forest cabin with a patter of moccasins close behind, despair and terror had been turned into hope and confidence by the mere sight of the Union Jack flying above the fort and over the roofs of the town. And, once having arrived—then, quite instantly, these family hermits were in the midst of many, many people and the cheering noise of life.

It had been quite bewildering to them at first. The newcomers were often shy, silent, and suspicious. Also there were many hardshpis to be endured. There was scant food at first, and it was difficult to find shelter. But then an amazing thing happened. They were not simply left to perish by themselves, while the woods brooded over their fate. They were helped to continue to exist by other people, by "strangers".

Colonel Bouquet, some other officers at the fort, and Garrett were in reality the helpful "strangers". It was due to the colonel alone that an authorized ration for the inhabitants had first been forthcoming from the commissary stores. He had first seized upon the Indian goods and supplies to distribute them the year before, when the situation had been desperate. Then the army had been prevailed upon to help. And finally, marvel of miracles, the provincial legislature having authorized some militia, now undertook both to arm and send provisions to the starving frontiers.

"They think they've lost their souls, anyway by voting for soldiers," said Garrett. "And I know they're good and scairt. But if Buckey wins down the Ohio, they'll all turn calm and holy and careless again."

"That they will!" agreed Captain Smith of the militia. "Bury me deep, sir, but you're tarnal right! It's only the fear of death and God A'mighty brings Pharisees to their reason. And there's more Pharisees at Philadelphy than in hell and Jeesusalem together. No decent man would go there even for to be hanged now—and . . ."

But then Captain Smith began to roar. For the very thought of Philadelphia made him rage like a lion, and he foamed madly about Indian traders.

Yet actually the news from Philadelphia, Garrett knew, was not quite so bad as all that. And Garrett really knew. For he it was who had co-operated with Bouquet and Ecuyer in organizing supply, in hiring wagons, and bringing all the influence he could find in Philadelphia to get help for the frontier, and for his part of the country in particular.

Mr. Gladwin had greatly helped. The merchants had assisted. They consigned goods to Garrett with the prospect of payment extremely remote. The Friends meetings made gifts of food, clothing, and cloth. Some of the traders even "lent" their horses and drivers, since they were now idle, for mere wages and subsistence. City churches took up collections. From Arthur St. Clair came a gift of ten pounds sterling. The Penn family remitted certain rents, and the Quakers in England eventually bestirred themselves. Alarmed authorities brought supplies. A depot was formed at Carlisle where the militia was to rally, and where it was hoped eventually to bring the Indian captives, if Bouquet were successful.

All this had taken time and untold correspondence; demands, and arguments by Colonel Bouquet. Ecuyer even went east once, instead of west, to start the wagon trains and pack horses moving. He returned, and then disappeared westward again, leaving Burent to further transport at Bedford under Captain Ourry.

But even before the break of weather in 1764, wheels had begun to roll and pack horses to slither and slip westward. Herds of beef cattle and hogs were driven through as far as Bedford. There they were killed and salted down for hauling to Fort Pitt, for the road from Bedford to Pittsburgh was still a tremendous hazard. The mountains stood, the enemy lurked, the drifts were deep. Now and then a convoy got through as far as Ligonier. Ecuyer wore himself out accomplishing even that. But from Ligonier only à trickle of recruits and provisions went through to Bouquet.

It would take open weather and summer to move the

mass of men and material for the Ohio expedition over the mountains to Fort Pitt. That was evident now, even to Bouquet. Yet for that very reason things tended to concentrate temporarily at Bedford. If one had any doubt of it, the lively noise of the place all through the day, and half the night too, was convincing.

It was a more hopeful noise now as spring came on. People were beginning to regain confidence. Their own numbers and the troops provided sweet security, at least in town. To the women particularly, the cheerful din of the village was constantly reassuring. Shy newcomers quickly grew used to it, liked it, and added to it. The eternal, depressing silence of the woods had disappeared. Women no longer lay at night with straining ears and nerves, listening to night birds, hoping all the owls were real ones, and that no murderous hand would furtively try the latch. They could sit by a fire now, knitting, and talking to other women. The children slept and were safe. The worst to be expected was that mister might come home drunk. There was a lot of liquor about. But a man couldn't do just what he liked to his family in a town. People came and asked what in God's name was agoin' on. Besides, a woman would have a comforting nip by the fire herself—and pass her jug along.

Also there was plenty of food in town by the turn of the year. More than most people had even seen before. There were potatoes, salt hog fixin's, and white flour.

Some complained about the white flour. They wanted samp and good yellow meal. Presently there was mother-of-yeast in fifty crocks about town, and then the white bread went better. If you had money you could get a bit of molasses or loaf sugar at Pendergasses'. That was *mighty* fine. It was rumoured that Mrs. Pendergass herself drank real tea. But some people exaggerated.

Still, it was an elegant house she had. If you were lucky enough to be invited upstairs, you saw wonders. It was like a house down east or old Virginny way. There were niggers and Injuns for help. You certainly learned things at Mrs. Pendergass's. Only a few attained the height of upstairs, however. Most people got no further than the spinning room. But every respectable female went there. It was now the general meeting place for all the decent women in town.

The spinning room was a lean-to shed that stood against the dwelling house. There was a good puncheon floor in it, a rough chimney with a hewn-log mantel, and three windows that looked out up and down the river. They were the first windows with glass lights some people had seen. The wonder of the place, though, was a painted German clock with a silver bell that struck every half hour.

And then there was the complete equipment for carding, spinning, and weaving scattered about the room. There were wool and flax combs, spinning wheels, two looms, and a jig for knitting stockings. It had been Garrett's ambition to rig the big loom to a water wheel. But he had never gotten to it. It would have required a millrace and a dam in the river, and the boys were married and living in their own cabins before he could undertake the labour.

Many a hank of yarn and good wide yards of linsey-woolsey and close woven cloth had come out of the spinning house, nevertheless. In this respect Mrs. Pendergass had driven her girls hard, and some of the neighbours' daughters too. The Indian boys and young darkies had been put on the big loom. Sometimes the beam and shuttles went all day long, while the clock mercilessly struck the hours. Mrs. Pendergass had upward of twenty people to clothe. The place became an establishment, almost a family factory. As Mrs. Pendergass grew older, Bella had gradually taken her mother's place in the spinning room as mistress of the floor. By force of circumstances she had now also become mistress of ceremonies and dispensatress of hospitality to strangers.

For it was this "hall of the fine arts of spinning and weaving" that was now thrown open to every housewife in town. And if the men congregated at the bar of the inn, the women gathered day after day, and gradually in increasing numbers, in the spinning room, where a fire burned, the clock struck cheerfully, the looms clicked and clattered, and the spinning wheels whirred. On cold afternoons the spinning room was generally crowded.

Open the door of the place even for an instant only a crack, and such a stream of talk, laughter, cooing sounds and titters; such a buzz and maze of fast-flowing words fairly stumbling on one another's heels flowed outward over the threshold that any mere man who came there was washed backward into the yard again like a chip in a flood.

And, in fact, the men were not needed at the spinning room. There was nothing they could do there, and they knew it. One peep told them that—open the door a little wider, and an appalling silence broken only by the *clipclap* of the looms bade them a reverse welcome, and seemed to say, "Well, after all, what *do* you want?"

Now, although this gathering at the spinning room was all quite natural and inevitable, it was also unexpected and enormously appreciated by the women, who had never had any place that was essentially their own to go to before. Most of them, indeed, had never had any women friends at all. A nigh neighbour, at best eight or ten miles away in another cabin lost in the forest, a brief foregathering of females at some wedding or at a husking or quilting bee was all they had known. On the far frontier not even that. Only a room in a dark cabin with the mister, where a woman made her own company, if she ever got any, by giving birth to it and teaching it to talk. Old Mrs Pendergass had been eminently successful in thus providing herself company. She and her daughters really understood how people should be managed as few others could. They had conducted life in a crowd in their own family for a long time.

It was Bella Pendergass who had learned most from her mother in this regard. The experience of many Indian alarms, when the family and all their neighbours had again and again been driven in to live near the fort, had given Bella much practice. She was completely devoted to her mother and not interested in mating. She was not cold. She had simply not been awakened to male necessity as yet, and all her energy was employed and found satisfaction in a purely female marshalling of domestic events.

In the spinning room during the crowded spring of "the '64", Bella arched the fine neck of a virgin palfrey, covered with a chestnut mane, and whinnied in the dust of a storm of work and gossip. Too frail to come downstairs frequently any more, her mother participated vicariously in all that was agog in the town by means of her daughter's mouth. But Mrs. Pendergass was not too feeble to advise. She was still, in fact and through Bella, a one-woman steering committee for the suddenly swarming neighbourhood. And to be just, most of her suggestions were benign and wise. Law, of course, to Bella.

Let us say it was "Bella", then, who had first sensed the possibility of the spinning room and had begun by inviting a woman here and there to come in and do her work. Garrett had been prevailed upon to send down to Harris's for a load of flax and wool. It was probably the most importantly laden wagon that ever reached the town, and the most profitable, although its burden was largely given away. For it was not long before the news of the pleasant place to work, of the comfort and warmth of the fire, tansy tea and company in the spinning room, spread throughout the village. One woman invited another.

How Bella contrived tacitly to convey her permission to extend the circle gradually, and in the right direction, can hardly be reduced to words. The process was akin to that by which one ant conveys to others the fact that sugar has been spilled. The news is spread, and the workers assemble. Out of the ambient nowhere ants appear sufficient for the task, by a mere touching of antennae—but no hostiles or strangers are ever given the contact. And so it was with Bella and her spinsters. Presently the room was busily and pleasantly full of women from all about, working and talking hard.

From the first there had been a certain prestige about going to the Pendergass spinning room. One primped. One combed and smoothed the hair. One washed and darned the holes in linsey-woolsey. One put on a house cap or ribbon, if one had one. One wore stockings always, and the best fitting. And invariably one looked one's self over for fleas. Carefully, for the town swarmed with them. And when one was to be seen by other people in company it was nice to be appreciated for one's self alone.

Besides, the Pendergasses were known to be elegant. Elegant—and clean. One lived up to that at least in the spinning room, whatever one put up with in the dismal quarters about town. Bella Pendergass actually smelled like a lady. Lilic-water, it was rumoured, was the cause

255

of this. Only one faint whiff of virtuous fashion from the metropolis, it set the female world at Bedford on fire and the spinning room circle on a pinnacle of ladylike grace and sanctity.

Few had ever dreamed of even sniffing such a world. Indeed, its very existence in these woods was unexpected, astonishing, disconcerting. But oh, how blessedly desirable! And when one went to the spinning room, of course one left the children behind. One went there to be nothing but one's self. One wasn't "mom" in the spinning room any more. One was Mistress So-and-so.

And once there, a sudden fountain of sisterly conversation long unsuspected, dried up, or left behind in premarital, girlish moonlight, welled up in the heart again; broke out and bubbled; gushed; rushed together into a river of rapid living waters of talk that overflowed and refreshed and revivified the whole glum village of Bedford. These lodge meetings at the spinning room had their secrets, too. But they were really important, because everybody soon knew them. They were not selfishly kept. No talents for spreading them lay buried in napkins. Every talent was put to work making interest fast.

And, good Lord, how interesting it all was!

Even the men soon found that out. For, of course, certain overtones of the spinning room were confided to them by their wives—and others. Nor was there anything idle about this talk. On the contrary.

It was Bella and several Mrs. Macs, for instance, who, finding out how many babies were soon going to be born, proposed to do something about it. They arranged to have the women who best understood survival of arrival present at the moment. They even got Dr. Boyd to help at difficult births—and for an army surgeon he learned a great deal.

256

Also it was Bella and two Mrs. McPhersons, along with dark Mary Sheean, the Irish papist, who practically constituted themselves a committee to find quarters for the forlorn refugee families in town. They put the men to work building cook sheds and family shelters near the hospital lot. They begged the use of cellars, lean-tos and haylofts. Animals were crowded to one side in barns to make room for human families, until temporary shelters could be built.

Mark Pendergass and his chest of tools was thus in constant requisition. Harried by Bella, and followed by Salathiel as an amused assistant, Mark dashed from one place to another notching logs, fitting doors, patching cracks against the weather, and framing roofs over crazy shanties—even showing some people how to split their own shingles, until it seemed to him he had built half the town himself. And for all this trouble he got no pay.

"It's all for the love of God alone," explained Mary Sheean, whose own red-headed brood of ragged young Celts had found shelter from the weather in a wagon shed. It had a slab front added to it provided with a window, which the boys stole from the fort. This nondescript *shebang* became Irish headquarters, where potatoes were forever roasting in a mud-and-stick chimney that frequently caught fire. There were a good many Irish in the village, Catholics, much despised by the Presbyterian Macs, although everybody's children played happily together. There was no stopping them. The Irish at least were grateful to Mark and his charitable gang of axe and adzemen for helping build them in. But Bella was simply inveterate. She drove her brother, until Mark complained that his sister was worse than his wife in always finding something to be fixed up. Garrett only laughed.

"Keep at it, Mark," said he. "Your sister's dead right. Get some more of these idle, wenching lads to help you. The babies can't be born in the snow. That's plain, ain't it?"

So Mark cursed, spat on his hands, and kept at it.

By early spring no more families were arriving and everybody had some kind of shelter, even if it was only an old tent "borrowed" from the commandant, and boarded in with slabs.

To tell the truth Captain Ourry* had been most helpful to the inhabitants whenever he could. Bella and her women frequently appealed to him. He had practically turned over to them the distribution of town rations. In that way he found that what public food was provided went to those who needed it, instead of being hoarded or sold. He soon had every confidence in Miss Pendergass, "a most respectable female". Some others weren't. Some of the bound servant girls, the runaways especially, plied an ancient trade with the garrison. The Welsh girls were the worst. They sang a great deal, and cheerfully spread the pox.

"Garrison life in the winter," said Dr. Boyd philosophically.

Boyd more than any other man was of "some use", insisted Bella. She even told her mother she thought Dr. Boyd "understood". He had once been asked secretly to meet the assembled sisterhood in the spinning room. Babies. The subject was delicate but visibly pressing. Dr. Boyd's suggestions were masterpieces of practical in-

---

* Captain Stewart was commandant at Fort Bedford during the absences of his superior officer, Captain Ourry. When Ourry returned he reassumed command, and Stewart became adjutant. The old records seem confused about this point, but are not in view of the above explanation.

uendo. Of course, no one could mention the subject
irectly. He called babies "recruits". By pure indirection
 kind of surreptitious midwifery was organized. Dr.
 oyd told how it was done in Edinburgh, adding some
 bservations of his own. In March there were fourteen
 recruits" in the village, who arrived successfully. Only
 ne of the mothers died. In cold weather there was not
 o much birth fever, Dr. Boyd noticed. Not so much as
 sual.

But the young children, boys and girls, were even a
 ore pressing problem. Lonely youngsters from the cabins
 ad soon discovered each other in town. They abandoned
 heir families, except for food and sleep, and ran wild.
 he fort and village, long prepared to defy Pontiac and
 is warriors, was now taken by mass assault from the
 ear by small boys.

A host of fierce urchins dressed in coonskin caps and
 heepskin nether garments defied the cold weather, chil-
 lains, and the sentries at the fort, who, not being able
 o shoot them, fraternized.* Boys swarmed at parades
 nd guard mounts, begged food, stole. They rode slab
 leds down the glacis and the steep village street. They
 layed soldiers and Injuns. They fought furious snow
 attles and snowballed everybody and his Majesty's offi-
 ers. They haunted the stables and picket lines. They slept
 n wagons, and crawled under the pest hospital. They
 lid on the ice of the river. They broke through it, and
 ad to be rescued by long ladders and half-frozen dra-
 oons, who crawled out after them.

A shinny game that kept perpetually breaking out on
 he parade directly in front of headquarters finally drove
 aptain Stewart, the adjutant, to take violent measures.

* A somewhat similar situation a few years later brought on
 he "Boston Massacre." At Boston, the soldiers fired.

259

An official "bull" breathing anathema on the boys and dogs appeared in the form of general orders. It proclaimed a curfew and imposed fines on parents and owners whose offspring and dogs remained visible, or even audible after retreat had sounded.

But Captain Stewart's indignation tripped him into a too enthusiastic official prose. In a general order that soon became famous he had directed his sentries to arrest any dog caught in the fort, on sight—any dog which appeared to be *"about to bark"*. It was that phrase which proved the captain's undoing.

Seventeen howling curs held prisoner at guard mount next day, and Ecuyer's undisguished chuckles of delight as the tall Highlanders solemnly explained to the frantic Captain Stewart that, "Ivery tike under *arr*rest undootidly appeared aboot t'bark, sir"—for a time forced the adjutant to take to messing alone in order to avoid a storm of ironical congratulations. Chaff, eventually from official quarters, descended not lightly upon his head. The shinny game removed itself to the moat, but it was cheered on from the battlements. And Captain Stewart felt distinctly that he was losing what everybody now called "Captain Stewart's War".

The curfew gave him surcease by night, but his days were long and filled with an agony of ingenious juvenile acrimony. The honest and sensitive young officer was soon the butt of his best friends at the fort and the object of general hostility in town, even though the seventeen dogs had all been reprieved. He was popularly supposed to be longing for the massacre of young males, preferably in the cradle. For it seemed only natural that a man who threatened to shoot dogs might also wish to murder children and the Irish women clinched the rumour by calling him Herod. So "Herod" he became—to the unholy joy of the whole garrison. The name proved apt, for Captain Stewart was a nervous-looking, refined aristocrat with a thin mouth.

It was really not so salubrious for Captain Stewart.

Just before retreat—and curfew—large gangs of boys accompanied by loping, leaping, and frantic mop-eared hounds appeared before the south bastion of the fort, where there was a splendid echo from the high ramparts. There they shouted horrid things in unison. What the echo repeated about Captain Stewart was inevitably overheard by the garrison, and caused even strong sergeants to simper at attention. It was *most* difficult to issue an order muffling an echo. Not even official prose would accompany that. And the dogs barked on.

The echo from the south bastion soon proved to be a powerful one. In a rude manner it repeated public opinion, and reverberations of it were eventually heard rolling back and forth even in official correspondence:

> Tell Captain Ourry at Bedford to put an end to the troops of arch [*sic*] young rebels who so plague the garrison there. The petty pilfering of the public stores by pets of the soldiers must stop. His Excellency is annoyed and thinks Ourry too complacent with the inhabitants. He instructs you . . .

wrote headquarters to Colonel Bouquet, and Bouquet wrote back to Ourry at Bedford. There a far from complaisant commandant conferred heatedly with his adjutant.

"Pets!" exclaimed Stewart bitterly, "pets, sir? While I'm called 'Herod' by every mother in town and forced to drink alone at Pendergasses' in Coventry, sir, I'm now censured by headquarters for being complaisant! What are

261

your orders, captain? I shall be only too happy to enforce them. Perhaps if a few boys were hanged in chains? Shall we erect a tall gallows and inform his Excellency that . . . that . . ." Captain Stewart choked.

"Now, now, captain," replied Captain Ourry in a mollifying tone, "*I* am not censuring you. I was merely calling the situation to your attention. I have no orders. I have every confidence in your own ingenuity."

Captain Stewart snorted, saluted, and withdrew.

Over a tall drink of brandy he confided his troubles some hours later to Surgeon Boyd in a quiet corner of the hearth room at Pendergasses'.

"He wished merely to call the situation to my attention," drawled Stewart, referring to the conversation with his commanding officer with elaborate irony. "As if *I* didn't have the situation called and bellowed out at me everywhere I do. It's that damn echo, you know. We can't fire on children from the south bastion just to prove we aren't complaisant. What!"

Boyd laughed.

"For God's sake don't laugh," cried Stewart despondently.

"I'll tell you what, Stewart," said the doctor after a bit. "You're not going about this as a widower like myself would. You're a bachelor. And so it hasn't occurred to you that the thing to do is to get the women on *your* side."

"Really! What do you want me to do? Marry that echo?"

"Oh, no, I'm really being practical. You have a revolt of boydom on your hands. You're being stung to the quick every day without recourse, and you're getting morose about it. Now why don't you go and talk with the Queen Bee of the hive here? I mean my old and much valued friend and fireside companion, Mrs. Rose Pendergass."

"Why, I'd talk with the devil in horns and tail, if it would do any good," growled Stewart. "But look here, Boyd, ain't this just another of your damned Jacobite plots to put a hoax on one of the king's men? Frankly I'm not in a mood just now to be had just for tickling your funny bone. Really, I've had to put up with more than you think."

"On my honour it ain't a plot," replied Boyd. "But you are in a delicate condition, captain. You admit that. And so I suggest you talk it over with Mrs. Pendergass. All that you'll find is a wise old woman with a Devon accent thick as cream."

"I once hunted on Exmoor," said Stewart, less doubtfully. "Well, lead on, lead on. But if word of this ever gets about, by God, doctor, I'll call you out."

"Never a word from me," laughed Boyd, as he rose to show the way to the dwelling house.

Taking his hat and his reputation in his hands, Captain Stewart reluctantly followed the surgeon over the Bridge of Sighs into what he called the "women's quarters" next door. Mrs. Pendergass was at home. In fact she was drinking real tea.

And that was why—to anticipate only a little—it finally came about that a school was started in the official precincts of the fort itself in one of the vacant barrack rooms. "Captain Stewart's Academy," Boyd insisted upon calling it, thus putting the credit for its foundation where he wanted it to lie. It was ably presided over by one Malcolm Hume, lately discharged from the grenadiers as an invalid, because both his feet had been frozen and one had finally dropped off at the hospital—slowly.

"But the most important thing is that Mr. Hume has

survived his feet," explained the surgeon to Yates one day, "survived through sheer obstinacy of disposition, and with both hands. And that is about all that most schoolmasters ever do have for to recommend 'em. But this gentleman is also possessed of the highest possible diplomas for teaching the art of writing. He is legally certified of great cunning in letters generally. He had the king's pardon for forgery, royal seal and all."

"Ah, I think I might recollect the case," said Yates, "under another name. 'Twas a note of hand of my late Lord Belasyse tripped him up, was it not? The dead man it seemed must have come back to sign it. It was a mere awkwardness in date, a kind of ghostly error in forgery brought the thing to light. Not the handwriting."

"Yes, that was it. And it was young Belasyse, the heir, who procured the pardon," laughed Boyd. "He said he hated to see a prince of copiers hang just for imitating a peer."

"The note was for only seven pounds," murmured Yates.

"By George, you *have* a good memory, Yates, haven't you?" said Boyd, looking troubled.

"Oh, I can forget, too," replied the young lawyer—"when advisable."

"Do so in this case, I beg you," said the doctor earnestly. "To tell the truth I became attached to this poor fellow Hume while his foot was coming off. And I have fond hopes for both him and for his school. The Lord knows a school *is* needed here. I just took advantage of the stew Stewart was in with all these poor little devils in order to get it going."

"You have nothing to worry about from me," said Yates, "only—"

"Only, what?" demanded Boyd.

"Why, I wonder you didn't pick me for the place," said Yates. "I could have quelled all your little devils with a single glance."

"Lord!" cried the doctor. "Why, I never even thought of you!"

The school, however, flourished under Mr. Hume. Roughly at first, and then steadily. Mr. Hume proved hard as flint, but he struck sparks that kindled a light in darkness. Long after the Indian troubles were over, when even the fort was gone and the king who had pardoned him was dead, Mr. Hume continued to provide a copperplate hand for succeeding generations of youths to copy from the best schoolmaster in all the valley. The past forgot him. His present was always honourable, for in the future he never wrote any other name but his own, even on his pupil's slates. Thus "Captain Stewart's War" ended unexpectedly in planting the first seeds of learning at Bedford—but for boys only.

The girls as usual were left to their own educational devices. And, as usual, out of sheer circumstances and the varying incidents of existence they provided themselves with a preparation sufficient to continue life successfully. Theirs was an informal and instinctive method of acquiring the ways and means of existing with all the reasons for doing so taken for granted. It was an education by imitation of doing rather than by word of mouth. It was self-generated, and the practice began with dolls and ended in grandchildren.

At least that was the way it seemed to Surgeon Boyd one bright, snowy afternoon as he sauntered down from the military hospital on the hill to Pendergasses' in the valley. He was badly in need of a hot dram to pull himself together, "to narrow himself down", as he phrased it. For on occasions, particularly after screaming amputations, the circle of Dr. Boyd's awareness became hugely wide, intolerably vast.

He seemed to be able to think of everything at once; to see and to hear petty details of what was going on everywhere. Yet with each item always related as a part to one agonizingly overpowering whole. And in this vicious circle of relating parts to a whole, and the whole to the parts, while his mind vivisected the world into its various organic functions, and yet kept telling him and explaining to him how beautifully one part fitted into another—he was walking down from the hospital to get a drink at Pendergasses'.

By God, he needed one!

There were only a few ways he could stop himself talking to himself. He could talk to someone else, like Yates, and let *him* reply. That stopped it! Or at night he could write in his commonplace book; get a whole section of himself out of him and into the book and locked up. Jail for Chatterbox! It was a nice big book with a brass lock on it. But it was nearly full now of explanations of the relations of this thing to that, medical notes, geological and botanical data, philosophical arguments—downright, barefaced metaphysics.

His secrets.

Probably a record of what was wrong with him. He had thought of that, too; noted it, and locked *it* up in the book. He was tired of thinking. He would probably never be found out if he just burned the book when it was full. He had thoroughly disguised himself as a surgeon. Other people thought he really was one. He hid his philosophy. Why, he had almost successfully impersonated someone else to himself! But sometimes, sometimes the world all opened up for him again, wide, clear, with a terrific immensity, inviting itself to be endlessly commented upon, while one thing suggested another until—he was walking down from the hospital to get a drink at Pendergasses'.

And, since it was a very clear winter day with the sunlight glaring on the snow; horribly clear in contrast to a kind of melancholy sombreness within him, all the small details of everything that was going on were projected upon the dark retina of his mind with a preternaturally clear-cut brightness and an automatic memorability that forced him both to notice them minutely and to try to put them each in place. Particularly, he noticed what the girls and women were doing in the village. He needed women. He missed his wife bitterly—and the little girl. Cholera. Bombay.

Most of the small girls in this village seemed to be nursing dolls, too. Anything would do for a doll. A log with a whittled head—the carving was not important. A corncob with beady eyes did as well, or a double-pronged root. Anything! Anything wrapped in a bright rag. But these objects upon which to lavish affection had other clothes; delicate, gossamer-spangled robes in which the tender fancies of tiny women swaddled their imaginary offspring. Anybody with half an eye could see that rags were really elfin splendours.

How any cocksure philosopher might be struck dumb with astonishment, thought the doctor, to be able to observe what he was now suddenly aware of—that underneath the grown-up human life of the village was a sub-race of gnomes, babies' babies, misshapenly beautiful, with starlight streaming from their eyes; with bright berry mouths kissed passionately by little mothers; hushed, whispered to, put to sleep, wakened, dressed, spanked, and sung to until they came to life in queer corners where female children played at keeping house in empty barrels or held pavilioned courts under the royal drapery of their mothers' lousy, moth-eaten shawls.

And, if our strolling philosopher were not of an entirely mechanic or logic-chopping turn of mind, mused the doctor, if perchance he wore a pair of farsighted and yet focusing spectacles over the bridge of his nose, instead of a sneer, why, then he might reflect—even in such a savage country as this was—that out of extreme delicacy emerges ruthless strength; that most little white girls remember all by themselves, even when alone, a dim green country where their as yet unborn children walk and haunt as dream sprites secret lawns of deep moss and tiny forests of fern fronds. A land of dolls, trolls, and fays, bright with magic morning. The original, northern, elfin homeland of the race.

Cool and mysterious it is lying far in the secret past. Delicate, but yet immortal and natively recollected. Out of it mighty commonwealths of men eventually erect themselves and walk into the sunset, making the land to flourish, and then to smoke and vanish behind them.

"For," said Boyd aloud to himself, "the fierce son of woman arises out of his mother's green country and marches forward into the flaming destruction of the future years."

Having said it, the doctor suddenly recollected himself, looked around to be sure he had not again been overheard muttering nonsense, and made hastily for the door of the big hearth room at Pendergasses', and a chair by the fire. All that old Garrett saw when he came in was Dr. Boyd as usual: a rather sturdy, red-faced Englishman in a worn surgeon's uniform with rusty spots of old blood on his faded scarlet sleeves, a man with troubled blue eyes. What he wanted was a long drink, quick.

Garrett gave it to him and excused himself for a moment, remarking that he would have to step out and put an end to the infernal racket that was always going on next door.

"You're not liable to put an end to *that*," mused the surgeon. "It's not infernal, it's human. And I'd like to bet it's going to go on here for the next thousand years or so—at least."

The contents of his stone mug now put an end both to Dr. Boyd's muttered remarks and to his thoughts. He looked relieved, and the wrinkles about his eyes relaxed. The noise next door at the dwelling house increased. Dr. Boyd laughed confidently. For whatever he might think of his more recondite cogitations, he felt quite sure that his last observation tha tafternoon was quite right. The din next door might well make even a philosopher curious as to what was going on there.

Rightly considered, the din next door might even be said to be memorable. The noise there certainly promised to go on for many years at least. In the Pendergass dwelling house was concentrated more life, vigour, and various promises for the future than under any other roof in town. In that respect it was unusual, in all others typical of the intense domestic life of the neighbourhood when driven in on itself for mutual safety and shelter from Indian raids. Only at Pendergasses' there were more people in one house than usual, and it was a bigger house.

Altogether, there were eighteen people who had found shelter under the dwelling house roof, including Garrett, who always slept there at night in the big family bed with old Rose. Only death finally parted them. But Garrett was the only man who did sleep in the house regularly.

Besides the old couple, there were now only women

and children in the dwelling house. All of them, however, were members of the Pendergass tribe, except Diamond, the slave girl, who nursed everybody's babies, and little Liza Shockoe, a blond orphan child of three winters, taken in to be mothered by everybody during the troubles of '64.

Bella and Susan Pendergass, Garrett's two unmarried daughters, had the room next to their mother's on the upper floor. Their sister, Mrs. Polly Murray, a widow, the mother of Salathiel's friend Nat, occupied the hall with her young son, Martin. In a small room at the end of the same hallway slept Phoebe and Arthur Davison, also Garrett's grandchildren. The two Davisons were only "avisitin' over from Fort Loudon," where their mother Rachel lived, father William being a prosperous tanner of that place. Thus most of Garrett's more immediate family were on the same floor close to old Mrs. Rose, who loved them all, and was constantly having them in to talk to her and sit by her chair.

On the floor underneath in four rooms and a large entry slept and dwelt the "in-laws": Charles's wife, Chloe, a sick and childless woman; Emma and Clara, Matthew and Mark's wives with their children, five in all. There were Emma's "little Garrett", Jane, and Edward, ranging from four years to eighteen months; and Clara's twins, Frank and Thomas aged two, the envy and pride of the whole family. Little Liza Shockoe was just tucked in. Mat and Mark Pendergass were thus by force of circumstances temporarily separated from their wives and slept downstairs at the inn.

"But that is just as well, for the time bein'," said Garrett. "I don't need to tell you why. You're just across the bridge away, and you'll not be in a constant *ding-dong* of babies. Till ye *kin* git back to your own cabins, it'll kinda be more decent and restful all round."

One peep into the "women's quarters" was sufficient to make even an ardent husband agree. There were plenty of beds and trundle beds there, packed close, but no place for dalliance. In fact the dwelling house was almost entirely given over to the children, who swarmed.

Up and down the wide stairs in the lower entry, and all day long, crept, played, and scrambled the babies and young children of the house. They also invariably had infant friends in from the village, whose mothers were only too glad to leave them there whenever they could. Then, too, there were pups and kittens; occasionally a miserable chicken or a duck or two to make Roman holiday for the infant populace, and to add to the squawks and screams, the pounding and racing of feet, the wails and clatter which emanated from this tribal nursery in the lower hall.

At the top of the stairs sat the black Diamond picking tow or sewing, quelling quarrels that became too violent, and snatching up youngsters who fell down stairs bump by bump or required liquid or solid attention, comfort or reproof.

Diamond did well with an Ethiopian tact and a soft, soothing voice which seemed made to comfort and reassure infancy. Casualties were mostly minor. But the entry for all that was a frantic place, a mad mêlée of small children, where a modest kitten could hardly get its business done in a corner before it was snatched back by the tail into the maelstrom of never-ceasing play.

Sometimes Phoebe came to take charge. She would tell stories and say rhymes, aided by young Arthur, with all the pack perched below her on the shadowy stairs, their eyes fixed expectantly and lovingly on her face. Or sometimes it was one of the Pendergass sisters, Clara or Emma,

271

who relieved Diamond. All the women passed through the entry at some time during the day, even Bella and Sue. It was the main viaduct of the household, and the incidents of its traffic, and what could be glimpsed through the door when it swung open into the wagonyard, were news and wonder to the children. On good days they played in the wagonyard itself with the papooses and pickaninnies; with the entire animal population of the place.

Cooking went on in the outside kitchen and the yard; washing, candle, and soap making. Beyond the big gate wagons with chimes of ringing horse bells went by on the road. Somebody was always cutting firewood with an axe or sawing planks in the pit. The only flock of tame geese in that part of the world hissed, and chased everybody. There were horses, cows, pigs, and poultry. There were the cabins of the Negro slaves and the Injuns to wander in and out of—and friends there. There was a blacksmith shop, and a small tanning pit and shed. An elk or a bear brought in by Captain Jack or Salathiel usually hung nose downward from the slaughter bar. There were dogs, pet coons, and rabbits. Altogether it was not a bad place to commence life in—the yard.

There you could watch the women coming to the spinning room in the afternoon. At times, if you were both big and good, you could help with the work in there. And just before sunset Grandpa Garrett called everybody into the house by the fire downstairs to read from the Good Book. Then there was hot corn-meal mush, milk, a strip of bacon, Now-I-Lay-Me, and bed. The best of it was you never had to sleep alone. You were not afraid when you were at Grandpap Pendergass's—and there was a war. No Injuns could git ya, and there was company. Lots of little cousins, and uncles and aunts. There was plenty to do always.

Certainly there was plenty for the women to do—always. But they, too, like the children, after the terror of the flight from the outlying farm cabins was over, tended not only to make the best of things, but to enjoy and profit by the experience of being at Grandpa Pendergass's. There was also company for them. There was the warm security of the tribe, and the solid comforts of the establishment. There was really less work to do than when they were alone on new clearings with their husbands. For the women parcelled out the work among themselves. And the whole place functioned as one family under the able direction of Bella and the experienced advice of old Mrs. Pendergass, to whom such a crowded crisis as this was an old story.

Above all, there was a certain abundance, even a wealthy feeling about being at Grandpap's, for the trade and ample supplies at the store brought to hand many things and materials which were not available or only the rarest of luxuries at a combination home and blockhouse in the mountains.

For instance, there was plenty of wool and flax. Plenty of it! That meant comfortable clothes. And there were candles, and soap, butter, and milk. It was not necessary to go to bed at sunset. People sat up at Grandpap's and enjoyed the evenings about the fire with a nip of hard cider, a bite to eat, plenty of talk, and even card games. Why, it was fun!

Perhaps that was why there was a fine air of security and hearty happiness about the place that in future times made stories of it a golden legend in the family memory of the tribe. Undoubtedly in "the '64", when everybody was at Grandpap's, there was a note of confidence, a cheerful excitement, a higher pitch to the women's voices at the dwelling house than usual. There was plenty of talk, and plenty of things to talk about night and day. And the men weren't always around, either. They had the inn and the store, the war, and jobs about town to keep them busy. The women could get their heads together and hatch something out. As for Grandpa Garrett, he could be counted upon to sympathize. It was all right to have him sleeping in the house. He was a wise old man, and he helped.

Bella was responsible to a great extent for the smooth way in which life went. No one was jealous or puzzled about her. It was instinctively understood that Aunt Bella was not going to marry. The whole family were in a way her children, and what she did was for them and not for herself. Everybody understood that and acquiesced in her leadership. She had tact. Her orders were phrased as personal requests. She consulted you, and then you had to do what you yourself had advised. That was Bella's way.

Everything, as it were, marched. Hers was a triumph of tribal housekeeping. The cooking, the sewing, the spinning, the cleaning and washing, the making of clothes, candles, and soap went on with a plan from day to day, and cheerfully, where each woman had her part and share. If matters became difficult, there was always Grandma Rose, who presided over the whole house afar off, but as a court of final appeal when disputes threatened, and as the dispenser of nostrums and rewards to young and old alike. You knew when you came to Grandma's room and sat down by her chair that she would understand—that the trouble whatever it was would be settled. She could giggle a difficulty into a joke. She was old, but she was still amused.

Her cheerful joking was sometimes a bit hard to understand. But you accepted it, for Grandpap and Grandma were both Old Country people. They had known and they were still in touch with the far world beyond the mountains, with Philadelphia, and with "home"—England. Everything you couldn't make yourself came from there —in a wagon. So you listened to old Garrett and Rose, because they knew. And they had read books, too. Grandpap got letters!

How it would be when the old folks died, many people wondered. Aunt Bella, it was understood, would probably get the dwelling house, and Uncle Charles would certainly be left in charge of the inn. Bella was the only one who could run the house, since Aunt Chloe was sick, and Charles was only a good trader and storekeeper. Most people were content to think of Bella as remaining in charge of the old place. It would seem natural. It would still be in the family. Only Aunt Sue still remained to be taken care of. Everybody wished she would finally make up her mind and marry. It was funny she hadn't. She was the darkest and handsomest of all the Pendergass girls. Everybody, even Grandma, wished Sue could get her cards and her Bible to agree about picking a man. It was said a number of young fellows had asked her. Yet she never said yes.

There was always something a bit mysterious about Sue. You couldn't quite make her out. Even her sisters didn't really know her. And there was young Phoebe Davison, too. She and her brother Arthur were Grandma's favourites. It might be just as well if Phoebe would take it in her head to marry. She might be managed into the idea. That big Albine boy looked hopeful. But he seemed to be holding off. Or maybe Phoebe was just too shy and young yet. She could wait, but Sue was getting along.

As for Uncle Charles, nothing was to be feared from him. He could be counted upon to run the store well and look after Aunt Chloe. She needed looking after. They would never have any children. That was plain. Aunt Chloe was in a bad way. She had a lump growing under her arm that didn't get better. And she was often so queer now. She sat cross-legged like an Injun squaw and moped, her hands in her lap. People in the village whispered about her.

All these things were talked over between the women at the dwelling house. The plans for the coming year were pretty well understood. Before summer came and everybody went back to their cabins, if the troubles were over, both Sue and Phoebe ought to be married off and set up for themselves. Aunt Chloe could be taken care of by one of the Injun women at the big house easily enough. She made no lively trouble. As for little Liza Shockoe, she could be farmed around among the family until she was old enough to be bound out. It was Sue especially, and perhaps Phoebe, who must be put in a way of settling down. The younger Pendergass boys would, of course, find girls for themselves. So all of them agreed. Such was the general view of things to come.

It would have been all the more curious perhaps to have taken the quite individual view of things of Aunt Chloe, who was so silent now. There was nothing cheerful about the dwelling house to her. Indeed, the presence of many people there was an agony to her when she was first forced to endure them. She now no longer noticed people. She shut them out from her mind. She had tried to narrow her world down to a peep through a crack. Or something—something like a lid over her brain gradually, slowly grew towards the front of her head. It felt like that. It made the crack she peeped through grow narrower and narrower. It was like living in a house with the shutters almost closed, where only one beam of light came in. So in the dark room behind her forehead Chloe existed, silent, trying not to move, torpid with terror. She had only one feeling now. It never changed. She was slowly growing colder with a bodily fear. She sat.

At one end of the corridor where the children played she often sat cross-legged on the floor, where she had squatted first thing in the morning. One hand lay on top of the other in her lap, and her eyes were narrowed to slits. The lump under her arm burned, but it seemed to be burning someone else. She felt it as another person's pain. If she could only get far enough away from herself, the burning would stop.

To her the hall where the children played was a vast corridor. It seemed a mile to the door, a long, long vista diminishing to a point of light, where incomprehensible shadow-figures of the children grotesquely gestured and postured. The noise they made was not a noise she heard. She heard someone else hearing it. It, too, was far away like a sea breaking on a distant beach, roaring in whispers. Almost as far away as the door, which, like the spot of daylight at the entrance to a mine, gave mysteriously on the outer world.

She could still remember that outer world, but dimly. She tried *not* to recall it, for her pain was there. And she would leave it, hide from it; withdraw and be unfindable. She had one constant fear. Charles might come through the door. He could still arouse her. She loved him. But for that reason she was horribly afraid of him now. He might bring her back to herself, to the full terror and agony of life. So she watched the door at the end

277

of the corridor with narrowed eyes, waiting, waiting for him to appear there. Charles had not yet returned from his trip to Fort Pitt. But he might return any day. Chloe knew that. Let him beware if he came back now. She could still defend herself.

They would rouse her at suppertime, make her eat, and put her to bed. It was hard to understand what was the matter with Aunt Chloe. Dr. Boyd said he could do nothing for her. He had shaken his head ominously when they showed him the lump. Grandma would soon have to be told all about her. Poor Aunt Chloe!

Sue also had her own view of things which she succeeded in keeping absolutely to herself. And that was the wonder of it in a big house like her father's full of other women and prying children. But she was a woman of great ingenuity, of careful, physical slyness. She was like two people, she told herself. But to everybody, to everybody but Nat Murray, who was a nice boy and kept his mouth shut for his own reasons, she was just openhearted, temperamental but biddable Sue Pendergass. The other person was sulky Sue, nervous and tightly-drawn, liable-to-snap-at-you-Sue just before the regular crisis—when "she had to have her stomach let down".

She absolutely had to have herself attended to or she couldn't stand it, the tension and breathlessness, the feeling of crawl. Her hands shook then, and she was no good. She couldn't get along with herself or anybody else unless she had her stomach let down regularly, and Nat Murray did that for her neatly and pleasantly. There was no comment or nonsense about it. He just knew the signs when he was needed.

They had a wordless understanding about it. After he was through, everything was fine, clear as a whistle for Sue. If Bella had been married she might have suspected something. But she wasn't. Bella was always the same, apparently. And ever since Nat's father had been captured, and the Murray cabin at the water gap burned, Nat had always been about the house a good deal of the time. Besides, it had all started a long time ago with Sue. She and Nat hadn't exactly been little, but they were young when they started to fool around. That was the way Sue had discovered what was the matter with her—and the cure. It had all happened just about the time when things first began to turn grey and spotty before her eyes sometimes.

But Sue wasn't in love with Nat. It was just helpful to have him around, because she quite understood it would never do to have any somebody let her stomach down for her. A man outside the family might get excited about it and talk. And Nat was always so kind. In fact, she wondered at times how it went with him. Once she asked him. He was so quiet.

"I'll bet you don't know what's agoin' on, Nat," she whispered.

"Oh, yes, I do. I can feel it very plain," he said.

And that was the way it had been for a long time. But lately—lately it had been different with Nat. She heard he had been running after some Irish girls in the town. Maybe that was it?

Anyway, last time, only two months ago, he wasn't her quiet Nephew Nat any more. He had used her. He had even been rough about it, and held her down when she, when she . . . and now for a long time she hadn't needed him. She wouldn't even speak to him, in fact. But there seemed to be something there, growing.

It was characteristic of Sue that she said nothing about that either. She felt well, even triumphant. And as soon as she became sure of what had happened she determined to make it all right, to have no trouble about it at all. Bella and Mother need never know. And she would even fool Nat so he would never be able to laugh at her or say a word to anybody. She intended to get married, and to get married quick. All she had to do was to play right into Bella's hands, who was always urging her to get married. She could say yes to some man, and then let Bella hurry the wedding.

Everybody would be mighty glad of a wedding while they were all in the same house together. And there were now plenty of beaux hanging around for Sue to choose from. In a way she was a catch. After that last time with Nat, Sue understood now why the boys were so interested. She pondered carefully and picked the best candidate.

About the end of February both her cards and her Bible kept telling Sue every day to marry young William Tredwell, the farrier's son. He certainly had been bothering her a lot lately, and in other ways than one it was a relief to say, "Yes." William was delighted with his sudden good luck. Bella and Garrett were downright happy when Sue told them. The news ran through the household, and everybody started sewing baby clothes for Sue.

"And about time they were doing it," she thought.

Nat never batted an eye. Anyway, he would not be around much longer. He and Salathiel and the twins would soon be off with Captain Jack stalking the Injuns as soon as the weather turned. That might be any day now, and that suited Sue well enough. The sooner the better. She even had time to think about helping Phoebe in her affair. It was about time young Albine declared himself, all the women thought. But Phoebe, the silly, only blushed when Sue talked to her and would do nothing about it herself. She had spent a good deal of time nursing Yates. Maybe she liked him better? You couldn't be sure. But it was something for Sue to talk over with all the other women while her wedding clothes were being made and fitted. Mighty elegant stuff her pap gave her, and in these times! But Garrett was very pleased, that Sue was getting married.

"Sue, I believe you're getting fatter," said Bella one day while she was fitting her.

"Fat and sassy," said Sue. "I'm that contented!"

And when she came to think it over, she was. William Tredwell was strong, a dark, and a tall youth. It might be different with him. Anyway, he wouldn't wait long after they were married. She could be sure of that. So he need never know, since he was marching west with the militia. No, they could be married before the roads over the mountains were open, in the big hearth room, early in March. There would be a big crowd, all the family, fiddles and a jamboree. She went about the house singing. She refused to worry, and she was never sick. Some girls are lucky.

As for Phoebe, she found in the absorbing preparations for Sue's wedding a profound satisfaction and comfort. She felt she was only rehearsing a prophetic drama of her own wedding with Salathiel, that would come afterward —someday. In a short while Sue's approaching wedding seemed to Phoebe almost like her own. She didn't stop to consider. She simply dreamed of a wedding. It became the favourite scene in the starry pageant of her constantly recurring reverie, a trance of springtime happiness by day, and of April longings and tender hopes that flushed her young cheeks and breasts at night, as she lay thinking of her wedding—and Salathiel. But it was in this vivid mental picture of her wedding that all her longings centred. And in Sue's nuptial preparations Phoebe tasted it all in reality and lived it in advance. You could have told that by the way she smoothed Sue's wedding skirt down and draped her bride's shawl. It was like a caress to life, like the brushing of a nesting bird's wing against a pussy willow—for Sue's skirt was of velvet. Old velvet, long cherished but unfaded, the gift of her mother. And someday there would be such a wedding skirt for Phoebe. Who could doubt it? The very thought of it made Phoebe shy and happy.

It was really a question whether at first Phoebe Davison was not more in love with love, and a wedding, than with Salathiel. He, of course, had started it all. And it *was* pleasant to have him about the house, and so near her just across the bridge in the inn at night. She had often watched the light in his window. Coming and going from nursing Yates, when he had been so ill, she had frequently met Salathiel in the hallway at the inn. She had even learned to manage that a little. After a while, they had come to stop and talk with each other. In her grandmother's room when Salathiel came to visit she had even sat close to him, quite close. But these meetings, the actual tall and overpowering presence of Salathiel, were almost too real, too disturbing.

In Phoebe's dream of their wedding Salathiel was just quietly "there". It was her bright bridal dress that stood out against the misty, imaginary greenery where the pageant went on. Phoebe was not so disturbed as the others that Salathiel had not spoken yet. She felt sure; she felt she knew. She knew that he loved her. And time seemed to halt and to hover, as it were, waiting for *her* occasion.

Meanwhile, Sue was being married sure enough, and the whole family at the dwelling house were absorbed by that. So busy and so preoccupied were all the women over Sue's fast approaching wedding that Phoebe's affair,

282

for the time being at least, scarcely entered into their thoughts at all. Even she scarcely noticed how little she actually saw Salathiel. He was out hunting or he was busy about the place. They smiled at each other when they met, and that was enough. Besides, Salathiel and Captain Jack and the twins had something mysterious under way. Salathiel told her they might all be gone hunting for a while when the weather broke. So in Phoebe's mind both weddings, Sue's and her own, went on to the exclusion of much else that she might otherwise have felt going on about her. She baked cakes and sewed. And her eyes shone large and happily, looking into the future.

And then one day the weather changed. It was only a week before the wedding.

The first soft, melting breeze of the year came lazing up the valley from the south. The ice broke. The sound of the river began to lap and gurgle again past the Pendergass door. As the snowbanks in the valley went out, the rushing Juniata began to sing and to hiss over the big stones in its bed. Higher in the mountains the snow still lay deep, but the country would soon be open again to those who cared to follow the lower game trails along the streams and valley. The spring wind curled in Captain Jack's nostrils like smoke, and a great impatience overpowered his mind. Yet he was dark, stern, and gloomy. The blood fit was on him. The forest called. No house could contain him. He must be up and away with hatchet, rifle, and knife.

"Git your packs ready," said he to those who were to follow him to the cabin. "Thar's a deed to do, and you to be made ready for it. Happen we'll be gone two months. And say no word of it. I'll not be tarrying for any girl's wedding. Keep your mouths shut."

He looked at Nat Murray significantly. Nat wondered

if the old man knew. Well, it would suit him all right to go. It seemed to suit Sue. She hadn't even a kind word for him any more.

Past the middle of one night about the beginning of March, Phoebe awoke suddenly. There was no wind, but the river seemed to be louder than ever. There was a rush of dismal sounding water that seemed to be trying to din an important secret into her ears. She felt it. Something was going on. She could hear the men stirring about in the house next door. Once the tones of Yates' and Salathiel's voices talking quietly came to her ears. Now and then a candle passed his window. She got up and looked out. Mat and Mark, and Nat Murray were in the yard below talking together in low tones. Captain Jack came out and joined them. They seemed to be waiting. She could hear Garrett saying something from the back door in a cautious tone. Suddenly she knew what it meant. The men were going! Captain Jack was on the war path again.

She moved swiftly and without thinking. She covered up Arthur warmly to keep him quiet, and slipping on a wool cloak and a pair of old moccasins, she made her way across the bridge and opened the door into the upper hallway of the inn.

For a moment she thought Salathiel had gone. The only light came from under Yates' door. Then she heard them both talking. They were saying good-bye.

"Good luck, Sal," said Yates. "*I'll* be all right. You bring yourself back with the spring. It will be a long time. Demme, I'll miss ye! You don't want me to say anything to Phoebe, then?"

"No," said Salathiel emphatically.

They were talking about her!

She put her hands over her breast standing there in the dark of the hall. Now the door was opening.

He came striding down the corridor. At first she thought he would pass her without seeing her. Then he saw her and stopped short just at the top of the stairs.

They stood looking at each other in the dull-red firelight from the room below that was just reflected from the ceiling. In the faint rosy glow, which seemed to flow from her clothes and face. Salathiel saw his angel waiting for him. Her long golden hair fell over her shoulders shimmering, and her eyes were tender with sleepy love. She was his. He could take her. He knew that. This was the great opportunity. Once once. Probably never again. Yet he mustn't touch her. It was forbidden.

He swayed towards her, driven . . . held back. He *couldn't* tell her. Not now!

"Are you goin' away, Sal?" she whispered in the half-dark.

"Yes."

"You'll not be here for the wedding?"

"No . . . but I'll bring *you* back something, something for you, Phoebe."

"Oh!" she gasped. "Oh, that will be beautiful, beautiful!"

"Like you!" he exclaimed, and drew her to him.

"Oh, Sal," she said after a while, "oh, Sal, I only meant to say good-bye to ye."

"Ain't I asayin' it?" he blurted.

Then he kissed her frantically again, and blundered downstairs, dashing a mist of tears from his eyes. He met Garrett in the hall below and almost passed him without speaking. The old man paused in surprise. Then, just in time, Salathiel turned and came back holding his hand out awkwardly.

285

"Oh, Mr. Pendergass! Sir, I want to thank ye for taking me in here like you have." He gulped. "'And thar's something I must tell ye. I guess maybe I ought to tell Miss Phoebe first . . .'"

"Now, now," said Garrett, laughing and looking up at him as he stood in an agony of embarrassment in the firelight, "I guess what you have to say can wait a bit, son. Can't it? Bring yourself back here. Be tarnal keerful. Your pap, you know . . .'"

The old man's face worked.

"Now git along with you, git along, or you'll keep Cap'n Jack waitin'. And he ain't in a mood for that!"

Salathiel darted out, slinging his pack and gun.

And then, instantly, all the warm world of the house behind him vanished.

In the wagonyard Captain Jack, Nat Murray, and the Pendergass boys stood waiting. The cold sheen of moonlight glittered and glanced from the long barrels of their rifles and the hatchets at their belts.

They moved out silently on moccasined feet.

Only Phoebe, her white face pressed against the window, saw them go. For a moment a sudden premonition of terror changed the happy beat of her heart.

She went back to bed, and clasping her sleeping brother close, lay and shivered. The patches of moonlight on her crazy quilt slowly turned to darkness. Somewhere on the distant slopes of Will's Mountain a panther screamed.

Salathiel was there.

15

Death at the Salt Kettles

MEMORY is the orphan child of dead events, the off-spring of haphazard circumstances. Let some sight, sound or odour re-occur, a familiar tone of inflection in a stranger's voice, and a whole area of the past is born again to mind, overwhelming often; a feeling, moving dream of lost reality. How essentially mysterious is this faculty, how unpredictable by philosophers! Conscience and consciousness have their unconscious roots in the process. In the end, we are all left helpless orphans of the past; to others, enigmatic dancers to a forgotten tune.

The scream of a panther—

What is that to most people—to those who have never heard it; never hunted amid mountains where the great cat calls? But to Salathiel Albine it recalled always and forever "Death at the Salt Kettles", the grim and stealthy doings of a certain wintry spring; green buds, and red massacre. Part of what it was like to be a white man from then on found voice for him in the merciless lion of the mountain, flashed in the moonlight from the bared fangs of the wolf.

Salathiel had come to learn many things at Captain Jack's cabin, to be a pupil in a stern school. As they flitted up the valley that night from Pendergasses's the panther screamed and the harsh echoes replied from Poorhouse Mountain. There seemed to be several panthers hunting that night.

Phoebe Davison was not the only one who heard them.

There were seven in the brotherhood of arms at the cabin. There was a vacant bunk for someone who never joined. But in that empty bed, as though such things were equivalent to another companion, they kept the tow, the patches, the ramrods, lead, and bullet moulds for readying their rifle-guns.

From the first it was a decidedly silent brotherhood. The moody blood-fit lay heavily on Captain Jack. It rolled out from him like a dark cloud, enveloped them all, and settled down like a pall. No one questioned why that should be. It seemed natural. Just as the panther's scream had set the key. Captain Jack's moodiness seemed to provide the proper atmosphere for what they were preparing to do. His all but palpable cloak of darkness was not the kind of covering they cared to peep under and investigate. It was taken for granted, and yet—and this was strange—all of them felt that what lay underneath it grinned with a fixed expression of expectant glee.

The first thing Captain Jack did was to strip them of every last unnecessary article. The Pendergass boys especially had brought along certain small luxuries, a pack of cards, even a small bag of tea and a pot. These, and some fancies contributed by the women, things that had been brought despite a previous warning, were now made into one small bundle and returned the next morning by Mark, without comment. Salathiel sent back the silver watch Captain Ecuyer had given him, for Phoebe to keep for him. Sid and Cal McClanahan, who had kept lone guard at the cabin for six weeks past, looked on at these proceedings and laughed. They laconically sympathized with the "old man's" Spartan rule. Indeed, Captain Jack's discipline was more than Spartan; it was North American.

For Captain Jack now relapsed completely into the life of the forest, and of the forest as he had known it without even a frontier forty years before. No one, for instance, could have surmised from the life they led at the cabin that there was a strong military post and a thriving settlement only a few miles away at Bedford. For the seven at the cabin, the town, the fort, Pendergasses's had for the time being ceased to exist. The log hut, hidden in a small cuplike vale on the east side of Lookout Mountain "a league back from town",* might have been lost in the Ohio wilderness a month's travel westward, so far as occupants went.

The place was lapped about by folds of hoary forest: huge-boled chestnuts, ash trees, red maples, and white oaks. There was a never-failing spring, a few sink holes in the limestone full of snakes, sumacs, and young sycamores. Some lonely open glades like green lanes led

---

* Captain Jack's cabin near Bedford seems to have been situated close by the spring on what in the nineteenth century was Judge William Hall's farm at "Echovale". It was in the garret of the "manor house" there (since burned) that Garrett Pendergass's diary was found in 1902, in a child's cradle among some household goods said to have been seized to satisfy a debt many years before.

through the forest, under a spread of mighty walnuts in the direction of the "Stinking Springs".

Down these "lanes" the deer fed even in the winter. There no one had come yet. It was still a pristine and dewy valley. There was not even a path or a trail, except that worn by dainty cloven hoofs, for the new human tenants had taken good care to wear no telltale trace to their door. Only a light blue mist shimmering hazily over the top of the chimney when they cooked marked their occupancy of the cabin.

"Looks like a house that the yellow varmints forgot to burn,"* said Captain Jack, "but ef they do come now they'll find seven kinds of trouble at home. Wisht they might!"

But that was too good-wishing to come true. The kind of trouble those at the cabin were looking for would not come to them now. They would have to find it. The Indian war parties that traversed the country were no longer searching for lonely cabins to burn. They had made a clean sweep of most of them long before. They were now all intent upon waylaying small convoys, or ambushing wagons, expresses, and working parties along the road. And in this work they were only too frequently and dreadfully successful.

It was characteristically Captain Jack's plan to meet them and then outreach them at their own game. When the open spring weather should come, he intended to bring retributory sorrow to many an Indian village, and to lay lethal ambush along the trails and forest traces that led back toward the Allegheny valley over the western hills.

* "Yellow varmints"—most of the older frontiersmen always spoke of the Indian as yellowskins. Redskins seems to have been an English rather than an American designation of the Indian.

Meanwhile, until the snow melted, he would practise and repractise those at the cabin until they were letter perfect in every detail of their work. He would indoctrinate them with his own spirit. And above all he would teach them to hunt as a pack.

"Makum all one hatchet," said Cal McClanahan, grinning.

"And that's the idee, and don't ye forgit it," replied the old man. Captain Jack was beginning to feel his age at times. The days of his lone raids were over. But those who came with him now he still wished to control like younger limbs of his own body and mind.

After nightfall they kept watch two by two. It was no mere plodding sentry-go. It was an art in itself of scouting in every direction through the darkness around, and waking the relief when the time came, noiselessly. It was constant vigilance by every sense.

"Trouble comes by night, and death at early morning," said the old hunter. "Many white men perish confidently in their sleep. While the deer browse and the moon whispers to her dead, that is the time for surprises. Yet to be surprised is the greatest disaster of all."

It was only now and then that Captain Jack talked. For the most part he was silent. But when he did speak he expected his words to be remembered. The rest of the time he appeared to be intently listening rather than to be simply negatively quiet. Every night before they turned in he told them a brief story out of his own experience. One night it would be an incident of white massacre, the next how the Indians had in turn been overcome. Thus he alternated, yet he never varied.

There was much to be learned from these talks; from the deep voice that growled on in the darkness while they lay listening in their bunks. Hatred was there; skill in attack and retreat; the ways of men and beasts in the forest; what to do to survive in the wilderness—and a great confidence.

"Only one thing the Injun can do better than the paleface. He hath a far keener nose," Captain Jack would say. "For the rest, don't forget ye be far smarter." He generally ended on that note.

Then they would go to sleep, pondering.

Salathiel compared all that the old man said with his own forest upbringing, and saw that Captain Jack was right; that he was wiser than Nymwha and keener than Kaysinata. And in thus thinking over the past he remembered again, as he lay in the darkness looking up at the top of his bunk, the dead child he had buried near Pittsburgh; how his father and mother and the baby had been murdered. He even dreamed one night of the lost days in his father's cabin when he was a small boy. The brindled ox came and smelled him. He heard his mother scream far off, "underground". But this time when he wakened he was a white man and not an Indian again.

In the mornings, after they had eaten and rid up, Captain Jack always read a fine, bloody incident from the Old Testament. He would open his worn copy of the Good Book on his knee. But Salathiel saw that he opened it anywhere; that he knew what he "read" by heart.

Then they would get to work with the rifle-guns. That was where the two McClanahans came in.

Rifle shooting with the brothers McClanahan was the art of a devoted lifetime. Their astonishing perfection surpassed that of merely good shots in the same way and to the same degree that the performance of a musician of genuine genius outsoars and distances the skill of merely talented and hard-practising professionals.

Sid and Cal McClanahan were brothers not only in blood but in craft.

They saw to it that each rifle of the newcomers was carefully fitted to the firing habits of the man who shot it. But not until those habits had been carefully corrected and re-formed. Everyone spent hours, entire mornings, in aiming practice from all positions. They drew beads on things near, far, and in the middle distance.

Then they shot at marks.

Next the sights were subtly filed, shifted, blacked, or brightened. The balance of a piece was carefully changed. The habits of each man and the peculiarities of his rifle-gun were almost piously discussed. And of grease, powder charges, patches, and flinting there was no end of experiment and proof by trial. Every man had his own bullet mould, and each learned to cast and pare his own bullets to suit best the barrel of his piece. Of nice readjustment of trigger pulls there was no end. And then one day there *was* an end. All these preparations were suddenly over.

"For either we've larned ye, or we hain't," said Sid.

"The rest of shootin' is all shootin'," insisted Cal.

So they shot.

They shot in the morning. They shot most of the afternoons away. And towards the last they began to shoot in the twilight, and even after darkness, at dim blazes on the trees.

"It takes a kind of second sight shootin' after nightfall," admitted Sid. "Oncet we knowed a man that ist shot at noises. And he alers brought 'em down, too. Didn't he, Cal?"

"Yis, sor. He went blind slowly, and he tooken the sights off his rifle-gun and ist shot with his ears. He got

293

to be the best night hunter on all the Conococheague Branch," replied Calvin, loyally supporting Sid.

"Lots o' long ears along that old creek," said Captain Jack sardonically, "ef'n they believe all what you say."

" 'S fact!" asserted both the brothers together—and only then the laugh went round.

But such lighter moments were rare. Mostly they were all deadly serious and hard at it from sunup to starlight.

The sound of firing in the clearing was continuous, but the racket caused Captain Jack less anxiety than might be supposed. It was not likely that it would carry far. There was a peculiarity about the deep cove in the mountain in which the cabin stood. The high front of the forest rolled all about it and above. From the heights only an echo was to be heard. Even that seemed to be somewhere else, muffled, and far off among the hills. "Echovale", Captain Jack called the place, and the name stuck. Nevertheless, they kept careful watch while the firing went on.

This shooting practice was Salathiel's great opportunity for perfecting himself in the use of his curious gun. The McClanahans were doubtful at first of a double-barrelled rifle, but they became respectful after trying it out. They put on a new double rear sight so that each barrel could be aimed singly, and they corrected the left barrel, which shot low, by changing the grip of the piece. Albine they found a more than decent marksman. Sid especially spent much time and effort on him. And it was now, too, that Salathiel practised for hours at a time his trick of loading while running and turning to fire. He always used cartridges for this stunt and thus reduced to a final minimum his motions in loading. He cocked, bit off the cartridge, rammed it home, primed, whirled, and fired the piece.

294

"I might be as good as four guns in one for a while, if I keep on," he said hopefully.

"Liken you mighten," admitted Captain Jack, who was impressed by Salathiel's perseverance and improvement. He and the two McClanahans had at last been converted to what they called "Albine's stunt".

"Try makin' a ca'tridge for primin'," suggested Mark Pendergass one day. "Make a kind o' powder pill to fit the fire pan. It's your powder horn that takes up most of the time loadin'."

After some trouble they succeeded in making a small paper pellet of powder that crumbled in the pan under pressure of the thumb. That cut down the time for loading almost a third. They all felt elated by this invention. Some of the others began to use the pellets, too. Albine persisted in his practice. Eventually his skill seemed uncanny and he was enormously proud of it. It was the one thing he boasted about like an Indian.

"Lieutenant Francis said this gun would bring down Fortune, when he gave it to me," Salathiel was fond of repeating, while patting the stock. "She's a good-luck piece, I do aver."

"Good luck and straight shootin' generally go together," admitted Captain Jack. "But it won't do to depend on your gun alone. Sometimes powder gits damp. Keep your hand in by throwin' your hatchet and knife, too. Don't forget 'em. They're good weapons in wet or dry weather."

So at a peeled post set up near the spring, hatchet and knife throwing went on as a kind of game whenever there wasn't anything else to do. Nat Murray excelled at this. He won most of the tobacco in camp and sold it back at monopoly prices. Even Captain Jack was driven to gathering sumac leaves for his pipe, until Nat relented, seeing that without the weed everybody's temper grew short.

Two weeks of this kind of work and they had all taken full measure of one another and were now impatient to "have it out with the varmints". But Captain Jack delayed. He was well enough satisfied with their individual progress, but he was not quite so sure how well they could act together. He spent the last blustery days of March in expeditions through the hills to the eastward, hunting, and living in the forest as though entirely surrounded by enemies.

There was enough real danger to lend a vivid reality to this practice of swift night moves, of sudden feigned attacks, of swift assault and retreat, and of scatterment and rendezvous. Above all they learned to move forward or to retire, to close in and to scatter out according to a careful system of signals of animal and bird voices perfectly memorized, with one set for use by day and another by night. The last deep, wet snow of the season fell, and the supplies they carried began to run out. But they ended by tracking down the "painter" on Will's Mountain, which had been crying there so regularly.

It was an all-day and all-night chase. The big, tawny cat eventually took refuge in a high tree in a swamp. They could easily have shot it, but it had been agreed that there was to be no firing, and Salathiel brought the beast down from the limb where it crouched by a beautiful swift throw with Kaysinata's war axe. The razor-keen tomahawk buried itself in the animal's brain.

"Good for you, Sal," said Nat Murray generously. He had tried first and missed.

Even Captain Jack was satisfied with this performance. Even in his opinion they were all now "one hatchet", and he led the way back to the cabin.

"Rest up and git ready," he said. "We'll be leavin' as soon as the snow melts off, and it's set to turn warm now. I'll be leavin' you for a little. I'll be away until tomorrow evenin' at the fort. Sid McClanahan's in charge."

They spent that evening and the next morning patching moccasins, casting bullets, furbishing rifles, and making up their packs for a long, hard raid.

They dressed now in nothing but deerskins and blankets. They wore leather stockings, breechclouts, skin shirts with deep pouches, and a tied, thong belt from which hung knife, tomahawk, and tobacco pouch. They slung their powder horns and bullet bags across their shoulders by baldricks, and they carried their rifleguns with a greased leather cover over lock and breech.

The blanket pack was made square rather than long or oblong. It was a mere bundle lashed with rawhide thongs. It contained a tinder box with flint and steel, an awl, a packet of needles and thread, a small sack of corn meal, salt, a slab of bacon, and a thin iron plate, bowl, and horn spoon. These latter articles had all been supplied from Garrett's store and were quite unusual. The whole bundle was slung over the left shoulder. Extra powder horns were carried by some, and a few flints and small gun parts. Everyone had a pipe and a fine-tooth comb. The last evening they anointed themselves with bear grease, hair and all, before the fire.

"Hit's the white man's war paint," said Sid McClanahan. "Sovereign agin wind, sun, rain, and cold. Some folks prefer rattlesnake ile."

Then they ate heavily, slept, kept on sleeping all day—until after darkness Captain Jack returned with news.

They had now been away from the town for nearly a month and he had quite a number of items to tell them,

297

both general news and personal messages. They sat, listening eagerly, while he furbished his rifle and made up his pack in the same careful and deliberate way that he talked.

"Wal, men," said he, "I slipped into the village last evenin' like a fox raidin' a hen coop. And nobody saw me, and not a dog barked till I was plumb thar. Only in this case some people was right glad to see the old fox. Garrett and Mr. Gladwin, Yates, and Dr. Boyd was havin' a noggin by the fire. So I said, 'Make it the same, Pina,' and they all like to have slopped their swipes, for I'd come in powerful soft.

" 'How are ye, ye old murderer,' said Garrett, and the rest agreed.

" 'I'm gloomy fine,' says I. 'Happen, if yer don't keep that door barred, ye might all lose your har some night.'

" 'We maunt,' said Garrett. 'How's your den o' mountain foxes doin'?'

" 'Tolerable for cubs,' I told him. 'What's the news in this hole in the woods and stronghold of the cra-own?'

" 'You tell him, Yates. You're a lawyer. You're used to talkin', and Dr. Boyd ain't,' said Garrett, and went over to bar the door, laughin'. So this is what I gathered up out o' sundry quips and quiddities from Mr. Yates. Pendergasses' news firstly:

"Nat, Sue's married after a big feast and fiddlin'. She went west to Pittsburgh with her husband in the last big convoy over the mountains, three weeks gone. So you can rest easy, Nat.

"Mat and Mark, your wives and children and the twins are flourishin'. Your brother Charles ain't so healthy. When he came back from Pitt four days ago, his wife Chloe was so tarnal glad to see him she up and drew a knife acrost his throat. Happen it was on

298

the right side. They've got her tied up in old Pina's cabin, and Dr. Boyd sewed up Charles pretty neat. I'll tell you about the letter Charley brought back from Buckey at Fort Pitt in a minute. Meanwhile, Albine, here's some news special for you:

"Yates said to tell you he's doin' all right. He's got special orders to do land and boundary surveyin' in these parts for the Proprietors. Him and St. Clair is in it together, I hear. They're out runnin' lines in the village now every day with Mr. Lukens, the province's surveyor, and some of the royal engineers. He said to be sure to tell you your old friend, the Reverend Jim McArdle's come to town to preach . . .

"What's that, Albine?

"No, I didn't see Miss Phoebe. I didn't see any of the women that evenin'. And I went up to the fort airly next mornin', 'cause Captain Ecuyer's come over the mountain from Ligonier and I wanted to talk with him. It ain't likely he'll ever cross the mountains agin. But I did git to talk with him, and what he had to say consarns us all.

"Captain Ecuyer showed me Buckey's letter to him that Charley brought back from Fort Pitt. The colonel has authorized us to act as independent rangers and scouts, but not more than ten at a time. We're to be able to draw rations and ammunition, and we're to git the same pay as labourers on the military road. That's two shillins starlin' a day. We're not to be carried on any militia roll or as part of any command. We're to be our own consarn. Thar's no oath required, but we're to take advice and directions from Captain Ecuyer, and to sarve for six months if he wants us. I'm to be responsible for ye, and ye are to abide by what I say. Now do ye understand, and do the articles suit? I'll take silence for consent. Anybody kin quit now and nothin' will ever be said by any of us. Remember, you're puttin' your lives in peril. Now I'll wait for a moment to hear."

Captain Jack stopped lashing his pack and stood waiting expectantly. A sombre silence, unbroken except by the sound of their breathing, filled the room.

He waited a full minute and then began tying his pack again.

"That's *good!*" he said. "That's a fine Pennsylvania, silent Quaker oath."

"*Fightin'* Quakers," insisted Mat Pendergass.

"Yes, *fightin'!*" agreed Captain Jack, taking his rifle down from its pegs on the wall. "And seein' that's the case, let's start now!"

A suppressed hum of approval met this sudden suggestion, while they tumbled into their equipment eagerly and slung packs.

"Put out the fire, Albine. And, Murray, you wedge the door. Reckon the par*fume* o' that painter's hide will help keep most four-footed varmints away. He-cats stink powerful."

A few minutes later they swung up the hill in single file. Captain Jack led, while the McClanahans brought up the rear. The night was moonless, but a frosty clear one. From the head of Lookout Mountain they gazed out over the town and valley below. Northward the ridge of the Alleghenies tumbled across the horizon before them, outlined by melting snowbanks near the summit, twinkling with setting stars. Only a few lights winked fitfully in the village below. Captain Jack halted and stood looking at the distant mountains for a moment.

"That country is still demon-hanted over yonder," he said—"and I'm growing old!" Then he muttered a favourite saying under his breath:

"All the King's horses, and all the King's men
Kin never grow har on a scalped head again."

"Promise me," he cried, turning on them suddenly in
the starlight—"promise me you'll never spare a *single one*
o' the yellow varmints that falls to your hands!"

Going down the line in the darkness, he made them
promise him this solemnly man by man.

They struck off on an old trace that led them south
of the village, and then straight towards the mountains
and the setting stars.

Two nights later found them camped in a deep stream
fissure on the western slope of Chestnut Ridge, nearly
twenty miles north of the military road west of Ligonier.

To recite the bare chronicle of the weeks in the forest
that followed would be eventful, but tedious. Although
it was a time full of incident, danger, and surprise, it
was the same kind of incident frequently repeated: the
waylaying and cutting off of small war parties of Indians
making their way eastward from the villages of the
Ohio valley to harass the Western Road, or to raid far
eastward over the mountains among the more unsuspecting and securer settlements.

There were many such raids and many small war
parties that fateful spring of '64. The Indians were both
bold and desperate. There had been no trade in nearly
two·years. They badly needed horses, powder, and lead.
Under these sporadic onslaughts the frontier writhed
and shuddered, waiting until Colonel Bouquet could
move down the Ohio and carry the war home into the
heart of the Indian country; to the very capitals of
trouble, the Shawnee villages on the Great Miami and
the Muskingum. Then only there might be peace. Mean-

301

while, especially through April, May, and June, there was a constant petty, but merciless warfare.

It was not in Captain Jack's tactics merely to patrol and protect the Western Road. That was the final objective of his campaign. But his strategy comprehended it in a much larger plan which included forays and attack, surprise, and terror, the ambushing of a large number of the enemies' war parties over as far-flung a spread of territory as possible. This, in order to give the impression that a really large force of rangers was being employed to guard the road.

In short, to put it technically, he proposed to screen the entire northwestern flank of Bouquet's communications from Ligonier to the Allegheny valley, and to carry conviction to the enemy that at least a battalion of scouts and woodsmen were involved in the task. That was essentially the scheme he and Captain Ecuyer had agreed upon at Fort Bedford. And by its very nature it involved several things: especially, that the small size of his force should never be seen; that they should never strike in the same vicinity twice; and that they should attack about the same time apparently in several places. In a word, rapid action by rapid movement was Captain Jack's game.

That was why Captain Jack had kept his party down to seven expert, carefully trained assistants. Add only a few more, and he would have had to carry or to cache supplies and move much more slowly. He preferred to multiply his force by time rather than by men.

And the event proved him to be right; even more to the point, fortunate. In six weeks' time his "Fighting Quakers", or "Mountain Foxes", as they were more usually called, stopped four war parties on their way eastward, and three more plunder- and scalp-laden bands coming back from the settlements. One party was twelve strong, the others ranged from five to nine. From none of them did a single brave escape to carry the tale of their undoing. Their horses were sent to Ligonier, and their scalps went into Captain Jack's "bounty box", with the date and whereabouts of their taking off.

To be sure, it would take some time for the effect of these lonely forest disasters to reach down the Ohio. But Captain Jack counted upon that, for he did not wish to make his enemies too wary too soon. Yet nothing travels so fast and so far as the rumour of mysterious catastrophes, and before a new moon had gone through all her phases, squaws were wailing in many a village in the Ohio Valley, and wise-looking, but puzzled chiefs sat exchanging sonorous views over their pipes and the ominous fact that so many notable braves, who had recently departed eastward, neither returned nor sent messages explaining their whereabouts.

Nor was the discovery, towards the beginning of May, of six scalped Hurons, all lying in a single grave along the bluffs of the Allegheny, notably reassuring. Their trail ended there and none seemed to lead away. But no one, not even the Mingoes who found them, maintained that Hurons buried themselves. Suspicion was thus sown between the tribes as to possible treachery among themselves.

As a late spring burgeoned quickly and gloriously into a warm May, raiding suddenly ceased. Convoys between Ligonier and Fort Pitt began to roll freely and unattacked. Captain Ecuyer, completely worn out by the harassments and fatigues of the preceding winter, finally collapsed at Fort Bedford and was carried to the corner room at Pendergasses', where he afterwards died. But not before he had written to Captain Jack at Ligonier and to Colonel

Bouquet at Pittsburgh with a final spurt of valedictory triumph in his pen:

. . . I am now at last laid firmly by the heels. But I take comfort in thinking that the work in which we have all been engaged together may now go forward to its hoped for conclusion; that the road westward, opened with such bloody toil, will remain so for all time to come.

With that thought in mind I can at last lay aside my mountain chariot cheerfully and take to my bed with resignation, even in the face of a lingering and perhaps a painful end. Never were shillings better spent than the few that have been so parsimoniously lavished upon thee and thy rangers, Captain Jack. But shillings are not our reward. You and I and Colonel Bouquet must find both our rewards and monuments in Heaven—though not in the usual way.

I mean that we shall be forever memorialized by the blood and gold in every dawn and sunset that renews itself across these forest lands in days to come. And we can at least trust Heaven not to fail us there, unless what I see out of my west-looking window even now is only a divine chicanery.

For it is now, as you may well surmise, the hour of sunset, and I write this same letter to both of you in a moment of relief after a long day of rigorous agony. I have therefore asked Mr. Yates to make a copy of it to be left by the express for you, Captain Jack, at Ligonier. Do both of you hereafter please address your directions and occasions to Captain Ourry, for I avow that I can do no more. I hope only that I may last to take both of you by the hand here at Bedford before the night of my total darkness comes. So be it. But in any event, let me remain as ever,

Your humble and obedient servant,

S. Ecuyer

Captain Jack, as the endorsements show, received this letter at Ligonier, but at the "Allegheny Entrenchment", at the top of the mountain, where they probably stopped the express from Bedford on his way westward. They were watching the road there for possible "lurkers" and had taken three scalps near Ray's Dudgeon only the day before.

That affair in Captain Jack's estimation cleared the road, at least for the time being. But their luck had now begun to change. One of the four lurkers had managed to escape. He was a Seneca, and after six hours he had outdistanced even the tireless McClanahans. So the news of their small numbers would soon be spread abroad. The Six Fires of the Long House, and the villages on the Muskingum would hear.

As Captain Jack sat on a rock at the top of the Allegheny Mountain, thinking of this and reading Ecuyer's letter, he determined to give the secret, bloody work of that memorable spring his own indubitable signature. He preferred to be remembered other than by sunsets. At least, he admired the blood in them more than the gold.

As he looked about him at the exceedingly tender spring foliage on the mountaintop, his inner eye was reminded of something and roved backward to that idyllic scene of a river, a high cliff, canoes drawn up peacefully beneath it, while smoke ascended lazily into a smiling, blue sky—all of which had once flashed so powerfully into his imagination at Pendergasses'. His thin nostrils distended slightly while he pondered.

Finally he called his fellow workers about him by a low whistle.

"Men," said he, "we'll be returning to Ligonier for a day or two to refit and sleep. There's a powerful big work to do. It's at a place called the Salt Kittles, nigh a hundred miles from here. We make tracks now."

On the sunny afternoon of May the seventeenth, 1764, as grim and savage looking a band as ever emerged from the sombre gloom of the forest appeared before the now carefully barred and watched gate at Fort Ligonier. Evidently Ecuyer's memorable enforcement of discipline in the winter of '63 had been effectual, for it was only after considerable parley, and not until some of them had been personally recognized, that Captain Jack and his men were finally admitted carefully one by one.

Certainly, there was nothing in their appearance that was reassuring to anxious sentries. Only their dense beards still proclaimed they were white men. The rest of their faces, even their hands, were blackened with charcoal. Out of these hairy, sooty masks, their eyes and teeth gleamed wolfishly, keen and hungry. They were lean. Their deerskin clothes were patched, grimy, stained, and rain soaked. They had now been living in and on the forest for nearly two months, engaged in an incessant man hunt day and night, in which while they were hunters they might easily become the prey. They had covered on foot hundreds of miles of country, crawled through dense thickets, scaled mountains, waded streams, and swum rivers. There was a mass of scalps in Captain Jack's "bounty box", and only a couple of charges left in his powder horn.

The garrison and the miserable inhabitants of Ligonier gathered about them, as they stood before headquarters, and looked at them silently and with cold chills. A child started to cry. It was the only, and a proper, comment on their appearance. With the best will in the world, no one could regard these bearded strangers, which the forest had given up as though even it could no longer contain such murderous night prowlers, as ordinary friends and kindly neighbours. They were too obviously specialists and veterans in extermination to engender any immediate applause, no matter how necessary their services were. A couple of crow feathers, which Salathiel had stuck in his hair, were like an unpleasant surprise. They made horror seem jaunty.

"Mon, mon, wauld ye look at the cloots they hae for breeks," muttered some of the kilted Highlanders from the detachment in garrison. Even the militia was squeamish about welcoming them into barracks.

But into barracks they went, while Captain Jack conferred with Lieutenant Blane, who had been sent back to take command of the post at Ligonier, where he had done so well only the year before.

Salathiel found that he had now little interest or curiosity left for Ligonier. All his friends of a few months before had been moved west to Fort Pitt. Even the company of Highlanders had been shifted. Only in what remained of the settlers' villages were there still some familiar faces. But there were no attractive ones. And in any event, there was no time now for prowling or investigation.

For after an hour's talk with Lieutenant Blane, Captain Jack emerged from headquarters to tell his men to "git what sleep ye kin. Spend the rest o' the time refittin', and git generally rested up. Because," said he—and he all but sang the phrase—"thar's a great work to do!"

So they slept like tired hunting dogs, they ate, went to swim under the walls of the fort in the Loyalhanna Creek, and then sat about on their beds in one corner of the barracks, repatching their sorry clothes and moccasins to make them last, if only a couple of weeks, longer.

The militia gathered around to watch them, marvelling openly at their infinite care with their rifle-guns and shooting kits, laughing, while they trimmed each other's beards. But they grew respectfully silent again when they reblackened their hands and faces, or went out onto the parade to snuff candles and cut feather edges at impossible ranges. Nat Murray and Albine gave a demonstration of knife and tomahawk throwing, against which there was only one complaint. Few who told of it afterward could expect to be believed.

"They ain't jest or'nery partic'lar and pecooler in their doin's," admitted one of the militia sergeants, an old rifleman and hunter himself, "they're downright exactin'. They're *hit!*"

And with this opinion all agreed and had little to add, when Salathiel put on his specialty of running away from a mark and firing backward at it by timed paces with his double-barrelled gun. He was quite glad to be able to show off before such a large audience. But no one laughed at him for that. For, as Mat Pendergass pointed out, "it *would* be kind o' dangerous followin' him up with hostile intent. Wouldn't it?" And there was no gainsaying that.

Albine had come up out of the creek new washed, and a shining young giant. His yellow beard and hair threatened to become one gleaming halo. "An awful temptin' scalp," said Sid McClanahan. So Salathiel soon took special care to tone himself down. He braided his now quite long hair closely into a club queue. He shaved, blackened his face and locks to look like midnight; blackened himself from the waist up. For in the warm weather he now went about again like an Indian in breech-clout and moccasins, except when actually on the trail. The red turtle still sprawled on his breast, and he put back the black crow feathers in his hair. His hatchet-shaped face and relic of an ear, his long rifle and the hatchet and knives at his belt left nothing in grimness to be imagined. Captain Jack was proud of his "young giant", but none of the rest resented it, for in their recent raids Albine's skill in the ways of the forest and the Indian had been scarcely less than that of his leader. Only a sure ripeness of judgment, a certain inveterate determination were lacking. But Captain Jack supplied all the determination any of them needed, and more.

Indeed, in this brief interlude at Ligonier Captain Jack seemed little less than exalted and under the compulsion of a fanatical zeal for smiting the heathen in which even he surpassed himself. He took little sleep; seemed to need none. Most of the time he spent with Lieutenant Blane, explaining and perfecting arrangements for the projected attack. He at first repulsed, but at length succeeded in imbuing that somewhat too careful and phlegmatic officer with his own fiery intensity of purpose and confidence. Nor was this at all mysterious.

For in the surprise attack on the Salt Kettles Captain Jack saw the crowning effort of his career, and probably, too, his last and most notable feat of arms. He was not unaware that old age was stealing rapidly upon him. The last two strenuous months especially had confirmed his reluctant admission of the fact. He still concealed it, how-ever. His moodiness vanished and he joked grimly. But he knew. And he intended to finish the long chronicle of his bitter wars against the savages by a final memorable incident. With one final blow he wished to press his signet so firmly into the wax of events that his seal would remain forever distinct and visible at the end of the document—red and dangling.

In fact, the thoroughness and scope of the coup he had in mind called for a larger force than he could muster in his own band. And for that reason, more than any other, he had resorted to Ligonier to obtain the assistance of Lieutenant Blane and his garrison. The lieutenant had received strong instructions to cooperate. The plan finally agreed upon for the operation was simplicity itself.

At a point about a day's journey north of Ligonier, near the old Venango trace, where the Loyalhanna Creek emptied into the Kiskiminitas, there was a notable salt lick and saline springs or wells, to which from time out of mind the Indians had resorted in the late spring to boil down salt in their largest kettles. So ancient was this custom, and so important the salt, that even before the white man had arrived, tribal warfare had been suspended to admit families from many tribes and regions to encamp peacefully at the Salt Kettles for the brief operations of the season. There was even a certain tradition of friendly rivalry and feasting about the occasion.

But it was not only its peaceful tradition but the lay of the land about it, which made the place so liable to hostile surprise. And upon both factors Captain Jack counted heavily.

The salt springs, or "wells", were situated on a low-lying, open flat on the north bank of the Kiskiminitas River. There, naturally, the Indians camped while making salt. But the opposite, south, bank of the river for several miles up and down was nothing but a perpendicular, rocky cliff, nearly a hundred feet high. The top of this escarpment, of course, completely commanded the encampment on the opposite flats below. And the Indians always clustered about the wells in a spot only a convenient, although a long, rifle shot across the river from the top of the cliff.

"Too far for a musket, but ranged for a rifle-gun. Liken they won't hev thought that over," pondered Captain Jack aloud to himself.

It was his plan to occupy the top of the cliff opposite the salt wells, under cover of darkness, to murder the Indian watchers found there, if any—and then at high noonday, and with complete impudence, to open rifle fire on the unsuspecting saltmakers below.

"The more of them there are, the less there will be when we git finished," he insisted. "God send aplenty to be thar, and a good flat light for sightin'."

In his mind's eye, and out of long experience, Captain Jack was sure he could foresee just how the Indians would act when the surprise rifle fire burst upon them from the top of the cliff. The squaws and youngsters would rush to their canoes and make off, either up or down the stream. Probably the latter, in order to go with the current. Whether they would try to gain the top of the cliff at some point and attack would depend on how many of them there were and how strong they thought their enemies to be. They might simply try to get away. It was to prevent this that Captain Jack had appealed to Lieutenant Blane.

The "Mountain Foxes", reinforced by six of the best riflemen from the post, were to open the attack from the top of the cliff. But two detachments from the fort, consisting of the more experienced woodsmen amongst the militia, were to occupy both riverbanks along convenient flats, one party some miles above, and the other

311

at the first swampy meadow below the Salt Kettles. The militia was to be in considerable force, about fifty in all, and if the Indians offered to stand ground and shoot it out at the Salt Kettles, they were to close in on them from all sides.

"Hope they do make a stand," said Captain Jack, "that would net 'em all at one swoop. But most liken they won't. They'll make a rush for their canoes lyin' on the river's bank, I've seen it happen that way before."

The details of this scheme were thoroughly explained, and with insistent repetition, to the officers and men carefully chosen to take part. Every possible eventuality was faced and openly discussed with the men by Captain Jack, somewhat to Lieutenant Blane's surprise. Each item of equipment and arms was thoughtfully checked.

"For ye can't just give orders in a case like this. Not if you reckon to have 'em carried out," explained Captain Jack. "Every soul has to make it his peculiar business."

And the old hunter of men succeeded in making it just that for everybody. His savage glee over the favourable prospect of the impending massacre was curiously infectious. "Not one, not a single yellow-belly must crawl away," he kept repeating. "Don't disappint me, boys, don't let the old man's repute be spiled." And once again they promised.

Meanwhile, the McClanahans returned from a scout to the Salt Kettles and reported that five pots were already boiling there.

"That means thirty or more savages, a number of families, and maybe more to come," they said. "Man, they're careless these days! You'd think Venango might have taught 'em a lesson. Thar's Injuns at the Kittles from several tribes."

"But all Injuns," replied Captain Jack significantly.

"All on 'em," said the McClanahans, grinning.

They waited till the 23rd of the month to make ready, and then started north on the old Venango trace, after nightfall to avoid any possible observation. Halfway to the Kiskiminitas, and about dawn, the force divided into three parties, a dozen rifles under Captain Jack making for the cliff above the Salt Kettles, while the other two detachments of about twenty-five men each branched off to the right and left to take up their positions on the river both above and below the Kettles.

Captain Jack and his men plunged directly into the forest and made their way slowly towards the cliffs, skirting the Loyalhanna Creek most of the way. The Loyalhanna joins the Kiskiminitas almost opposite the Salt Kettles, and there was an ancient trace leading in that direction, a branch of the Venango trail. The old hunter took his time and moved forward with infinite precaution. It would take many hours for the two flanking parties to reach the river. Their positions there would have to be taken up under cover of darkness. Even the slightest alarm would be fatal to the enterprise. Consequently, it was about an hour before midnight when Captain Jack cautiously reached the vicinity of the cliffs.

He sent Albine and the two McClanahans ahead to deal with any Indian watchers. But after a careful scout they found no one, and the entire party was soon disposed along the top of the cliff, in excellent wooded cover, and looking directly down and across the river at the Indian encampment at the Salt Kettles, precisely opposite. The dim glow of nine fires could now be counted, but all was quiet.

"They're just makin' salt," whispered Nat Murray

contemptuously. "They're not thinking of fightin'. Injuns ginerally do one thing at a time."

"Stop mutterin'," said Captain Jack. "Keep watch by turns, and between times git what sleep ye kin. No snorin'." So they watched and slept by turns that fateful night.

The morning of the 25th of May, 1764, dawned.

It was one of those balmy, crystalline mornings that in a belated spring swell the eager buds into a sudden burgeoning glory throughout the Pennsylvania mountains. The sky was a misty, curling blue, the atmosphere lens-like. Small breezes ruffled the cloudy bud clumps of the forest into light greens, saffrons, and red-greys. Birds twittered and flitted their way northward through the misty thickets. Down the face of the rocky cliff stock doves crooned. Fish leaped and splashed in the limpid river below. Westward an endless flock of wood pigeons passed northward hour after hour, their cloudy squadrons darkening the land. The sound of their wings throbbed at times like distant thunder. It could be felt rather than heard, like a soft breast beating under feathers; wild wings of the forest morning. From the valley below, the haze of the nine fires ascended easily into heaven; grew in volume as the Indians arose in their encampment and began innocently to boil salt.

Salathiel remarked it was one of the most beautiful days he had ever seen. The wasps began working in the warm sunlight. Butterflies lilted everywhere. A mile up the river a young stag swam the current and bounded happily away. From the top of the cliff, well screened behind the dense thicket that flourished to its very edge, the thirteen riflemen peered down at the leisurely activities of the Indian encampment below. In a murmuring talk the two McClanahans and Captain Jack, his

314

eyes fixed on the blank page of revenge flung wide open before him, conducted a discussion as to the range of sundry objects on the other side of the stream.

Looking across the river at the encampment below was to young Albine like gazing down a clear vista of time into his own forest past. Now that the range had been agreed upon he lay gazing through a notch he had made in a rotten log for a rifle rest at the familiar activities of the Indians on the flat below. He could identify himself with most of what was going on down there. He finally became lost in a reverie over the scene and the memories it recalled.

Squaws, waddling like Mawakis, fetched water for the kettles and pushed the ends of long sticks together under the boiling pots. In the blue shallows of the stream naked Indian children wandered, and pretended to fish. Some youths and warriors busied themselves repairing the plates of bark on the canoes, of which there were nine drawn up in a line along the grassy bank. Here and there papooses tumbled with one another and played with pebbles in the sun. In the background dignified forms, wrapped in faded blankets, stalked leisurely from one hunting lodge to another. A group of three chiefs sat smoking in the shade of an enormous maple tree. Some boys were busily skinning a small deer.

As the day advanced, the smoke from the kettles rolled thicker and higher. Yellow flames flowered under the pots. Now and then the shrill voice of a child broke the silence of the forest. The river rippled while the stock doves moaned—and Salathiel was back in the forest again, playing happily without thought, his daydream like an interplay of sun and shadows. At noon Captain Jack woke them all to attention by a low, tense command.

"R-r-ready!" he growled.

The line of rifles poked through the bushes. Everyone had his instructions. Everything was artfully disposed for rapid firing. In the heat of the day the Indians in their camp below had ceased to move about and sat quiet in the shade. They were so many still marks, unconsciously arranged. Each rifleman picked his separate target and drew a bead. Ten seconds passed, slow as a minute. The line of prone figures stiffened.

Captain Jack's rifle cracked.

Twelve others crashed in unison.

Flocks of startled birds rose swirling and crying along the cliff.

There was a brief interval of silence, punctuated only by the bark of Salathiel and Murray's rifles. They alone were concentrating on puncturing canoes. Their bullets seemed to drone slowly across the river. Then there was one terrific yell from the Indian camp.

The surprise had been paralyzing and complete.

It was for this particular moment that Captain Jack had waited and planned, for it was the precise instant upon which everything else turned. Eleven rifles had apparently found many human marks, to judge by the scurry of the survivors. But only two rifles had continued to talk, while Albine and Murray were putting holes in the bottoms of canoes. Meanwhile, the rest had reloaded and waited. That brief delay had given the Indians a comparatively quiet moment in which to recover and rally. They had underestimated the attack. They swallowed the reassuring bait of silence. Screaming fierce war cries, they rushed for the canoes on the riverbank.

"By the eternal," exclaimed Captain Jack. "they're ourn!

"Hold your fire, hold your fire!" he kept repeating.

316

They waited until the survivors of the first volley were bunched about the canoes and had begun to launch them. Then the pitiless rifles began to bark again. Yells of anger and consternation arose as several warriors dropped, and when water spurted through the bullet holes in the bark as the canoes shot out into the river. There were six of them.

But Captain Jack was now cursing, and black in the face. It had not been his intention to open fire again until the canoes were well on their way. One of the riflemen borrowed from the fort had not been able to restrain himself, and had precipitated the volley.

As a consequence many rifles were empty when the canoes strung out and passed directly in front of the cliff, broadsides nicely exposed. That was to have been their final moment of catastrophe, possibly of annihilation. The supreme opportunity had been lost by lack of discipline.

They tried to make up for it as best they could. They fired as rapidly as possible at the retreating canoes. But two of them had gone up the river, and four down. So the firing was divided. The range rapidly lengthened. Undoubtedly there were hits, perhaps several. Yet, despite the leaks, all the canoes that had been launched got away. They tried to follow them along the cliff, but the going there was difficult, and good aim impossible. In a few minutes they were all back again, and looking glum enough.

Captain Jack sat on a rock, nursing his still smoking rifle. The large blue veins on his forehead stood out, and throbbed as he looked at one Hawkins Poteet, a young, brown-eyed, dandy, raven-locked rifleman from the fort, who had fired too soon.

"Sir, the boys on the river will git 'em all yet," Poteet kept saying, unfortunately for him.

Albine thought for a moment that Captain Jack might strike him down. For a while the old hunter looked at Poteet, speechless. When finally he spoke he was hoarse with rage.

"Liken your pa didn't mean it when he got you, young man," said the old man witheringly, "just nervous on the trigger, liken you. God blast ye! Ye ought to be back home playin' pis-titty with the gals."

For the rest of his life the erstwhile Hawkins was known only as "Pis-titty Poteet."

Captain Jack's disappointment was so great, and his anger had so shaken him, that a few moments actually passed while nothing was done. Perhaps for the first time in his life he let his rifle fall forgotten to the ground. Then came a violent outbreak of firing down the river. The four canoes were trying to run the gantlet of the militia in the swamp. It sounded like a brisk engagement. Captain Jack sprang to his feet and was all action again.

"Albine," he said, "you and Murray and the McClanahans take keer o' them hidin' out acrost the stream. Go over there and do like I told ye."

With that, he led the rest off downstream in the direction of the firing, as fast as they could make their way through the thicket.

And so, by far the worst of it, the dirty work, was left for Salathiel and the three others to finish up across the river. Not that there was any opposition. In a way, that *was* the worst of it. What they did had to be done deliberately and in cold blood.

They had to cross the river first. It was much too deep to wade, even holding their rifles over their heads.

And at first they were not sure what might lie ahead of them on the other bank. There might still be some old warriors or active youngsters about.

So they left Sid McClanahan to watch and cover them from the top of the cliff, while they crossed. Then to avoid climbing down the face of the cliff itself, they cut back into the steep valley of the Loyalhanna Creek and came out at its mouth, where it emptied into the river. The gorge there was piled high with dead trees uprooted by old floods, and it was the work of only a few moments to thrust the heads of some of them together to improvise a brushwood raft.

On this they hastily slung their rifles, powder horns, and other equipment, and swimming behind it, pushed out into the stream, using the current of the creek to float them halfway across.

Not a shot was fired. The opposite bank seemed silent and deserted. The smoke from the kettles still rose calmly in the still air of the valley, high into the sky, curling leisurely. As they came out on the surface of the river they heard the firing downstream still going on intermittently. Not a sound came from the party above. Sid shouted from the cliff that all was clear. A few minutes later they were across and the deserted encampment lay before them.

"They're all hidin' out," said McClanahan. "You two start routin' 'em out, I'll begin here and wait for Sid to cross."

So saying, he began in a matter-of-fact way to scalp four dead Indians, who had been felled by the fire from across the river as they rushed for the canoes. He worked calmly, neatly, and fast. For a moment Salathiel and Nat Murray lay watching him, and searching out the ground ahead.

319

"That's two for you, pappy—and two for you, ma," said McClanahan, while his knife flashed. "And one for Sister Sue!" There was a sudden scramble as he knocked over an empty canoe, and his axe flashed. A young Indian, who had been hiding underneath, fell without a groan—"and one for Sister Sue!" repeated McClanahan. "Now you boys had better get goin'. Here comes Sid now. I'll wait for him. Best to hunt in couples." He laughed, and began to string the scalps on his belt.

So Salathiel and Nat Murray went up into the camp, where five half-huts stood, near the salt kettles.

There were two Indian crones sitting together in one of the huts. They were very old. They must have been brought along only to tend fires. They sat and said nothing. You could see by their eyes, which did not wink, that they already counted themselves as dead. Albine and Murray knocked them on the head. Murray scalped them.

"That's two for you, granfer," he said. "One for each foot you had burnt off." This, as a kind of explanation to Salathiel why he kept the scalps.

"Happen they'll most all be squaws here," he added, and spat.

"Come on," replied Salathiel.

They ranged out into the country behind the camp. It was a fairly open natural meadow in a great bend in the river, with small clumps of sumac thicket here and there. Trails in the thick, virgin grass of spring were not quite so plain as sentences on a page. But eyes could read them.

"Here we go," said Murray. "Two on 'em!"

The trail led, after a short distance, directly towards a remarkably huge specimen of a lone sycamore. They lay down in the grass, some distance away, in order to peer through the branches cloudy red with buds.

"Look out!" exclaimed Murray. An arrow had just buried itself in the ground some yards directly in front of him.

"Boys," said Salathiel. He could see them plainly enough now, dark and high up in the big branches, cowering close to the trunk. He remembered his days with the young Shadows.

"Jump!" he called in Delaware. "Jump and run!" One of them did. It was the boy with the bow.

Salathiel shot him.

The other youth set up a dismal calling and kept climbing about through the branches. Murray ran up and brought him down with his axe.

"Them's both yours," said Murray generously.

Salathiel took them. It was expected of him. He was surprised to find the two scalps gave him no satisfaction.

"One for your pa—and one for your ma?" said Murray inquiringly.

Salathiel nodded.

They went on to the next thicket. They flushed a young squaw there, who tried to run for it. Then she stopped and made pleading gestures. She even started to come back towards them. That was a little confusing, but Murray shot her. They didn't stop to take her scalp. There wasn't time.

At a distance of nearly a quarter of a mile the two McClanahans were now hellooing lustily. They had evidently found what Murray called the "main parcel". The flat *bang* of an ancient musket from a dense clump of hemlocks that stood like an island in the midst of the swampy meadow sounded more like defiance than a serious attempt at defence. It was the only shot fired at any of them that afternoon.

Sid McClanahan laughed as the slug bullet droned through the air overhead. "Nothin' but squaws and old men in there, I reckon. Maybe some childer, too."

"Damn hit, thar's more on 'em than we thought," observed Cal, wiping his rifle thoughtfully. "Even Cap'n Jack ought to be fed full when we git through with this. Pity they didn't all make tracks separate. Some on 'em might hev made it then, maybe." The others seemed to agree. This was the sole sign of compunction anyone showed at the Salt Kettles.

The four of them were now standing together a good musket shot back from the clump of hemlocks, listening. But no further sounds came from the small island of trees. An expectant and prophetic hush seemed to reign there. The breeze sang a kind of premonitory dirge through the branches at times. Otherwise it was now ghastly quiet. Downriver the firing had completely died away. They stood hesitant, not looking at each other, as though awaiting a signal. Then upriver a sudden fusillade broke the peace of the valley and the spell under which they seemed to be standing.

"They're gittin' 'em up there, too," said Salathiel.

"They'll git 'em all," said Murray.

"Come on!" exclaimed Cal McClanahan. "Let's git it over with here. The rest will soon be comin' back. Never mind that old musket in there. Scatter out first, and then we'll run in on them from all sides at once. I'll whistle."

So they scattered out, surrounding the clump of hemlocks, and then stood for an instant, waiting. Cal gave a shrill hawk's whistle, and they rushed in from all sides.

There was a green twilight under the thick tent of

the evergreens. Streaks of sunlight filtered through the low-hung branches onto the brown needles underneath. Cowering there in the wash of flooding shadows, like rabbits when a dog is near, the victims lay quiet. Some of the children whimpered. There were ten Indians in all in that dismal thicket.

On them the axe fell flashing, once. The only mercy shown was the swiftness of the deed. It was all over in a few minutes.

The four avengers walked away from the little island of trees, whose concealing shade kept the wild meadow still looking decent. They walked away silently.

From the height of the bank several canoes with the militia in them could now be seen coming around a bend down the river, nearly two miles away. The two parties caught sight of each other. The men in the canoes stopped paddling and waved their caps. Their triumphant shouting came faintly. Upstream all firing had now died away.

"Cap'n Jack will soon be here," grunted Cal McClanahan. "Hope he likes it."

"We've sure been right thorough," said Sid.

They were now walking down the riverbank to meet the oncoming canoes. Albine slowly fell behind the other three. It was his intention to have another look through the thicket where Murray had shot the young squaw. She had had a cradle bound on her back, he had noticed. And she had tried to come back for some reason.

Long afterward he came to regard his curiosity about this dead Indian woman as the cause of his greatest misfortune. And this was the way of it:

The dead squaw, still unscalped, lay only a few yards from the thicket, out of which she had at first broken in terror—and to which she had been trying to return when Murray shot her. When Salathiel came back to the place where she lay, he found, as he thought he would, why she had tried to return. He found what she had tried to retrieve.

The child was a toddler, just able to get about on his own feet, almost a crawler. He had evidently come out of the thick bushes, where he had been hidden, and found his mother.

He was quite happy. He sat in a small patch of white river sand, in the sunlight, and played with a string of bright almond-shaped beads, yellow with a red center. He made low, pleasant, and pleased noises in his throat as the beads slipped through his hands in a glittering cascade. Just a few feet away, but in the shade of the thicket, the dead woman lay on her side in the grass, her eyes half closed. She might have been dozing. But this was, momentarily at least, quite satisfactory to the baby.

Salathiel came upon all this suddenly, but stealthily, stepping through the grass on cat's feet like an Indian. The child looked up, paused, and held out the beads to him. The man didn't take them. He crouched down, watching. The child went on playing.

There was a curious suggestion about those beads. They showered like drops of blood from the child's hands in the sun. And at times they looked brown, hard, even jadelike, shaped like the eyes in the baby's smooth Indian head. That topknot! Here was the rattlesnake's egg hatching—hatched, and playing in the sun.

He squatted for a moment, watching. An ugly compulsion was on him. It grew. He was close to the ground, alone, looking around again at the tall grass and towering trees, the immense depth of shadows, the strange, high sky. A child's vision of things. It all rushed back upon him. He remembered. A cold terror gripped him, complete and paralyzing. He heard his mother scream. Something broke in his head. All the tenseness of his horror was suddenly expelled through his muscles, the muscles of a man now.

He struck the child in the nape of the neck a lightning blow with the hard side of his hand. It died instantly. It died still clutching the red, amber-colored beads in one hand.

He got to his feet. He looked about him, surprised to find himself in a familiar world again. Why, it was over! No one need ever know. And that babe of his mother—that other child he had buried near Pittsburgh —himself—his own stolen self—all his pain and terror had been given back again. It lay still with eyes closed, asleep forever on the ground. He would return later and bury it; get it out of sight.

What had he to do with this? Nothing. There had been a motion of his right arm. It happened like being hit on the kneecap and kicking out. It had relieved him. Somehow it had done that.

He left both the child and the squaw lying there. The shadow of the thicket was creeping over them both. He walked down to the riverbank and said nothing. Nat Murray looked at him enquiringly. But there was no time for questions just then.

The first of the captured canoes was coming in from downriver filled with jubilant militia. They gathered together and fired a joyful volley. The cliff re-echoed the crash of triumph. From both up the river and down the careless crackle of rifle fire answered back this *eu de joie*. All the fleeing canoes had been stopped. All the warriors in them had been taken. Their scalps dangled now from many belts.

325

Captain Jack sat in the bow of a canoe and the scalps were shown to him, one by one. Sid McClanahan told briefly of the clean sweep they had made in the encampment. The last of the flanking parties now came in. Three men had been wounded, and one killed. He had been in the party upriver. He had sunk in the stream when they had closed in on the last canoe. Who was he? No one seemed to know—or to care. It had been a small price to pay for so complete a victory.

Captain Jack's face shone with relief and satisfaction. He had succeeded, and succeeded notably. His ruse had been perfect, after all. Not a soul of all the Indians had escaped. It had been death at the Salt Kettles, death complete and final. The nine Indian fires still smoked peacefully in the face of the declining sun.

Such fires were slowly going out.

"Everywhere," growled Captain Jack. His desire was coming true. He had had a full taste of it. For the first time he felt avenged, his cup of hatred emptied. The men gathered about him on sudden impulse and cheered him. He thanked them calmly. His thanks were sincere. After him the good work would go on, safe in such hands as theirs. He, himself, might even go home now and wait in peace for the end. No voices would call to him from the shadows of the woods at twilight. No faces would mow at him from the flames on his own hearth. They had been atoned for, stilled by blood. The end could be peace for Jack on Jack's Mountain.

He turned away from them and went down to stand by the river of clear water that ran by the bitter spring of salt. His throat was still raw with powder smoke. He laid his rifle in the grass and knelt down to drink from the river. He drank deep, and thanked his God in his heart. But when he rose and stooped to pick up hi rifle again his hand hesitated. A tremor shook him. The long rifle-gun lay in the grass, shining, with many nicks on the stalk. But there would soon be rust upon it. The stalk, with its grim epitaphs, would rot. His work was over. He was of no use any more. The full realization numbed him. Finally he picked the rifle up and cradled it in his arm.

From that day Captain Jack aged rapidly. In a few months he looked and acted like an old man.

All of them crossed the river and camped that night at the top of the cliff. They made fires freely there, for they were in ample force, and victorious. They felt strong. The crackling flames leaped high, throwing a dark, orange glow through the woods. They ate the Indians' provisions gladly, bear's grease, and maple sugar from deer-head bags made by the squaws—their coarse, sweet corn pone. They devoured the small deer the Indian boys had skinned for them, and there was plenty of salt for that meat. They laughed in their beards, and boasted. Supper over, they sat about the clear fires and dried the scalps against the heat after they had spread them out on small willow hoops. There were thirty-eight scalps in all.

It was Nat Murray who insisted that there should be thirty-nine. Twelve warriors had fled downstream, and eight upriver. They were all accounted for by the militia. According to Murray's arithmetic, he and Salathiel and the two McClanahans had accounted for nineteen about the Salt Kettles, and they were now one short. Murray argued vehemently about this. He finally narrowed it down by elimination to the squaw he had shot by the thicket, and neglected to scalp.

"But I thought you lingered behind to do that, Sal," he said reproachfully.

To placate him, Albine acknowledged that he had not taken the woman's scalp.

Murray was angry. He seemed to feel he had been cheated. Finally, nothing would do but crossing the river again to make the work complete. Seeing that he was bound to go, alone if necessary, Salathiel agreed to go with him. He had grown to like Murray, and he wanted to keep his respect. Nothing else would have made him cross the river again.

All was quiet at the Salt Kettles. The last embers of the fires were dying out by the empty huts. Murray and Albine went carefully, but they went swiftly. It was a matter of only a few minutes before they found the little thicket again. It loomed up plainly in the starlight in the middle of the flood meadows. Neither of them could be mistaken about the place. But the body of the squaw Murray had shot was gone. They searched diligently for a while, but finally gave it up.

"Maybe we overlooked some on 'em," said Murray.

"Maybe we did," replied Salathiel, who was sure of it. He remembered he had forgotten to search through the thicket that afternoon.

And now the body of the child was gone, too.

But he said nothing about that to Murray. That was his own business, he reckoned. And he reckoned right. Even the beads had disappeared. He felt for them carefully in the grass. His fingers found where the child had lain. The beads were gone.

It was dark. Only the stars winked blindly. But for an instant he saw those beads flashing in the child's hands in bright sunlight.

He drew his sleeve across his confused eyes—and they went back over the river again.

"Reckon I was wrong," said Murray when they stood

by the fires again. But he looked at Salathiel reproach-fully.

They said nothing to Captain Jack, for neither of them wished to spoil for the old hunter a tale of death that, in his mind, was a perfect and complete affair.

Everyone always spoke of it that way. It was called "Death at the Salt Kettles".

16

Old Bonds Loosen

THAT TREMENDOUS DEEDS, that even ferocious crimes can be perpetrated, while no voice from heaven nor the lightning falls is always a surprise to the inexperienced and the young in evil. The legend of divine justice immediate and fell is too salutary and too consistent a piece of moral lore to be lightly discarded. Only a dim reflection of the harder truth, it is constantly being cherished into brightness; polished up. In even the simplest minds is lodged some memory of it. The indifference of nature to the best and worst deeds of men remains, therefore, a perpetual surprise to both reckless and violent doers. They do wrong, they wait—and nothing happens. They still seem to be one with the innocent. Relieved at their supposed immunity, they rejoice. Finally they become elated and boastful, dangerous even to themselves. They take credit for having exposed heaven's justice as a moral hoax, as a tale meant only for children.

Yet their escape is only an apparent one.

It is the long, retributory processes of earthly reality that are cunningly hidden from them. They become visible only in their final completeness, in the slow vengeance of cause and effect. Atonement, then, is only the mad medicine of romance. Some palsy, for example, overtakes the nerves and wills of strong men; the desert slowly lays red fingers upon chains of erstwhile verdant hills. Life gradually lessens. Men and the land they live in sicken together. The small, remote causes are long forgotten; lie forever hidden in a chain of events too complicated to be catechized.

Wait! wait! Wrongdoing is a deep, creeping, secret canker; not a surface boil to be easily seen and lanced. This the prophets have always said, and have been stoned for their trouble. It is the poets who have put the immediate lightning in the hands of just and angry gods. Silliness and the desert befall instead. The shadow advances by degrees. It creeps, it never leaps.

Each individual, every generation seems to escape it, until the last one. Catastrophe is a sleeping sickness from which few awaken. Perhaps, it is too long a process for a being of only some seventy winters at most to be truly apprehensive about. Responsibility to a millennium lacks piquancy, is individually faint. Maybe the poets are right; lightning were better. Law at least tries to abet the poets. Men escape actually only from their own fiction of justice, but their personal relief is none the less great. They seem to have circumvented punishment, and they rejoice greatly. And this is true of small deeds as well as great ones.

Certainly it was true of the seven grim individuals

who were returning across the mountains to the village of Bedford, in the spring of 1764. For even as they advanced through the forest their grimness seemed to drop away from them. They were in another, gayer mood. They might have agreed together to cancel care. They suffered from no doubts or compunctions. The scene of death at the Salt Kettles lay behind them; respect and appproval loomed before. They were happy to have proved themselves by so notable a slaughter. The scalps they were bringing back would be both profitable and acceptable. Their enemies had been warned and weakened. Vengeance had been full fed. So they felt appeased, relieved and satisfied, instead of guilty. They, themselves, were unscathed, and the rising tide of young summer seemed to bear them triumphantly on the crest of its green flood as it swept northward through the valleys and spilled over the mountaintops. Nature herself appeared thus to absolve and even to applaud them. For it was literally a laurel-decked, homeward path they trod. Mountain laurel, and rhododendron.

Captain Jack and his rangers did not return with the others to Ligonier. He had sent the militia back to the post with thanks and much praise to Lieutenant Blane, who, on his part, promptly seized the occasion for pouring encomiums on Captain Jack, and incidentally himself, in glowing official dispatches.

Colonel Bouquet at Fort Pitt was delighted. He sped the victorious news of the Salt Kettles to the troops still at Bedford, hoping it would also inspirit the new levies assembling at Carlisle. Ecuyer on his sick-bed at Pendergasses' was cheered by the glad tidings and the approval of his revered colonel. For a month all raids had ceased. Despondent settlers waiting at Bedford to return to their burnt cabins, and begin life over again, found hope renewed as the much magnified rumour of the affair at the Salt Kettles spread around and about. Before Captain Jack returned to Bedford it was being talked of even in Philadelphia as a good omen, as the fortunate prelude for Bouquet's Ohio campaign. Captain Jack was a hero, his men paragons. They were blessed and called wonderful. Meanwhile, where were they?

Meanwhile they were lingering in the Garden of Eden, enjoying their chosen reward. It was hunting, always the preoccupation of heroes, the prime anodyne of care.

They "lost" themselves in that glorious tangle of streams, hills, and mountains, where the western ranges and the Tuscaroras tumble up into the north between the Allegheny and the Susquehanna. Working slowly eastward, they followed the game traces and dim, seldom used Indian trails, as the chase led them through a region then little noted, deserted, and all but untrod. It was still matchless, virgin country forested with gloomy Titans, laced with patches of sunny mountain meadows, bled by a thousand silver runlets and rushing, roaring streams.

The deer rutted, and the moose called by swampy ponds. Small herds of the eastern buffalo still lingered among the remoter peaks and high, secret pastures. Deer amazingly swarmed. Their cast antlers whitened many thickets. The grey wolf sang by moonlight of the shadowed melancholy of his savage soul. Partridges drummed and boomed on hollow logs. Waterfalls whispered the days and seasons away. The beaver smacked flat the mud of his swampy dam, and barked.

Salmon leaped from pool to rapid, climbing by flowing water stairs high into the mountains. Trout swirled and flashed. In dark pools sunfish slowly fluttered, while food swept into their mouths. From high cliffs of vantage eagles saw the rising sun and yelped. Bears slouched sullenly about their rooty business. Long lines of elk filed gravely and sedately up the valley trails.

Here, too, the wood pigeon nested in crushing multitudes, his broken and sepulchral roosting trees limed bonelike by the droppings of innumerable generations, white islands in a sea of green. It was "God's Wilderness", so called by Captain Jack; so claimed to be and defended by the Iroquois, who seldom came there, but whose dreaded shadow guarded it. Difficult and dangerous to red and white hunters alike, it was wild perfection waiting to be ruined by improvement. "Never a plow had turned not any sod."

And it was here they lingered and revelled in lonely fullness all through the end of May and well into June.

Captain Jack was one of the few people who then knew his way thoroughly through this tangled maze of hills and upland streams. He had sometimes taken refuge here from Indian pursuers in the past. He had searched out the headwaters and capital springs of both the east- and west-running rivers, unmapped fountains lost in the unvisited fastnesses of lofty hills. The mountains did not march here in regular parallel ridges with broad valleys between, as they did farther south. Instead, there were horseshoe-shaped enclosures; "coves"; deep dales with a complete ring of mountains about them, where only one stream had broken through.

In such "holes" there was hunting beyond the dreams of old Nimrod himself. The thriving and undisturbed state of the beaver towns, whose dams turned miles of stream bottoms into swamps, was most eloquent of the lack of human trespass. For this animal was remorselessly shot and trapped at all seasons, by white and red man alike, to make London hats. But there were no trails here for trappers to follow as yet; not a sign of the small white bones that marked their skinning-lodges.

"We're poachin' on the presarves of the Long House," drawled Captain Jack, "and it's contrary to the king's proclamations, Gawd bless'm! But only the Lard will know. We'll leave no sign of ever bein' here. We'll vanish our way through."

It was not beaver they were after, however. They had no unseasonable profit or spoil of furs in view on this long journey homeward through the Garden of God. It was to be a sheer and complete escape from care. It became almost a boyish revel in plenty without work. In the face of utter solitude they gave themselves to the complete enjoyment of the body without thought. Without memory of the past or apprehension of the future, each day was in itself a complete and satisfactory now.

This was the kind of life which some men were to keep moving westward and westward in order to find over and over again, until the Pacific beaches bared their teeth in foam and the hope escaped them. And there was not a man in all the seven of Captain Jack's band who was not conscious of his luck of living in a faultless springtime; of joy in the effortless bounty of an existence without regrets and forebodings; of wonder at the overflowing, exalted magnificence of the hills.

They spoke not at all about it at the time. It was there. Their words were not needed nor expected. They would have been inadequate. But they dreamed and thought about it all the rest of their lives. They forever remembered themselves and each other in that wilderness as peerless friends, blameless in a land of wild fruits and venison, heroically at ease. Such were their memories later on when, as old men, they looked into the glowing embers of safe household fires. Even their grandsons believed it when they spoke of it then. They listened, and they, too, never entirely forgot. It was such a beautiful story—and it was true.

North of the Conemaugh it seemed as though no one had ever been there before them. The empty forest stretched park-like and endless, where there had been no underbrush for centuries. The rooted columns of its aisles and porches rose sheer and tremendous through the green, sun-streaked twilight, to a distant leafy ceiling. It was cool there always, and there was little game except black squrirels. There were few fallen trees. Only the crowns of these forest sovereigns were doffed to winter. They themselves appeared to have achieved immortality. They scarcely bowed to storms, and only lightning or whirlwinds could finally bring them down. Even in their "cemeteries", where the tornadoes had struck, they still stood upright, their bleached skeletons erect in death. But there were not many such places among those sheltered hills.

For the most part the forest floor rolled untrammelled for miles, soft under the whispering tread of their moccasins; brown leaves going down into black loam, with deep moss covering the stony places. Here were the silent sanctuaries of the land, haunted by some native spirit whose presence lonely men like Captain Jack felt and secretly owned, calling "him" by the name of the God of the Old Testament, or by no name at all, a vague, ever-present Manitou to the Indian, something all-powerful, mysterious, and of the shade. But it was not all shade.

Now and then there were successions of open, sunny glades where the light smiled, the rain pools glistened, and the grass grew waist high. It was between these grassy amphitheatres in the forest that the game trails led onward in every direction and eventually nowhere. And it was here in the reflected warmth of these sunny glades that early swarming myriads of locusts gathered in the trees about their edges to sing stridently. It was a year of that strange, gauzy-winged being whose cycle is seventeen summers.

Through these glades, forests, and mountain thickets, through the pond-dotted natural meadows, and along the bottoms of beaver-dammed streams, the seven Mountain Foxes moved circumspectly but choicely, selecting only what they called the "fancy places" to tarry and camp in. They made smokeless punkwood fires by springs of the coldest and clearest water in favoured spots. They slept under bowers of branches to keep off the night-gathering damps. They chose some small, perfect valley and loafed. They lived delicately, taking exactly what they wanted and no more. This restraint was due alone to the art of Captain Jack, who had long ago learned from his enemies to refrain from useless animal slaughter. They had only to stretch out their hands, and their legs a little, to find and take. So they were nice and particular.

They ate the choicest parts of young deer, the tender cheeks and belly steaks of salmon, the white flaky sides of fat trout. They feasted on the succulent paws of young bears. They had salt and a little maple sugar for flavouring, and they carried tobacco and corn meal in their packs. Smoke was a part of every feast, deep drawn and "tasted" by the tongue and nose alike. Tobacco flavoured the breath of life as salt did their food. Nat Murray liked a bit of gunpowder on his beaver meat or roasted duck, but Nat was peculiar in this. The rest were content with nothing to garnish the feast, or with "yarbs". And there were herbs for the mere finding: spearmint and sheepsower, strong cresses by cold springs, fiery wild horseradish, sassafras, wintergreen, and wild thyme.

In the stony brier patches on the southern slopes of hills some blue- and blackberries were already ripe. And there were patches of wild strawberries in grassy spots. They ranged from valley to peak, gathering and killing what they most liked. There were birds innumerable to choose from; fat wood pigeons and tender doves. There were ducks and wild turkeys. And in one place they found a great flock of wild swans resting, swimming about on a huge, shallow pond amid the island tops of beaver houses. Small birds they scorned. But they robbed the squirrel hoards of last year's hidden store and took their fat owners in the thickets or shot them from high branches. Their pots ran over. Their rifles and powder horns comforted them. They took fish by still waters, and wandering sought their meat from God.

They swam, slept, ate when they were hungry, enjoyed the warmth of sun-struck places, sat in the shade, groomed themselves with fine-toothed combs whittled out of hardwood. They discussed in drawling talk the advantages of the country, pointed out the best sites for thriving farms, wrapped themselves in their blankets nightly and went to sleep under a sailing moon.

It was clear, warm, fragrant, and enormously solitary. But it was never entirely silent. By day the voices of innumerable life; birds, beasts, and insects could be heard any time they cared to hearken. At night there were owls, whippoorwills, and many panthers. There was the sudden whirr of the rattlesnake always to be watched for. But he was the greatest of their troubles now, and not so great a one. Here were no Indians. Wildcats

338

might scream indignantly, the lynx squall; skunks were much more to be considered. For they had seven rifles and complete confidence in one another. Life was easy under the summer trees and the mild stars of heaven. They were masters of all they desired. They went where they listed—and the sun rode high.

For Salathiel this was living on as satisfactory terms as he could then imagine. Like all the others, he literally forgot everything but the day and hour at hand. Tired from the chase or by some solitary adventure with Mat Pendergass or Nat Murray, he slept dreamlessly. He even ceased thinking about Phoebe or longing for her at night. In fact, he forgot her and everyone else he had ever known, save his companions in those woods. No one else, white or red, male or female, seemed to have existed. It was full-time, no-time, now.

Even Captain Jack was now able to forget the past, and he was not anxious to think of the future. Indeed, he kept putting it off. He had lingered in this wilderness for some weeks, tasting for the while complete peace in the forest where he was most at home, deferring the hour of return when he knew things would go his way no more, when his work would be over and his leadership laid by. Only the gradual waning of ammunition forced him to move, as though he measured space and time by bullets expended. He edged slowly and reluctantly in the direction of Bedford. But at last he admitted that their powder was getting dangerously low. Only a few grains of it still rustled in the bottom of his own horn when he shook it.

And so one morning quite suddenly, by common impulse rather than by command, they started definitely homeward over faint, mountain game trails, guided by landmarks that only Captain Jack knew. They crossed high, wind-swept ridges where the rhododendrons still flowered in the tardy spring near the frosty summits. They plunged downward at last into the dense thickets of a valley forest, followed a deer path along an ever-widening stream, and came out of the green gloom of the trees one early July afternoon on the wide, middle reaches of the shallow Juniata.

Instantly it seemed to them they had escaped out of the wilderness, so sudden was the change. The quiet talk of the wide river, flowing strong, but sedately past innumerable boulder-stones, seemed domestic and familiar after the wild, headlong rush of shouting mountain streams. And accident contrived to confirm their impressions of nearing home.

The road to Bedford skirted the opposite bank, and along it, even as they watched, white wagontops came gliding through the trees. Sunlight flashed on the weapons of the escort, the muffled yoke bells of a convoy dimly chimed.

"By God," chimed Mat Pendergass, unable to control his emotions at such a cheerful sight of so much company again—"by God, you can't get them fellers to still their bells, not for no orders! God bless'm! Stottelmyer!" he bellowed. "Ho there, Stott!"—until the echoes along the river yelled and stuttered back again.

"Ho—ho—Stot—Stot—myer."

The startled and flustered convoy came to an instant halt. Men came tumbling out of the wagons with guns in their hands. It was some moments, and only after considerable parley and much shouting back and forth over the river, before the bearded wanderers made themselves known and certain of a friendly welcome.

But what a welcome it was, as they crossed above a rapid, leaping from one giant stone to another and

340

climbing up the opposite bank! The wagoners came swarming down to meet them and carried Captain Jack up out of the water on the shoulders of the crowd. None of them had any idea that the news of their exploits had preceded them. But it was soon quite evident from the hail of handshakes and backslapping that left their shoulders and paws sore. Even the young English lieutenant in charge of the escort actually came to congratulate Captain Jack, much to the latter's embarrassment. Indeed, they were all shy at first and could find little to say. The crowd seemed enormous. They had forgotten that there could be so many people. But a jug put an end to their embarrassment. The white whiskey burned them—and they talked. They talked with relief and like a house afire.

Mat Pendergass had been right. It was Stottelmyer. He and his stout wagoners were in charge of the convoy: ten wagons, and thirty pack horses; twenty beeves for the fort.

"Do ye think I wouldn't know that yoke chime any place I heard it, when me and Mark made it!" Mat kept exclaiming. "It's sweet as silver bells!"

Someone produced a fiddle in the fourth wagon, and to the sound of its gay rasping and the cheerful *bur-r* of a jew's-harp the convoy resumed the march and plodded on up the valley of the Juniata towards Fort Bedford.

They camped that night at the water gap. The fires leaped high and the jugs passed around. Only Captain Jack, who would drink nothing, sat taciturn and moody again. In this wild scene in the river gorge, even in the unexpected triumph of his return after his most notable campaign, he felt a sense of ending. Forbes Road would be opened now. It would never be closed again. Prophetically he felt that not only his lifework but the reign of savage terror east of the mountains was past.

Someone was playing a bugle, a fiddle scraped, the flames wavered, and the men sang. Even the outlying sentries of the escort sat in pairs and smoked comfortably. Their path westward was open and beckoning them on. They could lay plans now for homes in the new lands, after the war. It was only Captain Jack who was thinking of the past. The mind of everybody else in the convoy was content with the present or ranged the future. Salathiel was thinking that night as he went to bed in Stottelmyer's wagon of the cities he had not seen that lay eastward, of the great world by the salt sea. He was still bent on going there. He had not forgotten. He would talk with Phoebe about it—tomorrow.

Even a watched pot can boil over suddenly, while the cooks cry out at the disaster to their cooking. It seemed to Salathiel when he returned to Bedford that life would go on very much the same as it had the winter before. He had certain vague plans about how he was going to make it go. But nothing went as he had expected. His pot boiled over. There was even a faint sound of hissing in the hot ashes. Much that had been nicely simmering by the fire at Pendergasses' all the winter before was suddenly spoiled.

Young Albine was aware of a perverse direction of events almost as soon as he had swung off the wagon when the convoy came in and the thundering greeting of the crowd, which quickly assembled in the hearth room at Pendergasses', was over. The welcome home, heaven knows, had been hearty and genuine enough. But despite a deal of backslapping, handshaking, treating, and even rough but well-meant flattery, it was impersonal. It was simply part of the general welcome and approval which the village and the garrison wished to show to all of Captain Jack's Mountain Foxes, Fightin' Quakers—or how-do-ye-call-ems? It was one thing to be a bit of a hero, and respected accordingly, and another to find old friends, especially the only friends he had, curiously changed, and changed they undoubtedly were.

"How be ye, young feller? You've done well, too, I hear," said old Garrett, as though performing a duty. Somehow Salathiel failed to meet his eye. How he envied the greeting Garrett gave to Murray, as though Nat had been one of his own sons. Salathiel felt that when he had left for the cabin that night back in March he had almost become one of Garrett's family. What had happened while he had been away—and where was Phoebe? She had not come to meet him. Why not? Where was she? Could it be that McArdle had talked with her, or with Garrett? Probably.

He sat at the big table after the crowd had left, almost paralysed by the thought. How he wished now that he had faced the music before he left. But as he thought of Phoebe, her image banished everything else from his mind.

Phoebe! Phoebe!

It seemed impossible that even under the strong drug of war and the spell of the deep forest he had ever forgotten her, even for a moment. The months of hard living and danger, all the days and nights of hardship and absence, all his young, iron strength and longing for his golden-haired angel now flowed back upon him in an intolerable fire and tumult of longing to see her, to take her in his arms again and say he had come back.

Phoebe! Phoebe!

Every familiar angle of the house, every well-remembered scene about the river yard and spinning room

343

spoke of her. There was the place in the hall at the head of the stairs where they had said good-bye. He knew now that it was because of her that Pendergasses' had become like home to him. For that reason he had come to love the very curves of the hills about the village of Bedford. He knew he must find Phoebe now or suffocate. He must find her and live with her or something in him would die.

And all this tumult and dire necessity of emotion was a confounded surprise to him. Until now, until faced with not finding her, he had not really understood how hopelessly he was in love with Phoebe Davison. It had been a shy dream last winter, something too delicate to examine carefully and plan about practically. Somehow, somehow, their love would come out all right. Somehow he would get over or around that ugly difficulty about Jane; the threat that McArdle's coming to Bedford implied. He would explain how the marriage had happened. He would tell Phoebe now. She would understand. He would appeal to Garrett. He would run off with Phoebe if he had to! Of course she would come with him. He had to have her. He understood that now.

His return, the sudden entry into the hearth room, where he had first seen her, brought it all back to him intolerably, insistently, overwhelmingly. He know now that nothing else mattered. And yet, how *was* it to be accomplished? How? A premonition of unbearable tragedy turned him cold, then left him hot and restless. And this crisis seemed to have been forced suddenly and violently upon him by the very fact and simple act of his return.

After the welcoming crowd had come and gone, he still sat at the big table in the hearth room, pondering. He had gradually been left alone. Even the two McClana-

344

hans had relatives in town. Yates was away on a survey of the southern boundary eastward with Mr. Lukens, he had been told. Too bad! He needed Yates now. Over at the women's house next door he could hear the voices of all the Pendergass boys and Nat Murray, who had returned to their families, with the sound of laughter, excited talk, and the voices of happy children.

He listened.

The voice he hoped most to hear was not there.

Surely she would have come to look for him. She might at least have done that. He looked around the empty room. No, she was *not* here. And so great was his longng for her that for a dizzy instant he thought he saw her standing on the hearthstone just as he had seen her that memorable night when he had first entered the room.

It was a genuine hallucination, not a mere figment of saying to himself that he saw her. It was the kind of vision which men who had lived lonely lives in the forest sometimes saw. She stood there, alive. The vision of her that was in him had come out. It now stood on the hearth where she had once been. It was the vision which she had awakened in him. It was the dream which unwittingly he loved more than Phoebe herself. His sheer intensity of emotion projected it into the room. It was his young, new, and clear love. And she was maddeningly beautiful. Thus he saw her as he had once seen her for the first time. And once again he heard the voice of old Mrs. Pendergass saying, "You boys from the forest, you be like zailors home from the zea."

And then all this was dissolved into a mist in his eyes and a buzzing in his ears, and he saw only his huge, helpless hands gripping the hard oak table before him till his knuckles turned white. That table! Why, he had killed men with it!

He rose now, seizing it; actually shifting it from its ponderous base. He wished to rush with it, racing and crashing down the room again. His emotion and perplexity culminated thus in a sudden access of anger and blind action. But the table was really too heavy to be moved even by a young giant in a passion. It was like events. Its sheer weight and resistance brought him to himself again. He sat down and remained quiet for a while, breathing heavily, but looking affairs in the face.

Well, he would go next door and find out what *had* become of Phoebe.

He walked quietly enough down the passageway and out into the yard. All the Pendergasses were upstairs in the women's house. He could hear that Captain Jack and Garrett were there, too—in old Mrs. Pendergass's room, no doubt. Captain Jack was drawing away, and now and then old Garrett and the others laughed. There was plenty to tell, he thought. The others would be listening avidly, all of them crowding to the door. Outside there was only the lonely music of the river. In the yard, basking in the hot, June sunlight the chickens made dust nests and crooned with satisfaction. He saw that he had been forgotten. Probably they had not meant to leave him out. They had simply overlooked him. He would go up and brave them anyway. He would see.

He started towards the door, but just as he entered he met Charles Pendergass coming out. Salathiel looked at him, startled, for there was a great red weal across his throat, and he looked like the ghost of the man of the winter before.

"Why, Charley!" he said, and held out his hand. "I'm terrible glad to see ye."

Charles took his proffered hand slowly and looked at him as though he scarcely seemed to be there.

"Oh, yes," he said at last. "Oh, I know you! It's young Albine. I'm kind of forgetful sometimes these days." He pressed Salathiel's fingers spasmodically, and dropped them. They continued to stand looking at each other.

Salathiel felt ashamed of himself. He had had no idea that Charles had suffered so much. He, too, looked forgotten. He stifled the eager question that was on his lips to ask another. "And how's Mrs. Pendergass?" he asked. "Your wife, I mean," he added doubtfully and awkwardly.

Charley stood for a moment on the upper step, looking out over Salathiel's head. Apparently he saw something across the river.

"Why, she ain't doin' so well," he answered at last in a faraway voice. Unconsciously, he put his hand to the scar on his throat. "No, she really ain't doin' so well," he repeated slowly, so that his words fell like weights, one after the other. "They've got her chained up over there in old Pina's cabin. Ye ain't heard her screech, hev ye?"

"No," said Salathiel, "no, I haven't."

"That's good. I thought I did just now," said Charley. "That's why I come downstairs." He continued to stand on the step, feeling his throat helplessly.

"I'm downright sorry, Charley. 'Deed I am!" said Salathiel. "I did hear of your trouble, and I'm sorry. I'm really sorry," he kept repeating.

"I know ye be," said Charley, after a while. "I—I—hank you for it." He extended his hand again. Salathiel ook it, and he also took the opportunity to ask his own question.

"Where's Phoebe, Charley?" he asked breathlessly.

347

He had to wait a moment for the reply. Charles Pendergass looked at him thoughtfully and seemed to be considering his answer.

"Who? You mean little Phoebe Davison?"

Salathiel nodded emphatically.

"She's gone away," said Charles. "She went out to Pittsburgh to visit sister Sue."

Salathiel still stood there.

"No use askin' for her," Charles added. "Maybe you'd better not." He pressed Salathiel's fingers again before finally dropping his hand.

"I see," said Salathiel. "I guess I understand."

Charles Pendergass again nodded solemnly. "Gone away. You can't never be sure about women," he said. A look of mutual sympathy passed between them. The moment became painfully poignant. The plaintive voice of the river swept through both their minds, saying the same thing.

At that instant someone threw open a window in the inn building behind them and called out, "Albine! Salathiel Albine, come up here!" The tones of the voice were enormously familiar. Salathiel turned and looked at the upstairs window near the corner of the inn. Out of it protruded the well-remembered red face and half the sturdy body of the Reverend James McArdle, the mentor of his forest days. The wheel of time seemed to slip a cog backward, hesitate, and then go on again—now—with the voice. "Come up here, my boy. I want to see you, and so does Captain Ecuyer." Mr. McArdle appeared to gesture impatiently as he shut the window.

Salathiel turned away from Charley, and with a feeling of impending disaster tightening across his chest walked back into the inn and mounted the stairs to Ecuyer's room.

He had to pass his own chamber and Yates's at the end of the hall. He glanced into the two familiar rooms as he went by. They were empty, just as they had been when he had left to go on the raid. Both Yates and himself seemed to be away. He wondered if he had really come back. He braced himself for what was to come, and knocked at Ecuyer's door.

"Come in, sir," said the still firm voice of the captain, but in the flat tones of a sick man.

Salahtiel pulled the latchstring and walked in.

Mrs. McArdle rose from a chair where he had been sitting by Ecuyer's bedside and came over to meet him. He put both his hands on Salathiel's shoulders and said, "God bless you, my boy. I've never ceased to pray for you. Thank the Lord I find you here, and safe!"

McArdle's warmth was so real and his pleasure at seeing his pupil again so obviously genuine that, despite himself, Salathiel could not help but respond. The minister might be the cause of his undoing with Phoebe, but he had also "saved him alive" from savagery. The memory of many hours in the forest and Indian lodges, of all they had been through together, came back to Salathiel powerfully on seeing again the friend of his boyhood years. And so it was with great, although not without mixed, emotion that he took him again by the hand.

Possibly it was some awkwardness or hesitation that Ecuyer observed in Albine, or perhaps it was the sheer grotesqueness of the appearance of the two together, which now caused the captain to conceal a smile with a cough, and the cough with his hand. Albine was still dressed in the full panoply of a ranger, and McArdle, who also was no dwarf, in an old plum-coloured suit he had had conferred upon him somewhere, plus a clerical stock he had more recently borrowed from the

349

Reverend Mr. Puffin, the Church of England chaplain at the fort. At any rate, Ecuyer was both edified and amused.

"What a reunion it is!" he exclaimed from the bed. "You haven't grown any smaller, Albine," he said as Salathiel came over to greet him, "but you see I have. I'm withering." His thin fingers felt sensitively feeble in Salathiel's fist, and they suggested bones. "You can have no idea how a man entirely out of it like myself envies your strength."

Salathiel, of course, blurted out that he was sure the captain would soon be getting better. Ecuyer looked at him with eyes that now seemed to occupy most of his face, smiled, and made a quiet, little negative motion with his head.

"Hardly," he said.

There was an instant's silence.

"But let us not talk about *that* any more," the captain added, looking somewhat apprehensively at Mr. McArdle. "Now that you have come back, Albine, perhaps you will look after my body again for a while. Mr. McArdle has been devoting himself to saving my soul. Between you I might pass out successfully." He laughed with a sudden surprising gaiety. All his energy now seemed to be in his head. His eyes twinkled with mischief.

"But sit down, gentlemen, sit down!" he insisted, seeing their embarrassment. "Let us hear what Albine has to say. I hear he has been abroad in the wicked world. What news from the devil's kingdom, my lad? I've been hearing a great deal about heaven lately." He motioned Salathiel to take the chair beside his bed.

Now, there was only one chair in the room, and one very small stool. Albine was quick to take the captain's hint and sit down in the chair, removing an open Bible from it, and laying the still open book carefully on the captain's bed beside him. McArdle did not take any too kindly to the stool. It was quite a low one.

"Possibly there is another chair in the next room," said the captain.

"No, no," said McArdle. "I'll leave you now, sir. I know you will be desirous of talking with Salathiel. I hope he'll consent to what you want. 'Tis a Christian service ye might well do, even for an infidel, Albine," he said, and then turned to the captain.

"Oh, sir, do you now ponder well on what I have laid before you. The way is plain. The only way. I have left it open for you there at the fifth chapter of St. John."

"I'll consider it, McArdle. Indeed, I will," said the captain. "I'll ponder it carefully. But suppose you ask Mr. Puffin not to come until the day after tomorrow. I'll need a little time to think over *your* exposition of the matter."

Mr. McArdle nodded. He took this as a compliment to his own powers of persuasion, which deserved ample consideration.

"I'll tell Mr. Puffin," he said. "But remember, your time is short."

Ecuyer grimaced slightly as the minister went out. McArdle turned suddenly at the door and said, "Come up to the fort and talk with me as soon as you can, Salathiel. I've got something that nearly consarns you to relate. Maybe you'll know what I'm driving at. But good news," he added encouragingly, "on the whole, *good* news." He smiled, and closed the door as he went out.

It was Salathiel's turn to look disgusted. He struck the arm of his chair impatiently.

The captain laughed wryly.

"What's the matter?" he asked. "Is he fishing for your soul, too?"

"I'll tell you what's the matter!" Salathiel burst out— "that is, if you're not too ill to hear me, captain. I've got to tell somebody."

"For the last two weeks," replied Ecuyer, "a blessed numbness has come to my relief. I am cold from the waist down, but I no longer feel pain." He put his hands behind his head, leaned back on the pillow, and stared out the window a minute. "No, once more I can be interested in the difficulties of other people. The trouble with pain is that it makes you think only of yourself. I've been *beside myself*, as they say in English. And there is nothing quite so boring as that. It will be better to die than to go on that way. So I really would like to hear what you have to say."

"Before I came to you at Fort Pitt," began Salathiel, searching out his words slowly, "I was married to a girl named Jane Sligo. Mr. McArdle married us on an island down the Ohio one fine day to save woman-talk. We were running away from some Shawanee lodges on the Beaver, him and me, carrying along with us some captivated women and children to try to slip them through the Injuns into the fort. But we soon found we couldn't. So McArdle hid with the women and children at Nymwha's camp near the sawmill, while I got into the fort myself with Sergeant Jobson. The other soldier with us was scalped. We barely made it. You may not remember all of this. It was just before I came to serve you at the beginning of the siege."

"But I do remember," said Ecuyer. "And I also recollect that you thought me unfeeling not to send across the river for the captives immediately—and thus ensure their massacre with the probable loss of the rescuing party as well. Also, you wouldn't be satisfied until I let you go over alone to try to fetch your wife. I couldn't refuse you that. But you came back without her, and minus an ear, too. Well, where is your wife?"

"I don't know," said Salathiel, with an obstinate look.

"But the Reverend James McArdle evidently does," said the captain.

"Has he said so here?" demanded Salathiel uncomfortably.

"Of course," replied the captain. "He has been asking for you, and telling your good news. Your wife, it seems, escaped back to the inhabitants, and so did all the others. McArdle himself took them through the woods to Redstone Old Fort, while we were being besieged. It was quite admirable of him, I think."

"Oh, McArdle, McArdle, what a man he is!" exclaimed Salathiel, beside himself with exasperation.

Ecuyer leaned back on his pillows again for a while and looked out at the distant mountains. He waited for a minute to let Salathiel cool off before he said, "I know how such things are. I am truly sorry for you. To lose the one we love with all our soul is the worst of misfortunes. It warps our judgment of everything else. Nothing makes up for such a loss. All else that follows is dust or buffoonery, a play without a plot. It is not even much of a tragedy, for no one cares. At Geneva, when I was little, we used to pay a *denier* to look at a shadow play in a magician's tent. The most dreadful things frequently happened amongst the shadows. But they had no faces, so we children always laughed. Well, my little play will soon be over now," he added. "I have had my money's worth, and the magician will soon be asking me to abdicate my stool. The management continues; the actors and spectators change . . ."

Some of this seemed irrelevant to Salathiel. He was not thinking of Jane as the one he loved with his soul. And he was surprised at the feeling with which the captain had spoken. Towards the last he had been gesticulating, while he sat up. Albine had never expected Ecuyer to talk with him like this. All of their past formal relationship had dropped away. Ecuyer seemed nothing now but a sick man talking to a fellow sufferer. And he was even more surprised when the captain concluded with "Yes, I am *truly* sorry for you. I am sorry, because I understand. You see, my life was changed by a minister, too. *She* married *him*."

Salathiel pondered this. He now understood many things about the captain which had seemed strange before.

"And she loved you?" he asked.

"Oh, yes," replied Ecuyer. "But that doesn't prevent things from happening, does it? Your Mademoiselle Phoebe loved you, for example. Why, she as much as told me so when she left this packet with me the night before she married Burent. She was so completely miserable that she talked, and she had a good cry, poor girl —" Here the captain reached under his pillow and took out a small package wrapped in cloth. He held it out to Salathiel, who seemed too dazed to take it . . .

"Oh, you didn't know?" exclaimed Ecuyer. "I thought they'd have told you. I'm desolated to be the first with such news!" He appeared upset at the thought of it.

"Married Burent! Married Burent!" Albine kept repeating, trying to make himself understand the news. He fumbled with the package while his fingers began to undo it automatically.

Once again Ecuyer lay back on his pillows and gazed out the window with a faraway look. "I'm afraid I may have said too much," he muttered. "But someone would have told you before long."

"That little, brown man," Salathiel was saying. "Why, who would ever have thought of him? Burent!"

"But an excellent man," said the captain, "one of the most loyal and honest I have ever known. And he was here, and you were away. And you had said nothing to Phoebe, had you? McArdle's news must have come to her as a terrible shock. Burent had Garrett's permission to ask her. He told me himself he had long had his eye on the girl. I knew nothing of your affair at first, nor did he. I think you should at least have spoken to Garrett Pendergass before you left. He came to me, after he had talked with McArdle, and he was much cut up. He had greatly admired your father, he said. And he had thought of you almost as a son. But Garrett also loved his granddaughter. I would still speak to him," said Ecuyer. "You do owe it to him, and to yourself."

"And Phoebe?" asked Salathiel miserably. He did not tell Ecuyer that he had tried to tell Garrett that night before he left.

"Mistress Burent went west to Fort Pitt about the beginning of May. She had been married only about a week. Yes, it was McArdle who married them. Burent has at last received his commission, thanks to Colonel Bouquet. He will be in charge of completing the fleet of bateaux to take the troops down the Ohio this fall. They have married quarters in the environs of the fort, I hear. They are safe. That is something." He paused a moment and looked at Salathiel significantly. "Do not try to follow them, I beseech you," he said earnestly. "No good can possibly come of that now. It will be best to think of Phoebe as finding happiness with a good man, but . . ."

355

"Lost!" exclaimed Salathiel.

"Yes, lost," whispered the captain.

Salathiel's face worked, despite himself, and like a boy he buried it for a moment in the bedclothes. His forehead rested on McArdle's Bible.

Ecuyer felt an affectionate impulse to place his hand on Albine's head to comfort him—but the remnants of Salathiel's shorn ear showed through his hair. The captain instinctively withdrew his hand. His sympathy must remain understood, or not understood—as the case might be. In any event, he was sorry at having inflicted pain.

"Do not hate me for what I have told you, Albine," he said. "I have my own selfish reasons for asking you that, too. I wish you would come back to me for a few days. I need you. It will not be for very long."

Salathiel got up still grasping Phoebe's little packet. He would have liked to cut off his head, because his face had betrayed him. For a moment he could not answer the captain.

"But you *will* come back?" asked the captain plaintively. He looked up like a sick child. "We're both quite alone now, it seems." His voice trailed away.

"Of course, I'll come back!" exclaimed Albine. "God A'mighty, what did you think! I'll stay to the very end."

"That will be it," said Ecuyer, reaching up and clinging to his hand. "And *to the end* how we all keep thinking about our own precious selves. Now, take your love's bundle and see what's in it. Not hope, I'm afraid. It's only the silver watch I gave you, I imagine. I thought I heard it tick. If so, it passes between us again at a great moment, eh! What? Now go, but come again in the morning, won't you?"

Salathiel promised and slipped off to his own room down the corridor to be alone, and to see what really was in Phoebe's bundle. He closed the door quietly behind him.

Left alone, Ecuyer looked at McArdle's Bible where it still lay open on the bed, at the fifth chapter of St. John. He smiled feebly, for he was tired. He knew that whole Gospel by heart. His grandfather had long ago made him learn it in Latin. He closed the book impatiently.

"Bon Dieu," said he to himself, "why is it these ministers think they can bait a trap for my soul with the stale cheese of everlasting life? What a lure! Sleep, my St. John, sleep is the lure for a tired soldier. Poppyseed!"

He lay watching the sun setting behind the hills, as he had watched it every day now for several weeks. He grew drowsy. But any sunset now might be his last. Dr. Boyd had said so just before he left Bedford for Fort Pitt. Now, there was a man for you, thought the captain. No whining. No prayer dust on his knees. He had a respect for a dying man. Ecuyer wished that Surgeon Boyd could have stayed with him till the end. "He might have kept those heavenly foxhounds off my trail just before I have to go to earth," he muttered. "He had a way with him."

"Merde!" he exclaimed aloud. "How they close in on one at the end, these ministers! How they worry the exhausted quarry! They'd catch the faint steam of my last breath on a mirror to call it a confession of faith . . .

"O Lord," he prayed, "if it be possible, rid me of thy faithful servants, the Reverend James McArdle and Mr. Charles Puffin."

He waited as though for an answer. The room seemed to grow even more silent. Outside the sibilant rush of the river became audible, the twilight deepened.

"Thanks, Holy Comforter," said Ecuyer, grinning into the darkness.

"I know," he whispered to himself at last, "I'll get human help. I'll fight to the end. By God, I'll send for the village schoolmaster!"

He let the Bible slip off the bed to the floor.

The sun had by this time plunged far behind the hills. In the glowing gloom of his lonely room Captain Ecuyer painfully composed himself for sleep as best as he could, even though it might be his last one.

Back in his room, Salathiel found everything just as he had left it over three months before. His small belongings and the few extra clothes he had were waiting for him. Then he became aware that they had all been carefully put away and nicely rearranged. There were also new white curtains tied in with gingham strips, and a box with withered violet plants in the window. Arthur, he knew, had painted that box for Phoebe. The plants were dead, the earth about them dried. He crumbled the dust through his fingers.

So she had come here while he was away. She had kept the room garnished against his return. And then one day she had stopped coming. It must have been weeks ago. He shoved the small, painted box full of dead leaves and black violet blossoms behind the curtain. A gay little coffin.

Doubtless, at Fort Pitt the quarters of Mistress Burent shone—and had living blossoms in them. Yet it still seemed incredible. It actually made all six feet of him feel weak. He sat down on the bed and slowly unwrapped Phoebe's packet. It was carefully done up in an India kerchief he had given her. It pained him now inexpressibly to remember that this kerchief had been his only gift to her. She might have kept it, he thought.

The silver watch Ecuyer had given him, and a carefully folded and sealed letter fell out on the bed. He broke the seal with his thumb and spread out the paper. His strong hands trembled. Traced in the round, clear hand of Phoebe, in her grandfather's best red ink, and written out fair like a school exercise, he read:

To Mister Salathiel Albine
Dearest Sir—

Please find enclosed in these soft Folds the Silver Watch you did send for me to keep for you until the Time might catch up with us again. But what did I hear today! Oh, my Heart is stopped and stilled like a small Bird frozen in his Nest. That I did love you, I confess. But now there will be no Time showed on this Dial for us to pass together. I am going to marry Mister Burent, the Cooper. Now all our children will be the little Brown Man his. Oh Lord, Mr. Albine. I can say no more, I *must* go away. Do not try to find me, Sir. Do not I pray You. And I will always think of You as a true Man if you let me alone, yet try to think of You no more, as do You of me.

Give this Kerchief to your Wife when you do find her, and say nothing to her either. I opine You did not mean to be so close mouthed with me always. For that Reason I do not give You back your Kisses. The Watch I leave with Captain Ecuyer, because your Friend Mr. Yates is gone off Surveying for a while. I was indeed left alone—but now have taken good company for Life, if no more. I would it might

have been better, and bite my Tongue. So farewell—
and no more 'till we do meet as Angels.

Yours once,

Phoebe Davison

Fort Bedford Village, at my Grand'f'ter Pendergass
House. Old May Day, A.D. 1764.

And that was all.

But that was entirely too much for a hardened, scalp-
taking, child-murdering, young woodsman like himself,
who was not at all prepared for what violent feeling
could do to him. It was tremendous medicine. He knew
he had lost his mate—and so the rest would be as Captain
Ecuyer had said. It was a bright, bright moment of
brilliant agony, and he sat there on the bed while the
large muscles in his arms and legs twitched, and the
sweat came out in cold beads on his face.

Finally, he began to struggle to repossess himself, for
it was panic at the assault of what seemed to be an
unknown person within him, one who was violently com-
plaining and twisting under punishment, that brought him
to his feet and started him walking up and down the
short space of the room, until he went hot all over and
then unaccountably weak and cold.

He sat down again, full of shame and astonishment at
what had happened to the big body, which he had always
thought was his. He was scared fairly humble by that.
For a moment he forgot the cause of unease in pure
preoccupation with the effects. That helped. And when
he next glanced at Phoebe's letter he was able to take
it up, fold it without reading it over, and quietly drop
it in his old pouch along with other trinkets of the past.

A certain self-pity, defiance, and anger had now risen
in him. Twilight was falling, and his room, like Ecuyer's,

was fast turning dark. But he didn't mean to be left alone there, no matter what had happened! He guessed at the time, and seizing the silver watch, set it, and wound it with its little key and with a certain bravado. He shook it.

The watch suddenly began to go.

He could feel it in his big hands, ticking away against his pulse—he could feel a long, lonely lifetime beginning to flow steadily forward. And it was then, and only then, that tears came to his relief. His shoulders shook, and leaning forward over his knees, he sobbed like a child . . .

After a while the worst was over, and he belonged to himself again. He then made careful preparations. He put on the best clothes he had, and transformed himself from a Mountain Fox into at least a presentable frontier gentleman. He carefully removed every evidence of the late grimy and bloody business he had been engaged in, from beard to clothes, and prepared himself to go downstairs into the hearth room as much another man as possible.

He intended to look everybody, including old Garrett, full in the face. He would have it out with the old man *now*, and with McArdle too! And he would stick by Ecuyer until the end. After all, Ecuyer was the only person alive he really cared about; loved, you might say, —and he was dying.

He was glad now that Yates was away for the time being. It made things much simpler. Yates would have had a great deal to say, probably. He closed the door to Yates's room, as well as his own, as he went out. Those closed rooms seemed to belong thoroughly to the past. He looked in on Ecuyer quietly before he went downstairs. The captain was asleep, breathing faintly. He closed that door also.

Without faltering, he passed the hall landing where he had said good-bye to Phoebe, and taking the turn on the stairs, found himself in the hearth room again.

There was no feeling that that cheerful room belonged to the past. No, it was very much in the present! Garrett and Captain Jack were having supper at the big table together. He stood for a moment quiet and tense, breathing in the familiar, homely atmosphere of the place.

Besides Garrett and Captain Jack, there was no one else in the room, except sleepy old Pina, who had been serving them. It was a warm summer evening. All the doors and windows stood wide open. Outside he could hear the subdued music of locusts and crickets. Far, shrill voices from the village came floating over the deep undertone of the river. Only a small cooking fire glowed redly in the depths of the chimney. A full moon dreamed on the stream outside.

Nothing could have been more peaceful and seemingly substantial and everlasting than the long, dark, quiet room at this hour of evening hush. And in the midst of it, in a halo of gold candleshine that made a flickering circle on the ceiling, the two grey-haired old men were leaning back smoking their pipes, their dinner dishes pushed to one side. They sat there with an air of completion, with such a friendly understanding and venerable ease that Salathiel envied them from the depths of his homeless heart.

He had never seen Captain Jack looking quite so content. He seemed decidedly older, but his tenseness and grimness, something in the steely set and angle of his jaw had relaxed like a strong trap that has been sprung. At that moment he actually reflected something of Garrett's warm serenity. They were talking quietly over their glowing pipes; smiling unconsciously at each

362

other with candid eyes—and Salathiel would not have disturbed them for the world.

No, he thought—as he paused again for a moment at the door of the back hall, watching them affectionately, such scenes were not for him. He had lost his place at that table of plenty and board of peace, fumbled his welcome there. It would be better if he found lodging in the village now—or wandered back alone into the forest. He could always do that, he remembered. After a while, he could build a cabin in some remote cove of the mountains and live by hunting—after Ecuyer was gone. He turned to go silently before they saw him.

Outside in the wagonyard some moon-fooled cockerel broke into a ridiculous, gargling crowing, followed by a faint clapping of immature wings. It was a positively abortive, untimely, and useless defiance of the universe. Yet there was something comically gallant in the voice of that boy chicken—and both the old men removed their pipes from their lips simultaneously to laugh.

"False dawn, and a young cock dreaming," rumbled Captain Jack.

"Aye, moonlight! Do you remember?" replied old Garrett, looking up with a swift smile of recollection lighting his lips. "Do you remember how it was once? I jealoos I'm prejudiced to young roosters in the moonlight—" and he stopped short, startled by the apparition of Salathiel towering in the shadows by the corridor door.

"Albine! By godson, where in tarnation hev ye been?" Garrett shouted. "I've had young Arthur looking for ye all over town this afternoon—and not hide nor hair. Come over here and sit down! You been mopin'?" He looked at him closely. "All primped up, eh? What fer?"

"Oh, I've been visitin' with the captain," said Salathiel,

trying not to show his vast sense of relief at having been summoned to join them; at being invited back into life again. They must never know how he had doubted that they would take care to speak to him again. "Ecuyer wants me to take care of him again—well, until the end," he explained. "And I've been with him most of the afternoon."

"So you got my poor Phoebe's letter then," said Garrett in a tone so low that it seemed almost an aside.

"Yes, I got it," acknowledged Salathiel, and his eyes twitched.

Garrett saw that and looked away, embarrassed. "I kinda thought ye might be up to somethin' foolish this afternoon, young feller," he said. "I've been worried about yer. Thought ye might have packed up your kit without sayin' nothing or seein' me, or . . ."

"No, no," exclaimed Salathiel. "But I didn't know how you might take it. Mr. Pendergass, I *did* try to tell you that night I left. I was sartin goin' to tell you I was married—and you—well, you stopped me."

"That's what I figured out afterwards," said Garrett. "But not until James McArdle came around clangin' his tongue agin the roof of his mouth like the clapper of a church bell. What a convinced talker he is. He begets trouble—and then he wonders. I'm sure he has no idea what his tongue hath done now. But what could *I* do when you yourself managed so ill, boy? You should have told Phoebe long ago. It was terrible hard on her. I do blame you much for that."

"I meant to tell her. I always meant to, and yet I couldn't bear to for fear of hurtin' her. And I wanted her. I needed her bad." He ended somewhat dismally and desperately.

Garrett nodded. "Now I'm right glad to hear ye come

out flat-footed that way," he said. "My granddaughter, Phoebe Davison, is a lovely gal! I can't blame you. Tell the truth, I'd kinda hoped"—he checked himself suddenly —"well, well, I couldn't bear to tell her myself, and it took my old Rose to face it. She it was told Phoebe. And after that I couldn't forbid Burent. He's a good man, you know."

"Yes, he's a good man," acknowledged Salathiel. He wondered how often he would have to admit that. Next time the words might stick in his throat. He wished Garrett would have done. Captain Jack was all ears.

"Course, the Burent business was a great surprise to me," Garrett rattled on. "I did remember afterwards that he'd been hangin' around. But it was the women finally fixed it, I guess. After Sue's wedding I suppose there just had to be another one. And Phoebe was a proud little soul. She wouldn't let her disappointment disappoint them. And this July she'll be seventeen. Oh, well, it will be all right after her first baby comes, Rose says." But here Garrett paused and shook his head.

"Gal trouble, eh? Gal trouble!" remarked Captain Jack. "I didn't think you were in it quite so deep, Sal. But sooner or later it comes to us all. Now, my advice would be to find that young wife of yours and straightway go to bed with her. That's the cure, and that's what it all comes to in the end."

But Garrett shook his head again.

"Maybe so," he said. "But don't try to tell that to my Rose, Jack. She'd say there was a time when you knew better."

"Maybe I still do," admitted the old hunter. "Maybe I did—once." He shifted uneasily under some too poignant memory. They were all uneasy now, talking so much about women. It was old Piña who came to their rescue by plumping down a great dish of steaming stew before Salathiel.

"Lord! Here we've been talking nothin' but gals, gals to this young wolf, and I'll bet he's nigh belly-starved. Eat your dinner, man! It's a good one," insisted Garrett, easily reverting to his rôle of host out of pure habit.

So Salathiel fell to without further urging, and found that even if he had lost his love he still had his appetite— and that it was *not* so difficult to return to life, after all.

Indeed, afterward he went out and sat on the door stoop overlooking the river, where Garrett and Captain Jack smoked and gossiped, as old men will, tilting their sturdy chairs back against the grateful coolness of the stone wall, while fireflies flashed up and down the valley and two lanthorns hung like fixed stars somewhere above the dark ramparts of the fort.

It was a noble July evening, warm and cool, with light airs drifting through the calm. Out of the placid reaches beyond its upper bend the river poured itself forever past Garrett's door, talking in low, liquid tones of some wild secret of the moonlight. It was a secret too lovely to keep, one which Phoebe, like the ever-flowing river and time, had—and had carried away with her. And for that lost balm of love-in-quietude his heart yearned and grieved, and he listened, letting the sad sound of rushing waters speak for him and carry away into the darkness his melancholy which, although always passing, would also, he knew, always be there. What he could never say for himself, the river that summer night was saying for him in the solitary moonlight. He heard it and listened understandingly. The shape of his thoughts he covered slowly with a pall of blue tobacco smoke that hung like a haze of requiem incense about her deserted door.

Good-bye, Phoebe, vanished Phoebe Davison, farewell . . .

After a while he began to hear another conversation that was going on. He turned to it for homely comfort.

It was Garrett's tongue talking, a tongue that had caught a gift of true garrulity from the passing stream—its magic capacity to keep on retailing in easy bursts of liquid conversation, punctuated by half-stifled ironical laughter, the sprightly news of the neighbourhood along its banks; the differences in the sameness of events in the country it so thoroughly drained. For old Garrett had not lived by the river and with his wife without being much affected by both. It was of news of the neighbourhood, and after the peculiar manner of the river, that he spoke that evening. He ran on.

With a deep undertone of wisdom and wise solemnity, for that matter, if you cared to listen. And it was in that way that Salathiel learned what had been happening at Bedford Village since he had been away:

How the faces and the character of the garrison at the fort continually changed now as reinforcements went forward to Bouquet; what that gallant colonel had said to Captain Ecuyer, when he had come east going to Carlisle; how reluctantly Surgeon Boyd had gone west when his turn came to take charge of the hospital at Fort Pitt. "Where the pest is ragin'," said Garrett. "Poor Boyd had a premonition he will never get back. Oh, well," sighed Garrett, while he knocked out his pipe, "some people do think too much to be happy."

Yates might be expected back at any time—Salathiel was now glad to hear. He and St. Clair were surveying land grants and engaged in some scheme for settlement after the troubles were over. "Even Buckey has took up five hundred acres somewhere in this valley, I hear." St.

367

Clair, it appeared, had got himself appointed a surveyor too, and Yates would go to Philadelphia soon on some legal business connected with the project.

Albine pricked up his ears at that. So Yates was going to Philadelphia! He might want company.

The lodge had grown so that they were holding meetings now out in the hills. "It's not entirely safe yet," admitted Garrett.

"No, but it's summer," laughed Captain Jack.

They spent some time talking over the notable siege that McArdle and Mr. Puffin were conducting for the capture of Captain Ecuyer's soul. "Maybe we ought to come to this relief," drawled Captain Jack.

"He ain't asked for it," replied Garrett. "I think it helps pass the time for him, to tell the truth. Not much time left for him to pass, if Dr. Boyd was right. And he mostly was. Thinnin' out of the blood. Gineral weakness and no hope. A slow passing for a great little man!"

"Aye," growled Captain Jack, "by far the best o' them all!"

They sat silent for a while, thinking of Ecuyer in the room above and listening to the river.

"You can be a help there, Sal," said Garret after a while, poking his thumb at Ecuyer's room. "I'm right glad you've agreed to stay on with him. He misses Phoebe. She was a fine little nurse."

"I'm stayin'!" said Salathiel.

"Will you be goin' after that wife of yours, do you think?" asked Garrett presently.

"I'll think a long while," said Salathiel.

"I know, but I kinda wish you would," persisted Garrett. "Tell the truth, Charley ain't doin' so well since his wife cut his throat acrost. And the other boys are all bound for to settle out. There might be a place for you here if you cared to linger. Years ago I tried to persuade your pa to stay with me. He might have done better by you, ef'n he had. Now you're back, in spite of him and t'Injuns. Kinda looks like fate, doesn't it? Well, I'd like to see your children, too, tumblin' about my door here, even if they bean't Phoebe's. It would make me feel that things begun away back yonder are bound to go on. That's a good feelin'." Garrett coughed a little, and cleared his throat.

Salathiel was so surprised he made no reply.

Only the river continued to prophesy in an unknown tongue.

"Now thar's a proposition for you, young'un," said Captain Jack at last. He knocked out his pipe with an air of finality. He and Garrett rose and went in. Salathiel heard them laughing about something as they went upstairs. He sat on, alone with the river in the moonlight.

All that he could remember presently as he waited, dozing or spellbound, on the cold doorstep, was two voices saying:

"It's not entirely safe yet."

"No, but it's summer . . ."

And what a summer it proved to be.

17

Summer

THE MEANING OF A DREAM—often there is something in it deeper than reason can fathom. Like weather,
it operates through feeling on mood. Even with its
cause unnoticed or forgotten, some mood prevails—and
thus the actions of a man at certain moody seasons of
his life forever afterward puzzle him. Reasonably, they
are inexplicable. The key to them has been lost. Those
old men's voices Salathiel heard talking about summer
in the moonlight, for instance. They plumbed deeper
than he thought. His moonlight had been sadly darkened,
but summer went on.

And into the ripe, hot mood of it he drifted, unsettled
as to the future by the loss of Phoebe, strangely at rest
with his savage past by the killing of the Indian child.

Between those happenings he was left footloose. Old ties had ceased to bind. Familiar scenes irked him.

Temporarily he was listless. Only the uncertain lingering of Ecuyer kept him at Bedford. He ceased now to make plans for himself. While he waited for Ecuyer to die, he seemed ambitionless. It was even a relief to be able to devote himself to the captain. For the time being, there seemed little else to do. He did not care whether he found Jane or not. Somehow or other old Garrett and Captain Jack, talking that night in the moonlight by the river, had stated his case for him. "It's not entirely safe yet." "No, but it's summer." That was it exactly. Nothing was certain, except the season.

It was not that he remembered their words precisely. He soon forgot their smaller meaning. But the mood they had evoked remained with the season that made it. Summer—summer in the mountains poised heavily, hot in the daytime, cool at night, at once fierce and delightful. It lay draped along the high ridges in a flame of eternal green, alive, brooding, and waiting. It seemed to be waiting for some change that must come soon, and some with a vengeance.

For that change, and without knowing it, Salathiel waited, too. It was one of those seasons of quiet crisis in a man's life, when, for reasons which he cannot entirely fathom, he knows he is temporarily stopped. He waits. He no longer tries to foresee or control events. Some depth of wisdom tells him to submit his case to fate. So the time went with Salathiel that summer, and so it was that events temporarily took hold of him.

Let us piece them together and make a chronicle of that summer as nearly as we can. Once more, we cannot be sure of the precise order of events. The journal which Salathiel had been keeping before he left to go raiding

371

with Captain Jack he resumed again when he came back to Bedford in the summer of '64. But he was never much good at keeping a journal. His entries are mere fragments and asides about what went on. Sometimes the briefest of notations does for a day, e.g., "This day Yates returned with Mr. Lukens, the surveyor, and St. Clair"—or, "At lodge meeting in the woods above the springs tonight. Saw Burent there, but durst not speak to him. He returns to Fort Pitt." And later on we find, "News of Jane"—what news, we cannot tell. But piecing it all together it must have been about like this:

The seven in the brotherhood of Mountain Foxes did not hold together very long, it appears. Ecuyer was in fact essential to them. He was the only king's man with whom Captain Jack would deal personally—and everything with Captain Jack was personal. As Ecuyer languished, then, so did the brotherhood and his plans for employing them as rangers. For a brief while they seemed to have been used only part of the time in local scouting or as messengers in the vicinity of the fort. For a week or two Murray and Salathiel kept watch on the road from a post established on the high, sphinx-like front of Lookout Mountain. They had a spyglass and a rough pole for signal flags up there. All that they did was to report the passing to and fro of convoys and armed parties. It was nothing more than alert loafing. At times the Pendergass boys came to receive them. Then even that nominal duty ceased. Captain Jack returned to his cabin at "Echovale" and resumed his lonely life there. Occasionally he returned to Bedford for a talk with Garrett or to be present on the evening of a lodge meeting. Eventually, we find him receiving pay for himself and the "services of his gallant rangers", when Captain Ourry stopped at Bedford on his final trip to Fort Pitt with the main force of the new militia levies for the Ohio campaign.

Meanwhile, besides tending the captain, there could not have been a great deal for Salathiel to do. Indeed, had it not been for Ecuyer's miserable plight he would probably have gone to live at the cabin with Captain Jack. As it was, he lingered on in his room at Pendergasses', alone, and moody enough in that hot July weather.

"A melancholy fit for two days past, and little sleep," he notes about this time in his journal. "The captain worse today, and McArdle pressing me to be going to seek Jane. Heat like the dog days already. I never felt the like, and in these high hills, too. Swum in the pool near the mill at Nogle's half the night. I hear Yates is at Loudon with St. Clair. Sent a note to him by Sid McClanahan. He and Cal both leaving for home. Murray busy coortin' a Welshwoman. Much alone now . . ." etc. Some days later he makes one stark entry without comment: "I need a skwaw." In short, a certain young man seems to have been sorry for himself and is here probably diagnosing one of the symptoms of his case. There can be no doubt, too, that at this time McArdle was the reverse of helpful. Our journalist frequently protests.

Off and on, Salathiel must have seen a good deal of the Reverend James McArdle during that hot summer weather. Undoubtedly he saw him when McArdle came to argue with Ecuyer, which was almost every day. And the diary also notes several long talks with him at the fort.

The Reverend James was living at the fort then with the Reverend Mr. Puffin. Bouquet had found McArdle most helpful in explaining his lists of the numerous white captives, and for his minute knowledge of the western

373

tribes. The colonel had detained him to go with him into the Ohio country as an interpreter. The lists, which Salathiel had saved, were proving invaluable, and McArdle was in official favour. In the interim, while Bouquet was at Carlisle, the two ministers had set aside their minor theological differences to plan a mutual recruiting campaign for the kingdom of God. Between them, they were trying to organize a "woods preaching", for the conversion of the Bedford townspeople and the garrison. The plans for that great preaching fell through at the time, though they held it the next summer at Carlisle. Salathiel, however, got a lick of the tongue now and then by way of a personal sermon from both clerical gentlemen. In their opinion he much needed it. McArdle, in particular, was indignant to find that Salathiel was not enthusiastic about going after Jane. He felt that his own services in rescuing her were not appreciated.

McArdle had in fact worked well and hard to save Jane Sligo and the other women and children the summer of the year before. He made this all quite plain now and in some detail.

After Salathiel had left him, he said, he had waited for nearly two weeks near Nymwha's camp for some word of rescue from Fort Pitt. After that he was afraid to wait any longer. The Indians were closing in all along the river during the worst days of the siege, and at any moment the presence of himself and the women and children with him at Nymnwha's camp might be discovered. Indeed, it was finally due to Nymwha's care and cunning that they were not discovered and massacred immediately. Three days after Salathiel had reached the fort Nymwha had guided them by night southward over the deserted plateau behind Pittsburgh and hidden them in a slate cave. There for some days they had existed most miserably on nothing but parched corn. The woman with the cancerous breast had died and was buried at night. Otherwise they were afraid to show themselves, or even to light a fire.

Nothing further having been heard from either Salathiel or the commandant, Nymwha had at last taken his own horses, and picking the refugees up one evening, had guided them on a long circuit as far south as the Great Meadows, where he left them in McArdle's charge to take them the rest of their way to Redstone Old Fort, on foot. Luckily the country was deserted, and the trace to the Old Fort plain enough. They finally arrived, starving, but safe, about the end of May, and were kindly received by the garrison and the family of one Captain Cresap, a Marylander, who took Jane and the other women and children in.

All of this McArdle insisted was due to the "marcies of Providence" alone. Yet he was inclined to claim a considerable share in the divine credit for having invoked it by the power of prayer. And he was also surprised and even sorrowful that his "favourite pupil", as he now called Albine, seemed to show a lack of moral understanding in not immediately improving the occasion.

For there was no doubt that Salathiel could easily find Jane, the minister insisted. She was probably still with the Cresaps at Redstone, only a few days' journey through the forests from Bedford. There were a number of other refugees and escaped captives at the Old Fort, he said, and even if Jane had gone back to the inhabitants, even if she were in Virginny, Salathiel could still follow her up.

So McArdle kept reiterating. He was inclined to discount the fact that Salathiel had already lost an ear in trying to return to Jane. As he pointed out, he had himself long ago lost both ears just for being persistent. What was one ear spent in a good cause? Nothing! More disconcerting than that, it soon became evident that McArdle regarded Salathiel's marriage in the forest as a true piece of frontier romance at which he had benignly assisted. He wished now to see that romance properly consummated. He read Salathiel a lesson on marital duty, followed by a homily on the joys of marriage. In short, he persisted notably, and he finally extorted a promise that as soon as he could Salathiel should go to Redstone Old Fort to fetch Jane.

Now all this business with McArdle that summer was quite complicated for Salathiel. He admired his old friend greatly for his bravery, his zeal, and his determination. He had an old-time affection for him. He knew that he owed him much for his education, and he was grateful. For these reasons he did not refuse to go after Jane. He was even willing to admit that as a matter of duty he should. But at Bedford that summer Salathiel saw another side of McArdle; his blind and persistent pursuit of the soul of Simeon Ecuyer to the very brink of the grave.

It was at once a ludicrous and a merciless exhibition of theological zeal. Salathiel had grown wise enough now to understand that. It was now a year and some months since he had left the lodges of Kaysinata and the bodily simplicities of the forest. The time for him had been crucial. It had not been wasted. In that long year he had learned more than he might learn all the rest of his life. The field, which McArdle himself had harrowed and sown, had sprouted, had grown into tall grain. It was not ripe grain yet, not ready for the harvest. But it was no longer green. More had happened to Salathiel in that year than McArdle could imagine.

He was no longer a fallow field, nor a callow mind. Much of Ecuyer and Johnson, something of Yates, Garrett, Dr. Boyd, Captain Jack, and many others had been transferred to Albine. He had listened avidly and learned well. He had been married, and profoundly in love, and he had lost both his wife and his sweetheart. He had seen much fighting in a cruel war, and dipped his hands deeply in blood. Initiation into the lodge had aroused him both morally and mystically. He thought clearly and arrived at his own decisions. Physically, he had grown and hardened into a graceful giant of a man. And all this was a blank page to McArdle, who continued to address his "favourite pupil" as though he were still the Little Turtle.

This was unfortunate, critical for Salathiel, to say the least—for in the forest of life he had now reached a place where there was a weblike meeting of many trails. He could not see far down any of them, nor well imagine the numerous difficulties ahead. There was no guide to be consulted. To the questions he shouted at the silence he received no answer, save an echo that seemed to question him back. Yates was away. Garrett and Captain Jack had spoken. It was summer. After a springtime of sudden and violent growth, he was tired. That summer at Bedford he paused for a while in a kind of limbo of doubt and inner inertia. A push down any trail might start him rolling like a stone in the direction given.

Here was the great opportunity for the teacher who had done most to guide him thus far. If McArdle had only been a bigger man—if he had been only a little wiser! But he was not. He was as Salathiel now found him. Zeal had made him blind; official recognition, pompous; authority, harsh. And the world is not so contrived as to make it necessarily easy for heaven to collaborate in smoothing the future. Hell also has its say.

And so it was by the humane example of an "infidel", rather than from the eloquence of a divine, that Salathiel learned that summer; that he had some questions answered.

In the corner room above the bar at Pendergasses' Simeon Ecuyer lay dying.

The manner of Captain Ecuyer's taking-off was this: His ancestors had striven for generations to contrive that he should be well-born, and in his death he hoped not to belie them. Fate had denied him the honour of snatching him suddenly from the field of battle. Nevertheless, he was determined to overcome that and to compliment both his family and his profession by perishing in bed, since he had to, like a brave soldier and an intelligent man.

Now, there was neither false pride nor sham resignation in the captain's own estimate of his fatal situation. He felt that life had denied him its greatest satisfactions —and yet that his days were not sufficiently prolonged. He thought that the end of man is at best a dismal one, and his own no exception. Still, he had not wasted the time that had been given him. He had done his best with it, professionally and in the service of others. Now he must surrender his forces in the face of an all-powerful and ever-victorious foe. But he was determined, if possible, to extort at least the honours of war from victorious circumstances. He intended to be carried out, not like a penitent ninny, but rigid on the shield of his own experience, composed in the face of things, and with the tempered sword of Truth grasped to the last.

Ecuyer died about sunset on the evening of July the twenty-ninth, 1764.

In an age which can scarcely paint an oil portrait without resorting either to sly or to bestial caricature, whose all-absorbing occupation is to dishonour and destroy life, men despise themselves and hate others for being beasts of prey. To them the death, the mere manner of the demise of an individual may seem, if anything at all, puerile. But they are not honourable men who thus dishonour themselves, and it was not so in July, 1764.

Times change, and time keeps changing. The estimates of other days are valid, too. Ecuyer esteemed mankind for a few simple virtues; because men are always ingenious and often heroic against their certain defeat. And, as a man, he did not intend in his death to dishonour his kind. Especially at the last, he would not act like a fox, before the face of his Maker. He wished to give a thoroughly mortal performance. Nor would he spoil his part by assuming, or permitting others to libel him by giving out, that he was nothing but the helpless fœtus of an angel.

In all of literature, French or English, classic or divine, the captain had one favourite line. It was that notable aside of a cripple:

"Play well the part, for there the honour lies."

And since the captain was an honourable man, he found all the more satisfaction in this precept, because he felt that by and large a man's part in life is forced upon him, and he picked for it by the Great Manager of the general show. So that what finally matters is how one acts and interprets his rôle. It was only McArdle and his like who thought Ecuyer an atheist.

That there is a Manager or a Management, Ecuyer

felt certain. Not reasonably sure, he was convinced by experience. Perhaps this conclusion was the inevitable inference of a soldier from the grand analogy of military life; perhaps it was the result of a million observations by a discerning mind. Who knows? Certainly it was the prime reservation of a quiet soul. But it was a reservation, the sunny mental preserve of a philosopher. Not closed to fellow huntsmen, it was barred and banned like a strongly fenced park against the moonlight pot hunters and poachers of religion.

As his hour approached, Ecuyer was afraid of one thing only. It was not of the hereafter, rather it was of the possible malevolence of the present.

He was afraid, although he was not frightened, that the processes of dissolution at work in his carcass might make it appear at the last that his body was the abode of something less than a man. He feared that pain might pull his strings like those of a marionette and force him to make his exit jerking and dancing to a scurvy tune that Death often whistles through his teeth. He feared that. He knew that when the automatic obtrudes on the rational it is always horribly absurd. And horror frequently demands the relief of laughter.

It was, therefore, with a feeling of relief, so profound it almost amounted to gratitude, that some days before he died he found the agony which had threatened to control him was turning numb, as nothingness advanced upon the citadels of life from his feet upwards. His worst sensation was soon that of slowly turning cold. And this, although it could only presage the end, he yet could not help, under the circumstances, regarding as an improvement in his condition. In fact, the constancy, even a certain serenity, which Salathiel always remembered as havng accompanied the captain towards the end, was probably due to this small, but important alleviation. If the sound of the jester's bells was still heard in the closing shadows, it was only a wind from nowhere that now seemed faintly to jangle them.

So the western window stood wide open in the summer weather, and Ecuyer looked out calmly at the distant mountains. He could still enjoy the view. It even reminded him of home. He could still think clearly, lying in bodily peace. Surely this was a mercy. He counted the red ball of the setting sun each evening like a last bead on the rosary of existence. He hailed another morning with surprise and joy. In its last brevity life was again made childishly wonderful. Especially in the late mornings, as the heat of the day mounted, it seemed as if the energy which had been withdrawn from his extremities was being re-concentrated in his head.

That at least was the way it appeared to those who came to see him. To himself it seemed as though his mind floated, free from internal sensation, alone in his head. Free will freed at last, he thought. To the very end he saw and heard well. Feeling went first. The thing that Salathiel remembered most about this time was that, day by day as the summer grew hotter, Ecuyer turned cold.

That final time with Ecuyer lingered always with a strange quality of its own in Albine's mind. Possibly because he had just returned from the forest, it affected him more vividly than it might have otherwise. But even so it would have been intense and memorable. For either the captain was awake and his mind keen and almost feverishly active, or he was asleep and exhausted; towards the last, unconscious perhaps. So it was a time of poignant waiting, and there was not a great deal for him to do, except to be there when Ecuyer awoke.

Yet that meant most of the time, since he slept fitfully.

"Good!" the captain would say. "Now, I do not wish any more to be left alone. It is extremely kind of you to stay with me." He repeated this many times.

Altogether, from the time he returned until the captain died, Salathiel was with him ten days and nights. On some mornings Bella Pendergass came to relieve him, but Ecuyer was not so pleased to see her as she expected him to be. His eyes would follow her about the room full of a solemn mischief, and then he would ask her like a Frenchman why she had never married.

"You will be lonely," he would say, and shake his head warningly at her.

After that she came only briefly to dust the room. Some of the settlers' children occasionally brought in wildflowers and stood shyly while he thanked them. Then they would run like young deer.

Captain Jack came over once from the cabin. He talked for a while about old times before many whites had come into the country, and how it went in the forest when he was a boy.

"I have been thinking much of the days when I was a lad, too," said the captain, and then went on to speak of Switzerland with the wistful eloquence of an exile. The old hunter listened raptly, until Ecuyer finally grew silent, overcome by regret.

"Oh, it's best to be young," said Captain Jack, shaking his head knowingly. "An old man grows tired of himself."

"So I am lucky, then, you think?" smiled Ecuyer.

"Probably," replied Captain Jack, "unless those ministers be right." He grinned at Ecuyer, and then his expression suddenly changed. "Captain, you are the only man in a red coat I ever knew that's bound to be saved, if there's justice on high," he burst out. "You've

382

been a terror to the enemy and a comfort to the poor, harried people of these hills. Brother, we'll miss you sorely." He shook Ecuyer's cold hand with emotion, and departed.

"There goes an honest old fanatic," said the captain, "and a brave and valuable one. I feel I have been promoted."

There was also a letter from Colonel Bouquet which Ecuyer would often ask for. He read and re-read it several times. He would laugh as he conned it over, and once there were tears in his eyes. Finally, he burned it over a candle.

"My compatriot is a great man," he said to Salathiel, while the paper curled in the flame. "Bouquet is by far the best general officer they ever sent to these colonies. If he should ask you to serve him, I would advise you to consider it carefully. He would remember you for having brought in the lists of the western captives. They have been valuable. And Bouquet never forgets any service rendered, no matter how small. That is a trait rarely found in a man of the world."

He paused for a moment to crumble the ashes of the letter thoroughly.

"I also shall remember you," he said significantly—"for not leaving a broken man to die alone in a strange land. May there be someone to do as much for you, if you die without property. Even the corpse of a rich man draws crowds—but flies arrive for the same reason. You have no idea, at your age, how rare it is for anyone to do anything out of simple kindness of heart."

Salathiel was surprised by this outburst, which may have had something to do with the burnt letter, but was unexpected.

"I have nothing else to do with my time, sir," he answered, trying to avoid praising himself.

"But time is the best gift of all," asserted the captain. "It's the ultimate commodity. If anyone takes it away from you, you have lost your life before you die. I ought to know. I have been hired most of my time."

"But Captain Jack would call it 'well employed'," replied Salathiel.

"Perhaps," sighed the captain. "And yet . . . *work for yourself*," he snapped suddenly, "or else die early! By the way, isn't Mr. Yates expected back soon?"

"Not for a fortnight, I fear."

"Much, much too long for *me* to wait," mused Ecuyer. "Lawyers who travel far abet delay. And after a while with them is never soon. The fuse of my carcass will not sputter long. Bring me pen, ink, and foolscap now—and some sealing wax. I must sleep first. But remind me, please, when I do wake, of the task for my pen. And let no one come up to see me this afternoon."

This was about a week before Ecuyer died, the 21st of July, since the curt, holographic will, which the captain drew that afternoon, is so dated.

As the principal item in the captain's estate was his horse, no lawyers appeared to help him divide it equitably. But he was not left without benefit of clergy, so to speak. The ministers came regularly every morning about eleven o'clock.

Ecuyer was at his best then. For a few days he seemed positively to enjoy disputing with them. They were both sincere in thinking he was bound for the fires, but that a deathbed repentance and a declaration of faith might yet save him. They laboured hard to obtain both, sweating in the molten summer weather, and at thought of the hot wrath to come. McArdle did most of the talking.

384

Mr. Puffin occasionally supported him, but confined himself for the most part to urging Ecuyer to partake of the sacrament. That alone would be sufficient, he said.

McArdle's pleading was directly from the Scriptures. And in that Ecuyer met him text for text. It was over the interpretation of Holy Writ that they disagreed. That invariably took them into theology, and a clanging argument. And there McArdle was lost in realms he had never glimpsed before. Assisted by the captain, his own logic led him into fearful traps. Afterwhile, Ecuyer would stop, laugh, and explain to him some horrid dilemma.

"So you can see, Mr. McArdle," he would say, "it would scarcely be advisable for me to submit myself entirely to your judgement in so delicate and eternal a matter, when you are quite hopelessly confused about it yourself."

"I warn you, sir. I solemnly warn you," McArdle would trumpet indignantly through his nose. "Your time is short here—but how long there!"—and he would then paint a fairly competent picture of hell.

"Repent before it's too late. Only *say* you believe, I beseech you," pleaded Mr. Puffin, who on one occasion went down on his knees.

"Surely, you would not have me lie my way into paradise," said Ecuyer.

Scandalized, they would leave him at last—but only to return next day, fortified with new arguments and texts. They were not going to let Ecuyer be damned easily, for word of the battle they were waging had got about. Not only the captain's soul, but their own reputations as converters were now at stake. People watched their comings and goings for nearly a week, dubiously. There were arguments in the village pro and con. One

385

day a small crowd of the Pendergass boys and their friends gathered under the captain's window, after the ministers went in. They listened, and heard Ecuyer laugh. Garrett put a stop to such gatherings, calling them shameless. He thought the same of the ministers, and said so. But it was not so easy to stop them. They had the force of much pious opinion behind them, and he was only a tavernkeeper. Besides, Ecuyer himself seemed to suffer them gladly.

The truth was, the captain had let himself in for more than he had at first anticipated. He was now failing faster than he had supposed he might. The time soon came when he could no longer argue, nor take pleasure in doing so. The two ministers took this as a sign that he was weakening, which he was, and redoubled their efforts. They prayed together at his bedside long and hard, and the holy clamour was considerable.

Lord! thought Salathiel, if Ned Yates would only come back! He'd stop it!

It was not possible for Albine himself to do anything with McArdle, who vehemently reproached him for remaining silent at such a crisis in the captain's spiritual affairs.

It was only three days before he died that Ecuyer finally called in Mr. Hume, the schoolmaster.

Mr. Hume, like McArdle, had lost both ears, although not for an unworldly reason. Mr. Hume had once stood in the pillory for forgery, and though he now concealed his mutilation cleverly with a deep, Saxon wig, the iron had entered his soul and he was glad to aid the captain —for a small fee—and out of the rare hardness of his heart. He had been prayed over himself extensively in preparation for the gallows, and then brutally pardoned. He had lived to resent being saved.

The last time Mr. Puffin and McArdle came down the corridor to Ecuyer's room, they found Mr. Hume sitting by the window eating an apple, and the captain propped up, waiting for them, too. Salathiel with his arms folded sat near the head of the bed. Ecuyer's eyes snapped, and he smiled at the ministers. Two empty chairs had been set in the middle of the room, awaiting them.

Now, there was a certain air of formal preparation about these dispositions which was not lost on either of the men of God. They had hoped for a formal repentance, before witnesses, and they sat down expectantly in the chairs, facing Ecuyer, but trying to suppress any signs of triumph at being about to pluck the ripened fruit.

"Gentlemen," began the captain, "this is a somewhat *eery* occasion. I have assembled here the kind of audience which I think you do most deserve." He paused.

"Ah," said Mr. Puffin, exhaling with relief.

"How d'ya mean?" demanded McArdle, inhaling suspiciously.

"Why, there are five here present, but amongst us there are only five ears," said the captain. "And from now on my own also will be closed to your appeals. That would leave only three ears for two of you to preach at. I do thank you for your efforts on my behalf," he added, "but don't you think from now on you can find more and other ears elsewhere? I beseech ye to do so."

In the silence that followed, Mr. Hume lifted his wig, confirming the captain's count, and began to laugh. Mr. Puffin, to do him justice, rose to depart, but McArdle was not to be daunted. Ears or no ears, he drew a Testament from his pocket and began to read it.

"This is my beloved son. Hear ye him," he shouted.

"This is my esteemed friend, the schoolmaster," roared

Ecuyer, summoning the last of his strength. "Hear ye him."

McArdle paused with astonishment both at the voice and at its pronouncement.

"Mr. Hume is prepared to submit on my behalf an incontrovertible piece of human wisdom—if you persist, sir," said Ecuyer. And in fact Mr. Hume had laid down his apple.

McArdle still waited for a moment, looking about him. He was not sure yet what the captain intended. Then he flushed angrily and began to read again from his Testament.

"Mr. Hume," said Ecuyer.

"Two times one is two; two times two is four; two times three is six . . ." began Mr. Hume in the indestructible tones of a schoolmaster. McArdle flipped the leaves of his Bible with exasperated astonishment, and fixing on the fifth chapter of St. John, resumed desperately.

Under the low ceiling of the room the two men seemed to be intoning a liturgy in which the bald facts of the multiplication tables warped themselves through the woof of the rich prose of St. John, weaving a kind of Gregorian chant. Ecuyer closed his eyes and composed himself as though for a long nap.

At "seven times one is seven", McArdle closed his Bible with a clap and stalked out. Mr. Puffin awaited him somewhat sheepishly downstairs.

Mr. Hume completed the eighth table all alone—and stopped.

The captain opened his eyes and looked at the two empty chairs.

"The rest is silence," said Mr. Hume aptly.

"I hope so," said the captain.

"Albine, bring me my little leather purse out of the top drawer yonder; also brandy and three glasses." The captain filled the glasses himself.

"To the success of your future secular instruction," said Ecuyer. They drank the toast together, after which Mr. Hume received a gold piece gladly.

"To your very good health, sir," cried the schoolmaster, and drained his glass. They all laughed. Even the captain. "Also, at your service," said Mr. Hume, pocketing the piece.

"I hardly think I shall need you again. My health, as you may have heard, is really not so good." Ecuyer shook the man's hand. "Good-bye," he said quietly.

Salathiel put the purse back in the bureau, and stood the empty chairs against the wall.

"Albine," said the captain thoughtfully, "when I die that purse will be yours. There is not much in it, only what's left of my last pay, but I want you to promise me this. Do you remember that Irishman we hanged at Ligonier?"

"Of course."

"Do you remember his name?"

"Yes."

"Well, save a guinea for me out of that purse, and the first time you run across a Roman Catholic priest give it to him to say a mass for that Irishman's soul. Promise?"

"I promise," said Salathiel.

"*Finis!*" exclaimed Ecuyer, sinking back into the pillows contentedly. Almost instantly he fell into an exhausted sleep.

The ministers came no more. Salathiel was now prepared to deal with them if they appeared. But the last days of Ecuyer ran out swiftly and in peace. He received no more visitors, except Garrett and old Rose, who came to his room the day before he died and sat with him for a while.

Salathiel left them together and went to his own room. He was in no mood then to encounter Mrs. Pendergass. The gentle, friendly voices sounded on for some time together on the other side of the wall. When he returned after they had left, the captain was smiling, and there was a small spray of wild roses in a bottle on the window sill.

"And now," said Ecuyer, "no more! Not even the officers from the fort. Keep the door fast closed against the world and stay with me, my friend. Fetch me no food. That is all over now."

Salathiel locked the door and sat down to begin his vigil. He saw the captain expected to die that night.

But he was still alive in the morning. Salathiel then settled him as comfortably as he could in the bed. The captain seemed to have entirely lost the use of his legs.

After that Salathiel did not leave him for an instant. He used the vessel in the captain's room, for he was afraid Ecuyer might die while he was out. The day was fearfully hot, but Ecuyer shivered, and signed once to pile the bedclothes on him. In the afternoon he asked to have the bed drawn nearer to the window, so that he could look directly at the mountains without turning his head. He had himself propped up until the light fell full on his face. He seemed to feel the sunlight, and put his fingers to his cheek.

"That is better," he said. "Farewell, Albine."

As the afternoon advanced, the heat in the room became intolerable despite the wide-open window. But Salathiel did not dare open the door. It was probably Bella who came and knocked timidly once. He went softly to the door. "Wait," he whispered. He thought he heard her tiptoeing away. He squatted down close by the bed now. The captain began to speak softly in French. Salathiel sweated. The captain was not talking to him. His eyes glowed.

About sunset Ecuyer began to twitch with his hands. The signet ring he wore dropped off and rolled under the bed. He sighed ever so deeply. Salathiel rose from the floor, where he had been squatting, and leaned over to look at him. At that moment the sun was setting behind the Alleghenies. Its rim dipped. The room suddenly went grey. Ecuyer's head fell to one side.

Salathiel stood in the gathering twilight and wept silently. He was utterly and painfully alone.

Long after dark he began to hear the river and the crickets again . . . outside . . .

Summer!

There was a song called "Past Caring and Past Faring", which the musicians used to play at the fort, and there was a wild, tuneful bubbling of the flute that ran all through it with a devil-may-care Irish lilt to accompany the melancholy melody, like white gulls rising from dark waters. Salathiel never heard the song again or elsewhere. It passed westward into the forests with the grenadier musicians who played it. But through the hot summer of '64 all the garrison and village at Bedford hummed it, whistled it, and the Welsh girls trilled it by moonlight, sitting by the river, with their grenadiers, under the walls of the fort. It expressed perfectly the mood of the moment; the long waiting, the sorrow of past troubles, and a hope of venturesome, audacious escape in the flute notes. It was the first catch that sang itself into Salathiel's heart. And no wonder.

It was in the air.

The grenadiers had played it as they came back in quick time after they buried Ecuyer. The captain had had it all—the slow music to begin with, the horse with the empty reversed boots in the stirrups, the flag-swathed coffin, the three good volleys at the end, one for each Person of the Trinity. The white powder smoke from the gleaming muskets drifted across the face of Lookout Mountain like the flick of a handkerchief disposing of dust in hot weather—and time went on, while Ecuyer lay there in an unmarked grave, looking out over the old Shawnee Hunting Grounds into the sunsets.

There was no churchyard in the village then, and they had laid him high up under a cliff, safe from wolves, underneath the talus. The Masonic brethren in their aprons had turned out under Garrett; there had been a company from the Royal Americans; and the grenadier band. Mr. Puffin, despite McArdle's strenuous protest, had read the burial service, mindful of the arrival, expected at any moment, of the courteous but lionlike Colonel Bouquet. A controversy with him was not to be thought of by a poor parson, especially one who was chaplain to the forces.

And so it was all over. All over for Ecuyer, that is. Salathiel was very much left behind that summer. Phoebe was gone, the captain had vanished, Yates was away.

To be sure, Ecuyer had left a little property, mostly personal belongings. And these, much to Salathiel's surprise, the captain had willed to him; a purse with about thirty pounds in it, the horse, the wagon; all his chests, books, firearms, and clothes went to "my young friend, S. Albine, as a token of my esteem for his devotion, and with an admonition that he take good care of my faithful mare, Enna". His sword, the land in Maryland, his gold signet ring, and a small box with a sealed letter directing the disposal of its contents, Ecuyer left to Colonel Bouquet.

There was much difficulty with the garrison quartermasters over gaining possession of the ark. They seemed inclined to stand on the well-known nine points of the law. But one night Salathiel borrowed a team from Stottelmyer and dragged the big wagon away from behind the hospital, where it had long been idly standing—and then the shoe was on the other foot.

Garrett let him put it under a shed in the river yard, where it stood out of sight, and out of the troubled, troublesome minds of quartermasters, like a big tent on wheels, safe, and ready to go—but as yet Salathiel had no idea whither. He put all his new-found possessions into the stout chests in the ark and locked them up. Quite a fortune for a young woodsman! That is, he now had something more than the clothes he wore and his rifle-gun. He hung about waiting for something to happen.

But nothing happened.

The weather grew hotter as August began to slip away. There was a lodge meeting in the hills, scantily attended. Mrs. Pendergass sent for him and wept about Phoebe. He was depressed. He felt not a little guilty and miserable. It was impossible to say how much he missed Captain Ecuyer. McArdle gradually became unpleasantly insistent that he should keep his promise to set off to find Jane. Even Garrett, who remained his firm friend, also thought it was the right thing to do. The Pendergass boys were all planning to return to their cabins before autumn, and were much absorbed by their preparations to do so. It was partly his own mood, partly circumstances—but everything at Bedford now seemed quite the opposite of what it had been only the winter before.

He took to swimming in the river a good deal at night, and grew morose and restive. Finally he saddled the mare, took the rifle-gun and his raiding kit, and set off to see Captain Jack at "Echovale".

At least they would let him alone there. He could range the woods with the old hunter until Yates returned, and then find out his plans for going to Philadelphia. Hunting in the forest, he might be at peace.

He started about dawnlight one morning, but when he got to the cabin Captain Jack was away. "Conococheague" was scrawled in charcoal on the door, and that meant the old ranger had left to go to his even more lonely cabin on Jack's Mountain. He might or he might not return soon. Salathiel seethed with disappointment. After a long run of luck, everything now seemed to be going wrong. Was a perverse fate dogging him now?—he wondered. He decided, if he decided anything, to surrender to events and see what would happen.

In fact, there was a moment standing before the closed door of Captain Jack's cabin when he ceased to will anything at all. Perhaps for a recent graduate from the woods, for a mind used to the quiet of the forest, too much had been forced upon him lately to digest. Anyway, he let the reins go slack and sat there looking at a closed door.

He sat on in the hot sunshine. The mare stamped. The flies bothered her. Finally she moved off.

He laughed, and let her have her head.

She took the trail up the side of Will's Mountain and let herself down gingerly into the Springs valley beyond. They struck Shober's run after a while, and the new wagon road through the forest to Fort Cumberland, which ran along it. It was good going there in stretches, and the mare began to trot.

Salathiel did nothing to check her. She was headed south for Fort Cumberland. She might have turned back to Bedford, but she hadn't. He laughed again. The road to Cumberland was one way of going to Redstone Old Fort.

That evening he made a small supper fire somewhere near the Cumberland valley and sat smoking contentedly. He had humorously made up his mind that, while McArdle might be wrong, the mare must be right, and he might as well press on to Redstone Old Fort and ask about Jane. He wanted a woman badly. And, after all, Jane was his wife.

He sat trying to recall to himself what she was like. He had met her in another life, or so it seemed. He could hardly remember her face now. Yet he had only to look into the fire to see Phoebe's gazing at him from the embers like a clear picture. Well, he would make the best of it. He would find out at Redstone Old Fort who and what awaited him.

But he would take his time about it. He was alone in the woods again. Away—and his own master. He found he liked that. Why had he been so anxious to learn what other people wanted him to do? And who made the rules they were always pressing upon him? He hobbled the horse, put out the fire, and went to sleep looking up at the stars and clouds moving across the branches.

Now that he had killed that Indian child he could go to sleep peacefully enough. He need never fear hearing his mother scream again. That thought occurred to him the last thing, and very deep down, as he drifted off into the serenity of oblivion.

The next morning he knew he had found himself again. He wakened whole and keen. Not a single disturbing sound came to steal his attention. Not a leaf rustled. It seemed as though the weather had paused. The mare rolled in a patch of sweet fern and then lay contentedly looking at him. He yawned, and stretched happily in his blanket. Good Lord, how much freedom he had been missing! He sat up eagerly and caught intangibly, but none the less certainly, the first aloof freshness of autumn, a tang of unmistakable crispness in the air.

Summer was over. He had come through!

Somehow that summer had posed him a difficult crisis, had even threatened to stop him. But he felt he was over the crest now, free, and a man. As he breathed in the vigorous hint of autumn to come, he knew it. It had taken the loss of Phoebe, death at the Salt Kettles, the passing of the captain, all that and much more, to pour the molten metal of youth into a sterner and more enduring mould. And now the die was cast.

He would go on with what lay before him, no matter what. He could do it. He desired change, and a conviction of great change lay upon him. Suddenly he knew what it was, even if he could not tell yet how it might come to pass. It would happen.

Wilderness, farewell!

18

Wilderness Farewell

BY NOON NEXT DAY he was at Fort Cumberland, where he lingered only long enough to obtain some tobacco, of which he had come away short, and to exchange news. Here for the first time, and from a Virginia storekeeper named Crump, he heard talk of the stamp tax and trade troubles with England. A red-headed young man by the name of Drew roundly denounced government and the Parliament, standing on a whisky keg in Crump's barrel room. "Are you a Whig?" he asked Salathiel. "You look like one." That seemed complimentary—or was it? He was in no mood to go into the matter. It appeared remote and might, for all he knew, lead to a brawl. So he drank with the red-headed man instead. The whisky was fine, ripe juice, and he rode off westward along Braddock's Road in the afternoon sunshine feeling happy and free from care.

The Cresaps were still at Redstone, he had learned, among other things. Also he had told them at the store he was going after his wife—and afterwards that stood him in good stead. No one at Cumberland knew anything about Jane.

Braddock's Road was scarcely more than a track through the forest now, but it had been kept open by pack trains and a few salt and powder wagons that went to Redstone by way of the Great Meadows. There Braddock was said to be buried in the road, close by Colonel Washington's old entrenchments at Fort Necessity. Just west of that the road crossed over the Laurel Hill and pitched down into the valley to the cabin of Henry Beeson. He, together with his sturdy neighbours, Windle Brown and Frederick Waltzer, had occupied the valley since before Braddock's defeat.

Beeson was a devout Quaker. The Indians respected the Broad Hat for his peaceful honesty. They had long ago made a private treaty with him and scrupulously kept it. Alone of all the cabins in the district, and through decades of war and peace, Beeson's chimney never ceased to smoke. His cabin lay only a little more than sixty miles west of Cumberland, but Albine took a good ten days to get there, taking time off in the woods to loaf, swim, hunt, and smoke his fine Virginia tobacco.

At the Great Meadows he camped for two days, well hidden from the road, and let the mare get her belly full of grass. Enna was a fine, young roan with two white socks on her forelegs, and Salathiel was now grown very fond of her. Both of them enjoyed themselves thoroughly at the Great Meadows. Early September had laid light fingers on the foliage, and in the early morning the mountains smoked. By midday there was a deep-blue haze in the distance. He went about now feeling like the king of the world. He even began to grow careless about concealing himself. He realized it, but he didn't care.

At Beeson's, however, he was brought up short by an encounter that changed his life.

The trail branched at Beeson's. Braddock's old road struck off almost due north to Pittsburgh there, yet that part of it was now all but impassable. It had lapsed back to a trace. But Colonel Burd's track, the other fork, which led westward to the Monongahela at Redstone, was now become the main road for the Virginians and Marylanders to reach the west-running waters. Beeson's stood exactly at the fork and there a roof and entertainment was to be found. There were even cows and a patch of ploughed fields and open meadows in his big clearing. Salathiel stopped at Beeson's for the night, as did most other people on their way to Redstone.

It was after dark when he arrived, and supper was long over. Friend Beeson, however, welcomed him, helped him to put up the mare in the shed by herself, and remarked casually that it would be much better to leave her there than in the stable.

"For," said he, "there are three old Senecas have been camping near the farm for a fortnight past. They'll not harm me nor mine, but a stranger's horseflesh might tempt them, and they usually come at milking time to the barn. They're as fond of the warm, new milk as kittens be."

"I'm fond of it myself—with a little whisky in it," laughed Salathiel, who had already taken a notion to the obviously simple and kind-hearted Quaker, his broad hat and equally wide smile.

399

"Right thou art," said Beeson. "Come in and I'll see if I can't contrive something for thee. We'll at least warm a bowl of mush, even if it do be late. Liza, Liza, put a knot on the fire," he shouted, as he went into the house, leaving Salathiel to finish rubbing down the mare.

"Amy," Salathiel heard him call from inside the cabin. "Where'st gone to, woman?"

"I've gone to bed, Henry," replied a pleasant female voice, probably that of Mrs. Beeson, Salathiel surmised. "I'm plumb dickered out. No use thy calling for Liza. She left this morning and took her bundle. Cleared out without so much as a thank-ye-kindly. I've been doin' her stint all afternoon while thou'st been down at the byre. Have we company?"

"Young feller from out Bedford way. I'll tend to him myself. Don't thee rise now," he said affectionately.

A few minutes later, when Salathiel came into the cabin, he found a bowl of hot mush and a jug of new milk on the table, with Mr. Beeson sitting by smoking his pipe. A flickering rushlight tended to lighten the gloom.

"Thou'lt have to provide thine own liquor," said the Quaker, glancing at the milk a bit deprecatingly. "I never keep whisky here on account of the Injuns. They don't bother us so much when they know there's never none on the place."

"Do many of them come here these days?" asked Salathiel.

"Quite some, off and on. But they never did harm us, nor we them," said Beeson proudly. "It's been like that from old times now. They know Friend Beeson and his farm."

"It's a pity there aren't more like you, sir," said Salathiel. "I do aver there'd be less trouble, if 'twere so."

400

"Aye," agreed Beeson sighing. "We've always tried to do what we can. These last two years have been the worst of all. Many fleeing from the heathen wrath have passed through here. They go as they come, too," he added, a whit bitterly. " 'Twas a poor papist girl came only a fortnight ago come First Day, half naked. She ran off through the woods from somewhere nigh Fort Pitt. She'd been lost. She offered to work for Amy, and she was sartin in a bad way. Wouldn't say exactly what happened. I didn't press her. Injuns, I guess. It's best to let 'em forget, if they can. Wal, we fed her and guv her an old linsey-woolsey, and a mighty good bed— and now she's lit out without sayin' a word!"

"Maybe the Senecas you spoke of scared her off," suggested Salathiel, stifling a yawn.

"Maunt be. I hadn't thought of that. She was mighty scared about suthin' most of the time."

"I suppose you've seen a good many others like her," suggested Salathiel, with nothing particular in mind.

"Lot's on 'em!" exclaimed the Quaker. "Why, 'tis only four months ago Captain Cresap and his good lady brought fifteen poor souls through here, takin' them downcountry to the settlements. They'd been gathered in at Redstone Old Fort for over a year, and victuals was gettin' scarce. Women and children all. Some on 'em had been captivated, I hear . . ."

"What!" cried Salathiel. "What's that?"

He was very much awake now. He began to talk and to question Beeson rapidly. In half an hour he had told his own story of his search for Jane, and obtained every last bit of information he could from the Quaker.

There was no doubt of it. Jane *had* left Redstone with the Cresaps, and gone downcountry with them. The old Quaker not only remembered her distinctly in the crowd

401

of women and children, who had stayed with him over-night, but he also recollected her unusual name when it was recalled to him.

"Mrs. Albine! Yep, that was it! Some said she was a widow. And a nice, upstanding, yellow-haired, clean-faced gal she was."

As to where the Cresaps had taken her and the others, Beeson had no idea. Probably to Baltimore, he thought.

"For it's easier to git nurture for orphaned little ones in a town like that, and t'others kin bind out and git keep on some of the big plantations along Tidewater. At least so Captain Cresap says," remarked Beeson.

"Well, I'll ride over to Redstone tomorrow and find out from Captain Cresap himself," said Salathiel determinedly.

The Quaker laughed. "Thou't not do that," he said. "The captain and his lady passed through here agin, goin' back to Baltimore, only last afternoon. Why, I wonder thou didst not meet them on the road from Cumberland."

"I stopped to hunt at the Great Meadows," explained Albine angrily. "To think of it! They must have passed me, and I never knew it. Damn it, I do have the worst luck with women!" he burst out. Which remark brought in a mild request from the Quaker to refrain from profane swearing under "this roof".

So Salathiel went to bed in Beeson's loft, and slept on the news, profane swearing and all. There was no use going on to Redstone Old Fort. No, he would have to turn about and follow Jane downcountry, clean back to the settlements—maybe to Tidewater or Baltimore. He had a good horse and some of the captain's money along, luckily! He'd go. He wanted his woman now. He needed her. It was a long time now—and he didn't relish what Beeson had said about some people thinking Mrs. Albine was a widow.

The bunk in the loft to which Beeson had showed him had the fishy fragrance of a woman about it, and he realized that it was probably the one in which the girl, who had run off that morning, had slept only the night before. But it was a "good bed"—as Beeson had said. It had a deep feather mattress. Under the low roof, and in a dark loft, he slept late.

In fact, it was fully an hour after sunrise when he came down next morning, and both the Quaker and his wife were out at the barn milking.

He helped himself to some side meat and hominy, which stood warming in a pan in the ashes, and then took a drag at his pipe. He felt calm and happy, quite content, now that he had made up his mind to go downcountry after Jane. He would wait till his host came back into the house, settle with him for his lodging, give the horse a good feed of oats, and depart. Now he would be going to see the settlements, at last, and with an object. When he found Jane they would . . .

The shape of his pleasant daydreams glimmered and faded, came and went in the blue coils of smoke, wreathing from his morning pipe. The weed he had picked up at Cumberland was sweet Virginia stuff. Yes, he and Jane would probably end by taking up land somewhere, and then . . . he yawned.

A white fan of sunlight lay across the room from the open door. It was going to be another hot day. Indian summer seemed to be coming before fall was over. Down at the barn old Mrs. Beeson emerged from the milking shed, carrying her buckets on a yoke, and accompanied by two Senecas. She went down to the springhouse. The braves were both old warriors, he noted, dirty and pretty ragged. Friend Beeson appeared next, driving four cows to pasture. The broad brim of his hat flapped in the wind, and his dog barked at the small dun cows, heading them towards the pasture gate.

Not a bad life on a farm like this. Something like it in the future might do, provided there were children about. He could always go hunting if it got too domestic. He began to make pictures to himself of a cabin somewhere in the hills. The smoke curled lazily from his lips . . .

The shadow of a head crowned with a feathered turban fell across the doorway. Whoever was there had come noiselessly, and now stood quietly listening.

He shifted his rifle from the table before him and laid it across his knees without making a sound. He sat still, every nerve taut, his hand on the trigger and the two barrels covering the door. The shadow on the threshold remained . . .

"Go away, Little Turtle," said a familiar Indian voice after a while. "You heap bad man, I know you."

That roused him. In two strides he made the door, leaped past it, and whirled about.

Leaning against the wall of the cabin, unarmed, and with folded arms, stood old Ganstax, the Mingo, the Seneca chief whom he had last seen at Frazier's cabin near Pittsburgh. He was drawn up to his full height and his eyes glittered. He looked at Salathiel and the double-barrelled rifle with utter contempt.

"Go away," he said imperiously.

"Thou art an old fool, Ganstax," said Salathiel to the chief in the Algonquin tongue. "It is time for thee to tremble—not to command." He touched his rifle significantly.

Ganstax smiled. "You no kill big man," he said in

English, "you kill squaw; you kill baby!" He spat on the ground at Salathiel's feet.

So that was it! And so now he had a blood feud with the Senecas. That meant a private war with all the Six Fires of the Long House.

"My people have heard of the great Little Turtle and his brothers, the Mountain Foxes," continued Ganstax. "They have heard of their mighty deeds. Me show um dead baby!"

"Good!" replied Salathiel, burning with hate. "I will send them more, by and by." Then the devil prompted him. He drew out his purse. "Ganstax, Chief of the Senecas," he said. "Here is a New York shilling for you. Buy firewater for your brave people—and they will forget."

The old chief tensed himself against the wall.

"I'll not kill you here at Beeson's," he said in his own tongue. "This Broad Hat is a man of honour and of peace. I have smoked and shaken hands with him."

Salathiel laughed and patted his rifle. "Twin eyes, she never sleeps," he said significantly.

He turned on his heel in contempt and walked away, leaving the old chief standing there against the cabin wall.

He saddled the mare swiftly, keeping a wary eye for any more shadows falling across the sunlight. For a moment he suspected Beeson of having given away his presence at the farm. But a little further reflection convinced him that he did the honest Quaker an injustice, and that Ganstax must have seen him when he rode in the evening before.

Had Ganstax been at the Salt Kettles?—he wondered. He might have been. There was that one thicket he had failed to search through. But what did it matter now? Ganstax knew, and so did the Iroquois. Well, it was not his intention to wage a war with them alone, not now at least. He had other ends in view. And continuing to live was not the least of them. All this fled through his thoughts as he saddled the mare.

He rode out of the shed without attempting to conceal his departure. Ganstax still stood with folded arms by the cabin door. The other two Indians were down at the springhouse at the foot of the hill. Drinking milk! He laughed. Snakes liked it, too. He clapped heels to the mare and dashed off in the direction of Redstone Old Fort. At the end of the farm lane he saw the Quaker coming back and waved to him to wait.

"Mr. Beeson," he said, "here's what I owe you for my night's lodging. You've earned it. Your good reputation, I think, has saved my life. My fame with Injuns is of another kind. Happen those Senecas are old friends of mine. Do you see?"

"Meanin' it ain't healthy to tarry, with them here?"

"Exactly. I'm going to Redstone Old Fort. Tell them that, will you?"

"I'll tell them what thou sayst," said the careful Quaker. "Stop by again when they ain't around."

"Maybe," he replied, and started off down the road westward.

Once in the woods, he urged the mare into a gallop. Some miles along the road to Redstone he came to a deep creek. He plunged in. But in the middle of the ford he turned the mare's head downstream and swam for some distance with the current, and around a bend.

Two days later found him back at the Great Meadows again, after making a long circuit eastward, far south of Beeson's, and over the Laurel Hill. He was heading east again for Fort Cumberland, and so far he had seen nothing of the three Senecas. He thought he might venture to light a fire tomorrow.

"Tomorrow, and tomorrow, and tomorrow" . . . What was that thing that McArdle used to quote so much—something not from the Bible, but just as good? Ah, yes—"and all our yesterdays" . . . How true!

Lately he had begun to think a good deal about the future. The death of Ecuyer had made it painfully clear how mortal a man is. And he was still young enough to think that life was tragically short. He might die early, too, with all the Iroquois so anxious to assist. It was fine autumn weather, a grand, clear, starry night. But, despite that, he felt uncomfortably lonely and friendless that evening at the Great Meadows—without a fire—and the unfortunate Braddock buried some place near. He had better be hastening to see all he could of the great world beyond the mountains, of places where there were people, cities, ships, and the sea. Otherwise, it might be too late. He was doubly satisfied that his search for Jane would take him there directly. And he would be right glad, tarnal happy, to find him a companion for all his tomorrows. Somebody, b'God, who wouldn't up and leave him! He and she, they'd go over the hills of the world together hand in hand, and *then* home. Oh, yes, he supposed so—home at last . . . When he awoke it was tomorrow again, tomorrow in the silent forest.

Enna rolled and snorted in the deep grass, kicking her white socks in the air.

He saddled her eagerly and rode back along the road to Cumberland, trotting, galloping when he could, hungry for a cooked meal. Even if they had followed him, he must have left Ganstax and the others behind now. They *might* have gone to look for him at Redstone. One more night in the woods alone . . .

He pulled up suddenly.

Along a muddy stretch in the sandy bottom where he was passing were the firm, graceful footprints of a woman going his way. She was no squaw, with that high arch and the narrow-pointed tracery of delicate toes. Like a lady, he thought. But a little lame, or worn out walking in bare feet.

"Liza!" he exclaimed—that girl who had run away from Beeson's.

She must be on the road not far ahead of him. He wondered if she would try to hide while he passed.

He set off more slowly, watching her footprints in the sand and dust. They led on. Once he saw a snag of her dress on some briers. Here she had rested by the road. She rested often, he noted. She must be tired and hungry by now. He urged the mare forward. From the top of the next hill he saw her. She was sitting on a log with her bundle on a stick beside her. She rose hastily at the sound of hoofs.

"Liza!" he shouted. "Wait, gal, wait!"

For a moment he thought she would run into the woods. But seeing him so close, she evidently thought better of it and stood waiting. He galloped down on her and drew up . . .

Liza?—No, no, it was the Irish girl he had seen being whipped at Frazier's nearly two years before.

He sat staring at her in astonishment. She was gaunt, starved, and haggard. But she was still darkly beautiful.

"Frances! Frances!" he cried at last.

"Aye, meself it is. And maybe this time you'll be after givin' me a lift, Mr. Albine," she said quietly, looking him straight in the eyes and trembling—but not from fright, he thought. He leaned down and caught her hand and held it.

408

"Happen this time I will," he said humbly. "But you'll ride like a lady," he added proudly, while he dismounted.

"In that case you'll be actin' like a gintleman," she countered.

It was the only reservation she made, and in a weak voice. But he liked her all the more for it, and for not surrendering too abjectly even in desperation.

He began tying her pitiful bundle to his saddle rings, and laughed encouragingly.

"I'll make ye no false promises, proud woman," he said, "but I will cherish ye like a man. Climb up and see." He patted the saddle invitingly.

Without hesitating further, she put her hand on his shoulder and mounted. The mare looked around at her new rider in surprise.

"Where were you agoin' to, Frances?" he asked, half teasingly.

"Why, I was goin' to seek *you* out at Bedford," she said. Suddenly big tears ran down her face. "And now I've found you on the road," she sobbed.

"So you have," he said, overcome by sheer amazement, and began leading the mare up the stony hill just ahead, walking her.

He never doubted the girl's assertion, nor thought it strange she had kept him in mind. He had never forgotten her either. He might have gone back after her to Frazier's if it hadn't been for Phoebe, and the war—and Jane!

At the thought of Mistress Jane, now, he frowned. The widow Albine, eh! Well, why not?

He looked again at the tall girl in her bedraggled linsey-woolsey sitting there in the saddle. For all her rags, she rode with dignity and grace. He remembered the lovely form those rags covered. Her lustrous black hair swept back into a loose coil from her pale forehead. Her wide, grey-blue eyes met his own frankly, but appealingly. Her eyes were wonderful. The cheekbones stood up high in her wan, oval face. She was quite peaked and worn, but still with an undaunted air about her. Her mouth was sad, but her lips were bright and smiled at him bravely.

"Frances," he kept repeating, "Frances, Frances," trying to realize her actual presence, and that he was not alone on the long road through the woods any more.

"Yes, what is it?" she asked.

He had not intended she should answer him.

"Lord, I'm glad I've found ye!" he suddenly blurted out. "I'd like to put a kiss on your mouth."

"I'll save it for you," she said. "I'm a tired woman for your kissin' now. Belike I'd not be able to give it back to ye."

He felt ashamed of his outburst after that. He saw her feet were puffed and bruised, and her long legs bleeding in several places from thorns. She needed to be taken care of. He strode on more impatiently, making Enna step out into her best walk. He was afraid to make the mare trot, for fear the girl might not be able to hold on. How weak she was he could not be sure. She needed sleep and food. He could plainly see that she would not have been able to walk much farther alone. She needed to rest and soak her swollen feet in a cold stream. It was a good forty miles to Fort Cumberland yet, and they would never be able to make it under two days—walking! In the far distance a storm was brewing. Thunder grumbled and groaned.

He stopped for a moment to ponder, trying hard to remember the local lie of the land ahead. He had

410

hunted at a place near here on his way down. Frances looked at him apprehensively. The mare stomped.

"Maybe ye'd better reconsider, Mr. Albine. Might be ye don't know what you're after taking on," she said uneasily. "I'm no package wrapped in silk and ribbons to bring ye good fortune, even if ye did find me like lucky money in the road. I'm trouble—and it's the divil's own time I've been havin' in the hell of a world."

"Why, I don't doubt it," he said, looking at her. "But don't you misdoubt me. I'm only tryin' to make a plan for us."

"Oh!" she said. Her eyes widened, and she asked mischievously, "Goes thinkin' so hard?"

"No!" he said, nettled at her unexpected implication. "But good thinkin's always still."

She bit her lip, seeing she had scratched him deeper than she intended. Then she leaned forward in the saddle from weakness. "I only meant I've got to rest soon, and get somethin' to eat somewhere," she explained. "It's a long time since I left Beeson's, and me walkin', and afraid of every shadow that flitted across the way." She swayed a little and caught herself.

He jumped up behind her, and holding her firmly in the saddle, they moved off at a more rapid walk. How unfeeling he had been. He must remember she was not a squaw. He gave her a drink from his flask and felt her grow warmer gradually. She sighed afterwhile and leaned back contentedly against him.

"The crature makes me head spin," she said—"and me heart beat hard. Feel it?"

"Yes—" he laughed encouragingly—"I think I do—not that I'm *sure* you have one," he whispered.

She looked up at him enquiringly. Then she turned about as far as she could and gave him a kiss.

411

Something went to Salathiel's head, too.

"That's right," he said gravely—and gave her kiss back to her.

"And now, if ye can only hold on by yourself, I think I can find a roof to cover us even if it storms bad. You could rest a bit too. Hear that thunder?"

"It's growlin' far away," she said.

"It's a big September storm comin'," he answered. "And in these hills ye can get an icy drenchin' on a hot day. It's best to take shelter when we can. But I'll have to lead the horse again."

She accepted his decision without demur. "I'll hold on," she assured him.

"Good!"

They rode on, and he pressed the horse to a faster gait.

"This is it," he said, dismounting. "I thought we'd find it soon."

They had come to the place he had been looking for, where a lively stream came down out of the hills and crossed the road at the bottom of a steep dale.

He turned up the creek, leading the horse for some distance along the gravel bars and boulder bed of the stream itself. The thunder rolled much nearer now. But he knew where he was going, for he had sheltered comfortably here on the way down.

Presently the stream curved sharply back into the hills and they passed the site of an ancient beaver dam at the throat of a glen. The old ponds behind it had long been drained, and there the stream had filled in the level, making a smooth, wild meadow some acres in extent. Through this the creek still wandered from one deep pool to another. At the upper end was a fall over an outcrop of rock nearly ten feet high. The valley ther

412

was one mass of maidenhair fern. Short-stemmed grasses covered the floor of the place under tall buttonwood trees, with high feathery clumps bordering the stream. Even in her fatigue and hunger the Irish girl looked about her with visible pleasure.

He lifted her out of the saddle and carried her up the hillside well above the level of the meadow and the creek. The gaunt buttonwoods made an open grove there. Many of them were hollow and the abodes of countless grey squirrels that peered at them and chattered. A cheerful hammering of woodpeckers beat a staccato tattoo against the monotonous swish of the waterfall. Halfway to the crest, where the stream had once cut through the hill, a giant coal seam lay exposed between its double outcrop of slate. It was like a black cliff. But it had crumbled in places and spilled out its dark treasure fanlike over the slope below. There were hollows weathered in it, "rooms", with shiny walls of blue coal that ran back at places twenty feet or more into the hill.

" 'Twill be dark here," he said. "But at least it will not be cold comfort."

The leaves of many autumns had drifted in and covered the slate floor. He stood listening for the possible whirr of a rattler, but the place remained silent, and he laid her on his blanket in a leaf-packed ledge. He swept a space of floor clean down to the slate, and arranging a nest of stones swiftly, filled it with lumps of weathered coal, and kindled a flame. In its rocky basin the fire soon became incandescent and threw a bright light and a grateful warm glow against the damp walls and the low, black ceiling of the place. She watched him, revelling in the relief of being off her feet, and filled with a strange sense of security and protection.

"I'll find you a much better house later," he assured

her quite seriously. "But this is safe, high shelter at least. And it's coming on to storm for sure. Sometimes there's sudden floods in these valleys."

"Sure and it's a roof, a hearth, and a fire you've found us already," she said in her musical Irish tones. "What more do ye want to thank God for?"

"Meat to put on the fire, for one thing," he answered. "Now I'll be leavin' you for a bit. Lie easy and don't be scairt. I'll be back soon."

"I'll not be tremblin'," she replied. "Do ye know why?" She laughed, and drew from the bosom of her dress the small pistol he had given her at Frazier's nearly two years before. "Sure and it was a grand gift ye gave me. Better than ye knew. I'll tell ye about it—tonight."

"Good gal," he said, giving her a reassuring nod. Then he mounted Enna and rode off through the grove of buttonwoods. She lay quiet, waiting, a look of new peace and relief on her face.

The thunder rolled ever nearer, the lightning dazzled. Gusts full of the freshness of the oncoming storm tore by through the trees outside. She heard him fire both barrels in rapid succession somewhere down the valley. Then in a few minutes he was back again with two fat grey squirrels dangling from his saddle and a great bundle of long grass curved across the mare's neck. He tied Enna as far back in the cave as he could, and cast the fresh fodder down before her. He built up the fire again generously with large lumps of coal. It smoked densely and then began to flame and glow. Enna munched.

Frances lay watching eagerly the meal now in progress. Outside the first sheets of rain tore down the valley. There was a brief patter of hail, and then a violent deluge began. They heard the note of the waterfall rise gradually over the noises of the storm to a steady roar. Trees crashed. Somewhere on the mountainside above, the lightning fell with a stunning smack. The roof above began to dribble and drip here and there through the slate.

"Never mind," he laughed; "the only thing we have to worry about here is not the water, but setting the mountain on fire. Down the Ohio I know a hill that's been aburnin', the Injuns say, for nigh a hundred year. French trappers kindled it long ago."

"I'm not mindin'," she said. "Where do ye think I'd have been now, if ye hadn't happened along?"

"That's so," he said. "You might have been caught in a rush of waters." He looked at the little meadow below them in the valley already beginning to flood. An even more furious beat of rain began. "This storm looks like the end of the world!" he exclaimed.

"Only the beginnin' of it for me," she said.

"All right," he answered, without noticing her earnest gratitude; "now come over to the fire and eat."

They feasted on roast squirrel and hot johnnycake, while the storm raged on.

Afterward he gave her some soothing herbs he had gathered to bind on her feet. They sat quiet, close together in the glow of the fire. He, too, was grateful they had found so firm a shelter. It was no ordinary thunderstorm that blustered and blundered on through the trees. It was the great tempest that harried all the southern mountains towards the end of September, 1764. "Frog storm," the settlers called it; for in the brief, hot weather that followed, "frogs come out and hollered gin like it was spring".

Darkness gradually closed in and the fire in the cavern peered out into the stormy night like a wild, red eye from a black socket. But no one was there to see it, except those who tended it. And for them it shed only a mellow and comforting light . . .

Over a hundred miles northwestward, at Pittsburgh, Colonel Bouquet also was congratulating himself that the new troops left Bedford in time to avoid the "summer tempest" and that he had all his men and munitions over the mountains at last. A few more days would see him ready to leave Fort Pitt. His helpful friend Ecuyer would be sadly absent, but Mr. Burent had the bateaux flotilla ready and the colonel could now move down the Ohio and into the Indian country beyond, secure in his line of supply. The Reverend James McArdle accompanied him to interpret strange tongues . . .

But in the coal cave west of Fort Cumberland McArdle's favourite pupil neither knew nor cared any longer how fared the Indian war. He had made a truce with life at last, even though he found it in strange places and along forbidden paths.

The great storm passed. The floods subsided. The sun came out again, and the forest glowed in a Joseph's coat of tattered autumn colors. Salathiel and Frances tarried on in the valley. The season turned into Indian summer—and for them into an Indian moon. They slept in each other's arms—for there was only one blanket, Salathiel explained, when the time came—and they slept well. If any Senecas or others followed them, the great storm had washed out the last vestiges of their trail in both stream and road. No matter how long the "truce" they had made between them might last, they would always remember their first days together in that valley with the eternal voice of the little waterfall. And in the frosty nights, about the great coal fire in the heart of the hill, Salathiel heard from the woman who lay beside him:

THE STRANGE AND OUTLANDISH STORY OF
FRANCES MELISSA O'TOOLE

First Night

"Me mother was a woman from Drogheda, with some claim upon respectability, for the first thing I can remimber is the sunshine and long shadows under great trees, and bein' carried into supper past the flashin' windows on the tirrace of a great house. He was a tall man that carried me. A bright red beard he had. He spoke only English, and of him I remimber no more, or whether he was my father or another. But I lived there with me mother in the first time of me life, when waking to sunlight in the morning was only to find meself alive in a dream of many colors—that young I was, and so innocent.

And I can remember the far sounding of church bells over Boyne water from the town. And a drive there in a cart, with the houses, the staples, and the paple, and the name of the place that tasted so sweet on me lips: Drogheda! And what else was it God put in a baby girl's mind but the sad sound of huntin' horns at evenin', and a great pack of speckled dogs that once scared me heart out pourin' down a lane past me, while I sat on a high bank and watched a forest of wavin' tails go by. That, and the feel of dew on me bare feet in the mornin's; me bed with a bright painted angel on it, and the face of me mother, and small things she would be sayin', her gay laughter—and then *all that no more!*

For whether she was the mistress of the house that I soon came to think of as a lost heaven, or only a genteel housekaper about the place, I never knew. One summer's night in a time of moonlight she wakened me, hushed me, wrapped me warm, and carried me out to a low-backed car standin' under the gloom of the trees of the park. And thin we drove off into the misty hills with her cryin', and stoppin' now and thin to listen, and beggin' the man drivin' us for the love of God not to strike a bright light lightin' his pipe.

I went to slape after that, but we were still jouncin' along nixt mornin'. All the rist is a mimory of long lanes, hedgerows, and greenery; of drivin' many days, and of rain and hunger, and a great smokin' town we came to at last, noisy and full of pigs and paple.

I came to know well the word that passes for the name of that town on the lips of men, for I lived there till I must have been all of fourteen year. But though 'tis marked on the map of Ireland plain as a mole on a lady's lip, 'tis naught but a suburb of hell, where the divil walks up and down the dock streets, lettin' the say braze play on the scorchin' fork of his britches and the itchin' palms of his hands. Mariners, soldiers, and hoors; gintry, and marchants, and prastes; drays that go thumpin' the stones!

Shall I tell you how the chimney pots reek till the dirty fog drips off the slate roofs and the grey stone houses look like the faces of tearful sluts? And how the crimps walk up and down and in and out, and the bumboats ply, takin' the white bums of girls out to the fightin' cocks of his Majesty's ships? Ah, 'tis a fine, brave city with the dirty Union Jack flyin' over it, and privies that smell like slave ships; its

418

streets full of the heavenly breath of gin. For they drink more of hollands there than they do arrack or native whisky. Gin's the gum in their mother's milk to make their souls and bodies stick together.

And it was to that fair place we had come, and there me mother brought me, a baby girl with nothin' but half a glint o' the misty green hills o' faery Ireland in me eyes.

'Twas a country mimory that faded soon. What-iver was me mother's trouble, and what come upon her, God only knows who lets evil walk the world. But we were in a pretty room, at first, with plenty to eat and china, and white curtains blowin' in and out o' the windows, and a nice, young thing to look after me. There was a tall man, too, with a blue coat and gold buttons and one epaulet used to give me a penny and chuck me mother under her chin. And then there was none of them or of that, but only a great, twilight loft somewhere, and me alone in it, lookin' at cobwebs and cryin' most of the day, locked in, and with not even a wee pot to whisper in when I had to. So I cried unheard in me own slops, till I laid me down to die.

'Twas out of that perishin' place me "Great-aunt" Olive McCallister, a woman with a voice like an admiral and a big boy's moustache, come to fetch me one day, which she did after gittin' the man that was with her to shiver in the panels of the door and open it from the inside. And there I was, still able to crawl, and live long enough to bolt what they fed me downstairs with a horn spoon, which was pap with a dash of gin in it.

'And niver mind what's overtaken yer nice mither —and don't ye go askin' after her now, darlin',' said me great-aunt, who cleansed me off in a barrel of rain water, whisked a wisp of a dress on me there and then, and took me to be baptized around the corner fer good luck in name givin' and the savin' of me small soul.

'O'Tooles or not, it's like yer paple were bloody Protestants,' was all the light on me past I iver got from me Great-aunt Olive McCallister. Howiver that may be, my great-aunt was a pious Catholic herself, despite the Ulster Orange name of her.

But otherwise she was a bold, bad woman afraid of nothin' in this world but a great hulk of a sailor-man they called "Captain Turk" on account of the blue beard and bristles on him, and a way he had of tirin' out all the girls in the house whin he come home from the say after a long voyage to eat and drink everything up till the very rats would squake. And then he would gather up all the money in the place, excepten' the bad shillin's, and beat the yellin' hell out of me Great-aunt Olive. All that he iver brought her was love, three monkeys, swearin' parrots, two black eyes, and a consumin' hope that whin he was home he would go away, and whin he was away he would come back again.

Otherwise, me "great-aunt", who liked to be called by that name or she would pinch your bottom sore, kept as dacent a love-tavern fer gintlemen and highly prosperous mariners as there was in all Cork. The good drink she sold chape in the bar below, but she charged so high for carryin' worse liquor up-stairs to the girls, that Venus and Bacchus was kept apart by the tariff, alow and aloft, and so iverybody slept the quieter.

It was only new patrons or Scots that complained

of her sober policy. The rest, ships' officers and the gay young buds and heirs of marchants about town, rejiced in somethin' more than the usual gentility her arrangements promoted, and the fancy riputation they got for bein' seen there at all.

I'm spakin' now of the high days at McCallister's, you must know, whin only the knock of a gold-headed cane would open the door, and the money rowled in; of days before the linen trade was stopped, and the colony ships from sivin seas come glidin' like flocks of white swans in convoys up the river Lee. Thim was the roarin' days on the dock streets. And I'm glad me childhood fell in such good times, for it's naught much else but misery I've tasted since. In thim days there were tin girls at McCallister's, all dressed in silk like India queens, and fresh linen for ivery guest, and plenty of China tay, and fine victuals and drink galore, and two fiddlers and a cook."

Second Night

"There was three of us young things at McCallister's, waifs me great-aunt had picked up from garrets and cellars like meself, she kept to run errands, sweep up, and impty the slops, or turn the spit. And ye must not think because Great-aunt Olive was a madam, she had no charity in her heart, or did wrong by the poor childer she found. 'Twas just a way she had of bringin' them up for her house service. And if she worked us hard, she was niver cruel. We had a good place to slape, Jinny and Maggy and me, in the low room under cast-off fancies the girls giv us, and all tips from

421

the gintlemen for runnin' an errand she would lave us kape. Many a baitin' I've taken since from the pure in heart that I niver got at Aunt Olive McCallister's. And if you're still thinkin' black of her, I'll tell you this, too. When we got to be big girls she sent the three of us waifs to school two afternoons in the week to the nuns, who learned us to read and some needlework. She only stopped us goin' when we got bigger, and the young fellows started follerin' us in the street and whistlin', seein' where we come home to.

Now, what she had in mind for us I don't know, whether good or ill, for about the time me breasts begin to grow the good times at Cork was all over, whether on account of the wars or the wise new laws of Parliament, only a balladmaker would iver know. But that hard times was come, and money scarce as hair under a baby's armpit, was plain as a dog's bad habits.

Great-aunt Olive would never turn any of us into the street no matter what. But the landlord watched the calendar like a snake lookin' at a bird, and with the same marcy. So for rent the jewelry wint first, and thin the silks, and thin nearly everything else, till the house was as bare as Lady Godiva above and below. And not a Peepin' Tom came even to look through a keyhole at us. The only men that came callin' now were bailiffs.

Can you think what it was with thim divils waitin' to snatch us and sell us into the plantations as soon as iver we run into debt? Maybe you'll not think so black of Great-aunt Olive aither, whin I tell you she kept thim divils off, and niver borrowed a shillin'. She got praties into the house at night, fresh out of the ground, and the peat to roast them with, because she knew somethin' about a gintleman with an estate in the country would pop spuds into the mouths of her ladies o' the night, and young, vargin sarvants to stop their hunger and the tongues of them from waggin' in Cork about himself playin' farmyard and bellerin' in our best parlor like a mad bull. All me Great-aunt Olive had to do was to go out and stand by the park gates with the golden griffins on them and gintly moo like a cow to remind him. And nixt day a wagon of praties would set off for McCallister's.

'Twas a rare device in a hungry year. And we might have weathered the bad times and all. For five captured French officers on parole come to board with us and were charmed to share our spuds and nakedness. There was one nobleman amongst them had gold. And I heard him say he would rather encounter hot Amazons in Ireland than cold mermaids in the western say. Poor soul, he was wounded in his secret parts after a sea battle with the bloody British, and it was only for the gay company of us that he hired the whole house, and for livin' cheap. But he was like a gift from Paris smuggled to us. Some of the furniture was bought back, and there was meat with the praties again. He had chocolate for breakfast and I had the lees from the pot when I brought it up to him in the mornin'. So times seemed gittin' better, and we might have yit had another coy peep at the veiled behind of Fortune, whin all our high hope was brought to the ground with a horrid crash. 'Twas me Great-aunt Olive's favourite form of male misfortune looked in on us at the wrong time. I mean that bloody mariner they called "The Turk" come home again.

Howly saints and angels, what a rantin', reckless sorrow of the world was Captain Turk! A voice on him like a mountain waterfall, eyes like two dirty caverns, and a beard would rasp the hide off a shark even when he shaved, which was not often. And the rest of him was all in iligant proportion, all a fit expression of his black heart and devistatin' character, so that what me Great-aunt Olive found to comfort her for bein' a woman in such a man was past findin' out even by sagacious philosophers. A night with him must have been like bein' trampled by a hairy unicorn on the lip of a volcano. And ivery day in his company surpassed the last one in unexpicted troubles, like the divil himself was flippin' the calendar of hell over, writin' choice bits in his own diary. 'Tis only the splindid liberálity of the high God of heaven could afford to let a man like Captain Turk sail up and down spoilin' the ways of the world. What his ship was like, if he iver really commanded one, is past all human thinkin'.

Well, 'twas himself that came home now, askin' a bit of change after a tedjous voyage to Roossia. And he meant to git his divarsion by baitin' the peaceful expression off the dirty face of the old town. Howly Mither, I well remimber the day when he come stormin' up the stairs, with the curses rowlin' out of his blue beard like bugs from a mattress, roarin' for me Great-aunt Olive McCallister to, 'Close the house, b'God! Close it!'—and callin' all the girls by their own pet names, and ivery other, to come and help him say his black mass on their hands and

424

knees, and welcome him home. Many were called, and all were chosen.

As for us three young ones, we hid in the cellar till the tramplin' overhead and the scrames and chivyin' of the girls and the furniture died away, and we heard the bottles begin to smash out in the street, which was a way he had of gettin' rid of old glass and havin' a bit of a lark with the citizens passin' by. Drink soothed him at first.

Now, I've not told ye the half of it, or all I saw at McCallister's, for, of course, the captain had come home before, and gone away. After which, when things was prosperous 'twas still possible to pick up the establishment again and have the glaziers put in the missin' window lights, and buy lotions for bruises. But his comin' home the last time was a final calamity to me Great-aunt Olive. It was fatal as when a bitch dies before her pups are weaned, leavin' the litter to suck the blue dugs of death. Did ye ever hear a little family like that whimperin'?

That was the kind of noise we made at McCallister's in the proud city of Cork, the last time Captain Turk come home and was hanged for his troublesome gusto. Not that the hangin' stopped him at all. 'Twould have made them dizzy at a rope walk tryin' to twist the hemp strong enough to strangle such a man.

The first thing he did after baitin' me great-aunt unmarcifully as though she was married to him, was to kick all the Frogs out of the house entirely stripped of their clothes, and to sind them hoppin' through the streets to the scandal of iverybody, and, as it turned out afterwards, croakin' to the magistrates—even if they was only French foreigners and naked in a strange land. After which he locked all the doors and stopped the windows, lit all the candles, and held his own kind of hell's carnival for two days and nights, till every bite of victuals in the house was bolted entirely and the cellar drunk dry as a famished place in the desert or the bald spot on an old man's scalp. Thin, seein' the thirst of sivin camels was made one in him, he sinds me out with hot curses and all the pewter shillin's in the house to buy up foamin' pitchers of beer.

Now it was while I was out tryin' to pass bad money for good malted liquor, which is a hard thing to do in Cork, that the constables come for Captain Turk, bad cess to them. They had a warrant sworn to by an English friend of our French nobleman, and, since there was six men for the law and only one actively forninst it, after a terrible hour of roars and riot they took him like a wild beast, bound up in a tablecloth and foamin' off to the gaol. But not before he had thrown Tim Kelly, the best lookin' man in the day watch, down our stape cellar stairs and broken his back, so that he died before Father Magillacuddy could be found. And him all the time in a tavern almost acrost the strate!

The rist of the story I'll tell you whither you belave it or not. 'Tis a curious tale. But there's many a man must have found the truth hard to swallow, if Lazarus left a handsome widow behind him the first time. You'll soon be after seein' what I mean."

Third Night

" 'Twas the death of the poor constable in

McCallister's cellar that evintually landed ivery girl in me great-aunt's house in America. For Captain Turk, or 'Hugh Throstle, of the town of Deptford, master mariner', as the indictments called him, was tried for the murder of poor Tim Kelly, and sintinced to be hanged. And the verdict was had with little trouble to the crown.

Ivery girl at McCallister's was a witness at the trial, glad of the chance to tell what a divil of a man was the Turk. The trial was the most attended of the sissions, for Cork is full of Kellys as a wine bottle of wine. And all the gintlemen and macaronis come in crowds to watch the doxies in the witness box and ogle them, and to hear what the McCallister had to say for herself, and laugh at the deep voice of her, boomin' out tistimony for the crown like the guns of Dublin Castle. For 'twas now that Olive McCallister herself seen the chance to sind Captain Turk off on a voyage from which he would niver return, and she made the most of it. The Turk listened to her witherin' tistimony, and asked only one question, out of all he had a right to be askin'. But even that was objicted to by the crown's attorney as facetious and irrelevant.

'Do you love me, Olive?' was what the Turk asked the McCallister before the cruel face of iverybody, and her under oath.

And she stands up and says, 'Yis, you incarnate divil, I do, but I'll gladly see ye hanged, for all that!'

'That's all any man would want to know, me lord,' said the Turk, and grinned like a death's-head at all of us, includin' himself.

'Irrelevant, but *not* facetious,' said his lordship. 'Tragic, I'd say, tragic!'—and all the gintlemen in curled wigs laughed long and hard. And a few minutes later his lordship, after enjoyin' his own wit imminsely, and complimentin' the fair witnesses for aidin' justice, puts on the black cap.

So the Turk was hanged by the bull neck of him, and half Cork seen him swing. And the law, and even the Kellys, was satisfied. That was about six o'clock on a rainy Irish Thursday evenin'.

Now it may seem strange, but there was no one from McCallister's wint to see the poor captain fightin' in the noose. For 'tis a terrible thing I have to tell, but me Great-aunt Olive was a woman wild with joy at the thought of bein' shut of the Turk foriver and a day. She had the shutters closed on the day of the hangin', and a fine funeral supper set on a long table in the hall. And ivery girl in the house, and the French officers she invited back, was all settin' down by six o'clock under a brutal glare of wax candles, amid a forest of tall bottles towerin' over all the game could be poached for miles around, to cilibrate her liberation and ginuine sense of relief.

And, as a great joke would make your ribs clash togither for laughin', there was an impty chair set at the head of the table for Captain Turk, with an impty basket in it to pile the impty bottles in to his impty mimory.

When the news come he'd been turned off at last, that funeral supper begun with a shout and the clash of knives on dishes and a fusillade of poppin' corks. There was drinkin' of toasts to the poor man that was no more, and the mad feast wint on with only us three scared waifs listenin' in the kitchen, and snatchin' off what we could from time to time.

God only knows how it would have ended, for one

of the French officers made a mock funeral spache fit
to call down the lightnin'. And he was jist sittin' down
to a wild burst of applause—whin there came a crash
like the crack of doom, all the panels leaped out of
the front door that was kicked clane out of its sash,
and we heard a horrible, husky voice like a hoarse
ghost cryin':

'Close the goddamned house,
Close it!
I'll be waked all alone, all alone,
By the only woman I love.'

And then, seein' me great-aunt was like a dead
woman already at the gruesome sight of him, he
begun to croak the names of the other girls, callin'
thim to come to him by name like he always used
to, one by one.

That was the ind of McCallister's. The Turk
closed the house foriver. No one could iver make
love there agin. It withered their prats to think
what had happened in it. For such a screechin' broke
out, and such a frantic fleein' into the street, and
a flittin' of wild Bedlamites, their eyes stickin' out
with the horror of the nether world in thim, there
was that night as brought the neighbours into the
streets with their bloody nightcaps on. And for thim
girls that had their names called by a walkin' dead
man with a great, sore weal under his left ear, and
a blue, swollen face with red, burnin' eyes in it, there
was no pace for many a day and bad slape at night.

Ah, yes, it was himself risurricted. And he made
off with me Great-aunt Olive.

He rowed her in a boat down the river past
Haulbowline dockyard, we heard, and out to a

429

foreign ship. And they was gone with the tide, before the magistrates could be made to understand or belave what had happened.

We was all had up for conspiracy in a gaol delivery. But no one pretended to belave it, exciptin' the jury. 'Twas no delivery, but a carnal risurriction. The Turk had just come to in his coffin, whilst the tired hangmen were out havin' a drink. He shivered the lid entirely and kicked out the sides of it.

'Twas nailin' him down that waked him up, they said."

Fourth Night

"As I was tellin' you, we was tried for gaol delivery, just the same. And the magistrates was not to be moved by anything so simple as a plea of innocence, and the mere lack of ividence to prove us guilty. 'Twas remimbered against us we was a troublesome lot, vagrant bodies, and hoors; and there was always a handy way of turnin' a bit of cash by sellin' poor girls off to the plantations.

A company of London snatchers made the wardens a comfortable offer. And for sivin pounds apiece, and the payment of fees and fines, we was marched down to the docks one evenin' about candlelight and delivered over body and soul to the gintle marcies of Captain John Lang of the bad ship *Doncaster*.

I heard afterwards that the French nobleman made an offer to buy off the three youngest of us that had brought him his chocolate in the mornin's. And, if so, it was out of the kindness of his gay heart. For he was fixed so that even young vargins like the three of us waifs could have been of small interest to him. But we'll pass that, because divil a bit of anything else did I hear of credit to man or beast till ye gave me the pistol at Frazier's to protect meself. And that, mind you, was in America.

Of our crossin' of the western ocean I'll only say this, that if I die and go to the low pit of hell, 'twill be a haven of the blest compared to the dreadful hold of the foul ship *Doncaster*. Besides the unlucky thirteen of us from the house of McCallister, there was three hunder and sivinty-five other souls aboard, reeved from two villages in Donegal, where the Saxon landlord was makin' a deer forest to blow his lonesome horns in and rally his sniffin' hounds. So away we sailed down the river Lee, with the hatches battened down, the sailors cursin' above, and a sad Catholic hymn reachin' only the ears of the saints and fishes from the decks below.

What winds of agony puff fat the sails of vessels sailin' to the New World's shore! Trade winds they are, big with the curse of profits for those who shear His lambs.

Nigh two hunder of us died on the way over in nine starvin' and famishin' weeks of baitin' with the storm winds to and fro. And a leak drove the rats amongst us, and one midnight there was cries of fire. But they doused it and sailed on.

We was fed by contract, but the less they fed us the more they made. 'Twas a nice calculation made in English pounds and pence aginst the days of voyagin', and our flesh and blood; and how much a rimnent of the survivors would bring at New Castle on the Delaware.

431

That was the port we was bound for in Quaker Penn's dominions. But we landed at Lewes further down the bay, as divil a bite was there left or a cup of water when we sailed through the capes.

So at Lewes it was the marchants come aboard, some with broad and some with fashionable hats on. They stood on the poop deck holdin' their nice noses, and watchin' what was lift of us bein' washed down at the fire pumps, naked as the day we was born, men, women and childer.

This give their worships a fine sight of the marchandise they was bargainin' for, and a glimpse of the high ribs of famine like risurriction day in the potter's field, all at the same time. But it was like findin' heaven for us, who was past shame with sufferin', seein' the sunlight agin, and the nate, little town with its white staples and green, swampy shores smellin' of new-mown hay and the guts of fishes.

The man that bought me time was a Mister John Copson of Philadelphia. And he was not so bad a master as such coiners of flesh and blood go. He was lookin' for young paple with a long time to sarve. And so I was picked out with three spalpeens and five colleens to his fancy, the youngest on the ship.

We was taken ashore in his honour's barge rowed by negars, the first time I iver saw any of the race, and, bless God, given a full meal of iysters so big they was like swallowin' a baby, and piles of hoe-cakes, and all the frish milk we could drink. Which was like manna from on high, for we was starved and famished both, and some showin' signs of scurvy. Two of the lads made themselves sick stuffin', till a factor of Copson's drove the slave woman cookin' for us away from the griddle. Then we was locked up in a brick stable with iron bars on the windows and deep straw on the floor. But it was dacent enough, and clane.

That stable was about all I iver saw of the fine town of Lewes on the Delaware—a glimpse of the river with the white ships sailin' by, and firin' their guns when they anchored.

But before I left I saw we was not the only ship had come over from Ireland. The Ould Sod was pourin' the childer of St. Patrick through the capes of the Delaware like the souls of the just crowdin' past the pearly gates when purgatory lets out.

Mister Copson gave us new clothes, even shoes and stockin's, and put us to work hired out to a rope yard for profitable ixercise, till the day of the big sale for redemptioners. It was about a fortnight till they held it on the steps of the town hall, with a crier ringin' a hand bell, and a couple of hard-voiced Englishmen for auctioneers, like a county cattle market.

There was paple gathered from all over, gintlemen, townsmen and farmers, come in to buy up their help and pick up their indentured sarvants.

I had high hopes at first a prosperous lookin' marchant from Philadelphia would take me. He gave me a wink. But his wife was along with a smile on her like a pint of vinegar in winter would have wilted a lead statue of Cromwell. And so that man went home with no young maids, but took an old body with the wrinkled face of a dried mermaid.

Then I stood up on the steps with Jinny and Maggy, the two other waifs from McCallister's,

433

while the big, lyin', black-hearted auctioneer cried out we was three orphans raised by the holy nuns and expert needlewomen and flax spinners.

And that was the cause of our partin' and undoin', for it was not for embroiderin' that plantation owners, farmers, and tradesmen in the crowd would be buyin' our time for. And so it turned out. A glove tanner took Jinny and Maggy. Meself it was that was finally left to the last, standin' there on the steps with a dirty ribbon in me hair I'd found in the muddy strate of the town, and weepin' that I'd never see Jinny and Maggy agin, who was both like sisters to me.

Then the little man rung his big, brass bell for the last time, and the auctioneer changes his tune and cracks me up as a big-boned lass fit for field work or cow tendin'.

'Sivin year to sarve, likely lookin', healthy, with sound white teeth. Only fourteen year behind her. The last of the bloody lot, goin' cheap. Goin', goin' . . .'

And with that a Pennsylvania German with a head like a round shot bids me in—sivin year of me life and labour—for six hunder and thirty pounds of tobacco, and that sot-weed not of the best leaf."

Fifth Night

"Me new master's name was Witmer Hogendobler, a farmer he was, lived west of Lancaster near 'Smoketown', in Penn's province, with a stone barn like a castle and a wealth of fields every way you looked, all tinded by his family and the rist of the cattle on the place. His daughter, Mimsy, about

434

me own age, had died from the strain of bein' a Hogendobler the year before, and it was to fill her place that he bought me time out. They were all moon-faced Germans late from the Duchy of Cleves, spoke no English, and made me go to a heretic chapel ivery Saturday, which they held was Sunday, and listen to sarmons praisin' virginity.

The rest was stark work from starlight of the mornin' to twilight of the evenin'—work in the fields and house, in the kitchen and barn; spinnin' and weavin' and saltin' and picklin'; and milkin' and cheese makin' and butter churnin'; and lamb tindin' and wool cardin'; and sewin' and washin' and scrubbin'; and hoein' and weedin'; and butcherin' and sausage makin' and brewin' and bakin'—and all—till I was like to go zany with it and me tired fate drap off the ankles or the hands of me grow blue on me wrists. 'Twas a year before I could twist me tongue or me ears to their talk. And thin I got no good of it, for they had nothing to say but what one pig might confide to another about the spacious news of the sty.

Ochone! 'Twas a bad time, takin' it all in all. And the thought of sivin year of it was twice as long as double etarnity. Sometimes I thought I was in purgatory bein' purged of me sins, havin' to watch thim eliven Hogendoblers settin' about a table eaten' their weight ivery month in flesh and vigitables with their little eyes papin' out over the top of their fat, rosy, moon-shaped faces. Eatin', I say, as though they'd been hungry for ginirations and was tryin' to make up for havin' had to ate each other in Germany durin' the late lamintable French wars.

I heard about the "dragoons" all the time, for the

thing they was most afeerd of was soldiers. They'd run and hide at the rumour of them. It was that finally put a hope and an idea in me head of tryin' for liberty, that tired I was of bein' a slave. Or belike, the ample fare had put courage in me heart more than fat on me bones. For I'll not say they did any-thing but stuff the guts of the entire family and me, and a couple of hired hands, like the cattle in the barn, and for the same reason.

As for baitin's and drubbin's I had plinty of thim, till me ribs was sore. Let the work lag or the harvest go slack, and there was farmer Hogendobler with a hickory cudgel would drum on your sides like a shillalah at a county fair, till the lofts was full of corn and fodder, and the family of bruises, ivery autumn.

That was the only wages I iver got, and the only sympathy was from some of his sons or daughters had been kicked in the same place by him.

And so it wint for three year, each long as a tailor's table. I was goin' on to be sivinteen, as near as I could tell. And not so hard to take, if a big boy would try.

But divil a coy look did I git in Lancaster County; not a prick for me conscience to worry about on their Sabbath afternoons when we was idle. For the mistress kept her eye rollin' even in chapel, and her head could turn clean around back on her neck like a doll parrot, without even twistin' her bum on the bench. Maybe I was lucky, for I've heard 'twas not so on all the farms in Pennsylvania. But I got restless, and kipt me eyes open. And what one day did I see but me deliverance in gold buttons and a scarlet coat come ridin' down the Lancaster road on the way to Carlisle.

I was bindin' barley sheaves close to the highway whin I looks up and sees a king's officer, one I well remimbered at Cork, disporting himself at me Great-aunt Olive's in the auld days. And so I runs to the fence and climbs over it to meet him, and I says as he rides by on a fine horse a bit ahead of his men —'The top o' the day to ye, Captain Harold Williams. It's a long time since I brought tay and cinnamon buns up to your honour and Bessie Killykelly in the early mornin's at McCallister's.'

And with that he draws rein—and I threw me sun-bonnet back.

'Demme—If it's not little Cinderella from old Olive's house,' he spit out, goin' blank with amazement.

I looked at him boldly, and I could see he liked what he saw, too.

'Grown to a fine lass, b'God!'

'And you as handsome as iver, but a captain now,' says I, curtsying with the barley sheaf in me arms.

'And what the divil are you doin' here, me gal?' he asked.

'Oh,' says I, 'Oh, do you care, Captain Williams? I'm sold for sivin years' slavery to a dirty Palatine peasant and his graspin' family, and if ye iver got a kiss from an Irish girl in Ireland warmed your brave English heart, you'll remember it now and not lave me here to perish. Me name's Frances O'Toole— and I've got nice, grey eyes like your own!'

'You have!' says he. 'We're both damn handsome paple. But the divil a guinea I have to me name

437

after Philadelphia, and I'm ridin' west to the Indian wars at Carlisle.'

'You've got wagons though,' says I. 'And ye might ravish me off to Carlisle, and nobody be the wiser.'

'I might,' says he, makin' his high-stippin' horse to wheel in the road and come a full circle around. 'I might,' says he, 'if you hold your tongue like a wise woman, afterward—and wait here now.'

And with that he trots back down the road to the rear of the column, where I see the white tops of baggage wagons slippin' along through the trees.

As for me, I threw the barley sheaf over the fence to kape from breakin' the heart of the farmer, and crouched me down with the reapin' hook still in me hand. I waited till the cavalry iscort trotted past me, sayin' niver a word to all their bawdy chaff. Behind thim come the great four-wheeled wains, and Captain Williams ridin' by the first one. He gives me a broad wink, and I slip in behind on the first wagon, with the two drivers pretindin' niver to see me whilst kapin' their eyes on the captain. The last I seen of Hogendobler's was all the family hollerin' to one another about the cattle-liftin' soldiers, and speedin' in a wild stampede to the house and barn to bar the doors till they passed."

Sixth Night

"I must tell you now how, after flittin' from the farm near Lancaster, I come to ind up at Frazier's log tavern clean on the other side of the Allegheny Mountains in a worse plight than iver I was before.

'Tis a hard thing to get down on your luck. Misfortune comes back like a beggar, always to ask for more. You must know, howiver, it was no light o' love of Captain Williams that rode off in a big flour wagon. Nor was it the wink of his handsome grey eye that got me into a pickle. I was a disperate young girl. And me plight was brought home to me forcibly even before we got to the ferry on the road to Carlisle.

For hardly had the captain turned his back on us, and rode to his place at the head of the column, whin one of the ruffians that drove the wagon left his seat and come back under the canvas to try to have his own way with me.

He was no soldier. He was a hired wagoner, but he was no child. And I would have paid me maiden debt to nature in that miserable conveyance, if it had not been for the reapin' hook, that not knowin' what to do with, and not thinkin' to throw it away, I still grasped in me hand.

I give him the sharp point of it whin he laid hands on me. And I wint after him like a cat o' the mountains. I drove him back to the seat, and he bled all over the flour sacks in the wagon, and sat mutterin' and cursin' to his friend, and sayin' things low in his ear, while he bound up his wounds. After that the two of thim would turn around and give me black looks and a leer ivery few furlongs as we drove along.

So I could see how it was. They would give me away to the magistrates at the first place we come to, and git their reward from the farmer for returnin' his runaway girl. Whativer I was goin' to do, I must do quick. I must git out of the wagon I was in, and I must git out of the neighborhood of Hogendobler's farm.

439

'Twas a hot afternoon, and at a small hamlet we stopped to water the horses and give the troopers a rest. The soldiers was a squadron of dragoons, I should have said, escortin' fourteen wagons from Philadelphia to Carlisle. The wain I was ridin' in was the first in the train. Now, whin the drivers took out their teams to lead them to the town trough, I slipped out of the first wagon and walked down the village street like I was a slip of a girl on an errand, goin' from one house to another. But whin I got to the last wagon, and found no one was lookin', I whisked into it and covered meself up under some big sacks.

Prisently the train began to move again, and I could hear me two former friends up front inquirin' if anyone had seen me. By the luck of an orphan no one had. So they must have concluded I'd give them the slip in the village, and their hopes of collectin' the reward had gone glimmerin'.

At the ferry, Captain Williams come inquirin' after me again. And there was no doubt he was ginuinely disappointed, for he give the two drivers in the first wagon the hell of a bad time. And seein' the blood on the flour sacks, and the ugly dog I had wounded lickin' his wounds, he had him out for a floggin', tied up to his own wagon wheel. After that there was a gineral uproar amongst the hired drivers in the train, cursin' me and the cruel Royal officers.

You can be sure whin I heard that, I lay quieter than ever. To be discovered, with the resintment of the drivers hot agin me and Captain Williams, would have been pure disaster, and maybe as much as me life was worth. So I stayed tight, covered up by sacks of biscuits and greasy sides of bacon, hot and thirsty and sufferin'.

Two days later we rowled into Carlisle in a cloud of summer dust.

By that time I had come to the end of me rope intirely. I had to get out of the wagon for food and relief, and hardly had I put me two fate on the ground, when I was nabbed by the little bearded man that drove it.

Now I'll not tell you all the trouble I had. 'Twould make a lawyer give an honest sob. The gist of the matter was that the man who drove the wagon caught me—and that he was old Frazier himself.

Luckily he was on older man with a grey beard and thoughtful blue eyes. And I saw that me only chance to kape from fallin' into the hands of the other drivers, or of bein' turned over to Captain Williams, or sint back to the farmer for the reward, was to make meself valuable to Mister Frazier.

I found he was somethin' more than a hired driver. He had a contract to take six wagons over the mountains from Carlisle to Fort Pitt. He kept a woods tavern on Forbes Road near Pittsburgh. His wife was no good, or worse. And he badly needed a hired woman to do the gineral work.

Blarney and delay are the hopes of the disperate. All this I pulled out of him whilst tellin' me own sad story, standin' there by the wagon in the starlight, while he smoked a pipe leanin' against a big, yellow-painted wheel and lookin' at me kindly enough. I think I plazed him.

'Very well, me fine gal,' says he at last, 'sarve the rist of yer time out with me at the tavern, and

I'll see ye over the mountains without sayin' a word to the authorities.'

'If you're not lookin' for anything more than the work of me hands and honest labour, Frazier,' says I, 'it's a bargain. I'll be your indentured maid, but nothin' more.'

'No, no, I meant nothin' more than me words,' says he. 'But you'll have to put up with the old woman about the place. And that'll not be so aisy.'

'I'll chance it,' I said, not knowin' what I was sayin', or the half of it. So we shook hands over it like two men.

And that's how I come to be a sarvin' wench for Frazier in his iligant forest hostelry at the cross trails near Pittsburgh, and that's why you found me there when you and the captain come travellin' along.

Oh, 'twas a bad bargain I made with Frazier, though both of us thought it a good one at the time. Captain Williams went back to Philadelphia with his brave horsemen, and I niver saw him again. Frazier hid me at Carlisle till we started over the mountains. And after that, and once in the wilderness, I was like a bird in his hands.

But 'twas not him I had to fear, as it turned out. It was his crazy old woman. You seen how it was when you were there that day. But that was only part of it. Tomorrow night I'll be tellin' you what happened at Frazier's lonely log tavern in the western woods."

Seventh Night

"Now I'll tell you what happened at Frazier's.

442

And it's important for you to understand. For I wouldn't want you to be thinkin' I'd be after takin' shelter with you with a bloody murder on me soul. But that's what it come to—and this was the way of it.

From the very first there was no gittin' along with Mrs. Frazier. It was not so much what she did or said—or what I did. It was the way she watched me. A kind of a side glance from another person lay lurkin' under her lids. And sometimes, whin she thought I wasn't watchin' her, that other person would come out and pape at me, around the corner you might say, and I'd catch a full glare from her jist for a moment like cats' eyes staring in the dark. And I was the mouse. Oh, yes, I could see that. I knew.

But I tried me best all the same. I worked me hands to the bone. There was nothin' I didn't do. I kept the place nate, and there was many a mess to clean. I tried to plaze the customers, whether they were Injuns, traders, soldiers, or settlers. And I did plaze them. I plazed Frazier himself, for he said so. He was a fair enough man; subdued, and anxious to git along. He was thankful for what help I give him. He brought me some cloth for clothes and promised me wages for makin' his tavern go. Not a thing would his old woman do but sit by the fire and watch me. And there was no way I iver found of plazin' her at all. She said little, but she watched.

For a while I thought she was jealous, and so did the old man. He told her he'd bought me time at a regular sale of immigrants at Carlisle and brought me out to help her—and she ought to be glad of that. So she started to pretend she was, and that really scared me. I saw she was glad he'd brought me, but not for the work I did. What was it she wanted? I wondered. She'd lived alone in the forest with something under her eyelids, hauntin' her lonesome days.

And then one day it came out and walked. And a grisly thing it was. She wanted to tie me up and whip me and watch me squirm. She had the strength of a giant's daughter and an arm like a horse's leg.

She caught me just once, while the old man was away. I was off me guard and she nabbed me. I think now he saved me life by comin' home before she was lookin' for him. She told him I'd stolen five shillin's from under the stone in the hearth. But he never belaved that. I saw he knew what had happened. And then it was that I understood why he really wanted someone else at the cabin. He was afraid of her. After that I had the wings of quicksilver on me heels.

You may well ask why I didn't run away again. Injuns!

It was about the time the worst raids started. And divil a choice did I have but to stand Mrs. Frazier or run off to the woods to the savages.

Besides, the old man himself stuck it out like a soldier. Livin' with his wife, he was used to hard times. He bored loopholes in the log walls of the tavern, and arranged to rally some neighbours in for a garrison if a raid come. And I hated to desart him in the face of the inimy within and without. He was one of the oldest settlers in the Monongahela valley. So I stayed on, and so did he. And so did Mrs. Frazier. And that was the way you found us when you and the captain passed by.

Well, you saw how it was that day. 'Twas an accident brought her a timptation she couldn't resist. But after you left it was different. I had the pistol you loaned me. She knew I would use it. And I did. When Frazier left next day with the lead in the wagon for Fort Pitt, and old Ganstax ridin' along, leavin' us alone, I climbed into the garret and told the old woman I'd shoot her if she tried to come up the ladder at me.

So she stayed down, after a bit of blarney, and after a while I heard her outside makin' the big axe fly on the firewood. Now that was something she'd never done before. When Frazier come back he stood gapin' at her in surprise, and I didn't blame him.

'That's right,' he says, 'take it out on the wood, woman. It saves trouble and it makes kindlin'.'

And that's all he iver did say. He'd banged her head well against the wall for tryin' to whip me, as you may remimber. That seemed to stop her. And as time went on we both began to think maybe he'd knocked some sense into her brain pan.

I'll not try to tell you all the ins and outs of it as the months went by. When the spells come on her, and I seen her watchin' me, I'd show her the pistol was ready, and let it pape out of me dress. I slept with me eyes half open, and twice in the bitter night-time I started her choppin' wood.

Oh, there was several times like that. But somehow we kept the peace walkin' around one another, the three of us, like bastes in a cage, watchin', waitin' for one to jump. It was bad.

Still, I begun to think I'd get through it all right. In a few weeks me time would be sarved out. Then

445

I was to get the wages Frazer had promised me, in a lump, and a ride in his big wagon back to Fort Bedford. He was a man of his word, and I was countin' the days one by one till me bargain with him should be over. I thought how I'd be free then with a few pennies in me pocket, and able to go to find ye. I heard about ye from Mr. Burent when he passed through from time to time. I didn't know how ye'd take it if I sought ye out, but I thought 'maybe'. So I was already makin' up me bundle, and darnin' the holes in me poor stockin's, whin the cat jumped.

Arragh, it was quite simple, you might say! Instead of only choppin' up wood one evenin', after she'd heard me and Frazier talkin' about me goin' away, Mrs. Frazier chopped up her husband, too.

I seen it all happen, fetchin' a bucket from the springhouse.

He was standin' near the woodpile watchin' her wield the axe in the twilight. It seemed more like a mistake she was makin' than murder. After she finished up a log into billets she jist went on and finished up on him. Then she carried the parts of him in along with the wood and laid them out in the fireplace. An' thin she seemed to remimber somethin' and started to look around.

Maybe it was her backcomb she'd lost. But I thought she was lookin' for me.

She come to the door wipin' her hands off on an oats sack, and stood, peerin' out into the darkness with the light behind her.

Lucky for me I'd gone down to the spring! I might have been cornered in the garret, and I don't think the pistol would have stopped her any more. The terrible thing was the quiet way she went about

446

it all, and jist carried old Frazier in with the wood.

The last thing I seen of Mrs. Frazier was her standin' in the door, puttin' her bangs back in place, and pattin' them down nicely like she was satisfied.

I didn't wait to see no more.

I took the trace south leadin' to Braddock's Field, and I niver stopped goin' all night. I ran, and sat down till I got me breath, and thin I got up and ran again, niver mindin' the roots and briers that clutched me. Next mornin' I saw the Monongahela River over the top of a hill, and found me an old raft at the mouth of Turtle Creek.

The rist of the way I followed what's left of Braddock's Road, I chewed bark and et berries, I was in me old fur slippers when I left and they soon wore out. So did me two fate. But I walked on bleedin', with fear stalkin' behind me.

Once I thought I saw her in the moonlight, but 'twas only a mossy tree looked like a witch. I niver saw a livin soul till I got to Beeson's.

There I told them me name was Liza Magee, and I give them a cock-and-bull story. For all the time I was in mortal terror the old woman had turned me in at Fort Pitt for doin' the murder of Frazier. Even in these woods news like that gits around. And who would belave me own story against hers, unless they knew her? I'd cry out at the sight of her, too. I'd look guilty. Whin Ganstax showed up with his two warriors to drink new milk at Beeson's, I lit out before he saw me. I thought he might remimber seein' me at Frazier's. The rist I think you must know. Meetin' you on the road to

Cumberland is the only feast I've had in a sivin years' famine and luck."

It was a story full of tears and laughter, but an honest tale hot off the griddle of life. There was nothing smug about it—and she had told him all.

Into her past he had already tried to fit his own. As the days and nights had passed in the lonely valley, he told her everything about himself that he either knew or could remember. It was a comforting kind of lovers' confession in which they forgave each other, and resolved with the confidence of a mutual absolution to go on together, despite the world, evil, and bad luck. They would try actually to fit the future together as they had managed to accommodate each other's past. But their future would be mutual. They would share it, as they had already shared their bodies and minds and the days and weather in the dark cave by the fire.

He made her no promises. She expected and exacted none. They would go on, over the mountains, and downcountry to the settlements. They were agreed upon that, but not much more. The rest was understood and left nebulous.

The mountain nights were growing rapidly more frosty now. When the time to leave came he made her a pillion out of his blanket, and they rode out of the valley together on Enna; and took the road eastward.

Thus about the end of October Salathiel appeared once more at Fort Cumberland, with Frances ridin sedately behind him. He dismounted before the roug log building that bore a sign in homemade letters saying "Josh Crump—Gineral Store".

"Wal," said the proprietor of that backwoods empo rium, who was leaning against the doorjamb as usua

448

"wal, now, ain't that nice! I see ye've done found yer wife after all. Howdy, Mrs. Albine," he added, spitting out a large wad as a tribute to the lady. "How be ye?"— and he shifted his coonskin cap.

"Fine," replied Frances, and gave an ingratiating smile. "But I've been where there ain't much to be had. Have you got any boltin' for makin' clothes?"

"What d'ye lack?" cried Mr. Crump, automatically sensing a customer.

"Everything the Injuns didn't have," replied Salathiel, giving Frances a wink. "Step down, my dear, and have a look at Mr. Crump's marchandise."

"Aye, step right in, step right in!" cried Mr. Crump, removing his shoulders from the doorjamb at last. "Now don't you be blushin', mistress, I've seen gals lookin' much worse than you do, comin' in from bein' captivated. You're lucky to have found your man."

"That so?" Salathiel asked Frances in a whisper as she dismounted.

"Oh, I'm a lucky woman now, I know that," she said, apparently to the storekeeper. She laughed, while her eye ran along Mr. Crump's meagrely stocked shelves.

And so it was that the first of Ecuyer's small legacy to Salathiel went to buy calico and some other vital things for Frances Melissa O'Toole. Mr. Crump whistled when he saw gold pieces, and everybody in the dark little store was suddenly quite happy, including Salathiel and Frances.

It was surprising what a guinea or two could do. For the first time it was thoroughly brought home to Salathiel that he could "git" with his purse as well as with his rifle. So he "brought things down" from Mr. Crump's shelves which Frances "aimed to git".

They stayed with the Crumps for several days at Fort

Cumberland while Frances made new clothes. They could have done better buying at Pendergasses', Salathiel said. But Frances would not hear of riding into Bedford in a tattered linsey-woolsey and bare feet.

"I'm no naked blanket girl," she said. "I aim to be somebody." And in a surprisingly short time she appeared as somebody, and no denying it.

The transformation she brought about in herself in a few days with Mrs. Crump's shears, a few needles, and "hand blarney", more than justified her contention. A short woollen bodice made from scarlet "officer's cloth", blanket petticoats, an overskirt with flounces of bright calico, something white about the neck made out of nankin and stiffened with potato starch, a leather snood with an old slipper buckle on it—all this and a black straw bonnet gradually evolved in the back room of Mrs. Crump's dark cabin behind the store.

Meanwhile, the shopkeeper's wife looked on and tried to help by knitting Frances a pair of red stockings. There were no extra shoes in the place but a cast-off pair of soldier's brogans, and Frances rejected these for the neat moccasins Salathiel made her out of heavy rawhide. Finally there was a matchcloak pieced out of many squirrel skins, black and grey, to throw over her shoulders.

"Howly Mither," said Frances O'Toole, standing up in all her glory at last. "If I only had me a mirror!"

"And a ring?" asked Mrs. Crump, who had been wondering.

"Sure, 'twas the first thing they took off me finger," replied Miss O'Toole—"the red divils!"

Mrs. Crump nodded. It seemed extremely likely. She knew of girl captives who had lost more than their wedding jewellry.

450

"Anyway," said Frances, "I can still walk like a lady." And she proceeded to do so, while the older woman laughed with feminine pleasure and delight at the droll mimicry of fashion that somehow seemed genuine.

"Madam Cresap!" she exclaimed—"and to the life."

"Her!" said Frances. "Does *she* walk like that?" and Mrs. Crump nodded.

Then the Irish girl laughed.

If the mincing gait of vanished dock street ladies in the city of Cork and the fashions of McCallister's of nearly a decade before had bloomed again for a moment in Mrs. Crump's cabin—who at Fort Cumberland, in a gulch in the wildwoods of Maryland, would ever be the wiser?

"Mrs. Albine" could walk like a lady, even in moccasins. They all saw that. More important, they all said it, and that she was a fine, upstandin' Irishwoman with sad . . . no, with merry eyes. They could never be quite sure which. But they remembered them.

When Salathiel rode off to Bedford with Frances behind him again, Mr. Albine had learned something about what a needle and a woman can do for each other. He scarcely knew Frances when he looked at her now. But he was a proud young man.

"Look what I have, and be damned to you!" seemed to emanate like a challenge from his cocky manner; from the way he rode in his saddle, erect as a trooper; and from the way he let "Twin Eyes" sleep in the hollow of his left arm with a sparkle and a glint like Captain Jack's baby. Enna, under her double burden, stepped more gravely and sedately, as though aware of her new responsibility. Only there was nobody along the lonely valley road to Bedford to see them. Exactly what he would say when he got to Bedford with Frances instead of Jane, he wasn't sure. At least they would make a handsome entrance into town.

They laughed together over "Mrs. Albine" having been taken for granted at Cumberland. They had done nothing to confirm the impression, except not to deny it. It had not occurred to them that such a conclusion would be inevitable. They had simply accepted it.

"But what *will* you be sayin' at Pendergasses'?" demanded Frances, who like a woman, wanted the future made clear.

"I'll wait to see what happens," replied Salathiel. "It depends"—whether McArdle is there or not, he added, but to himself alone. He'd see. He wouldn't try to deceive Garrett. No, he had made up his mind to that. The rest must turn out as might be. Besides, Yates might have returned. He hoped so.

So they rode on through the late autumn weather, bright with the hint of November frosts to come, and the last painted leaves falling. He began, humorously now, to whistle the tune of last summer, "Past Caring and Past Faring", while he kept his eyes keen for every shadow falling across the road. You could never tell. It wasn't entirely safe yet.

About six o'clock they rode into the village of Bedford.

All that the "triumphal entry" lacked to be triumphant was an audience. Enna stepped her highest and best, snorting at the familiar scents of the neighbourhood. The young couple on her back rode with more dignity than their years demanded. But there was no one to watch them pass. It was dark, and Salathiel had forgotten that it would be, having left Bedford in the long summer days. Now the town seemed positively deserted. Only a few windows glowed dimly in the village. The rows of barracks lay silent at the fort. Even the hospital showed only a few lanthorns. Bedford seemed but the ghost of its former busy self. You could hear the river and the wind in the trees, it was so quiet.

Of course, he might have expected this. He knew what had happened even before he passed the first deserted sutlers' houses. The troops had marched west to Fort Pitt. The settlers had scattered to rebuild their cabins before snow fell. The life of the town—its garrison, all the hangers-on of the troops, the wagoners and wagon trains—had vanished. Instead, there was silence, and here and there a solitary candle burning behind a window. He was glad to find, almost surprised to see, a Highland sentry on duty at the gate of the fort as they rode past. Only the colored servants and the Indian help were in the yard at Pendergasses'. The ark stood lonely, towering under its shed. The only light in the "women's house" came from Mrs. Pendergass's room. It was a calm welcome.

But once in the familiar wagonyard, he sprang down and helped Frances to dismount. By the feel of her hand, as she climbed down from the pillion, she was hot and nervous. While a young darky finally answered his calls and took Enna off to the stable, she stood smoothing her skirt and re-tying her bonnet in the dark. He put his arm around her encouragingly and gave her a kiss.

"Don't worry," he said. And—quite worried himself—he pushed back the big door of the hearth room.

"Phoebe!" he thought—and then thought of her no more.

At the extreme end of the place near the hearth Ned Yates and Arthur St. Clair were having a bite and a bottle between them. There was no one else in the big room at all.

"Demme!" cried Yates, looking up at the sound of footsteps, and shading his eye against the candles. "Demme, if it isn't my old friend the Little Turtle—and? His lady turtle!"

He rose and came forward cordially, the curt dapperness, the all but preternatural neatness of his small person, was somehow set off and enhanced by the trim wig, and the black patch he now wore over his left eye. He contrived thus, inadvertently, to convey a hint of something deftly sinister in dark contrast to his good-natured grey eye and bright smile.

For a moment that evening, after a long absence, Salathiel saw his friend as a stranger again, and felt his enigmatic stare. He had recovered all his poise, but he was changed and matured by his tragedy. No use trying to deceive him.

"Yates," he said, "this is Frances."

She dropped him a curtsy, and gracefully. Only for an instant a smile puckered the corners of Yates's mouth as he bowed gravely in return.

"Congratulations!" he exclaimed—"to both of you!"

"You have a swift wit, sir, I perceive," said Frances.

"Oh—you perceive that," laughed Yates. "That *will* make it pleasant."

He took her by the hand and led her down the room to where St. Clair was still sitting at the table.

"Arthur, I want you to meet the young lady my friend Albine has had the good sense to bring back with him. Mr. St. Clair is our arbiter of elegance, fashion, and decorum in these parts, madam," he added solemnly.

Always a bit pompous, St. Clair invariably rose to the bait of a compliment, no matter how broad the hook.

He was wearing a small sword that evening—as he might have in Philadelphia. He rose now to confirm Yates's outrageous assertion, and bowed formally.

"Mistress Albine, 'tis indeed an honour to greet ye."

Yates kicked Salathiel a tap on the ankle. "Fast work," he whispered.

"Have ye supped, mistress?" St. Clair was asking.

"I'm hungry as a wolf's mother," confessed Frances. " 'Twas a long ride from Cumberland."

"Heavens on earth, sit down with us here then!" exclaimed St. Clair, pulling out a chair. "Albine, you've grown no smaller, I see. How's that double-barrelled gun of yours? Did you ever get it fitted with a single lock as I advised?"

"No," drawled Salathiel, "I've still got a trigger on both my barrels. You know, I rather like taking my choice in a double chance." He looked at Frances and laughed.

Yates nearly suffocated. He patted Frances' hand under the table. "Used the *right* barrel this time," he whispered. "Glad he got you?"

"Very!" she said, and blushed to the neck.

"Pina, Pina!" roared St. Clair impatiently. He was hungry himself.

The old woman came hurrying into the room—and all hopes of supper disappeared for the time being in her overwhelming excitement at seeing Salathiel and the girl he had brought with him.

"Do God, do God! Do bless 'em both! Miss Bella mus' be told. De bride mus' be welcome to de house." The old slave's voice trilled on with African fervour and excitement. Here was news, indeed! Her first announcement was directed to the entire yard, where she went to spread the tidings. And in another moment the hearth

455

room was invaded by all the servants of the place, black and red, great and small, staring, jabbering, and pressing as close to the table as they dared to see Marse Albine's new woman.

"Good Lord, we'll never, never get supper now," said St. Clair, looking annoyed at the hubbub he had precipitated.

"Where's Garrett?" asked Salathiel anxiously.

"He's gone to Fort Pitt on a contract—luckily," laughed Yates. "But Bella's at home, and ready for anything, I'll bet you."

At that instant Bella herself, with old Pina hobbling and jabbering behind her, came hastily through the corridor door.

Salathiel was forever grateful to Bella Pendergass for the welcome she gave to Frances that evening. Whether she understood that Frances was not Jane, he could never be sure. If so, it made no difference to Bella. The two women obviously liked each other from the first. In fact, it was he who almost spoiled it by attempting to explain: "Of course, she's not a *bride*. I've been married a long time, you know. I've just found her, and . . ."

Yates kicked him again just in time.

"Of *course*," said Bella, taking Frances by the hand. "Pina's an old fool. But you must forgive her. We all want you to be welcome here. My father will be sorry not to have been here to greet you, when he hears about it. Nigh the whole family's away for once, workin' out on the clearin's. But Mother's at home, and she'll want you to come over and stay with us—for the first night at least. Guess you'll have to have to put up with your old room again, Mr. Albine. I hope you won't mind. Mother and I will look after your Frances. She must be tired ridin' the woods. Have you any things, mistress?"

456

"Only what I'm wearin', ma'am," said Frances.

"Where ever did you find that habit? I never saw a handsomer one," exclaimed Bella, with obvious envy, as she led Frances over the bridge to the women's house.

"It's all out of your hands now, Sal," grinned Yates. "Bella and Mrs. Pendergrass have taken charge."

The three men sat down—looking at once disappointed and relieved.

"I make it a rule to ride a natural mistake as far as the first hurdle at least, Sal," remarked Yates, laying his hand reassuringly on Albine's arm. "There's no reason you *have* to tell them everything at first."

Salathiel didn't know exactly what to say, seeing how matters had turned out. He was both pleased and annoyed that Frances had been led off by Bella. He felt uneasy at all the excitement.

"Damn it! *Stop* that jabberin', Pina," he finally shouted. "Here! Give your family and all the big Injuns a go at some grog. And for Lord's sake bring us some supper. I'm starved." He slipped the old woman a yellow coin.

"God bless ye. God bless ye, Marse Albine. De good Lord send yah a hunder chillens, and all twins," cried Pina, bowing, wiping her hands on her apron, and shooing her progeny and the Indians from the room. "I'll dish yah up a hot mess in a little jiffy outside in de summah kitchen."

So it was over—and Frances bedded next door.

The rest of the evening he and Yates sat listening to St. Clair unfold his plans for a new settlement to be made at Ligonier.

It was a large scheme, well laid, exceedingly promising. St. Clair and Yates had been working at it all summer. "We've counted on you, Albine, to help get the first wagons over the mountains, as soon as Colonel Bouquet settles the frontier troubles," St. Clair explained. "That ought to be directly, for few doubt the colonel's success now, who know him. Yates and I will be looking after certain legal tangles at the land office at Lancaster and in Philadelphia for a while. Maybe you'll come east with us and meet the settlers we've been roundin' up. We hope so. You'd encourage them, I opine. You, and your double-barrelled gun!" He talked on. There were many details to be discussed. But before the evening was over their plans were agreed upon.

Salathiel was greatly pleased to find that both St. Clair and Yates had really been waiting for his return, and that they regarded his help in the new settlement as important. How curious that, after all the trouble of the year before with St. Clair and Japson, he was now to take part in helping them bring people to Ligonier. There was no trace of resentment of the past in St. Clair's manner. He was now all affability and business. He deferred constantly to Yates, and listened carefully to any suggestions. How times had changed!

The "undertakers" of the venture were to be rewarded by shares of land. Yates had not forgotten Albine in arranging that. Salathiel could see he owed much to his legal friend, "Mr. Cyclops", as St. Clair now constantly called him. Eventually the name stuck, and "Mr. Cyclops" became Yates's real name to many to whom Homer was pure Greek—and nothing more.

St. Clair was inclined to prolong the discussion indefinitely, since his own interests were so heavily involved. But even though he was going to bed alone, Salathiel wanted to stop before midnight.

"I'll put Frances in the wagon then, and we'll all go downcountry to the settlements together," he said at last. "When do ye start?"

Yates hummed something about the animals going into the ark two by two before answering. "Thursday," he said. "Day after tomorrow, if you can get horses for the ark."

"Wonder what Ecuyer would say, if he could see Mistress Albine going downcountry in his precious *voiture?*" Certain memories of the past twisted St. Clair's mouth momentarily into a wry smile.

"Oh, I don't think he'd mind," said Albine. "He'd not wish *any* of us to be lonely, I'm sure." It was now Salathiel's turn to kick Yates on the ankle. They broke up after a nightcap and went upstairs chatting.

Despite certain associations of his lonely old room, after the day's ride Salathiel stretched out comfortably. After all, Frances was safe in the next house. The move east had been settled. He'd get horses for the ark, somehow. With his ranger's pay and the legacy he had nearly sixty pounds in hard money. He had his rifle, Enna, the wagon, bright prospects, and Frances. Those last nights at Pendergasses' he slept well.

Circumstances soon solved the problem of finding two teams to pull the ark. Stottelmyer came through the town with a return convoy from Fort Pitt next day. He brought horses and news with him. Garrett had lingered at Pittsburgh to visit with both Sue and Phoebe. Colonel Bouquet had set off down the Ohio with his expedition. Nothing more would be heard of him for several weeks. He and his men had plunged directly into the western wilderness. The rest was fate. Stottelmyer's wagons were returning empty to Carlisle. He laid one up at Pendergasses' and lent four nags to Salathiel providing he would keep them for him at Carlisle until Stottelmyer could pick them up.

Salathiel and Frances busied themselves the next afternoon arranging things and re-stowing the wagon. She was delighted with the ark, "a rollin' shebang on wheels". Everything was in it; even Johnson's old valet kit and the wig-furbishing outfit. Bella came out to help, for she and Frances had rapidly become good friends.

"I do hate to see ye leavin' before Pap comes back," Bella kept saying. "It's right lonely already with the house so empty; with even Charley away! Mom ain't been feelin' so well lately, either."

Bella sighed. She could see long lonely days ahead for her at Pendergasses'. Wartimes had their compensations after all, she thought.

Salathiel and Frances had only one serious ordeal to face before faring eastward. It was saying good-bye to old Mrs. Pendergass. On the last evening they went to the house together and Bella took them up to the old woman's room.

She was sitting in her chair before the fire, as usual almost birdlike in her white cap and fragility, but still alert.

"Your cap's awry, mother," said Bella, putting it back into place.

"Let be, let be," said the old lady impatiently, while pinning her bright blue gaze on Salathiel and Frances.

"So you're goin' to leave us, Salathiel Albine, an take your girl downcountry to the old settlements," she said. "It's a fine lass you've found yourself. Did you know she looks like your mother? Ah, well do I remember her, a blue-eyed, dark-haired O'Moore." She patted Frances' hand affectionately.

"You're like your father Lemuel, Salathiel. You with an Irishwoman, too. But you go east—this time

"Everything seems to point that way, ma'am," said Salathiel.

"Aye," said she under her breath, "tides ebb and flow." He thought she had said something in disapproval.

"But we'll be comin' back soon, and stop off to see ye," he explained hastily.

Mrs. Pendergass laughed.

"You Albines are all alike," she replied. "You'll be comin' back soon, will you? That's what your pap said when he set out for the west-running waters—and he never came back again. I thought maybe you'd listen to Garrett and stay on here. But it's town life you've set your heart on, I can see that. Well, go and see the towns, get the smoke and the sting of them in your eyes. You're both young yet . . .

"No, no," she went on, motioning to Salathiel not to interrupt her, "I'll *not* be seein' you again. I'm as sure of it as that the woods be green in zummer! And that's the reason I called you both here, to give you a little zumpthin' to remember me by before you go."

She fumbled in her sewing box and drew something out by two faded strings.

"It's a babe's cap your mother knitted for me when my Matthew was comin'. Or was it for you, Bella? I forget now which of the babies it was. It was in other days. But I thought you might like to have it, Salathiel, to give your Frances. It looks a bit like an Irish bonnet." She sighed, and handed it to Frances directly.

"I'll kiss you for that, mother," said Frances, and she flung her arms around her, with tears in her eyes.

"Good-bye, young woman," said the old woman. "The Lord be with ye!"

She shook hands with Salathiel.

They went out of the room together and turned at the end of the hallway to look back. She was still sitting in the firelight, smiling.

They went to bed together that night in the wagon. The start next morning was to be long before sunrise.

But faithful Bella was there to wave the ark and its crew out of the yard. She threw her apron over her head as she went into the house again. Yates drove for the time being, having left his lame horse at Loudon two weeks before.

It was a still, starlit autumn morning, Guy Fawkes Day of November, 1764. The road down the valley glimmered before them with silver patches of hoarfrost. St. Clair followed some distance behind the wagon on a sturdy gelding. Salathiel rode ahead, curbing Enna in to keep pace with the party. He kept whistling the refrain of "Past Caring and Past Faring", until Yates shouted to him to "desist".

He laughed and began singing to himself instead. He had seldom felt so carefree and deeply happy.

Dawn overtook them at the water gap, where the Juniata cuts like a bright sword through the mountains. By the time they came through the pass the sun was rising directly ahead of them out of the misty eastern hills. A wide and magnificent sweep of wild landscape with the prolonged shadows of morning rapidly lessening, opened up ahead. The day suddenly brightened. The hills blinked and stood outlined against the oncoming glory. His pulse quickened in the growing light.

Salathiel was some distance ahead of the wagon now. He drew up, waiting for it, and rose in his stirrups to look about him.

Behind, the long western ridges curled with the frosty smoke of November. The road led on over many a shining hill before. It dipped and disappeared, and appeared again.

The wagon came in sight.

Yates and Frances were sitting on the big seat together now. Frances had taken over the reins. Salathiel shouted to her exultantly, and she shook the four horses into a rapid run. Yates began laughing as the teams stretched out and came to a gallop.

Oh, what a morning!

Oh, to be free in this great natural world!

Salathiel knew they would know what he meant—

He rose in the stirrups again and thrust his rifle sparkling in the sunlight towards the western mountains. He threw his other hand up open-palmed, eastward, in a wide, wild, happy gesture. Good-bye, wilderness; good day, tomorrow and tomorrow and tomorrow—

Farewell, and hail.

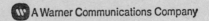